Book One of
The Prophecies of Rowe

Reappearance

Dennis J. Cooley

ISBN-10: 1546842578
ISBN-13: 978-1546842576

Reappearance

For Danielle and her artistic abilities amidst troublesome times, for Barry and his enthusiasm and encouragement, and for Anthony who helped me mentally spark the idea of this entire debacle

iii

The Prophecies of Rowe

THE NORTHERN LANDS OF

AMRUHN

1

ARNENN PASSED THE MANY BEATEN FOOD
crates and discolored whiskey barrels that were stacked
high along most of the inner-city walls, creating a sweet
yet pungent scent as warmth flowed through the dense
passageways. Inside, the many taverns and restaurants
were filled with hungry and thirsty customers whether
it be day or night. It helped him fall in love with the
homey feeling of Harpelle.

He meandered his way to the docks to help load
produce into the merchant boats before stepping onto a
beamed pathway bridging over a river in the northeast
end of the city. It's where he saw the familiar sight of his
cousin, but more like a best friend, Gjone.

Long and partially braided brown hair set over the
broad shoulders of a tall man in his early twenties. His
deep and brooding eyes under thick brows stared right
at Arnenn's face while carrying three large barley sacks
over his shoulder, awaiting a carriage boat. He called
out to him sarcastically. "Look who decided to be on
time again!"

Arnenn wore only a smile while reaching down to pick
up a bag of coffee beans lying next to his foot. Quickly
out of his hands flew the twenty-pound bag before
yelling, "Catch!" putting his cousin in a moment of
suspense.

As quick as possible, Gjone tossed his own bags into
mid-air and caught Arnenn's before throwing it right
back. With such fright, Arnenn dodged Gjone's throw,

but also fell into the River, almost landing inside one of the merchant boats passing underneath the bridge.

Laughs came from the surrounding workers and customers of Remma's Produce (Gjone's parents' shop) as Gjone himself projected an enormous snort of laughter that made Arnenn chuckle right back. Even in his moment of complete embarrassment, he couldn't wipe the smile from his face. There had always been a healthy camaraderie between the two, one that helped them in and out of trouble many times before.

Entirely soaked in his dark trousers, rolled-sleeved tunic, and leather boots, Arnenn's prominent features stood out. He had jet-black hair down to the bottom of his neck, a lean posture, and a wise, almost serious look. Yet he was pretty good at not concerning himself with matters of anything too serious or important most of the time.

Getting his cousin back onto dry ground, Gjone still laughing told him, "I need help stacking these stinkin' boxes of fish brought over by my dad onto that cart over there—seems to think my mom's going to be cooking a bunch of food for some gathering that he's putting on tonight."

"What do you mean, '*think*?'" asked Arnenn, confused while getting the water out of his hair and ears. He thought it a strange thing for Gjone to say because his mother practically never had a problem with anything of the sort before, especially when it came to helping her husband. Rayne did, of course, run one of the busiest River stations on the east end of the city, and his wife Jemma was always there beside him. She worked harder than anyone else and it seemed to most that she took great pride in it.

" . . . I don't know. Maybe she hasn't been too thrilled about the idea of my dad throwing another large celebration for all the employees since she doesn't believe they do much more than standing around, talking. Obviously no one works as hard as her so it's natural for her to think so. That, I would say concerns you as well, Cousin . . . since I was wondering if you were even planning on showing up today," said Gjone in his normal matter-of-fact way.

"Ha . . . well, it's all because your mom made me such a generous breakfast, which is more than I can say she did for you! Guess that gives me a pretty good out!" Arnenn followed in a shrewd way that was easily accepted by his cousin. Gjone knew he really only talked to him and very few others in such a manner: those he only knew well enough.

He continued by asking, "Besides, your father has sold more goods than any other supplier on the east end of town for nearly the last five years, has he not?"

Gjone agreed. "Guess you have a point. But I've noticed something different lately. Maybe she becomes a little fed-up with being expected to handle more than she already does . . . and I can see how that's the case with my father being who and how he is 'round here. But maybe not . . . it's like she's trying to avoid something lately. I've noticed her like this a few times before—like my dad's going to do something she doesn't care for very much."

"What could that even be? Your dad's out there sometimes, but he doesn't ever do anything *that* crazy . . . other than tell outlandish stories every once in a while."

"Yeah, I'm not sure. Maybe that's it. But it's just one of those things I can sense."

"Okay then . . . if you say so," followed Arnenn, postponing any further questions to begin helping his cousin. He knew the day would fly by like they always did in Harpelle, and he wondered why it was.

Perhaps it was the city's busy atmosphere where spirits flowed with ease and the food grown by its locals and the farms of the provinces attracted many people from neighboring towns, making it attractive for trade.

He remembered the reason he chose his summer stays to be in the quaint and prosperous place where the everyday citizens barely stopped doing their business in one way or another. They'd be seen working inside their small shops and pushing their oversized carts around, or carrying boxes in many directions while wearing their mostly tattered work clothing.

Harpelle was a bit cooler overall, and a friendlier atmosphere than that of his homeland Vidhera where he'd spend all other parts of the year as a Watchman of the Courts for his father. But Arnenn decided long before that he'd never had as much fun as when in his older cousin's smaller city, so why not spend his time in Harpelle having extra fun, making extra money, and doing something different than the usual while visiting his aunt and uncle's? Arnenn was only eighteen, not of age to take over his father's service. That did not come until age twenty-one, and he wasn't too fond of the job as it was. If Arnenn were given the choice, he would stay in Harpelle year-round.

More of a towered city, Harpelle could only grow south. Its northern, eastern, and western ends were engulfed by the longest range of mountains in all of Amruhn called the Cunnings (given its name by Cunning River that ran beside it), which dwarfed the city, not allowing it to expand in all directions. And

4

reaching to the River both east and west was a towering wall that circled the city's southern face. But, its many gates were never found to be closed.

The River, oddly, was given its steady stream not from a lake, but from a rocky ocean dam far north before running right through Harpelle where small carriage boats full of food and the shiny objects of distant lands, came to a stop before continuing southeast and down to a great lake of lightly salted water. And if those things or the vibrant personalities of the boat merchants weren't enough to make the city appealing to most folk, then the wood carvings of animal heads such as bears and wolves and cats sculpted deep into the buildings' structures, definitely were.

Most of those structures had been there since the city's beginning and were upheld by the thick wood and stone frames that made it beautiful and durable. It had a sturdy and guarded character, just like most of the people that lived there—especially those of the earlier days.

You see, Harpelle was founded hundreds of years before by those known to have strength and who respected the treaty made between man and beast. Cities in the northern parts of Amruhn were to keep watch over the realms of the Light-Beasts as the Light-Beasts in return, were to watch over the people's lands, protecting them from any threat that might exist in the wilds.

At evening's end, the two left the docks and carried home Rayne's boxes of fish. Arnenn was a bit more exhausted than Gjone by the time they neared the house—being not as muscular and rugged, or as good as his older cousin was at the art of carrying heavy things for long distances. But since smelling the various delightful aromas coming directly from his cousin's house, he didn't let himself lag a single bit.

Ready to indulge, Arnenn flopped himself onto a bench outside the house to take off his boots and felt the relief of freeing his toes as the cool night breeze rushed through his socks. The smells from inside contributed to his growing hunger, so he jumped up and strode quickly into the house.

It was a familiar sight, and one he enjoyed seeing daily. A staircase of thick oak beams just to the right cornered their way up two stories above the main floor as a kitchen below added a fourth. He always found his aunt and uncle's home a bit peculiar. The structure was similar to any other house in Harpelle: rooms never much bigger than thirty-five feet wide and stacked atop one another. But this house was a bit more crowded compared to the usual Harpellian's home.

The left wall was practically a jumbled library due to the mess made out of many columns of books and journals—some stacked almost to the ceiling and most older than anyone alive, all dusty and out of order. Arnenn always wondered what kind of disgusting insects might've lurked the wall behind the books, because some hadn't been moved since visiting his aunt and uncle's at the age of four.

Creating the primary gathering area was a thick wooden table that centered the room. It came within a close proximity of a fireplace made of stone set on the east end of the room while a single shelf above it held many plates, bowls, and cups. His aunt had placed small vases holding drooping plants wherever any room was left.

Speaking of his aunt, she came up the little stair from the kitchen below holding a large tray of freshly cooked vegetables that created a significant amount of steam in front of her brown hair. Jemma would normally always smile at Arnenn, but the look in her eyes would make him feel she was questioning something. So much so, it made him uneasy most of the time and wondered if she was a bit out of herself when he visited, afraid she never became very comfortable with the idea of him staying around during the summers.

Immediately striking up a conversation, she asked, "Are you ready for this big hurrah Rayne's putting on tonight?" She rolled her eyes about it with a partial laugh.

"I suppose I am . . . Gjone told me about it this morning but I had no idea about it until then. And I don't remember you saying anything about it earlier, either. What about you?"

"Well, Arnenn, your uncle has such excitement when he has an idea to do something. He's hard to say no to. And I really just go along with it most of the time because I don't need the opposite side of Rayne, which you know equals to him moping around for an entire week with disappointment. What can I say, though, he loves a good gathering, and especially when business is doing well, and that it is!"

He just said, "Okay, yeah . . . I guess you're right!" as he watched her walk out the back door. She didn't seem to be too upset about anything Gjone was getting at earlier, at least from what he could tell.

She was correct about what she said. Rayne was very likable. He had a presence that struck your attention along with the attention of your neighbor and even your neighbor's neighbor. He was somewhat charismatic. He could tell a story, and anyone listening would get utterly lost within it as if some magic existed in his voice or demeanor. His look helped it somewhat, too. Being large and slightly rugged with his great chin-only beard of brown and gray and eyes of discerning purpose spoke well for his stories of the past and of the old world or far-off imaginary lands—both inside and outside Amruhn.

His stories filled Arnenn's heart with such curiosity that he'd sense a slight pull from reality. He felt it before when listening in on some of his uncle's previous gatherings of the last few years.

He didn't know where Rayne heard or came up with most of the tales he'd tell, but perhaps they were from the many dusty books piled up in the main room. He'd talk about stuff such as far-away forests and witching magic, or great serpents and old kingdoms—very rare and unusual things to most people. But Arnenn had an adventurous spirit about him, so he loved Rayne's story telling.

After washing up from the day's work and redressing for the evening's festivity, he came upon the large patio rearing the house where a short wooden fence lined with benches wrapped around an oval brick fire-pit. Thick wooden beams that dug deep into a pond below suspended the whole thing where Rayne was grilling the fish and talking to his many guests about how well things were going that particular summer, and how having the presence of both his son and nephew around the docks had helped the shop significantly.

Many people were gathered, awaiting food and consoling with one another about goings-on around the realms of Harpelle. There were Rayne's employees, which also happened to be some of Gjone and Arnenn's acquaintances, a gathering of nearby neighbors, friends;

and even some men and woman of the Bear Guard had stopped by after their shifts since they, too, knew and liked Rayne very much. And many children played tag around the fire-pit while their parents consistently reminded them to not get too close to it.

All the people were celebrating such a good season of business and friendship, and a great cheer was on most's faces. Harpelle was doing well and many good things were available and in plenty.

Arnenn noticed Gjone speaking to one of his since-childhood friends that had recently been fathered into the Bear Guard. He went by the name Haulfir. He was a fire-red haired young man that stood sturdy in his tightly fit Guard outfit of black with the insignia of the Harpelle Bear Head in stark white on his left chest. His summer-yellow eyes didn't place well with his red hair as they shined off of the firelight, and there were seasons in which he looked a bit better, such as brown eyes in the fall.

Haulfir would constantly remind Gjone that he needed to join the Bear Guard and had always looked up to him more than his other friends. (Arnenn had always speculated that Gjone being bigger and stronger, was the only reason.) Gjone didn't seem to share in the same enthusiasm for it, though. It was either because he just didn't care to, or because he had so much to do helping parents around the shop most of the time, that he never entertained the idea too seriously.

As Arnenn walked up to the small gathering, he noticed Gjone's red-haired friend giving him an ignoring look. He knew Haulfir didn't exactly care much for him: him being the kingdom kid that decided to share his presence on a yearly basis for practically no reason other than the fact that he only "wanted" to. Haulfir envied the freedom.

Arnenn heard and watched him smugly bragging to Gjone and the others of the small group about the types of dealings he had with being on the Guard, all the way from keeping watch over the docks to arresting villagers for small and petty crimes. He wanted to laugh. He found it ridiculous how impressed Haulfir was with himself, but also thought it better to not rustle the leaves at his uncle's gathering. He really was never the type to do so anyway . . . mostly always too respectful.

Laughter absorbed the air as Haulfir told aloud, "I had to put that crazy old man that roams everywhere around the city into a cell just an hour ago. He drank too much to walk back up to his crappy hut, and none of us wanted to play an escort for the old loser tonight." He chuckled to himself before continuing. "We're allowed to make those kinds of decisions if we feel they are best. What about you, Arnenn? Are you able to make those types of decisions at the Kingdom City?"

The group of about seven younger men stared directly at him, awaiting an answer.

Arnenn found himself deciding against his original decision to not be rude and felt like he was going to say something stupid, which he did.

"Oh, yeah . . . I even throw guards into the cells overnight if I feel they're not performing their tasks up to par. You really have to watch them. It's crazy how cocky they become, too, especially the younger ones— have to keep them in line."

It came out in a very serious tone on accident and he felt silly and embarrassed saying it. He knew it was a bad response, but hoped he had somewhat pushed the point across to Haulfir's bigheadedness. Arnenn was never excellent at fooling-around-talk, so he hoped nobody took it too seriously. Gjone was particularly much better at that sort of thing than he.

Knowing it to be a lie, Gjone tried to hold back his laughter—even though it wasn't very funny. But, not laughing wasn't one of his greater strengths among the many he had.

Arnenn was a Watchman of the Kingdom City, but that only meant he'd survey the lands to report any weird findings outside, or close to it. He really couldn't throw anyone in jail and was no sort of officer of the law or anything even closely related.

Haulfir gave a scowling look but decided to let the matter pass. "Anyway, I'll be finding someone to take that old man up to his shack tomorrow morning. It definitely won't be me! I don't feel like walking the three-mile trail up to it, nor will I ever feel like it."

Without a moment's pause, Arnenn chimed in with, "I'll take him. I could use the hike. . . ." They all looked back at him in surprise. Even Gjone thought it out of the ordinary for his cousin.

"That's a guard's job," said Haulfir, annoyed to even look over at him again.

Arnenn couldn't understand why he would need to be transported to his house at all. He thought maybe it's because he was older, but he couldn't have been *that* old—maybe only in his mere fifties or early sixties.

"No really, it's not a problem. I actually know that old man. He goes by Throone; he's a friend of Rayne's."

Haulfir spoke again, hoping it to be the last thing he'd say to his friend's younger cousin. "I know his name . . . heard him saying it earlier in his drunkenness—we all heard it. He finally stopped before falling asleep. But fine with me I guess . . . go ahead and take him since you seem to be someone who obviously has things handled back at your mansions—"

"I'd like to give big-huge thanks to my employees! And really any of you, too, I suppose . . ." exclaimed the loud voice of Rayne before laughing as the food had been prepared and serve-ready. He partly scared all the members of his gathering before continuing with, "We shall have a feast tonight in my honor and I want you all to know how proud I am and how much I really appreciate your time and services around the shop, along with your friendship . . . but mostly your business . . . of course."

The crowd laughed along with him.

"We're really having such a better year than last and your efforts will not go undeserved! I want you all to fill your stomachs with food and ale and I'd hope you'd all stick around throughout the night! I'll be telling a tale; a personal favorite actually, one about my family that I myself, deem to be true!"

Arnenn believed he had heard such a story when younger, something of an importance that had to do with his family in at least one way or another. He also remembered not giving it much thought or care and he'd mostly forgotten all about it since none of it made any sense at the time. He was excited to hear it, however, and it had been quite a while since hearing a good tale told by Uncle Rayne.

He peered over and noticed the look on Gjone's and Haulfir's faces after his uncle's speech. It was the look of not wanting to hear another fairy tale.

2

RAYNE TOOK HIS SEAT NEAR THE FIRE AND began speaking again. "I know many of you have stories of your own and many books to read—just like I do, and I would love to be able to tell you the story I'll be telling tonight straight out of a book. However, there is a problem with that. You see, I've lost the particular book that holds this story. This book was, in fact, a journal filled with words I had received directly from my grandfather himself. He would tell me about this tale year after year when he'd come to visit us in the time of my youth—when we all lived in Vidhera.

"As I became older, he had unfortunately passed away, so I was never able to get all the details and the notes I kept were lost. Now, not so much the journal itself, though . . . I don't remember just losing it out of thin air, but odd as it sounds, the words and information that I had put on the pages seemed to just . . . disappear. It was entirely confusing to me! The journal just lost its substance altogether and I can barely even remember what it looked like. And I'm afraid that I have lost it entirely. Trust me, I've searched endlessly for it and have had no such luck in finding it. It's my greatest confusion ever! If you don't believe me, just ask Jemma! I've talked her ear off about it!

"A wandering merchant my grandfather knew, and that he'd come upon in his travels from time to time, would tell him about this story before he then passed it on to me. He'd also try to relay the story to my brother—

Arnenn here's father, but he never cared too much about the whole thing." He said that before laughing wildly. "With all that said, I wanted to relay to you the fact that this story may have some missing details. Nonetheless, I will tell it to you now, and as best I can and from what I can remember."

Rayne almost changed the sound of his voice to a deeper and more dramatic tone as his short hair fell over his forehead.

"There was a time that may have been very much like today, but hundreds of years ago, at least I was told so. And it was said that some type of evil creatures were killing not very far from where we live here in Harpelle. Now, whether Harpelle existed yet, I cannot say, but bad things were happening, and to innocent people. These creatures were explained as beasts wrought in black fur, or skin. They would also kill the animals of our forests. Yes! Even kill those that were known to be the Light-Beasts! . . . That's if any of you even believe in them. . . .

"No one knew where they came from, but the creatures were of different shapes and sizes. Week after week, there were more victims. But nobody knew how to find them. Some cities had absolutely no idea about the creatures' existence at all and would be surprisingly attacked and their homes, overrun. As time went on, it had become more and more common and word existed that there were some who figured out how to kill them. Other people wanted to know how it worked so that they, too, could keep themselves safe. However, killing them was no easy task! And those who'd figured it out were only able to explain that they were lucky and somehow caught the creatures the right way by spear or sword. There was very little or almost no evidence that these creatures were being killed at all, though, because it was said that if one were stabbed or pierced, they would only just disappear into nothing—there would be no trace of them afterward. Most people were hard-pressed to believe any of it because there was absolutely no proof of it being true. None at all!

"Unintentionally, it began to become a bit of a secret for those that were able to dissolve of them, and at the same time, many people were scared and gave up any hope to the matter. They tried to ignore the killings and the talk of the strange creatures, but it never helped. They just kept coming. The ones that chose to ignore them became more frustrated and rebelled against those who believed the creatures were real, while those not ignoring, quickly learned that the things were not just estranged animals, but maybe some sort of demons. I'm only guessing it sure didn't help their cause one bit!"

Rayne enjoyed another laugh with himself.

"Of course, dissension kept on drawing and before long, stranger and even bigger creatures started being seen in all corners of Amruhn that were of the same unexplainable likeness. These creatures—or demons if you will—would continue to overrun many villages; people would be driven out of even bigger cities and start to dwindle. Amruhn began to become a lost place altogether—nothing similar to today!"

Rayne showed to become more excited about it as he continued, the opposite of his usual serious story-telling style.

"Some that'd been run out of their homelands would keep together and create clans, or tribes, if you'd like to call them. And over time, they began to collaborate with one another on how to get rid of the black-wrought creatures, and there were even some who'd be able to have a deeper knowledge about what they were. These mostly became the leaders of the tribes. And there was talk of individual leaders who were more than just 'different.' They looked different, spoke differently, and were able to do things that others could not—rare abilities, unheard-of things! They also were said to travel together and unite more of the tribes. They would teach them how to fend for themselves and to regain back their towns and cities.

"Crazy enough, there were even clans that ended up siding against the others and alongside evil: the black-wrought creatures themselves! They would somewhat become like them, believe it or not. They would be swayed into it somehow!"

A friend of Rayne's jokingly shouted out in question, asking, "Is that where you and your family come in?" before getting out of his seat, walking over, and then patting Rayne on the shoulder while laughing. All the others of the gathering joined in with him.

"Perhaps it is . . . you'll just have to wait and find out, and also watch yourself, Frenn! I *could* be a demon for all you know—now sit back down, you old fool!" responded Rayne while giving him a friendly, yet warning eye before continuing.

"Moving on, many started believing different things of the past, things that they didn't believe before, and they also began to see the world in a very different way. It's true! They started to become more a part of Amruhn in spirit and felt as if they were accepted into a belief of the past with some new kind of knowledge!

"One thing that I was told by my grandfather and believe to be even more amazing is that old cities would seem to just . . . reappear: ones that existed long before, which were supposed to be only ravaged with the decay of time! As you can tell, even weirder things were going on in Amruhn and it was entirely changing. And while all of these things were happening, these rare leaders of the tribes spoke of certain people who'd already begun reuniting a lost kingdom, and started preparing for a war."

Arnenn was interested, but also drained from his hard day of work on the docks. He hadn't thought about anything else as he was lost within the story, but most of the time while listening, he'd also be looking out into the distance of the Cunnings that a full moon shined upon, lining their crowns and crags, or at the pond underneath the patio because staring at his uncle the entire time didn't make him feel the most comfortable.

Out of his peripheral, he noticed a frog sitting on dry land. It jumped toward the pond. But as it neared the water, the strangest thing ever was happening. Arnenn expected to see the water move—a splash or something, but instead, the frog had landed on dry ground; and where water had rested just a second before, there was then fresh dirt with small spring-red flowers protruding upward. He could see them growing numerously, dispersing throughout the area. They became brighter; and it was like the light of the day had almost come back to Harpelle. With that, his attention had completely turned from Rayne's story, to the new vision.

There were missing details of what was real while new things kept adding into his sight. Suddenly, an enormous structure in white and red stood far in the distance behind a girl that looked to be around his same age. She was in a garden where before, only a dry bed of land existed before the Mountains. Amazingly, she had different colors throughout her hair, almost in series of blondes with browns and glowing reds. He was entirely perplexed; completely fixated on her.

She wore obscure clothes showing dark leathers, blue silks, and possibly jute that wove in and out of stitched loops. He had never seen the likes of it on any other girl. Some fabrics molded to her body as others swayed around her when she moved, picking vegetables from the garden and placing them into a round-weaved basket. The girl suddenly looked up at Arnenn and smiled directly at him. He could almost feel her presence and found her breathtaking.

Anything after that was a bit foggy.

"Guess you lost interest a long time ago, huh?" asked Gjone as he woke his cousin from his strange slumber.

"What? I fell asleep? No, I was listening and then I saw—"

"—Saw what?"

"Nothing," stated Arnenn, thinking it best to keep what he'd just seen to himself.

"Yeah, well you've been asleep for a while. You should've seen your head hanging completely over the fence . . . it was quite the hilarious sight! You're lucky Haulfir didn't try anything funny."

Arnenn looked back out into the area of the pond and the field beyond it. All was as it had been before, just like normal. He also caught sight of a disappointed glance from his uncle, and he knew why.

Earlier, Rayne said that the story had something to do with their family, and he knew he wanted him to hear it, but as Arnenn pondered it, he really wasn't sure what to think with it being a story about demons and all: something quite unbelievable. At that point, he just wanted to be asleep in his comfortable bed because sitting on a wooden bench for the last hour or so made his back and neck quite sore.

As he stood, he could see everyone that had stayed to hear Rayne's story. Most people were shaking their heads in disbelief while asking Rayne more questions and some were laughing and making jokes about it, or about him falling asleep over the railing.

He began his way into the house, but before walking up the stairs to the bedrooms, he almost tripped over one of his uncle's dusty books lying out in the middle of the floor.

Jemma caught him right in time though, stopping him from falling straight on his nose.

"Be careful, Arnenn; I don't want our home being responsible for your injuries now." She chuckled a bit at her own comment before telling him to have a good night. He said it right back as he thought it must have been misplaced by one of the evening's guests going through the stacks to see if anything intrigued them. He picked the book up from the ground as he made designs with his fingers, wipe marks through the years of dust applied to it before setting it atop a shorter stack. He waved back to Jemma a good night and made his way up the stairs to end the confusing evening.

The next morning, Rayne, Jemma, and Gjone were already up and eating breakfast at the table as Arnenn paced his way down the stairs. It was the weekend, which meant the shop was not its busiest—at least for the Mourenrowe family that owned the place.

He knew he had slept quite later than his usual and also felt a bit embarrassed about the previous night due to falling asleep in front of everyone and feeling he had let his uncle down. But Rayne didn't have the same disappointed look on his face which he wore the night before, so Arnenn thought he must've already forgotten all about it.

He found out quite quickly that he was wrong as Rayne beckoned him over and spoke up. "It's a shame you fell asleep last night . . . really would've loved for you to hear the rest of the story. . . ."

"I'm sorry, Uncle, I was interested. I just don't know what happened! Guess I was more tired than what I thought. I was actually wondering if you'd tell me all about it some other time . . . if you wouldn't mind."

"Absolutely!" yelled Rayne. "I think it to be important for you to know your family's real history. Yes, that's right . . . I believe it to be real anyway, even if it's mostly just because I *want* to."

Jemma made a face at Rayne. "I had no idea you were planning on telling *that* far tale last night. If I had known, I would've told him to just stay in the house."

It was strange. Rayne only changed the subject.

"Haulfir told me you signed yourself up to take old Throone back to his house up on the hill. Sounds like an odd job and makes no sense to me; he's a perfectly able and willed old man if I may say so."

"I don't fully understand it either, but yeah, I did . . . and I made the decision in a split second. Guess I thought it would at least be something different to do. I've never been up there before," responded Arnenn, who had always enjoyed long walks on trails and pathways that led off to places he'd never seen before. Back at home, he would usually roam off and end up in some distant place around the City and become quite lost. But he loved getting lost in the forests outside and wasn't too concerned about knowing where he was going, for he never second-guessed he'd eventually find his way back home. He only wondered what more there was to be seen in the vast realms of Amruhn.

Arnenn enjoyed the distance between Vidhera and Harpelle. Vidhera was more than a hundred and some-odd miles west from his cousin's city, and that summer as a young adult, he took horseback for the first time (rather than just taking the ship from the shores of Vidhera that sailed east from the harbor, and then from there to the Cunning River's beginning in the North, and down, which was really a much faster way). But he enjoyed walking horse-side for a lot of the distance; it was how he thought best and cleared his mind. Besides, he would have to travel by land heading back to Vidhera just like he had always done before since there was no river heading that direction until reaching the Great Bridges. Also, he didn't care much for the idea of traveling alone with some random strangers far down to the Lake in some tiny boat just to have a full week's travel by ship through the Disdon to his homeland.

"How do you even know him?" he asked, suddenly becoming curious about Rayne's friendship with the old town dweller.

"Throone's just someone I've done some business with before. Come to think of it, actually—" He looked around and saw that Jemma had left the room, so he comfortably spoke of it again. "He used to talk to me about the tale I told last night. Well, more so years ago than recently, really. Anywho . . . he's lived in that cottage or hut or whatever you want to call it near the top of the mountain for a long time now. As long as I can remember. He told me that the small house belonged to someone far back in the time of my grandfather. Apparently, it's been there quite longer than anyone knows—perhaps even before Harpelle has

21

been here, but I'm not certain. Not everyone knows about it, either, since the many trees of the Cunnings hide it well.

"I'm not exactly sure what he does for work to be honest, but he said he's dabbled in quite a few different things over his years. He was never very specific about what, though. Perhaps he just saved up a lot of money long ago and is retired. But, sometimes, months and months go by and I don't see or hear a trace of him at all and then suddenly he'll appear again and grab some goods from me. So maybe I'm wrong. He either stays up in that place of his for extended periods of time or is off venturing somewhere else. It's really kind of strange and hard to keep up with. He seems to be a very sturdy old man, and given so, I'm not sure why you or anyone else needs to be 'walking' him home."

"I don't know, either. Haulfir said it's just because he drank too much last night. Maybe they feel it's their duty somehow?"

"He drank too much? Ha, that doesn't surprise me. . . ." commented Rayne.

He agreed with his uncle about him being a sturdy old man and thought that he just aged well, more than ever looking very timeworn.

After breakfast, Arnenn was ready to leave. He took a walking stick found somewhere in the house along with a small pack of apples that hung from his back before heading to the Guard Tower where the man was held, and which was the most popular part of the entire city.

About fifteen minutes after leaving his cousin's, he arrived at the Tower and came upon Haulfir with some of his guard friends just inside. It was very basic. There was a level atop a set of stairs where guards would pass back and forth while in between duties, which rounded a single desk. And the walls inside were white, which was not the usual for the wooded city. It reminded him of some locations in Vidhera more than anything else did in Harpelle, and he didn't care for it one bit. It wasn't too surprising, though; it wasn't the first time he had ever been there.

Pointing to Arnenn, Haulfir nodded to his fellow guards and said, "He'll be filling in for us today to take that old man in cell five back to his hut."

The guards chuckled, not very jealous of the task Arnenn had appointed himself. Haulfir just smirked and smiled for an extended amount of time which made Arnenn feel awkward and nervous while waiting for him to stop. But it just didn't seem to happen for quite some time since Haulfir was merely too over-confident in himself. Eventually, the young guard turned around and started walking to the destined cell. Arnenn followed.

"Hey, old man. . . ." spouted Haulfir. Arnenn could hear his guard friends laughing in the background. "Wake up! It's time for you to be taken home!"

Throone sat up and placed a hand upon his beating head in remembrance of the night before. Then, he looked at Haulfir and said, "young Arbowen, thank you for letting me stay here last night; you are very kind for allowing me to do so."

Haulfir quickly tried to shrug off the matter. "What are you talking about? No thank yous are needed. . . ."

Arnenn could tell that Haulfir's story of "throwing the old man in jail" was no more than Throone only asking if he could use a quick bed for the night since it was close to many of the main taverns in town.

Haulfir only stormed off, avoiding the conversation altogether. He went around a corner and was out of Arnenn's sight within seconds.

3

STEPPING OUT FROM THE LOWER CELLS OF
the Guard Tower, Throone spoke by questioning, "Well,
from what I'm guessing at here, you are supposed to
walk me home?"

He tugged at his short white beard and neck-length
hair that had tangled during the night's sleep as he wore
a cream colored and long-sleeved tunic with buttons
going from half way up his chest and continuing up to
his neck, which was tucked tightly into his trousers held
on by a thick leather belt. It was the everyday attire of
Harpelle, but worn very well for a man with the looks of
his age. His face gathered an almost whimsical sort with
a slightly curve-ended nose as the deep creases around it
stretched like thinned leather. They also ran along his
forehead and curved around his eyes that if had set any
deeper into his skull, would have handed over his rare
handsomeness, to just plain ugly.

Arnenn felt a bit timid around his presence for some
odd reason. It was one thing to have seen him dragging
himself around town like the usual nobody everyone
thought he was, but a closer look told the young
Mourenrowe that rethinking the way he'd speak to him
would be a most brilliant idea.

"Yeah . . . but all I know is someone was supposed to
take you and I stepped in because—well—I thought
you'd rather not have a guard take you," guessed
Arnenn.

"You're right about that . . . I don't need anyone to help me home at all, young man . . . but I suppose I could use the company, and I don't really care for the likes of the guards to be honest—at least most of the younger ones." Throone gave a good stretch. "I have most likely worn out my welcome in the area for the last few days, and perhaps I've spent too much time alone as is. I do feel a bit weary also, so I suppose you're right . . . I guess I really *can* use a little assistance," said the old man, ending the statement with a grin.

As they walked to the northern end of the city, they came across the many likings of Harpelle. Arnenn could remember his very first trips there during his youth when visiting his aunt and uncle with his father and being so excited about the interesting place where his slightly older and favorite cousin lived. Together, he and Gjone would run through the crowded streets while going on searches for all kinds of animals, playing games with the other children, and getting in trouble with the Bear Guard, of course—which explains why it wasn't his first time inside the Guard Tower.

Throone, however, had an appreciation for Harpelle that no one could share. He had been there longer than anyone else and he, unlike Arnenn, thought the city to be too overwhelming and crowded most of the time, especially in the summers. He remembered days when less of a merchant presence existed and when most of them were more respectable than the ones of the current day. Throone knew of many traders that came in and out of the city; some even from his old travels as one himself, but most of them he guessed had forgotten about him, and he, them. He did at least always have his little home atop the hill to get away from it all from time to time and no one ever thought to bother him when he was up there, which gave him great comfort.

He didn't dislike *everything* about Harpelle, though; he did enjoy the smells of the decent food and the city's charm just like Arnenn, along with the music that came from inside the taverns. It made him feel at home and he was glad that some he needed to keep a watch over had decided to reside there as well, even if he was more than partially responsible for it from time to time.

"Arnenn is it? Arnenn Mourenrowe?" asked the old man without letting him answer before continuing with, "What brings you back here every year to work on the docks? I have only seen you here in the warmer season. Is it because it gets hotter than you'd like in Vidhera around this time? Your uncle has told me that's where you're from, just like himself."

After making their way through most of the city, they crossed over the Cunning and headed to the last food crate infested outcrop of Harpelle by Remma's before coming upon the bent trees that hovered over a slight opening into a forested area of the Cunning Mountains. Then, they continued and entered it where Arnenn saw a narrow path of stair-like rocks ahead.

Arnenn answered by saying, "Yes, I am. I have always liked it here and my parents allow me to spend my summers away for a bit, and also yes to your other question, too. It gets kind of hot over there. Trust me . . . I wouldn't mind spending the entire year here if I were allowed."

"I see. Well, it does get mighty chilly here in the winter and sometimes the cold comes earlier when compared to other areas," said Throone. But he knew well enough that talking about the weather wasn't going to help him know the young Mourenrowe any better, and quickly decided to move topic. "Anyway, I take it you like your uncle?"

Arnenn thought it to be an odd question. "What's not to like?"

"You're right! He is indeed a man of great accord for this city—a wondrous soul he has as well, something I have always liked about him. He always seemed to share in my liking for things of old legend, that's for sure." He was beginning to feel better than when he'd awoken an hour earlier.

"Yes, you're right. I enjoy Uncle Rayne's vibrant stories. Not sure if I even believe half of them or not but they are at least interesting." One came to his mind right away. "I remember one a few years ago about giant sea creatures attacking islands or something. It was fascinating, but I don't remember any of it now. I do tend to get lost in them very easily, though."

Throone lifted an eyebrow at the comment which Arnenn couldn't see as the older man walked ahead of him. "That's good you do . . . most of those stories are more interesting than anything going on nowadays, at least I'd say so."

The trail underneath the forest became dense under clustered trees which made it darker as they continued farther up into the Cunnings. Arnenn was surprised that the woods he had always been in such close proximity to when being at his cousin's house had such an interesting and colorful character when inside. He wondered why he never actually wandered into it before—knowing his sense of adventure. He always thought it hadn't looked very appealing, but now realized that he was very wrong in his original assumption of it.

There was more plant life inside and amongst the underbrush than anyone would've guessed, and one thing he noticed to be very strange is that every tree they walked by showed to have a thin and black horizontal marking as if a burning stick of a passerby set the trail's direction. Other than that, the trail was very well put together. It was as if somebody (or the old man himself) had spent a long time making it a pleasure to walk upon with both natural and human-made staircases of rock.

Throone felt a little uncomfortable about the mostly unneeded presence, but Arnenn was a Mourenrowe: a family he was familiar with. He was going to get to know Arnenn because he would probably have to at some point in time, whether he wanted it or not. He already knew Gjone a little, but also knew he wasn't very interested in adventurous things such as his father. He wondered if this even younger Mourenrowe could be quite the opposite of his cousin, which he so far guessed to be the case.

"Actually," began Arnenn, deciding it best to keep some type of conversation going, "he was telling a story last night at his gathering about something of our family."

At that, Throone turned around while still walking. "You should be careful about what's presented to you about such stories from him. As well of a man he is indeed, such things are only of speculation in Amruhn." He looked ahead again.

"Right . . . I really just like to hear about anything different. Last night I dozed off and unintentionally fell asleep, but I didn't even realize it until Gjone woke me up, and I missed anything about my family's part in it all. It doesn't matter . . . just strange. It was like having an out-of-body experience or something."

Throone thought it sounded just about right. He had known for a long time that the members of Arnenn's family have a tendency to dream and to see things, although it usually ends up meaning nothing. He wondered why he should be all too concerned about this new Mourenrowe kid having visions—if that's what they even are. It sure wouldn't be the first time for it to happen to one of his kind. Why would this "Arnenn" be any different—or of any more a special significance when compared to all the others? Throone didn't want to do any more than he had done from time to time before, so he thought it best to only let the matter rest.

They didn't speak much more after that, other than Throone pointing out some of the wildflowers and plants prominent to the area of the mountain. The old man's speaking suggested that he knew a lot of things about nature, which Arnenn found intriguing as he listened intently and continued treading behind his heels.

After a three mile hike on the trail that was full of rocks they had to step up and over, Arnenn saw the figure of a small house condensed within a mass of trees with a slight ray of sunshine pointing down on it. Made of gypsum based mortar with a pointed roof of wood with dirt, moss, and leaf coverings, sat an almost suspended by some of the nearby trees, home. Arnenn thought the area was quite a pleasant sight, very green and exotic. It was different than the mostly barren-dry-looking wheat fields surrounding Harpelle.

Quite happy to be there after the steep and strenuous hike, and impressed by the endurance of Throone who'd glided up to his house with great ease, Arnenn stood awkwardly against his walking stick, awaiting whatever was to come about next for the day.

"Thank you for your company on this little trip up here. Please come in for some tea," said Throone, welcoming him eagerly.

"I think you more so accompanied me to be honest . . . you seem to have no problem walking up here on your own," said Arnenn as he made his way through the slightly tilted door of Throone's small home and saw a space inside bigger than what the outside hinted.

Quickly making his way over to pour water into two vase-style cups, Throone said, "It's just something you get used to after many years of enduring such type of travel. You are allowed to stay for a bit and take your boots off, young Arnenn. I can tell you need it. Any tea? Or is water just fine enough?"

Arnenn felt a bit hesitant at the thought of getting too comfortable in a house he had never been to before, especially with somebody he barely knew, but it did sound like a good idea for his poor feet. And heading straight back down the mountain right away didn't sound very wonderful, either. He placed them outside the door and while doing so, and saying, "Just water please," he could see parts of Harpelle through the trees to the south. It was a view he had never before seen: the city of Harpelle in an entirely new light. It showed more majestic than when compared to being inside of it. It made Arnenn feel even better about his decision to spend his summers there.

Throone found himself deciding that he couldn't help but question the story Arnenn had heard just the night before, even though earlier, he decided to ignore it. But he knew that wouldn't truly last long for him.

"You were saying something about the story your uncle was telling last night. You fell asleep, huh? Wasn't your favorite cup of interest I take it?"

"No, quite the opposite, actually," replied Arnenn. "I was very interested; believe I just had a long day which caused me to drift off." He felt like he had already explained it more times than ever wanting to as he sat in the seat Throone had pointed him to, right before the old man set Arnenn's glass down on a shaved tree stump made perfectly into a side table. He took himself a seat in a raged yet comfortable-looking chair.

"Well, you said something to the fact of having an out-of-body experience. You're not the first of your family to have such behaviors you know. . . ."

Arnenn was puzzled at the comment, but Throone let it pass as if it wasn't relevant, and not having the chance to question it, heard Throone say, "Oh, never mind that, your uncle would probably understand what I meant. It's not a bad thing by any means, and I am interested in this story myself, even though I've never been around for any of his storytelling times. Also, sorry for speaking in such obscure ways . . . I have had some odd days, and a good conversation about something that is actually *interesting* would be quite fitting for me. I hope you'd understand."

"Oh, uh, it's not a problem, Mr. Throone," Arnenn politely replied. "I remember parts about killings by some creatures and then dozed off around a part where people were different, and they were doing something to prepare for a war—I think. I didn't last very long into the story, to be honest."

"I can see you were paying close attention!" laughed Throone with a small cup placed between his legs. The tea inside it was almost spilling out the sides as it shook. It cautioned Arnenn because there was steam coming up from it, but the old man didn't seem to be too concerned about it spilling on him. What was even stranger is that

Arnenn didn't recall him doing anything to make it hot in the first place.

"What is it you'd like to know about this story you've missed?" asked Throone. "I wonder if I may remember any of it."

"You would know it, too?"

"I might know something of it, Arnenn," he replied, waiting cross-legged.

"Okay-uh . . ." He'd begun recalling out loud what he remembered before trying to ask any questions about it. "He said his grandfather, who I guess would be my great-grandfather, was really the one who knew it and had told him all about it. Again, there were killings by strange animals or demons, so he said . . . and people were divided and then—uh . . . I don't know . . . sorry, I don't know what to question about it yet, either, other than the whole thing, really . . . especially the demon part."

"There's no need to apologize, Arnenn. Really, nobody knows of it but a few. I myself came upon the story in my younger years, and quite on accident, too." Throone's face changed to a different intensity out of nowhere before he condescendingly said, "You probably wouldn't believe me if I told you how I did, and I probably won't be telling you, either! There may be a lot of things that you have no idea about, *boy*, even demons!"

Arnenn didn't understand why he responded the way he had. And he didn't quite know what to say back. He kind of only wanted to leave and most likely would have if it wasn't for his renewed interest the story. He wanted to at least know *something* else. But he only awkwardly looked around the house, taking more notice of its many odd and unique details.

The home itself was just one room for the most part. There were many interesting objects scattered on shelves or hung on stretched mantles that were unrecognizable, and in different colors they gleamed his way off the sun that came through the tiny windows. He guessed the objects to be either cleaning instruments or weapons made in odd shapes very long ago. Also, some items sat around the house in an unorderly fashion that must have been set aside for cooking, yet nowhere close to the supposed "kitchen." Throone also had a collection of books, such as Rayne did. There were not as many, but most were older-looking and sprawled out, lying open instead of closed and stacked. It explained why his little house smelled a lot like his aunt and uncle's, or like the stuffy bookstores back at home. He also noticed some of the pages to be marked with big, red X's.

"Yes, I'm a collector of such things—don't mind any of those bother of books behind you, just research that has resulted in nothing for the most part. I will answer you some information as I said I would." He repositioned himself more comfortably. "What you really need to know about that story is that it basically piles up to some embellished tale about demons and of the old world. Really, believe it or not, a part of the past coming back to life at some point in time. A fairy tale it is, yes, but a fairy tale that's led me to believe some of my own findings to be possibly true in their own funny way. You'd be amazed how some tales can have an effect on someone's life. . . . Just look at your uncle! Just the mere notion of liking such stories of legend has made him somewhat who he is; and I can tell he's holding on for something great to happen someday. I have always known it. I myself am awaiting the same, but I need not bother you with any of that just yet."

Throone paused before folding his hands together right in front of his face; his cup still set between his legs. "You were saying your great-grandfather would tell him these stories. I believe that. I am, in fact, the age to have known him in more 'youthful' days, you can say. Him and I would speak of such things . . . of course more people then, than today, knew or cared about stories as such, though still forgotten by them anyway. Today they really only do as well as fairy tales . . . and that's about it."

Arnenn thought it to be his turn to speak, but he was wrong as the old man went on.

"Also in those days, there was a slight cause to know that story. There was rumor of strange creatures running abroad not too long before your uncle was born. But by popular vote, it turned out to be nothing other than normal animals which were not of the Light-Beasts. There were also talks about colossal bear attacks, which are of course a real threat, but there was no real proof of it. I had my own doubts and speculations about the general consensus being false but they did very little. I also must apologize to you, Arnenn, but I believe some of your past family members may have been taken by those attacks."

Arnenn saw him give a sigh, like he held some type of disappointment over it. He thought to himself that there must've been more to this story in effect with people's lives in the past than he ever could have thought— perhaps Throone's life specifically.

"But there have always been rare sightings and attacks by large animals," Throone continued. "And there are enough of those stories to fill an entire year with! . . . Back to your uncle's story, and as he was probably getting at, the creatures kept coming, and over time there were great threats. The world started changing. A war came about and new kingdoms were founded, or 'refounded.' That's pretty much the story—the best I can tell it, anyway." He blankly stared when finished.

Arnenn sat in silence for a moment. He was shocked that it was all he knew, or at least all he had to say about it. He had to question it.

"You must know more about it than that—I mean, what happened in the war?"

"It was a war . . . what do you think happened? People killed each other . . . there was good vs. evil, the usual . . . what do you expect?"

"Wait a minute. So if this 'fairy tale' story is actually true, why haven't I heard much about it any time before?"

"It's as you and I said, young Mourenrowe, a fairy tale. Also, I'm not a storyteller myself. Besides, I may have said too much already. Any more interest from you on the subject and you may turn right into your uncle! What I said is simply where the story goes and that's really about it."

"You just said you may have said too much. You act as if you *do* know more. And you're the one who brought it up in the first place. . . ." replied Arnenn, quickly and anxiously.

Throone lifted his hands up to his shoulders while his eyes became much bigger. He said nothing else.

With that, Arnenn thought he should start heading back—for real this time as the old man was acting overwhelmingly rude. (He was beginning to see what many others might have seen in the guy.)

Standing and coming up with an excuse to leave, he said, "I should probably be going now . . . I'm sure Jemma or Rayne have things that they need help with."

Throone only nodded as he started looking around his little home himself, but as Arnenn came close to the door to grab his boots, he heard the man speak up again. "Wait, please come back in; take a seat!"

Arnenn paused and thought twice about turning around, but also thought the other couldn't be of any real harm. And he probably just wasn't very used to having guests inside his home.

"Let me apologize about my behavior. Please take a seat. I'll make you a quick bite to eat. I'm sure you must be famished—and I could also use some food myself!"

"I have some apples that—" began Arnenn before the old man cut him off, saying, "No, no . . . please, let me make you something of actual substance."

As Throone stood up and headed to the tiny table in the west end of the house again, he started talking with his face to the wall, moving his hands around and grabbing at things to prepare the food.

With quite the muted tone and echo, Throone spoke loudly, saying, "It is long since I've had company in my home and I'm sorry about my attitude with the story. You see . . . it's actually of great interest and importance to me. That's why I become a bit skeptical when talking about it. I just want to be careful, nothing else. I believe the story's real to be completely honest; it's just that if I say too much, people tend to think me 'crazy.'"

"I could've guessed that . . . stories about demons and such would scare anyone, including me! But it doesn't matter to me whether most people decide to believe it or not . . . what I don't get is that it seems to have something to do with my family, at least as far as my uncle says. How's it that my family holds some type of importance to this story, Mr. Throone? And if that's the case, why doesn't anybody other than my uncle know

I don't get it. I have never heard my father *or* ...other speak of it. No one!

"Just Throone is okay, Arnenn. We can skip such pleasantries between one another if you don't mind." The old man turned and stared at him for a few seconds before only partially answering his question. "Yes, Arnenn, your family *does* have a particular history in it, and you see . . . that's also the tricky part. Most don't know it because they've honestly never heard it, nor care to." He paused. "There are many families, Arnenn, that have history regarding this story. However, you are a very descendant of *Rowe*, Arnenn Mouren 'Rowe.'"

Suddenly, Arnenn felt an impact at the sounding of the name Rowe alone. An unexplainable jolt triggered while his hairs stood up over numerous sets of goose bumps. It looked like all the light in the room turned itself blue-like for a glimpsing moment. Quickly coming back to himself, he said the word aloud. "Rowe." It was as if that part of his name held some more importance.

Looking around as if he may have noticed it as well when walking back with the food, Throone asked him very excitedly, "Do you know why your last name is Mourenrowe, Arnenn?" Again, not giving him a chance to answer, he added, "I would say it's possible that one of your ancestors had the first name of Mouren and the last name of only Rowe, and had a very significant part to play in that war. Before that, your family's name was Rowe and that only. As far as my guessing goes."

Gazing past Arnenn and slightly edging his voice, he also said, "I have come across that in those books sitting behind you, Arnenn, though it was difficult to put the clues together—even if it sounds like it should be only too easy. And I lied . . . they have been quite useful in at least *some* ways. I do apologize about that. But this is no fairy tale, indeed. I *have* to be careful with what I say. I believe your ancestor played a part in that war of a particular importance. Maybe even beyond what you or I would believe! But do you see now why your uncle believing your family was highly involved, is very interested in this tale and even others of the sort?

"What else you would need to know is that this war wasn't the usual in many forms. It wasn't your act of warfare between one kingdom and another, at least not at first . . . it was between good and what was real of evil—a war between those that were of Light, and those that were of Dark."

Arnenn replied with a confused look as he noticed that the sandwich he'd been given was toasty warm, yet it never seemed that there was any actual "cooking" going on.

" . . . Dark? Is that what the creatures in this story, or war, were called? And do you mean *Light* as in the *Light-Beasts*?"

"Yes, and also maybe not entirely . . . or maybe there's more to Light and Dark than we've ever thought! I cannot be completely accurate about what Dark even is, Arnenn, but I do believe that it goes far back to a time we may have never heard about. And I believe that the war between Light and Dark is beyond all of our knowledge in many great measures.

Throone began questioning himself as to whether he had said more than meaning to, but he needed to let it out; he had held it to himself for far too long, again, and this Arnenn he was looking dead in the eyes was his new and prime suspected Mourenrowe. And there was something familiar about him, like some of his previous kin.

Still, he took a deep breath and calmed himself. He was getting too excited, just like before where it never turned out well.

"What this means for your future, I don't know. It may mean nothing at all and that's most likely the case. Do understand, Arnenn . . . it's best not to dwell on these things or to make your uncle any more excited about it than he already is, if you know what I mean."

"I don't intend to do that at all, but I have another question about something I just remembered. My uncle spoke of a journal he owned. He said his grandfather passed down information to him and he used it to make notes of the story, but also said that the information had disappeared from it somehow and it even changed from how it originally looked. Would you know anything about that? How could that even be possible?"

Throone pondered it in silence for a moment, almost with a stunned look. And Arnenn could tell he cared about it in a sense. But he only answered with, "No. That's fascinating . . . but what would I know about a missing journal of your uncle's?"

He truly had no idea about it, but was very intrigued, nonetheless.

"Books and information regarding any relevant matters to know in life do seem to disappear. I know from personal experience. And I've searched my own books and notes for lost information that has never reappeared. The truth is that it's a difficult story to come by and to many, it makes no sense and never happened, or their own ancestors easily forgot all about it.

"Also, there are perhaps forces in Amruhn that would want to get rid of this information; forces that want to rid the truth about the story which such books or journals might hold. It wouldn't surprise me to say the least. I have traveled Amruhn doing many different doings and have also been gathering any information I could when able, but it hasn't done me much good to tell you the truth. It has always been a keen interest of mine, though. But no, I don't know about the journal your uncle owned . . . perhaps it is of some considerable importance—and maybe it's not. See, some books or weapons can be substantial relics related to wars in the world. But let me tell you: Such objects are hard to come by and they could drive you mad by becoming an obsession if let's say, you were to go looking for them, like myself. Trust me in this; it may be best that journal of his stays lost for his sake . . . and for yours, too, might I add.

"I'm only deciding to tell *you* this because you may want to pass it on to your children one day, even if it's not very much. Still, it's important to have at least some family history, and I suppose Gjone already knows a great deal about it being the very son of Rayne, and all."

"It's all very interesting . . . are you sure there isn't more you know?" Arnenn asked.

"You may just want to ask your uncle. He may know something I don't," said Throone. Another lie.

They spoke of other pleasantries about Harpelle and Vidhera as they ate the rest of their sandwiches and after that, Arnenn said his goodbye and thanked Throone for the food as Throone in return, thanked Arnenn for his company.

The old man watched him leave while leaning against the rim of his door with his arms crossed. He hadn't found himself in such question for quite some years as the young Mourenrowe began his descent on the trail he had come up just an hour earlier.

The way back down was a bit slippery from the new rain that started the very moment he left. The area amidst the trail descending the Cunnings became dark for mid-day, and Arnenn found himself having to hold on to the nearby trees to step over the rocks and roots of the forest's floor, keeping him from falling; it continued for what had to have been a good twenty minutes or so.

Closer to the bottom of the mountain, Arnenn heard what was believed to be the roar of some great grizzly from far away. It startled him. He heard it again a few moments later, but it sounded different the second time. It was more human—as if someone from Harpelle (still about a half mile away), was shouting ferociously. He heard it in different waves, almost as if he heard it only in his head before it stopped. He momentarily paused to decide whether he should continue at a greater speed, or not.

He chose not to and came back to his aunt and uncle's house around noon and stayed in for the rest of the rainy day with Jemma, finding out that Gjone and Uncle Rayne had already taken off somewhere, something that had to do with trade near the eastern farms.

He thought about his little get-away from the inner parts of the city that day and was interested to hear more of the story from his uncle. For some reason, he felt a strange pull to it all.

4

AS THE CENTURIES CAME AND PASSED ON

Amruhn, old age became of the Keeper. He guessed the war had happened not long before he was born and always wondered if he was the first, or maybe the only of his kind. He was given a task to watch over those of Rowe using the magic, but he did not understand how to use it at first and it took him almost a hundred years to figure it out. It surely never made any sense as to how it was supposed to help.

From the droplets of the morning dew that fell from a leaf before landing directly on his nose, he woke in surprise. Suddenly, a spark ignited within the palm of the Keeper as the leaf turned to nothingness.

He stood. His legs ached considerably. He didn't know why he was in a forested area or what had even led him there, but looking around, he wondered why he wasn't inside it more often: A light stream of water filtered over a moss-covered stone sculpture of old, creating falls as it rummaged and danced through the stark-brown trees circled by many white and yellow lilies and small ferns. It gave a soothing sound to his ears and a comfort to his eyes as they adjusted to the brand new day.

Numerous greens surrounded the area, making the ground a soft net. He noticed the usual squirrel, rabbit, or hedgehog roaming about every few minutes or so, and even the small spiders creating webs in the above creases of the trees brought a sudden light and shine of comfort into his soul. He wouldn't have been surprised to learn he had come across the remnant of some ancient place, wherever he was.

What he remembered was little, other than being knocked to the ground before falling asleep—or simply just passing out. He sat on a rock near the grassy area where he had just awoken. He closed his eyes; it did not take long to catch a glimpse of it.

The memory rushed back into his mind—drawing in every moment and emotion. He remembered the patch of forestry before and how it looked nothing similar to when he had woke: Dried out, the stream of water barely dripped down the barren rocks while the trees' leaves became a lazy yellow, almost withering away amongst the somber dirt.

Then, he saw it.

Bending down the branches was the form of what was some ill-looking and enormous insect wrapped in a moving black—a cloud-like substance. It was almost as big as the canopies of the trees that swayed back and forth as it crawled from one to another.

The Keeper's feet remembered the leaves crushing beneath them as he walked backward and stared up in question. And the night sky had turned into a black abyss from the previous dusk, making it harder to see the creature before it jumped to the ground.

"I have come to devour you," sounded a voice through the Keeper's mind as the terror narrowed toward him. He had never seen such a creature or substance, but he knew exactly what it was, and also, what it meant. He had known a day like this would come and he waited a long time for it to happen.

The Keeper had been warned. But just as quickly, he was failing.

The creature of Dark was about to consume him, and he knew that if it succeeded in doing so, the line of Rowe would fail.

He stretched out his hand as the creature came closer. His fire ignited within as he grasped the monster, but his effort did nothing to stop it as it caught him off-guard, almost sticking him with the ends of its many claw-ended legs.

A shock of terror came over the Keeper as fatigue overtook him. He thought of how all his work and efforts had come to nothing throughout his long years, and would continue being nothing. He had grown lazy and weary; he was sorry for his attitude and prejudices. He thought of how he should've known better and given more truth to the story to all he possibly could, not just the Mourenrowes, whom more than most, were skeptical and unbelievers.

But just as he was about to unwillingly give up his life, a familiar sight came from above the creature—one that he had seen before, but at a time so long ago he could barely recall it. It came back to him at once: the one who informed him of his task, the Angelic Being he hadn't seen since the day he first came across his magic. It all came back to him, clearer than any of his memories of the time since.

Out of the black sky above and wrapped within a blue light, her arm of almost silver ripped back the Dark creature as a glowing blade went through it with great ease. It disintegrated into the air like ash and dust before disappearing entirely.

The Forest's night lightened up; the sky became vibrant with day again; grass came out of the once dry ground; the leaves disappeared and flowers bloomed across the area. He watched as the water level raised and trembled over the mossy rocks and stone. The small sector of the Forest came back to new life, such as it may have lived at a time long before.

Thankful to be alive, he looked up at the Being and was stunned by her beauty as she landed softly on the web of thick grass with only bare feet. She spoke as her golden blonde hair moved in a wind that did not exist.

"Keeper, this is the only time I can come through the Pull to save you. They are coming, and it has started." Her voice came in whispers of heavy breath with a vibrant ringing. She had lost much of her own energy through the travel.

The Keeper was completely overtaken by her presence, a presence he'd been long awaiting to see again, one he needed to see again.

"My lady, I have been waiting so long . . . so long here! I need answers! I will not disappoint you again! Not forget! I know it is here now—that it is happening." He paused and asked, "My lady, is it him?"

She walked closer and with an even softer voice, said, "Yes. He will make his mark, if not overthrow those of Dark, Keeper. There is great potential here. I saved you because I love you. And fully, I trust you in this task . . . much as I always have."

He didn't understand. He wanted to know more of his task; he never truly understood. He had to know more about everything—all of it. But as the Being grabbed and held his hand, his energy was drained from his body.

She was gone, and the Keeper slept in a long peace.

* * *

Coming back from the memory, he didn't know how long he had been asleep. He felt as if he hadn't moved for many days if it was at all possible. He looked around once more at the renewed forest that surrounded him and gained a new foundation of hope within himself.

The Keeper was ready, as if renewed and feeling young again, younger than he had felt for many long decades.

Remembering where he was, he had a look of sheer determination on his face, yet happier than he had been for many long years. Coming out upon the trees' ending, he ran faster than he had run for a very long time. Out of the Palendrian Forest, and back to Harpelle, Throone went.

5

SUMMER'S END MEANT THE EYES OF ALL IN
Amruhn turned the dark shade of autumn's brown. And
it was cause for celebration, just like every Changing of
the Season. And a celebration, it truly was.

The people of any and all places on Amruhn would
wake up to a new sight of each other. And on that day,
the tents would be set, the ales would flow outside the
taverns; regular work would mostly be halted and
glorious amounts of food and presents were shared. It
was always a surprise, too, for no one knew the exact
day the world would choose to give a new season unto
Amruhn. And it was different each year (though still
around every three months).

Also, there were no such things as birthdays, there
were birth "seasons."

All celebrations of an Amruhnian's birth happened on
the changing day and even further into the days
following. As a person of Amruhn, you celebrated the
season you were born, or better yet, your eye color at
birth, along with all others that shared the same. Arnenn
himself was born with eyes of green, so he wouldn't be
celebrating his nineteenth year for quite some time to
come, unlike Gjone, who had just celebrated his twenty-
second.

The Changing of the Season also meant something else:
the time for Arnenn to go home.

The last month was busier for Remma's than the
beginning part of summer and time to do much else

became limited. Arnenn hadn't been able to catch up with his uncle about any of the story regarding his family, nor had he seen the old man Throone again that reinterested him in it all, thinking him to be up in his tiny house doing whatever weird things he did.

His aunt and uncle were the busiest of them all. He and Gjone found bits of time off of work and were able to go off on some ventures of their own around the city with some of Gjone's random friends, but it wasn't very often.

Gjone would be questioned by his cousin about their family history from time to time, but shrugged most of them off saying the stories were more of his father's interests rather than his own. He told him he thought them interesting, but Arnenn knew that Gjone was not the kind of person affected by history lessons or far tales.

His cousin's lack of interest in the story, or being busy on the docks didn't keep Arnenn's fancy for the subject away, though. He found himself reading some of his uncle's old books for stories about anything tying into it, but had no such luck as he guessed would be the case. One thing he found interesting, however, was that he couldn't come across anything nearing around three hundred years earlier. Most stories from before that time came to some sudden end and barely made any sense, and then new histories weren't written until about a decade or so later; and those were mostly events of wars between kingdoms, cities, or villages with rulers that had their own selfish ambitions. Nothing of a war against great evils.

The same strange pull he felt reaching out to him from the time of his visit with the old man still existed within him. It is why he was looking into the books and journals; he hoped there was something he could find to do with demons or wars with strange creatures. He thought to himself that he was surely turning into his uncle, and was afraid of what his father would think or have to say about any of it.

His father was a good man, but one of strict integrity. Alandis Mourenrowe had always loved living in the Kingdom City with his wife Kershpa, both born and raised there. He was one of the Noble's chief advisors, a sturdy man, and it was for good reason. A great kingdom was that of Vidhera, the capital of all the northern lands of Amruhn, the land known to be that which the great beasts of Light had existed on long before any human capitalized the area. He was proud of his nation and his city through and through, somewhat similar to his wife: Arnenn's mother, Kershpa.

Since parts of Vidhera sat near the western coast, Kershpa loved to look out upon the waters of the Gathralim'. She would spend much of her time near its shores, having a love and respect for the underwater realms and its elusive creatures. She also spent much of her time helping others in the great city, those less fortunate: always living selflessly; and she was well known for her ability to do so. Arnenn received his fun-loving, caring, curious, and adventuristic attributes from Kershpa, and knew he could share with her anything about the wondrous world of which they lived.

Alandis, on the other hand, frowned at his son's wondrous mind, wishing Arnenn would have turned out more like himself so that he could fulfill his place on the Kingdom's Court as early as turning twenty-one. But as the years went by, and as he saw Arnenn's interests continuously travel elsewhere, he lost all hope that his only son may want to join the king's service at all. In fact, he knew that in Arnenn's mind, it was more of a duty than that which was his actual job to have little concern about most dealings of the Kingdom City.

Arnenn always wanted to know more about what surrounded the bordering walls of his homeland; and he would come home day after day to his mother, telling her all about his different adventures and findings—especially during his pre-teen years.

His father never shared too much interest in such subjects and it was more than obvious as he'd always reply with an easy, "That's great, Arnenn. That's great," which was the exact reason he wasn't planning on opening his mouth about any family history pertaining to things such as make-believe wars. However, he was very interested to know if his father knew at least *something* of the story at all. He thought he might at least have some of his own notes about it, but it was also very possible that he didn't, since Rayne joked that his older brother plainly never cared for their grandfather's stories.

It was true. Rayne was the only one who shared in his grandfather's interests; the only one of the family who left Vidhera as a young man, newly married, looking for adventure and something different; he left behind his brother and two sisters to live in the growing and joyous city of Harpelle.

Arnenn hugged Aunt Jemma goodbye, thanking her for another great summer stay and for all she had done to help take care of him before he, along with his cousin and uncle, left the house and headed to the stables to find him a horse for the journey north to the Great Bridges. They started west along the road that ran close to the Cunning and which wrapped the northernmost slope of the city. Arnenn watched the many different shapes of wooden boats from their neighbors to the north coming down the River with loads of different paraphernalia and/or foods. And he knew he'd miss the rich character of it all.

He pondered what his stay back at home would be like after leaving Harpelle this particular year and felt it would be the hardest of all the times he had to do so. There were unanswered questions about his uncle's story and there was also a connection his heart began having toward being in Harpelle that had never existed as strongly before. He even wondered if there was some item of importance he had forgotten or left behind as they walked on, but he couldn't imagine what it could be. He already wanted to turn around and go back to find whatever it was, though, and wondered if the old man was right about just forgetting the tale and if it were only corrupting his interest.

But he looked at his uncle and saw that even he, though very interested in the story and even other strange things as such, didn't seem to be driven mad or weary over any of it—quite the opposite, so it couldn't have been *that* big of a deal. Besides, Arnenn felt he had a right to know either way.

It was really beginning to bother him: how much of a straining task it was to get more of the story from his uncle or Gjone. Everyone else knew more than he since they never fell asleep during the story, and it was understandable; it was his fault he had. But why was it so difficult to just have someone tell him the rest of it? Especially *his* family members since it was about *their* specific family history. He thought he should have just asked someone else, anyone that was there that night— he probably would have had much better luck that way. But it was too late now.

However, maybe all of that wasn't the case. Maybe Rayne was ready to talk. He thought he should speak up and find out before leaving the summer behind for good.

"Uncle, we still never spoke again about that story you told the night of the gathering. I was wondering if you can tell me any more about it now."

"I wasn't sure if I even needed to say anything," said Rayne, squinting while blocking his eyes from the sun that had just peeked through a hole in the rain clouds coming their way. "Don't think I haven't noticed your head buried deep in my books, Arnenn. Thought you'd found something in there—something I haven't been able to find. So what's it that *you* could tell *me*?" Both he and Gjone looked Arnenn's way and awaited an answer.

"I found nothing!"

"Sure . . ." remarked Rayne, before laughing.

"I'm serious . . . I really haven't! I found nothing but regular historical events that don't tie in!"

"We know you talked to Throone . . . did you fall asleep on him as well?" asked Gjone, laughing alone at his own joke with no shame.

"No! What's the matter with you two?" fused Arnenn before chuckling. "I haven't seen Throone since that day! And actually, how do you two even know he told me anything at all?"

"You're not the hardest person to read, Arnenn. You give yourself away pretty easily. Besides, he came by the docks one day when you weren't around—most likely when you were deep in research. He told me he spoke to you about our family having a special history. He also asked me to keep a steady eye on you throughout your remaining time here."

"Keep an eye on me? What? Why? He doesn't even know me that well."

"Well, who knows? Are you for certain that there is nothing he had told you that would make you do anything unordinary?"

"Yeah . . . pretty sure . . . he didn't really seem to know that much anyway!"

Arnenn pondered if he'd perhaps missed something within the conversation he shouldn't have. It wouldn't surprise him if he did.

Rayne finally stopped fooling with him. "He also said he'd be leaving for a bit after he bought a small bag of produce from me. Said there was something he needed to be looking for, but he didn't say what. I have an idea, though; he did ask me about my journal . . . wanted to know if I may still have it. I had to disappoint him. I wonder what he would want with it now. I didn't know he cared for such things anymore. . . . Perhaps you two's discussion interested him again. After that, he rented the most ill-looking boat I've ever seen and began taking off quite quickly down the Cunning."

"Okay, well, anyway . . . what's all that I missed? I want to know!"

Rayne quickly pointed ahead at what they were approaching and only gave him, "I don't think we have the time, Arnenn. We have to get back to the shop—got much to do! I am very sorry. There is always next summer. . . ."

The conversation ended at that; Rayne ceased to bring up any details about it. His expression implied that he *wanted* to say more, but just held himself back for more reasons than the usual "being busy."

That was it. He was done trying; he had come to the point of almost aggravation, annoyed with it all. No longer was he going to care.

They had reached the outskirts of Harpelle and the road they walked came to a familiar cabin-looking building surrounded by haystacks used for feeding.

"It's been a pleasure, Arnenn, having you here again. Thanks for all of your help on the docks—when you were able to make it, of course. . . . It truly has made a big difference for business this year. Do you have everything with you?"

"Yes, of course, Uncle," said Arnenn as he thought about it, but then wondered why he'd be asking. Maybe he knew what it was he had left behind.

"No you don't," said Gjone as he pulled out a long knife from behind his back. It was an original Harpelle blade—the handle, a carved face of a wolf. It was a gift from Rayne two years ago at a particular Changing of the Seasons celebration.

Arnenn shook his head with a blank face. He knew Rayne and Gjone just *had* to share one more laugh about something else at his expense before he'd leave. He slightly laughed back afterward and shrugged it off, wishing he had a good comeback or at least something funny to say, but like usual, he didn't. (Knowing that after spending a good ten minutes thinking of what would've been great to say, it would finally come to him.) Arnenn only grabbed it back from Gjone and gave him a cousinly punch on the shoulder.

He said his final goodbyes as he picked out a horse who went by the name Narmor. He was quite tall and had the blackest shade of hair that any of them had ever seen, even darker than the very hairs on Arnenn's head. The stableman told them the horse was given to him by its previous owner who'd passed away just after; and who gave him the name when finding him as a young stray. He explained it stood for "Night Armor." They didn't know why—nor did the new owner. He was fully grown but young and a mightily impressive-looking stallion, so the name fit him quite well, well enough to leave no room for questioning.

Arnenn knew it was time to go and could only guess he had everything with him, even though it didn't match the feeling.

He and Narmor started walking west where he gave a final wave to his family members who shouted after him. "Give Alandis and Kershpa a good hello for us!"

He took one more glance back at his second home and his favorite city, sadly knowing he wouldn't be seeing any of it for almost an entire year.

6

THE FIRST DAY OF TRAVEL WAS TOUGH.

Storm clouds came the same moment he left the stables. The forest road to the north left the Cunning and rain came blazing down as he walked his horse through the mud of the wide-open fields. They came upon sets of scattered trees where paths were scarcely used due to the River that supplied better use to the merchants.

The land west was a bit denser and almost swampy in areas. Small clusters of trees gathered here and there but most were losing their leaves due to the new season, helping them appear bare and scary-looking.

Arnenn decided to wait out the rain after walking through the second small pocket where he ended up making camp for him and his new friend Narmor. It was in a ditch underneath a partly uprooted tree; it at least still held some leaves compared to most others.

Unable to make a fire due to the menacingly heavy rain, he huddled down within the ditch and ate some apples and grapes. He also shared them with his horse who didn't seem to be bothered by the rainfall. And with his back up against the wet dirt and roots, he found it hard to get comfortable, but kept his eyes closed and tried to doze off for a bit while waiting out the inclement weather.

When finally starting to fall asleep after a good fifteen minutes of shifting around, he heard the roar of what sounded like another great grizzly, and not very far from his camp. It was then followed by a high shriek of another creature. It startled him considerably, to the point where any luck for napping was quickly stolen.

He sat tight while in thought about what he had heard. He knew about some of the beasts, the wild animals that kept watch over the outer forestlands between Harpelle and Vidhera, and some of the other neighboring cities such as Alderhollow to the north (where he was heading for a nice stop).

One telling he knew about was how some of the animals were said to be friendly with man, agreeing to protect them from outside intruders or other types of animals that would for any reason want to harm a human. He heard they would typically keep a watch on those traveling as well, such as him if it were at all true.

He didn't know how or when this agreement came to pass and it sounded very outlandish to him and many others of newer Amruhn, but he heard it all before and for the most part, believed it true. It is one of the reasons why the Harpelle Guard has the emblem of a bear head and has always been called the "Bear Guard."

Not all animals were a part of this arrangement, though, some of the very same types of species were different. The ones said to protect humankind were called the Light-Beasts while the others were just regular animals: not necessarily good or bad to most people's knowledge. Humans were never able to tell the two apart other than the fact that the Light-Beasts were supposed to be somewhat larger. Still, there were little ways to know for sure and even littler reason for most people to give a care unto any of it. Certain sayings such as them possessing "magical abilities" gave people an easy opt-out of joining in on the belief.

Also helping was the fact that they were rarely seen, and if so, then only from a distance before running off somewhere else, not giving much ability for humans to lucidly think much about them.

Staying awake while the rain came down to a lighter drizzle, he became anxiously curious and bored, and wanted to investigate the noise. He walked by Narmor and patted his neck as he said to him, "Don't go anywhere, I'll be right back."

Arnenn grabbed the blade strapped to Narmor's back before walking through a highly brushed gorge that led to a small hill, not very far away. There was some destroyed and ancient-looking sculpture atop a hill, ravaged by time and staged within a small platform bare of trees. It was no strange sight to Arnenn, though, because it was quite common for all travelers to see such things in the middle areas. There were known to be run-down castles and statues that once consumed the now empty lands and some of its surroundings between the major cities of Northern Amruhn, known as the Sculths (scary lands of many beasts and strange things alike). A closer look at the sculpture showed him it may have been a man atop a horse that had stood on its hind legs.

Coming to its top near the sculpture, he saw more land than he thought he'd be able to, such as a road clearing out of the forested areas about a mile north. And at a creek below the hill, he caught sight of the beast he'd heard, which in fact, happened to be a bear.

It had already caught sight of him as well.

He froze and met the eyes of the beast unintentionally, unable to remove his gaze.

But the bear only looked away and continued down the creek as if losing interest while Arnenn slowly loosened his grip from his blade behind his back, assuming he wasn't in any imminent danger while giving a great exhale.

Walking farther down after a few moments had passed, he could see what looked like spots of blood on a patch of tossed-up dirt by the creek below. He knew the bear had killed or at least badly hurt something, but there was no victim or tracks of anything that had scurried off, or anything that had been dragged away. And after a good minute or so, the bear was nowhere to be seen.

Arnenn decided to make his way down to the creek to investigate what happened. As he neared the sturred patch of dirt where the bear's victim *should* have been, he continued seeing nothing. He was intrigued; but he wondered why he was investigating something that really had nothing to do with him at all. Still, he knelt near the patch and gazed down at the freshly turned dirt that settled itself before him.

What at first looked to be blood from yards away, proved to be more of a powdery substance similar to ash. Slowly, he reached down to touch it. And once his fingers made contact, he felt a jolt.

His ears were filled with loud screams of horror and his fingers burned as if they had caught fire before his feet flung him backward. There was a pounding like a drum, a fierce din inside some deep den—reverberating inside his skull.

Lying in the wet creek atop the jagged rocks, the sounds calmed and he was able to take back most of his composure, but the rackety noises absorbing his head were not yet finished.

A second sound then echoed inside of his ears. It reminded him of another one: the one when coming down the trail from the old man's house. In waves it came again; there was shouting and yelling. He could hear his name within it. He heard other names as well—

names he could not make sense of. But this noise wasn't consuming him like the first and had a familiar pulling sensation tied to it, which gave him the urge to go back to Harpelle.

It was again, the feeling he had left something behind, something he indefinitely needed.

He thought it best to only leave the creek and go back to the camp at once. As he stumbled back up the hill, moving farther away from the creek, he looked up and saw the statue again. It had changed. It now gleamed back at him in a majestic might. Renewed and unsullied and looming down on Arnenn was the shine of the knight on his horse of stone with a brand new, brilliant magnificence.

He had a weakening feeling and dropped to one knee as he put down his head and shook it, trying to gain back his normal consciousness, taking a few deep breaths to regain his composure. He believed he was losing it: seeing things that didn't actually exist.

Feeling sturdy again, he peered back up; the statue had gone back to its ravaged state. He passed by it, running quickly over the hill with no hesitation, going through the brush and undergrowth by the scaly trees—back to the camp, flinging himself into the ditch and hiding away where he sat confused, shaking due to the cold breezes and rain for many long minutes that stretched by like hours.

He pondered if it was all actually happening or if being out in the old and mangy land in the rainfall was evading his mind. He also wondered if the bear he had seen was even real or just in his head. His flawing strength had eventually put him to sleep after his mind raced with the multitudes of thoughts, trying to figure out what he was seeing or maybe *not* seeing.

When he woke again, the dusk was close to ending and he had lost out on much of the day. His mind had continued to race and sleep only clouded his thoughts and judgments. The only thing he knew for sure was that he wouldn't be leaving until the next morning.

He went through his bags and found some more food, ate some dried steak his aunt had set within his pack, and was able to create a fire since the rain had mostly let up. It helped him feel better. He used a blanket to cover himself for extra warmth since the darkness and rain of the night made it colder than what it should have been.

He stared at Narmor who seemed to be more than fine under the rain while grazing on some grass around the area. He was just about jealous of the horse.

Arnenn sat through the many hours of the evening, pondering the day's events and why he felt such a need to turn around. He thought about the screaming that put him into a frantic scare and consumed his ears, as well as the yelling sounds he felt were reaching out to him. He then dwelt on his summer stay in Harpelle as a whole, and the story about his family he had barely learned anything about, which continued to frustrate him even more.

A memory then came to mind. It was a memory that surprised him because he realized he'd not thought of it since the time it had happened. It was the very night of the gathering: the night of Rayne's story. There was the vision of the structure of unrecognizable shapes in red and white in a far distance, and there was the girl in the garden. He remembered her face just the same as when he first saw it: her hair of different colors, her obscure clothing, and her eyes that looked directly into his own. They set on a face of an almost exotic and rare, but very natural beauty.

He wondered why he hadn't given more thought to the vision of her since it happened. Maybe it was where he was missing something. He thought over it and tried to make himself see the same vision of her, but he eventually had to give up due to nothing happening. And he became worried about the forested area as he would hear the usual sounds of the wind through the trees and the small critters that scurried around making strange noises. It became more uncomfortable as the night stretched on, which was the most unusual for him. He held his blade close.

Drifting off, he only wanted to get through the cold and frightful night so he could leave once the sun first rose the next day.

A bit of a rude awakening, Narmor was tapping his hooves on the edge of the ditch. Arnenn's eyes pried themselves open and saw that the sun had been out for quite a few hours, and it looked as if his traveling companion was more than ready to get a start on the day, tired of waiting on his sleepy rider.

He splashed some cold water on his face he'd cupped from a newly formed puddle that was created by the night's rain. He also replaced the previous day's clothes with fresh ones that weren't wet.

After eating and having packed his things, Arnenn and Narmor started walking north again, and this time nearer to the main road instead of trying to use his common shortcuts and secret trails he knew of. He was happy to see zero rain clouds in the sky and he only needed to get through one more night before making it to the Great Bridges. There, he would boat back to Vidhera on the slow river heading west. (That is if the weather stayed as it was.)

He thought about the events again, but he was in better spirits that morning; they didn't seem to have such a strong tie to him anymore. The new and bright day was only bringing along new and bright feelings. He had mentally become more and more prepared to leave the memories of Harpelle behind and go home— somewhere he would likely be safe from strange visions or noises. Something normal.

Travel went how he'd hoped. The ground had already begun drying for the most part and his black haired friend was moving with a solid pace. He made his way onto a road that had some other travelers such as rare merchants with small carts who gave a great waves, as he also, would wave right back. He felt good to have his usual spirits with him and to look ahead rather than behind. Also, the roads were better put-together in the area closer to Alderhollow, making it more suitable for the uncommon traveler.

Some hours into the day, he and Narmor stopped for a short rest where he looked out at the terrain ahead that was mostly hilly and rockier than the flatter valleys surrounding many parts of the Harpelle's realms. With that, and the fact that Arnenn could see signs on the road pointing to the different directions of many small bricked houses ahead, he knew he wasn't very far away from Harpelle's sister city.

Alderhollow was a very well-laid-out town and of decent size. It was placed closer to the north end of the Cunnings than Harpelle and it was also where Arnenn decided he'd be staying in a room overnight, and not in another wet ditch underneath some old tree's ragged roots, or anything slightly similar.

After having some more dried meat and fruit, he started up the road and awaited a different one that would turn slightly east to his destined city. He could picture the sign he was expecting to be seeing soon: a large, white-wooden and squared sign with thick bold and black letters held up by a broad and impressive tree reading:

WELCOME TO ALDERHOLLOW: *The White Walled City*

He also remembered that for some reason, numerous smaller signs were sticking out above tall grass with arrows pointing in its direction. It was one of the many cute characteristics that made him like Alderhollow, though he had only ever been there once before.

It wasn't really a city entirely painted in white like its name suggested. It had its name due to the high cliff banks lining the River that were somehow covered in white. It was an exquisite and unique sight, but nobody knew or remembered what happened to make it as such.

Nearing the sign almost an hour later where vast open fields of farmland in green surrounded many roads that crossed, he slowed for a pass of sheep led by their stocky shepherd. When completely stopped, he suddenly felt the strange pulling again, and also, a presence looking his way.

Slowly turning his head to the right and seeing into the midst of the small and lonely line of trees that sat in the openness, there was another great bear looking straight at him, no farther than thirty feet away, but this time with an ultimate intensity in its brown eyes. Arnenn froze again, and strangely enough, he thought it could have even been the very same bear he had seen the day before.

The shouts inside his head started again. They came back, wave after wave and even clearer than before.

Arnenn . . . go back . . . GO BACK!

The pulling became stronger and the shouts became even louder, and in more waves they still rung deep in his ears. The bear gave a sudden roar and lifted itself on its hind legs while its mouth hung wide open, eating the air around it. It made Narmor jolt back on his own where in complete discomposure, Arnenn fell off his horse—flat onto the road.

The commotion caused the shepherd's herd to run in all directions where the man screamed, "What do you think you're doing here?" before walking up and prodding Arnenn with his walking stick as Arnenn only stared up at him in shock and confusion, constantly looking back and forth to the place where the bear was just a moment ago, and then to the shepherd where he could only say one thing. "Ss-sorry—sorry."

He looked back to the bear once more but it had moved on or completely disappeared; and he guessed that the shepherd must've been untroubled by the bear, or maybe didn't even hear it at all. But the shepherd and his sheep weren't his concern; he knew he had to go back to Harpelle immediately to figure out what was going on with him. He thought that if anyone would be able to help, it would be Rayne—or at least the strange old man Throone could be useful somehow.

He flung himself atop Narmor, saying once more to the shepherd, "Sorry," and then rode off so fast in the direction he had come that the man who stood shaking his head only saw Arnenn for a few more moments.

7

THE VERY SAME DAY ARNENN DEPARTED

the Keeper's home within the hills of the Cunnings, Throone mulled over the conversation that had taken place. Keeping still in his chair while the dark of his home shadowed every crevice within, he felt alone. It was a very familiar feeling.

Throone pondered his many years yet few findings, and rationalized if he had done enough—knowing it to be his purpose. But it wasn't as if he hadn't been trying all along: keeping an eye on them as best he could and even saving them from imminent danger from time to time. Many times he had been there to protect their lives, but wondered if he'd placed them in even further harm by not saying or doing enough, or simply by not being more persistent.

He continued in thought about all of the different generations of Mourenrowe he had come to know and befriend. He experimented with them, which equaled to some becoming mad with too much interest, or even falling into further disbelief. Eventually, he thought trying at all was an entirely useless act. He became frustrated with grief and sadness time and time again and grew angrier with each and every one of them. He wanted to know too badly why this was to be his, and *only* his task. And why all of his work and efforts continuously went to waste as they just died off one by one while he just kept living. How was he supposed to know when or *if* it would happen? And why should he bother caring anymore?

The Keeper grew bitter and found he'd need to leave it all behind and forget about the troubled family, live his own life; needing to find his own purpose, even though it unfortunately felt wrong to do so. At times he thought he was lied to all along; his spirit tossed around like a joke. But there were still parts of his being that he just couldn't ignore, which would continuously change his mind back to believing it all again.

He aged slow, much slower than anyone else, but in rhythms more than just riding the continuous slope of declining life. He remembered back when he was almost a hundred years old, yet looking like he was the age of others who were in their mere forties. Better yet, how was he able to create heat through his hands? He never heard of anyone else being able to do that before.

"WHO AM I?" he would scream to himself sometimes.

Adding to his difficult life, he couldn't stay in one place for too long. People would start to notice his agelessness, and he didn't need anyone's questioning if he could help it. It was a good thing he always had his little hut of a home to himself and that no one ever cared to want it except for him—that being the reason for its rough location.

Still, at times, Throone had to move for a few decades or so whether it be in Harpelle, Vidhera, or even towns that no longer exist today.

He thought about the journal Arnenn brought to his attention while staring at the tens of open books spread up against the walls of his home, giving little indication to the one he had been searching for all along. He did find *some* books that happened to prophesy events, but none of them tied into anything real or anything that could actually help him, just made up prophecies of future kings and kingdoms written by already kings who selfishly wanted to continue their prominent lines. There was nothing that played into the Mourenrowes' history or the war specifically. At the same time, he wasn't exactly sure what this book was really supposed to do or how it worked, or what he would do with it when finding it. He only knew he needed to seek it out. That's what she had told him—that is if he remembered it correctly.

Thinking it to be another useless and painful effort, it still ignited his soul to know about this journal Rayne had apparently attained at one point. Perhaps he missed something there twenty years ago. And now, it is the only object he had never been able to find. He wondered how something like that could have slipped from under his nose.

He left his home the next day for a couple reasons. One of them was to ask Rayne about the journal.

About two hours after leaving, he saw Rayne in a far back corner of his shop trying to handle customers while carrying more boxes of produce than he should've been. Eventually getting some free hands and a moment alone to speak to the old man and having to disappoint him, he explained that he had searched for it hundreds of times throughout the years, but had unwillingly lost it and gave up all hope in finding it, and long ago.

"Only in my far memory can it be found," said Mr. Mourenrowe as he kept himself busy and stormed off.

Throone just stood there, taking it for what it was worth, understanding that once again his luck had run out. But he wasn't giving up all hope just yet again . . .

there was still the second reason he had left his little home.

Purchasing some food from Rayne before renting a boat made up of the most common stock and beaten up pieces of wood, Throone left Remma's company to begin his travel down the Cunning River. He remembered a good friend from years back living in the lowlands near the Lake that ran a famous inn and thought he could pay him a quick visit.

From the harbor at Harpelle, the Cunning ran southeast along the Mountains as it traveled through tall and thick pines.

When daylight fell, he came to a different harbor on the outskirts of a town called Crennan of the Cunning (otherwise only known as Crennan). There, he grabbed a room at an inn called the Boarish Slug—an angry green slug with tusks was painted on all corners of its chipping walls outside that were right up above the flowing water of the River. It was fairly beat down and came with the heavy scent of the fish caught from it, which were stored to be served at the many bars and restaurants. Some of the men inside its bar looked just about the same as the painting of the slug—or at least gave off similar characteristics.

The town was mostly just a rest stop, and that was the one and *only* reason he was there.

Over time, Crennan became one of the main towns for the poor boating folk who were simply known by some to be "dirty merchants." They would stop and grab a room there for sometimes many days or even weeks at a time, and some even ended up buying small properties or renting a room at an inn until they practically took over the entire place. It was easy for it to happen in a town like Crennan, for cities more north didn't have very many places for the merchants to stay. Some even tended to live on their boats or were for the most part known as homeless; either by choice, or by the impending popular opinion of others.

It was easy to spot a Crennan-based merchant from far away. There villainous shaped hats, twisted beards, knotted hair, and grimy roguish fashions were found everywhere in the small town. (Also, due to their many outgoing natures, personalities, and knowledge of under-the-table items, they were quite the people to speak to if let's say, you were feeling down.)

Throone watched Crennan change more than any other city and also more than any other person had, but not in a good way. He could still remember what it looked like hundreds of years back as a child being no more than a small camp made up of rundown mini-houses as he would travel about with his foster parents of the time. It was the fastest growing city throughout all of Amruhn, yet, it never once improved on its looks.

It was downright in dire need of repair. The planks of wood on all the homes and shops were rotted due to weathering while overgrown brush and weeds took over the city's pathways. Pipes with rusted edges stuck far out over the inns of Crennan which leaked some sort of musty-green ooze. Still, most people there didn't seem to mind a single bit and made the best home of the place they could.

Anyone else traveling down the River that wasn't a merchant did anything they possibly could to avoid the city—and its people if at all possible. Throone himself tried to stay clear of the intoxicated boaters and remained in his room over the night, trying his best to drown out the loud noises from the bar underneath his puny room, rolling up small pieces of paper to stick in his ears and eventually falling asleep.

The next day, Throone got up as soon as possible to get a start on his day, and also, to get away from the fishy smells that he was unhappily getting used to. He spent most of his morning waiting around for the harbor workers to fetch him his little boat, learning long ago that if you weren't the common carrier, you pretty much came second, or even very last in respects.

He sat on a small bench while looking upon the great Cunnings just on the other side of the Cunning River itself when he noticed a strange stretch of black smoke behind some brush, settling near the ground. Throone fixed and narrowed his eyes to see if he could get a closer look, but suddenly, the smoke moved like some traveling fire. It disappeared quickly behind a patch of trees. Before he could give it any thought, he heard the sound, "Mr!" which came from the voice of a small boy maybe nine years old, working the harbor, probably the poor son of some Crennan-based merchant. Throone saw him paddling up his pathetic raft to the edge of the dock.

Before noticing, the boy had been staring at him, waiting for quite some time to get the old man's attention as he wondrously stared off into the trees like a fool.

"Oops! You caught me off guard there, boy!" he said as the youngster jumped out from the boat and then onto the dock, and then stuck his hand out for a tip. Throone stalled for a moment in amazement at the kid's lack of shame, but then smiled and handed him a couple of gold coins and said, "I suppose I'll need to give you two coins for having to wait on a dazing old man."

The boy ran off without hesitation to get to the next boat in line, taking no notice of his comment. Throone stared off at him, shaking his head, thinking again about what Crennan had become.

He paddled swiftly away and waited until he was out of range of the strong smells of Crennan to have his breakfast.

The land surrounding the River farther south had become less green in parts. Yet, tall grass danced from the breeze on the hills between the trees and rocks where the occasional deer would be seen drinking. The Cunning was always heavily trafficked, which made Throone believe most animals would be run off, but it was actually quite the opposite. It had him smile. He found a love in boating his way to the Lake where the Cunning swelled into one giant mass of flat water. The cities around it shared the richest of environments since they were the gathering place of all trade that came from the north and south and beyond.

Not only was it the gathering place of goods and the many boat merchants that traveled down the River, flooding the Lake's shores, but also of talk. Any happenings in Amruhn were more known by the people of the Lake than any other, and of all them, none knew information like Throone's old friend, Crowlis.

Crowlis Jepp was the famous inn-owner known far and wide throughout the Lake, as he himself somehow knew mostly every soul there in one way or another. One of the richest men in Filman (a city lying just at the mouth of the Cunning River's western end) was also a man that wore the grimiest clothes and had more personality than he did money.

Throone arrived in Filman late in the afternoon on the very day he left Crennan when happily disowning his uncomfortable raft that would eventually drift off to the massive ships on the Disdon's coastline. He watched the boat scouts take it roughly away before he entered one of the closest buildings visible.

The walls of the busy and crowded Inn at Filman were covered in bronze tapestries that were hanging from the high wooden ceiling of the main chamber where four stone pillars had a spiraling shape reaching up to its top. It was a very peculiar match, almost as if they had taken bits and pieces of older buildings from the Lake, along with remnants of abandoned castles, and placed them together—it's likely what happened. The people of the Lake made things work with whatever they could and most were experts in the art of being scavengers.

Throone saw Crowlis near the bar talking to a few of the regulars.

Crowlis loved to talk, and he found the best way to do that was to tend drinks for others at his inn that was originally run by his father; and where he would spend both day and night throughout most his life. Crowlis saw Throone coming toward him at once and a large grin appeared upon his face. He simply ignored the others he was previously speaking to as if they didn't exist.

"Oh my. Good ol' Mr. Throone!" said Crowlis while shaking the old man's hand and patting his side arm with the utmost excitement. "What brings you back here? It-is been yeeears, sir! Ha-ha—" stopping the chuckle quite suddenly, he jokingly pointed a finger at him before asking, "You're not on a-troubling business now, are you? You know that-I should be reporting old men such as ourselves—or more so the likes of you that-are up to anything of importance . . . you know it-is not good for us."

"You know that I have never had anything to do with any *real* importance, yet, Crowlis," said Throone, sarcastically.

"No? Just the-usual running off to save important people with important matters and . . ." he looked around and softened his voice, "and igniting fire-in your hands, may I add—" Crowlis said it in a soft voice right before he laughed harshly again. "What will-it be? I've got a new draft from the east of the Red Hills. They say it's the best barley around these days, you must give-it a try!"

"I would insist on nothing other than exactly what you'd suggest, Crowlis, and you know that well."

"That I-do, sir . . . at least somebody still listens to me nowadays. . . . So, what is-it that one old friend can do for an even older friend that he hasn't seen-in ten years? Might I ask? And, what are you doing in these parts so far away from your comfortable little cottage-like home in lovely Harpelle?"

"Well, I was hoping to talk to you in a less crowded environment," said Throone as he looked about. "You see I'm here because something, or . . . some*one* from Harpelle has me questioning things."

"Uh-oh, that sounds like the usual case from you . . . look, why-don't you go ahead and come over for tea tonight? In the meantime, have yourself a stay at any room you would like, it-is on me."

Throone sipped on his ale as he watched Crowlis go back to his gossiping with all the others in the bar—just as easily as he ignored them the minute before.

He meandered some of the sights of the Lake for a bit before making himself a very comfortable guest at Crowlis's home that evening. It was the largest room of the inn; it was located at the extreme top of the building. Some called it a penthouse, but with the way it was poorly designed as it hung to the edge and even down, it wasn't easy for most to agree.

Throone had to weave his way through many pieces of stuffed furniture to reach a set of purple chairs with golden beads on the far side of the room where Crowlis was waiting and waving him over.

He found Crowlis's place fascinating and delightful: the perfect place to have a good cup of tea.

Sitting down and leaning forward, Throone said to his old friend, "So, what strange things have you heard of lately?"

Crowlis found it abrupt and way too general of a question to be asked, but answered gleefully with, " . . . Just the usual really, other-than your visit, of course."

"What would you call *the usual* around here these days?" asked Throone.

The inn-owner set his cup down and placed himself sturdily within his chair. "You know how it-is. Not too different than last you were here. Many boat thieves lately, along with the typically disappearing wine bottles from Grusher's Cellar, if-you recall." At that he had a chuckle to himself. "And sightings of strange things here and there."

Throone thought about his sighting on the River: the black smoke he thought he had seen.

"Explain these sightings," he commanded with a severe tone.

Crowlis, being used to Throone's random spouts of aggressiveness that were just the same as many years before, didn't let it rub off on him and only explained, "There've-been some around the Lake late-at night, such as strange animals running close to the water and also up around our caves. Most say they're-just dogs and I believe them, too. I see all kinds of dogs running-around here every single day and night! But, I also heard about some woman being-bitten late at night about a week ago by something she couldn't see or explain when she was putting out-her fire. Apparently, the thing was quite the fighter. Luckily for her, she-was able to escape into her house. I'll take a bet that-it was some type of wild dog, but there are many animals that could do something like that I-suppose. . . . I barely even remembered this. If you had come a-day later, it would surely be cleared straight out-of my memory!"

"Indeed," said Throone as he paused. "Strange animals or creatures . . . that's definitely something that could be dangerous, or that could mean many different things— bad things if they would be the types of creatures I'm thinking of, but they're probably not. Still, you'd tell me if you saw something out of the real ordinary, wouldn't you?"

"Of course . . . no problem!" Crowlis yelled back in his usual quick-paced speaking.

"Crowlis, none of these things would be a joke to me and I wouldn't have traveled all this way south to this Lake of yours for no reason at all."

Throone was beginning to take Crowlis out of his usual excited tone of life, which the inn-owner did not appreciate very much. But even so, there wasn't very much he could do about it; Throone wasn't the same as some of the others he dealt with each and every day. It was actually quite the other way around and there were many good reasons as to why that was.

Crowlis responded with, "Yes, old man. You-know, Throone, you seem to be a-bit moody if I might say so, even more than before. What's to explain it?"

Throone looked stunned for a moment.

He found it hard at times to not talk "down" to people, being that he was so much older than everyone else; most to him were almost only children, though he never meant to be rude. He mildly stretched back in his chair.

"You are right, Crowlis, I am. Fact is, I really don't know how much I've been myself *at all* lately. Not that I really know myself that well in the first place—as I believe you'd agree, but, I've had some hard nights. I found myself putting down too many beverages. Believe it or not, I even had to ask a young guard for a cell to sleep in just a couple nights ago, and he seemed more than just willing to assist me from what I can remember. It has just become pretty bad overall. And sorry to be so intrusive . . . I've had a question growing inside my mind and it has stalled progress of allowing room for anything else to think about, which I have found to be typical of me."

Throone went on. "You see, a few years ago, I'd found out about a book . . . one of importance that is supposed to have existed some time before. I remember reading about it much longer ago than then, too, even before *our* dealings here, but I of course put the matter aside and had forgotten about it due to being interested in other findings. This time, I didn't forget so easily, and since, I've spent each and every day looking for answers to where it could be or reappear, though it ended up coming to nothing, which, of course, only angered me and led me to more feelings of uselessness. Young Crowlis, have you heard anything about odd journals or books being sold anywhere around this Lake at all?"

Crowlis had a bit of an intrigued stare before he spoke. "Sounds like it must be a very interesting read, whatever this book is, but I-have not! And what books may be sold around here-is not exactly my area of expertise. Is this why you've come all this way? And if so, how important is-this particular book? What's so special about it? And what's it called, if-I may ask?" He also had a love for rare artifacts such as his older friend.

"It is crucial to me, Crowlis, and from what I have read, it's supposed to be called the Orrumn . . . or at least *was* called that at some point in time. I don't know exactly why it was or even still *is* special, other than apparently being a book of prophecy."

He had Crowlis's full attention.

"As I've said before, I search because I feel a need to and that's why I came all this way down here, yes. The power I feel pulls me to do it as it makes me mad at the same time! All I know is that it exists somewhere. And somehow, I must find it . . . to help the Mourenrowes."

"Still-on about that family, are-you? Still believe some war-is coming?" asked Crowlis as he shook his head and secretly rolled his eyes. He lost interest in the whole thing at the sound of the name.

"Yes, I do! But whether I believe there is or not, is irrelevant compared to how it makes me feel! It's the same as my power! And Crowlis, there is another one! . . . His name's Arnenn."

Crowlis rolled his eyes again and this time Throone saw the expression in its entirety. The inn-owner remembered the last time his old friend Throone had come to him and started talking about one particular Mourenrowe member and how that turned out to mean practically nothing, and quite quickly, too. He wished well for his weird friend; and he also had a very high regard and appreciation for his impressive "wizard-like" abilities, but also wished he'd just put an end to all his ludicrous belief of things.

"Crowlis, you and I have been on many of our own out-there adventures and doings, saving these cities of yours. I can trust you in this, right? You are the only one I've ever confided in and that's risky of me—knowing that you know just about anyone there is to know and especially talk more than any other I've ever known to talk."

"Yes, old man," answered Crowlis, slowly. I haven't betrayed your trust yet, have I?" He looked even older and more worn than he whom he called "old man." Throone had confided in Crowlis with many things, though mostly on accident, and he never told him just how old he actually was. Fact, he never told anyone.

He gave into it a bit. "So what is it about this Arnenn character? What makes him any more different or special than the last one you came to me talking about? Rainer, was it?"

"It's Rayne," he corrected. "And this Arnenn I speak of said he might've seen a vision."

"Might have? Well, that sounds to-be some promising news!"

"Crowlis, stop messing with me! You must understand. When the young man said it, I felt it! It felt like magic!" he said, jumping out of his chair and hitting a side table, almost spilling his hot cup of tea. Then, peering down at Crowlis while his hands made different gestures around his body, he continued.

"It was like nothing I have ever felt before! I even almost saw it—like a blueish light! And then of all things, he started asking me about a journal of his uncle's which had somehow slipped from under my knowledge. Now, of course, I'm intrigued all over again, but I wasn't about to try the same old methods and tactics that drove me nuts like before! I knew I had to at least ask if you knew anything at all before I started looking elsewhere—"

Crowlis responded hastily. "If I remember correctly, you seem to find things in-the most obscure places of all. Perhaps you should just let-it come to you and enjoy yourself in the meantime: Relax. Throone, you may not be getting much older, which is strange enough as it-is, I must add . . . but you're also not getting-any younger."

Crowlis then stood up to pour himself some more tea, tired of his old friend peering down at him with his most overwhelming presence.

The Keeper decided there was no more he could learn from Crowlis which was unfortunate since he had come all this way, but he already knew there was a tiny amount of luck he had of his friend knowing anything about such a specific subject in the first place. He mostly just needed to get away from Harpelle for a bit.

"Crowlis, if you end up hearing anything, please send word. I feel the need to be deep in thought about all of this. Perhaps I will be spending some more time in my shack of a home mulling it over, or even take your advice and do nothing at all." He walked nearer to the window and stared out at the many lights and fires of the Lake with his arms crossed.

Crowlis confirmed him that he'd be keeping an eye and an ear out for it before his wife walked through the door, and where the conversation was practically over.

Next, Throone asked Crowlis if he could use a horse for his journey home.

"Absolutely!" he replied. "Just as long as-I see it again at some point in time—maybe within another ten years from now."

"That, I will try. And another thing, Crowlis. I need to have you and your men's support. If anything truly odd starts happening around these lands, I need your commitment to helping me. You are the most powerful person I know other than myself—in your own ways, at least."

"I wouldn't have-it any other way, Throone!" stated Crowlis as he nodded the old man out of his door and on his way, knowing he may not see him for quite a while all over again. It gave the inn-owner a slight sadness for him to be leaving so soon after only just arriving, yet, he was also partially glad to have him and his somewhat brutal personality gone for the evening.

As Throone walked down the hall, he heard Crowlis's wife Lune ask, "Who was that? He looked familiar," right before he also heard, "Do you remember how my friends and-I used to say 'the Skill of Throone?'"

The Keeper made a quick stop at a small campground next to one of the eastern stretches of the Palendrian before nightfall had come the next day. Peeling an orange and sitting on a fallen tree that had been carved into a lovely bench, he noticed something out of the corner of his eye: A wild stag with strange black fur was looking directly at him with the coming black sky surrounding it. It turned its head a bit to the side and looked back at him, and then again, giving notice for Throone to follow. It gave him nothing but a creepy vibe at first, but knowing well to trust most mammals without any added doubt, he followed the stag into the Forest's walled beginning. (Even into *this* particular forest.) He was then led through a small meadow of dried out grass and then near to an almost dried-up creek set back within the trees again.

About a quarter of a mile into it, and continuing along the creek, he noticed that the stag had begun to look quite different, almost as if it was shorter and wider than when he first started following. He couldn't be too sure, though; the black sky had begun to set all about which made it harder to see. He was a bit perplexed as to exactly what he was even doing—but he didn't care to give it too much thought, either. (Throone was easily found "just going along with things.")

He then saw something else. It reminded him of what he'd seen on the River just the morning before: the smoke substance, once again, which was streaming up from the bushiness of the Forest's floor ahead of him and even into the towering plantations.

He was cautioned, but it was too late; he was already led into an area condensed within dying trees where it all quickly happened.

The stag was out of sight. Or, it had turned itself into something else.

Before, and up above him within the trees, he saw what was guessed to be an enormous spider; or a similar insect that was much larger than the likes of anything it should have been, and it was completely wrapped in the smoke-like substance. He knew at that moment, that it was of Dark.

It was the night that the Keeper was almost killed; the night he was saved by the Angelic Being while the forested area changed from old to new; and the night when he fell into a deep slumber that continued for almost an entire month.

8

GJONE WAS AWOKEN BY THE SCRATCHING noises coming from somewhere inside the house before also hearing the light sounding footsteps against the creaking wood of the stairs. He knew them to have been his mother's; he recognized them since being a baby. By the time Jemma landed to the bottom of the flight, he heard a slight pause followed a rather harsh thud. It startled him. He sat quickly up out of bed and heard nothing except his mother's irregular breathing after that.

He raced down the stairs and saw his mother holding the steel pipe that had been leaning against the wall near the front door since before he could remember. It was meant for intruders, but the last time it had been moved must've been ten years ago, or maybe even longer than that.

"What happened?" he asked, barely able to see his mother in the dark room where no candle had yet been lit.

He started toward her, but she cautioned him: putting up her hand with, "Wait!" and, "Stop!" She pointed down to a mass even blacker than the darkness already around them. Gjone had almost stepped on it. It looked as if a large dog had fallen asleep on the floor.

"Uh, what is that?"

"I don't know, but I heard a strange scratching sound so I came down and this thing let itself in the back door. Must have been traveling by the patio and thought it would come in to see what's for dinner. I've told that father of yours to keep this doors locked so many times. Go wake him. You two need to get this thing out of here—right now! I don't want to touch whatever it is."

Gjone followed his mother's instructions without any question in his half daze of sleepiness. He began his incline on the stairs to wake Rayne who'd surprisingly slept through the commotion with great ease. But not a second later, Rayne's eyes opened wide due to hearing his wife screaming.

The creature woke and had a good hold on Jemma's leg after she had dropped the steel pipe in the opposite direction of the room.

Gjone ran quickly back to grab the animal by the neck and to get its jaws off his mother's leg, but the moment his hands made contact with the thing, the skin of his palms and fingers immediately felt a burning sensation. It felt as if he had grasped a hot pan of cast iron on accident.

Rayne practically fell down the stairs while adjusting his eyes to see Jemma lying on the floor, being bitten at the leg by something terrible—and his son on his knees, holding his hands up in torment. He didn't understand a single thing he was seeing when both began shouting at him. He was unsure of what to do but without waiting a moment longer, he grabbed a small book from the top of his dusty library collection and smacked the creature straight on the back with it. The thing lost its stability and crashed into the floor, no longer having a hold on Jemma's leg.

Having to ignore the burning pain on his hands, Gjone stepped up and over his mother to grab the steel pipe. Taking hold of it, he jumped over her again and with one hand, swung it directly down on the beast's back.

They thought it to be dead. But, it suddenly moved again, even after Gjone's astonishing blow with the heavy pipe.

Surprisingly, instead of Gjone, it looked at Rayne and snarled with a fierce anger as if the man had something it wanted. Gjone lifted up the pipe to strike down at it again, but this time with both hands—to really put it down.

It was no use. The creature quickly jumped back and out the door it escaped with great ease into the black of the night where the clouds were the moon's only company.

Rayne closed the back door which it had escaped but also opened the front door after hearing a knock and someone outside asking if everything was okay. They knew the voice to be Simeon's (their always-overly-concerned next door neighbor).

Before Rayne opened the door all the way, Simeon heard his voice. "Simeon! Go and get Stalk! Jemma's been bitten by something and we need him to take a look. But be careful—and quick!" he cautioned. "There's something very dangerous out there!"

"R—right away, Mr. Mourenrowe!" said Simeon. The man had wrapped himself in a green robe with small stars of gold all over it, almost asking to be attacked by something. He ran off speedily, holding his nightcap securely to his head.

"How does it feel?" asked Rayne, racing over to his wife with a wet cloth to wrap the wound and to stop the bleeding.

"It hurts, you giant imbecile!" she screamed with a frustrated and confused look as to why he'd be asking, breathing at unsteady rhythms. She was more in shock from the attack than the pain of the bite.

"Just keep breathing and try to calm yourself," said Gjone as he picked her up and helped her over to the closest chair that steadied near the fireplace.

After waiting for what felt like an eternity as Jemma slowly calmed her breathing to a steady pace, Simeon came back with a man who wore a small gray cap with no visor and a vigorously big pair of eyebrows that sat on the top of a tired pair of eyes. The well known doctor of Harpelle carried himself along with his case into their home. Seeing the wound, he looked keenly at the bite that wrapped almost all the way around Jemma's ankle. It had gone quite deep.

"Was it a large dog that attacked you?" asked Stalk as he placed the firelight of a candle behind a purple stone. The stone allowed the firelight to reflect and shine brightly through and out the other side so that he could get a better look. (A purt stone: a very common and popular stone used for light throughout all of Amruhn.)

Jemma looked up at Rayne and Gjone, unsure of what to say. Rayne spoke up for her. "You can say it was a dog . . . I guess, but it seemed much stronger—more resilient than any dog I've ever known to exist. We got it off her leg by hitting it with this book here." He pointed at the book lying on the floor, and then to Gjone's direction as he continued with, "And actually, that steel pipe Gjone's holding, too."

"So it escaped just fine after being hit with *that* thing? And by Gjone?" asked Simeon as he, too, pointed directly at the pipe. "If there's something that can handle a strike such as that running around town, we must warn others!"

"Well, let's be careful. And let's not make any quick decisions here to scare everybody in town half to death, Simeon. Fact, it's probably long gone by now, anyway," cautioned Rayne while looking out the back door and shaking his head.

"Well, how'd it get in here?"

Coming from the table, Jemma's pain-stricken voice sounded. "That would be due to Rayne here who I have told SO MANY TIMES to make sure the doors are locked at night!"

Rayne knew it to be true. He only kept a straight face showing slight embarrassment.

The doctor spoke up. "I agree with Rayne. It's best not to make anyone frantic. Also, the wound's pretty deep, but I'm giving it a good clean and wrapping it up for the night. You'll be okay, Jemma. Just try to stay off it for a bit and add this ointment here—don't let it dry up too much. I'll be back to take another look at it before noon."

He packed up his case and gave a slight tilt of his top hat with his thumb and index finger before tiredly waving his way out.

After Stalk's absence, Rayne urged Simeon to go back home and to keep the event to himself. He knew this to probably be asking too much of him because Simeon was one of those neighbors who would go out of his way to gossip about anything and everything that happened on the east end of Harpelle.

Gjone stared out the main window by the front door and watched Simeon go back into his house before looking to his parents. "One thing I didn't want to say while they were here is that something very, uh . . . "*off*" happened."

His parents gave him a look suggesting they were quite well aware without him saying so, but Gjone went right into it.

"When I tried to grab at that thing, it was strangely hot, and my hands felt like they were on fire! I thought they might've been burned at first, but they seem fine now. It was like there was a dusty or grainy—almost wet substance on my hands from it. Anyway, they're the same as if nothing even happened, now. . . ."

"Burning feeling? Son, that *is* very off, and I'm not sure what that could mean. I will say you're right, though; it does make things more interesting . . . and whatever that creature could be sounds like something I've heard of before."

Rayne stood still while studying his brain, a posture Gjone well recognized.

He knew what his father was getting at and even had his own moment thinking anything possible. But still, he didn't want to get caught up in the many possibilities of what it "could" have been, particularly with someone like his father. He immediately changed the subject and only responded with, "Yeah, it's crazy—I think we have already had enough excitement for one middle-of-the-night wake-up. My mind can barely function on what the heck even happened—and Mom, you need your rest, for sure."

"Don't tell ME what I need, Son. I have taken care of you since you were soiling your tiny clothes! And I have healed enough of you and Arnenn's wounds to equal up to this entire city's worth!"

Gjone knew how to handle his mother's abrasiveness and even found most of his to be from her. "I got it, Mom . . . let me at least help you up to your bed before you turn into a werewolf or something, since that's the path you seem to be heading."

"Let me help as well," said Rayne, timidly, knowing how unhappy his wife was with him about leaving the door open. He went to it again, and assured it was safely locked.

* * *

They had gone back to bed, but it took all three quite long into the night to actually fall asleep. It took Gjone the longest; he felt an awakening from the adrenaline rush of swinging the pipe at the creature, but it wasn't satisfying in the slightest. He didn't understand it a single bit. When he struck it with a steel pipe directly on the back, it barely did anything other than frustrate it even more. Gjone knew he had great strength, and he had already proven it many times before. It was really messing with his head.

It was him, not Arnenn, not Haulfir, especially not Cezz or Rimland, or any of his friends growing up that could throw large bags of grain clear across the Cunning, or lift practically anyone over his head and throw them over tables when getting in fights at the taverns with those who thought they could best him. It was, of course, absolutely ridiculous for anyone to believe they could. (By this, his friends gave him the nickname: Gjone, Throne-Thrower.)

He may not have shared the same adept skill sets as Arnenn or Haulfir with a blade, but he knew his strength and that he had it. And the night's events were an absolute blow to his ego; he knew it well. Even his mother was able to take it out for a bit with the same pipe. Also, it bothered him that after he hit the creature, it wasn't even angry with him, it pretended more upset with his father, who'd only hit it with a small book.

Unsatisfied and discouraged, he wanted desperately to find the creature; he wanted to wake up first thing in the morning and hunt it down. If it wasn't for himself alone, he was undoubtedly angered about what had happened to his mother; and he knew he must get revenge on the creature, and soon, whether it was just some rare and obscure animal, or even a creature from one of his father's stories. To him, it didn't matter either which way what it was—only that it ended up dead.

The sun rose, but a cloudy and rainy day was in store for Harpelle as Gjone awoke in a fright all over again. But this time, it was due to the sound of another knock on the front door.

He immediately remembered the event from just a few hours of terrible sleep ago. He jumped out of bed and just about flew straight down the stairs in a great frenzy, almost shaking the thick and sturdy house while small amounts of adrenaline still whirled within his system. He thought it looked too early for Stalk to be dropping by before slightly peering out the crack of the door, hoping it wasn't Simeon again, or some other random neighbor questioning the evening's noises.

All he saw, though, was Arnenn. He was standing on the front porch while dripping wet in the pouring rain. The water sloped over his hood that almost hid his eyes as he slowly brought up his hand to wave, knowing his presence would only confuse anyone in this particular house.

"What in Amruhn? Come in! What happened? Why are you back here again?" asked Gjone without pause as they grabbed each other's arms harshly.

"Gjone, you wouldn't believe it . . . I mean, strange things were happening to me out there! I needed to come back!"

"Strange things happened to you? You're not the only one who—" Gjone stopped as he was about to explain the night's happenings, but thought he should hear Arnenn out first. Maybe his story was more interesting. "Go on—"

"Cousin, I think I've gone off the maps or something! I've been seeing things, hearing things, feeling things . . . I mean, I saw a bear—and this weird thing happened—and then I saw it again! And then there was this yelling, and I just felt like I had to come back! It isn't right, Gjone, there's something here, or something out there that's just not letting me go home, it's hard to explain."

"Can you be a tad more specific? —Wait, actually . . . let me get us some food, and then you can tell me all about it. And try to be quiet. My parents may still be asleep," said Gjone as he headed down the little staircase that led to the bottom floor kitchen. He thought Arnenn might've been quite hungry with just making it back from his journey. He himself definitely was. He lit a match before going underneath.

Arnenn only sat waiting at the table before bending down to untie his boots. But when doing so, he looked about and noticed that there had to have been some kind of commotion in the room at some point when gone. He didn't notice the many things out of place when first walking in. The chairs were a bit out of order. The steel pipe that had always stood against the wall by the front door had somehow found its way to the ground. And there was also one of his uncle's journals of blank pages lying open on the floor. All of the other books that sat along the wall had been scattered amongst each other or shoved even more up against it.

As Gjone came up the stair from the kitchen with some bread, butter, and leftover cold chicken, he noticed his cousin looking about the room before peering at him with a wondrous gaze.

"—Yeah, so . . . last night . . ." said Gjone, almost under his breath.

"What happened in here?"

"Well, basically, my mom was bitten by some strange dog that found its way in."

"Ouch! She alright?" asked Arnenn. He was genuinely concerned.

" . . . Yeah, she'll be fine . . ." he said easily. We had Stalk come by and wrap her leg. He's supposed to be swinging by this morning, too. Guess my dad left the door unlocked and it somehow snuck its way in. I don't know exactly what it was in here for, but we think it was probably from the smell of last night's food. Something was very off with this dog, though, it wasn't that big or anything, but the thing was unyielding." Gjone shook his head while also saying, " . . . Took all three of us to fend the darn thing off." He wasn't acting *too* excited about it. He didn't want to lead on about the not-so-much damage he caused the creature.

"It had some kind of weird skin, too. I grabbed at it when trying to pull it off her leg. It just about burnt my hands off!"

"—Wait, an animal burned your hands? Let me see this!"

Showing his palms, Gjone said, "They're fine now. It's like nothing ever happened. It didn't do anything other than make them only *feel* like they were burning—even though they apparently weren't. It also left this wet and ashy substance on my hands that I was able to just wipe off. It was weird."

"Wow, that *is* weird . . . but Gjone, I sort of had a similar experience."

He had Gjone's full attention again.

"I heard a bear attack some other creature not far from the road; then I went and found the area where I believe it happened. I saw this blackish or dark reddish powder and when I touched it with my fingertips, I felt it burn them; and I also don't have any marks to show for it, either. This is crazy . . . I don't know what's going on with any of this."

He took a couple bites of the food as Gjone sat silently, waiting patiently under an awkward air, interested to hear the rest of what Arnenn had to say.

Arnenn spoke on after finally swallowing his food. "My head went out of reason. My ears were filled with screams. It was followed by another sound I've heard before—weeks ago. That sound has something to do with why I came back. There's something going on and I have to get to the bottom of it or else it will make even *less* sense to me. I'm telling you, Gjone, if I try to ignore it, it may just get worse!" He looked steadily at him. "What else can you tell me about that story your father told?"

Gjone remembered Arnenn's interest in the story from the night of the work gathering; it was really getting quite old to him. He couldn't help but feel a slight annoyance with his younger cousin about the whole subject.

"I get it if weird things are happening, Arnenn, but it doesn't mean it has anything to do with that story. You need to get it out of your head! Also, if you just *have* to know what happened, then basically . . . one of our ancestors helped defeat great evil while past magics came back to life. Okay? It's entirely unbelievable and I'm quite over hearing about it. Nobody believes it other than you and my dad!

Arnenn looked at him in shock at his response, and that it somewhat matched up with what the old man said.

"I'm not saying it does, Gjone, but some things seem to be connecting to it—like strange visions and—"

"Strange visions?" sounded the voice of Rayne while helping Jemma down the stairs. She tried keeping the pressure off her leg while sharing the same face with her husband. "The only strange vision I see is the sight of *you* being here, Arnenn," he said.

He helped Jemma into the chair that his nephew was using, who eagerly moved for her benefit.

"This really is an interesting sight. We thought we heard you down here . . . and had to come and see you for ourselves! What's going on? Why have you come back? Did you forget something? Thought you said you were set to go."

"Yes, I believe I may have forgotten something," said Arnenn as he thought he should put the matter aside for the moment, seeing Jemma in pain with her leg wrapped up and Gjone giving him a hard time about it all.

"Are you alright, Aunt Jemma? Gjone told me about the attack last night. Some type of strong animal—"

"A strong animal you can say, I suppose, but I'll be okay. Please make yourself at home, Arnenn, and go take a bath. Good grief! Have you seen yourself?"

"Oh, um . . . I guess I must look pretty shabby."

Gjone found himself alone with his father who was gathering some items from a tray downstairs in the kitchen. He decided to try and have a short talk with him concerning his cousin's well being, something he'd never done before.

"Dad, Arnenn's been acting different than normal lately, and now he says he's hearing and seeing things. And, of course, he suspects it to have something to do with your story from the party. Should I be worried about him? I don't know what his deal is."

"I'm not sure, but maybe it *does* have something to do with it, Son," said Rayne, taking a deep breath. "Just because you don't care much for it, which I completely understand, it doesn't necessarily mean that it isn't tied to that story. There are many things in the world, Gjone, that you don't know, and the same for myself . . . but for all we *do* know, that creature from last night could've been anything, and from anywhere. I'm quite troubled by it and you should be, as well! Also, we shouldn't discourage Arnenn if he's in any type of need or trouble and there must be a good reason for him coming back here. He's never done anything like this before and I even have my own questions I'd like answered about that story that I will not give up on trying to find, even with your mother stalling me from bringing it up around him for various reasons. Besides, since when have you been ill-mannered about him? Thought he was practically like one of your best friends. . . ."

"Yeah, well . . ." tried Gjone.

"Anyway," continued Rayne without missing a beat, "we are his family, and as you know, we are strong. So let's be strong for him. Now, I'm going to make your mother a decent breakfast, and I need you out at the docks before the end of the morning. In the meantime, tell Arnenn that if he plans to stay here for any amount of time at all, to write my brother and Kershpa a letter explaining why and have him do it before the last of the westbound carts go out this weekend."

It summed it up quickly for Gjone as he only just stared and listened the entire time. It was hard for anyone to get a word in when Rayne spoke and Gjone began to feel like it was another useless effort to explain the way he felt to his father.

It's not that Gjone was completely unable to believe such a thing; he'd believe it if he must. He was more annoyed with how the story was the only thing that came to their minds whenever anything "strange" was going on.

Stalk came back with new bandaging and also put some form of green gel on Jemma's wound that both Arnenn and Gjone had never seen. It was some new medical finding from the distant kingdom lands of the South. (Land not ruled by Vidhera.) Stalk said it would improve the healing process and none of them had any reason to doubt it. He left a hefty amount behind for all to use in case of any cuts or wounds, and for free as well.

Gjone thanked Stalk and hugged his mother. He then walked out the door with a hood on to keep his head dry from the rain. He knew he was going to be helping his father pull out the tarps to make working in the rain a little easier that day.

Arnenn, on the other hand, didn't plan to give any help on the docks or inside the shop; he just sat and wrote his parents a letter as to why he wouldn't be showing up at home for a little while longer.

> *Dear Mom and Dad,*
>
> *I am writing to inform you that I will not be coming back as soon as I thought I would. I had some complications on the road and had to go back to Jemma and Rayne's. There are some things that I would like to do here. I will fill you in more on the details when I am home.*
>
> *Hope all is well, and I miss you both. (Tell Jenkas that I miss her too.) Sorry!*
> *Love Arnenn*

Rayne left before Gjone, and Arnenn wondered why he didn't seem more interested in hearing what he had to say about his adventure or why he was back, but guessed that he was just too busy again, like always, or maybe Rayne was just very used to hearing about such types of matters.

He wasn't sure what else to think or even do at the moment, so he decided to walk the letter to the transit stop up by the Guard Tower, even though the rain still poured down heavy on the city. Arnenn would've loved more than anything to only have gone to the stop near the River, the one which was practically right next to Remma's, but the one by the Tower is what he always had to use after writing his parents letters—since Vidhera was west of Harpelle instead of east, where it could've been taken by the boat carrier.

He caught sight of Haulfir on accident. His now brown eyes made him look much keener and actually less brat-like. Still, Arnenn did his best to avoid him since he hated any type of awkward situation with those he was uncomfortable around.

After dropping off the letter, he headed quickly back to the house to be whatever help he could to Aunt Jemma.

9

SINCE RETURNING TO GJONE'S HOUSE, HE didn't exactly know what to do or where to turn to find out what was going on with him. He attempted the books again, but had the same luck as before and started to feel like quite a nuisance to his family members. Rayne still gave no response to Arnenn on the subject and Gjone was once again busy on the docks like the usual of late, because the changing of the season meant there was new work to be done.

It seemed that Aunt Jemma was at least happy to have someone helping her around the house for a few days while her leg healed, which made Arnenn feel like there was at least *one* good reason why he was still there. He would try to talk to her about Rayne's story at times, but she had the same look on her face, such as the many times before. And for the most part only nodded before bringing up some other subject like the shop or things that Gjone had going on, or asking him the very same questions that she had already asked throughout the duration of the summer: how the family has been doing since he was last home in Vidhera. It was becoming apparent that they had less in common than he thought and was reminded of his conversation with the old man that in one way or another, said that most people's interest in such things just didn't happen to exist anymore.

More days passed, and Jemma was happy to finally be getting outside of the house (and away from her ever-pressing nephew).

Her leg was doing much better when she and Rayne left early in the morning after the sun first rose to get down to the mid-city markets and enjoy some shopping of their own, rather than the general only selling of such items. She wore one of her pairs of long trousers due to not wanting any questions from people about her leg.

Arnenn and Gjone were still sleeping that morning after they had left; that is until it was Arnenn's turn to be awaked by a noise while inside the house.

There it was again, the same shouting he'd heard before. He knew immediately what he was hearing and that it was in his head, and not a sound from outside. He sat up and focused on the shouting; listening intently; trying his best to hear if there were any words he could make sense of. He was no longer going to let it frighten or consume him, but only pay close attention to it.

He heard his name again, but anything else, he could not understand.

His head started pounding; he was unsure of what to do next, but felt the same pull again. Something was trying to get him out of bed and down the stairs to where it was. He began walking and staying focused on the noises. The shouting came in waves; he heard his name again, much clearer.

His vision was blurry from sleep as he headed down to the main floor where all shined brightly due to the morning sun that beamed through each and every window.

At the bottom of the stairs, the pulling was stronger than it had ever been before. Something was almost magnetizing itself to Arnenn, calling for him to grab at it. But he did not know where or what it was at first.

The shouting became louder as if it was almost on him: tired of anxiously awaiting for him to find it, and to understand.

Finally, he took his leave from the last step, and saw it.

A book sat atop a stack of many others. It was the same one he had seen on the floor just a few of days prior, and that he himself put back in its place; and also the same one he passed over in his research many times before due to its blank pages, only, it must have changed a bit. It now showed to have a glowing blue trim that edged its way around all its sides and corners.

Almost unwillingly, he reached out to grab it.

Taking it in his hands, he noticed the newfound heavy weight for the small and empty journal he'd held before, knowing it was the object that had been pulling him in all along—somehow without question. The shouting abruptly stopped as he placed it down at the table and opened it to its first page.

He felt proud to be figuring something out, yet he was all too confused. It didn't help prove anything, nor did it make any sense. For what in all of Amruhn would a blank journal have to do with anything?

Arnenn stared at the blank page, wondering why he would've been led to this. But not a moment later, as if a ghost were drawing a thin line in black, the outline of an ancient-looking structure from the left of the page began to show through the paper. He didn't understand how he was seeing it, but he'd intently lost himself, enjoying every quill-like stroke as it created the figure. He saw bridges and ledges over tall walls with towers that towered even higher than what could be drawn within the confines of the pages. There was no color at first; it was only in black until a heavy white began filling in the bottom left hand corner.

He was keenly watching: gazing at its many details that kept appearing.

But then it stopped mid-page.

The shouting came in new waves again and all on its own. The right page he was looking at swiftly turned, and a new blank page rested itself before him.

This time, the drawing began on the right page instead of the left. And what looked like a snout atop a set of terrifying teeth began being drawn. The eyes and ears similar to the form of a wolf appeared on the page as it continued to the left, drawing the rest of it.

Arnenn then heard a creak in the wood and felt a presence right behind him, as if someone was watching.

Turning around quickly and with high anxiety, he saw his cousin.

Gjone was holding the steel pipe in both hands.

He was ready.

Arnenn only had a look of confusion and worry. But Gjone nodded his head and darted his eyes forward, looking past him. Slowly understanding, Arnenn finally turned his own head. And in front of him on four legs stood the exact same image he had just seen drawn inside the journal.

The back door had been swung open behind a creature of great terror. Growling a strange grinding noise, its black eyes looked Arnenn directly into his. The two young Rowes stared back at the beast: disgusted. Yet also amazed at what they were seeing.

The creature must have been a great wolf, or at least something similar: The black that covered it was neither fur nor anything that resembled hair. It had more of an ashy coat, and almost dripping wet at the same time while a remnant of smoke took over the air above it, suggesting its coat had just caught fire.

Gjone was certain it had to be the same exact creature that attacked his mother, and he understood why his hands burned while trying to grab at it in the dark. His fierce determination and remembrance of his failure to kill the beast set in. He squeezed hard the steel pipe in deep anger and ambition. He would not let the creature escape alive this time.

"—Um . . . Gjone. . . ." Before Arnenn could say anything else, Gjone had just about leapt over him to swing at the beast again. The pipe made its way down thoroughly, but the creature jumped backward and just quick enough, allowing the pipe to go straight through the wooden floor to create a nice hole.

As Gjone tried relentlessly to pull the stuck pipe back out of the floor, bending the wood the other direction, the creature had entirely escaped from the house once again.

Arnenn ignored the journal and ran up the stairs to grab the blades, and by the time Gjone had freed the pipe from the floor, Arnenn tossed him his longsword, keeping his shorter blade for himself. Gjone never dropped the pipe; he carried himself two weapons.

After the beast they chased out to the patio, catching air as they took sail from a bench: clearing the fence with ease. They landed straight into the water beneath with the creature still in sight.

Their bare feet were soaked as they followed it through the harvest-ready wheat field and they could see the path the creature had taken through the tall growths. The clearing was small before it ended at the beginning of an old plantation where they saw it race into the trees, unaware that the Rowes were following.

Skimming the ear of the creature and sticking right into a tree in front of it was Arnenn's short blade. Its head-end of a wolf stared directly at the beast that was once a wolf itself, angering it even more as it could feel the slight sting on the tip of its ear. The cousins also came to a complete stop and heard what sounded as if rusted gears were grinding against one another, ones that hadn't moved for ages. It was the sound of the creature's growl that was now heavier and louder than before.

"I'm guessing this is the same one?" asked Arnenn, restlessly.

Gjone widened his eyes with a slight grin. "You guessed it," and with a serious face, followed, "and it's the first and *last* time you'll be seeing it."

Turning around, the beast showed its ferocious set of teeth again. Its ears were pointed entirely toward its back. It started to run at Arnenn, whom without a blade became startled. Just then, he saw Gjone throw him the steel pipe out of his left, keeping the longsword held in his right, loudly shouting Arnenn's name.

Arnenn caught the pipe just in time to put it in front of himself as the beast's jaws surrounded it and missed his face by only an inch. The force of the creature's jump threw him onto the ground where he luckily landed on a thick patch of pine needles. He used the thrust from the fall to push the creature back behind him.

Gjone was ready. He ran in the direction of the beast and came upon it as it was just getting back onto its paws. The young Rowe swung his sword downright at the creature's belly where the blade had ripped right through it.

It snarled in agony, but only for a moment. The wound stayed as it was with traces of a black blood showing within.

Arnenn and Gjone stared wildly as the creature that should have died, was now ready to make its next move.

Arnenn threw the pipe at the creature to distract it before running to get his blade out from the tree. The creature dodged the pole easily.

Gjone was even more unsatisfied than before, and confused as to what to do next. Even so, he was not about to relent.

After withdrawing his blade, Arnenn saw the sheer determination in his cousin's eyes. The creature then turned its full attention to the big man with the sword, ready to have revenge of its own.

It began to circle him. Each awaited a first move.

The beast took its chance and went for Gjone who used the hilt of the sword to strike down on the beast's head. The astonishing blow made a knocking sound on its skull as it went face first into the dirt.

Again went Arnenn's blade, whisking by Gjone and sticking within the creature's rear leg.

Getting up again and yet squealing in pain, it jumped up at Gjone with what power it could bear on its best three. But before it could fully leave the ground, Gjone made a leap of his own. In all sky and no ground, the sharp end of his sword came down on the creature, diving far into its neck, brutally burying into the beast.

The creature only laid on the ground while squirming in torment.

They stared, waiting for it to die. But it just wasn't happening as the sword still stuck out of its neck. The creature bit at the air in their direction.

It only made Gjone angrier. He still wasn't satisfied in his thirst for revenge. Adrenaline ran through his blood at its peak. He would not feel assured until he crushed the creature and saw it breathe its very last breath.

Taking his sword out from the creature and tossing it aside, he grabbed the steel pipe once more. He again brought it up and smashed it down on the creature's body, relentlessly giving in to his determined ferocity.

The creature tried to escape its torment over and over again, but every time it attempted to move, another one of Gjone's swings came crashing down.

It was almost hard for Arnenn to watch while he stood back with a look of concern for the creature, but also for his cousin.

Finally, Gjone put to use the jagged and rusted edges that circled the base of the steel pipe. It went straight into the creature and created a clean hole that centered all the way through it.

It finally gave up; it was ready to die.

"—That's for my mother . . . and for me," Gjone said, breathing heavily. He threw the pipe aside while wiping his forehead.

They both stared at the dead creature. The smoke gave way, and its body turned to nothing but ash that fell to the ground where Arnenn and Gjone only jumped back in shock.

Shouts, hoorays, and praises came from inside the Ivory Nook that very same night. Now satisfied and highly impressed with himself by his victory over the creature, Gjone needed to celebrate with some friends, and also, some ale.

"That's correct, lads! Did you hear? Our man Gjone has taken down a beast! Gjone, Thrown-Thrower!" came

Rimland's scraggly voice, along with the many other voices that filled the small yet lively tavern.

The Ivory Nook was Gjone's favorite place to be, ever. Even as a small child, Rayne and Jemma would take him there. Many birthdays, casual get-togethers, even some sloshed nights were spent inside the tavern during recent years.

Purt stones lined the bar and walls, setting ample lighting around the room as the fire from small candles danced lightly behind them. Many young men and women worked the counters with a great cheer for their many customers and visitors of the Cunning as they rummaged its kitchen and gladly sampled its numerous varieties of ales. And as far as decorations, the Nook would be seen with damaged, salt-worn, and water-soaked river rafts that hung from the outer walls and ceilings.

What roamed through all's nostrils other than beer was the wonderful stench of wet rope as if a sea were nearby; and it mixed with the smooth scent of rare plant life set about and exchanged for fresher ones on an almost daily basis. It barely matched the character of the place, but was warmly welcoming.

The tables made of solid wood were hard to move around and it was for a good reason: Anything could happen inside the walls of the Nook, and no one knew it better than Gjone, Thrown-Thrower himself.

Sitting atop the longest table in the place, Gjone was entirely proud. "You should've seen this beast—it was unlike anything that ANY of you have ever seen in your lives! AND IT WAS STRONG! You should've seen me— and Arnenn!" said Gjone as he gave the credit due to his younger cousin. " . . . He stuck him in the leg with a quick throw of his blade—and when it tried to jump at

107

me, I ran my sword straight through it! This thing was SO STRONG! It wouldn't die! I had to beat it to death before I ran a steel pipe straight through it! And you wouldn't believe what happened after that. . . ."

"—Gjone. . . ." said Arnenn, shaking his head and widening his eyes at him. No one knew about his mother's attack, and he remembered his uncle telling him they were keeping it on the low in efforts to not put everyone in town into a great frenzy. In his opinion, telling them that the thing just disappeared was a little over the top. He himself was still trying to mentally deal with it all happening. It was simply too much to just start muttering about in public places.

Gjone didn't buckle under the pressure, though, and was already impaired enough to not care.

"—It's alright, Arnenn! Fact, as my father says . . . *'there are just things in the world that we cannot explain'* or something like that . . . ha . . . ha. . ."

He continued to say how the beast diminished after he had killed it. Everyone listened intently: amazed at what he was saying. And also amazed that he, the son of the man who told the great stories and fables and that was never thought to tell them himself was now doing that exact thing. Most of Gjone's friends were unsure if it meant they should believe him any more than his father, or not.

Rimland came back from the bar and shouted out with another, "Gjone, Thrown-Thrower!" as again, everyone else in the Nook responded the same. Even those that knew him not, continued chiming in. They were all very interested and began to speak of it among themselves.

Rimland was holding a great big pitcher of ale he poured first for Gjone, then Arnenn, and then himself before Gjone kept at it with, "We were even barefoot and in just our sleeping clothes! Ha—ha—" His laughter was more obnoxious than his usual.

"Congratulations, Gjone!" said Haulfir who ghostly slid through the door of the Nook, almost unseen. He had already heard the news from Cezz: the one who somehow always knew of all rumors and events right before anyone else ever did, sometimes before they even happened, from what it seemed.

"I see that Arnenn wasn't the one who killed it, of course." He made himself a seat at the far end of the table and placed his shined Guard boots atop it as he leaned back in his chair. It was the one and only way he took seat in the Nook.

"Hey—hey, if it weren't for him, I wouldn't have even had a sword in the first place," said Gjone, sticking up for his cousin lightly and laughingly.

Arnenn was unsure of what to say as usual. He gave Haulfir a scowling look of his own, uncertain if he was just joking around or not, but feeling uncomfortable either way.

" . . . I'm sure you could've taken it without a sword, Gjone," said Haulfir as he followed it with a great-big, "GJONE, THROWN-THROWER!" Again, the entire place cheered it back. "Besides, I heard you killed it with a pipe, not a sword."

"Indeed I did, sir," Gjone playfully confirmed. "I'm sure you've seen it, it's the same one that's been uselessly standing by our front door since the beginning of time! It finally came into use throughout all its rusting years as a terrible decoration!"

Arnenn decided to ignore Haulfir and his comment. "You think he did a lot of damage to the beast? You should've seen the hole Gjone put through the floor when it was in the house!" He said it while looking at everyone except Haulfir. All the rest laughed willingly.

"Yeah, my mom reamed me good for that one!" said Gjone, not embarrassed at all. Everyone else continued in with him. "I have to fix it tomorrow. But anyway . . . really, this thing was truly some type of monster. I got it good for biting her though!"

"Wait, so your mom was bitten, too? How did Cezz not already know about this?" asked Rimland. He had already had more to drink than even Gjone (which really, was no surprise).

"I don't know . . . all I know is that the thing got what it deserved!"

Within the large and busy crowd, Arnenn thought to himself about the book and how it drew the creature before he saw it in real life. He realized that he hadn't said anything about it to his cousin yet. And he noticed that it was quite a great idea to keep it that way due to how things were going with Gjone and his big mouth that evening.

Haulfir's direct voice sounded again. "It was probably after Arnenn for still being here." He crossed his arms while peering directly at him in distaste. "Aren't you supposed to have gone home by now anyway? Why are you still here?"

Arnenn first showed to have a nervous look upon his face before all the members at the table saw it turn confident. "I just had to come back." He was over Haulfir's playful malice. "And why I came back, Captain Nosey . . . is none of your business," he said plainly and calmly alike. All at the table had darting eyes and stunned faces.

Haulfir set both his feet onto the floor and immediately jumped up high from the table, snapping, "It's my job to know what goes on here, Captain Nobody-boy." He with his sharp eyes and wildly red hair slowly began moving toward Arnenn.

Arnenn never understood why Haulfir had to be such a jerk to him, or what it was that he really had against him in the first place. Haulfir's father was the only one who had any *real* need-to-know in Harpelle. Haulfir to Arnenn, was just his spoiled brat of a son, and he was seeing it now more than ever before.

Gjone was surprised to see his younger cousin talk back to his intimidating friend, but knew for years that he had put up with Haulfir's bad attitude and many unnecessary words, whether playful or not. The truth is, Arnenn never wanted to cause any trouble when in Harpelle since he was only ever a visitor, but also because he had an enormous amount of respect for his aunt and uncle allowing him to stay there at all. So he always made sure he didn't do anything stupid or out of his usual decent regard—anything that would keep him from visiting the place for another summer. But this time, it had finally caught up with him.

He stood up after Haulfir had already walked over to where he was sitting.

Gjone tried to stop him, but Arnenn had already succeeded in giving Haulfir a powerful push to the chest. It sent him tumbling back to the table behind. All watched him fall clearly over it, along with the people who sat around it (*and* along with all their food and drink, sadly).

The shock of it stalled everyone in the Ivory Nook. If it wasn't one thing he had just insulted and pushed a man of the Bear Guard, it was then bad enough that it was the son of the Captain, the Master of the Bear Guard himself. But Arnenn was over caring anymore.

The young guard jumped back up immediately with a brand new fire in his eyes, and even Arnenn's ignited with more ferocity. They had both finally had enough of each other.

It surprised Arnenn and any others watching how fast Haulfir got up and ran back over to him. Gjone tried to get in the way of his friend this time, but again, was too late.

Haulfir jumped at Arnenn and threw him straight to the ground. And with his fist about to come right down on Arnenn's nose, a hand stronger than his own had stopped it.

The young guard was then forced to stand up with a twisted wrist while being turned around to see the determined face of the old man he let sleep in jail one night—the same one who needed to be "walked" to his hut.

"I don't think so, young Arbowen," said Throone as he pushed Haulfir off of Arnenn and to the side as if he were only five years of age. "And you two," he said with the most grim face ever as he pointed to the two young Rowes, "are coming with me."

10

"I'D SEARCHED THE ENTIRE CITY BEFORE I finally found your parents, Gjone," said the old man with a most serious look in his brown eyes of season hidden under his hood. They moved at a fast and steady pace, and the moon was bright enough to convince them that purt stones were of little use.

Throone continued speaking as he sturdily drifted ahead of the two. "It'd just turned dark by the time I found them. They said they were heading back out to the city's inner circle to gather with some friends. They also told me about you two's little killing expedition, though they were reluctant to at first. I told them to go back home. It's the exact same thing you two are doing."

Arnenn and Gjone had never seen the old man so lively before, and they were highly impressed by what he did to Haulfir back at the Nook. They also felt a bit shunned for words by the sight of him like this, for the matter. He in return, didn't seem to be too impressed by any of their actions.

Rayne and Jemma were already at the table hastily eating their food when Throone walked right into the Mourenrowe residence without knocking. A thin sheet of wood had been laid over the newly decorated hole, making an eyesore of the entire room as they welcomed Throone in and offered him a seat where he politely declined and started pacing back and forth between the front door and the kitchen stair.

Arnenn and Gjone took seat at the table while waiting for him to say something about why he brought them home. As many candles flickered light off of the already blazing fireplace, Throone spoke up clearly. "First off, Arnenn, you shouldn't let your cousin say such things in public."

"—Uh, why would I be responsible for what Gjone says?" He was puzzled by the command.

"You should know better, 'Watchman,'" said Throone, pointing at Arnenn before making another turn between paces. "But thank goodness you're still here and that I didn't need to go searching for you all the way to Vidhera . . . I have had enough of a journey getting back here as it is!"

Gjone sat backward in a chair that was closest to the fire while eating what scraps of food his parents had left on the table. He asked with a mouthful of it, "Where were you? And what do you have to do with any of this?"

Jemma gave him a look of rebuke. "Manners, Gjone." She kicked him under the table, clearly disappointed that he had been off partying when she wanted him to fix the hole he had created, instead.

Throone ignored his rudeness. "I may get to that, but first, I must know about this animal that I would guess the *whole* city knows about by now."

"Gjone!" said a startled Rayne, "I thought I told you not to say a word!"

He sat silently with a blank stare before responding. "Everyone would've found out eventually, I mean . . . we live next to Simeon after all—"

Rayne started to reply to his son but was quickly cut short by Throone. "He has a point there, Rayne . . . but Gjone, it'd be best if this were spoken of no more from here on out. And how does Simeon know about any of this?"

Rayne answered. "He heard our commotion in the middle of the night and came over to check on us. The animal left by then; he stayed around when Stalk came to look at Jemma's leg."

"I assume you're alright now, Jemma?"

She shook her head slightly, saying, "Yes, thank you."

"Well good! I am glad you're okay. What you were attacked by could've done a lot worse to you. You are lucky! And Stalk is a great man . . . a great doctor he is!" Throone exclaimed in a burst.

The youngest of the group decided to speak up. "— Between us all, I don't think there's a need to continue calling that thing an animal anymore. . . ."

"Not that anyone *has* been calling it that—" said Throone, rapidly. "I heard some of your speech around the noise in the tavern. You guys said it was unlike anything you've ever seen, and that it was strong—a beast if I heard and understood correctly, which I'm sure I did."

"It WAS a beast!" confirmed Gjone before looking to his parents. "Mom, Dad, I'm certain it was the same exact beast from before. I saw why it almost burned my hands when I tried to grab it. Seriously! In sheer daylight, this thing didn't have fur like some regular animal or stray dog or something. It was like it was being burned alive. And there was . . . smoke coming off of it. It even had a burning or gassy smell to it like I thought I'd smelled before. And you're right, Dad, it actually *could* have been some kind of demon! Or something!"

Surprisingly, there was no sarcasm in Gjone's voice. Arnenn, Rayne, and Jemma thought it was strange to hear Gjone being the one muttering something like that. But they also thought it could've just been the ale talking through him.

"I wouldn't necessarily disagree with you on that," said Throone. "You two are lucky to be alive! I believe I heard you say you killed it with that pipe over there. Tell me, how did you manage that?" You could tell he was more than curious.

Arnenn spoke first. "He kept hitting it over and over, and then he came straight down on it with its edge and the pipe went all the way through it. But what happened after that was . . . ."

The two young Rowes looked at each other steadily. "It just vanished; it disappeared . . . entirely," finished Gjone. "There were only ashes left to the ground and then the pipe just dropped like it was never there!" He sat straight up with his eyes wide open, looking back and forth between his parents and the old man.

"Dark Dust," said Throone as he came to a standstill before resting his hands on top of the chair that had been awaiting his presence. The others stared sturdily his way. Gjone sat himself back down.

"That's what they leave behind, or better yet, what they are, or what they are made of. They are the beasts of Dark. Dark-Beasts. The very same ones from this story you tell, Rayne."

The room went quiet for a moment.

Rayne was stunned. "You know something of these beasts?" he asked with an excitement.

"Well, of course he knows about creatures made of dirt!" commented Jemma while shaking her head. "Why not? What's next? Are flying cats going to swoop in on us now? Do I need to grab a broom?"

Throone gave her and the other three a blank stare. There was no laugh behind his determined demeanor.

"Perhaps, Jemma . . . perhaps," he said as he suddenly sat down in the chair and settled himself into a more comfortable position. Changing his voice to a softer tone, he added, "It's best you all know as well. The only way that kind of beast—or 'demon' if you will—can be killed, is by creating a clean stab . . . or in your case, Gjone, a puncture: a hole that goes all the way through it. Which I must add, of course, that I am mightily impressed . . . Gjone, Mr. Throne-Thrower. But, you are a however a Mourenrowe, so it isn't all *too* surprising."

As Gjone sat with a grin and Rayne with a look of pride for his son, Jemma sat still, shaking her head at them and the situation as a whole.

"So why did it come in here in the first place?" asked Throone.

"We thought it was attracted to the smell of food the first time, but why it had come back, we don't know," answered Rayne.

Out of nowhere, Arnenn excused himself and walked over to a stack of books near the kitchen stair as if he was alone in the room.

"It may have something to do with this."

He grabbed a journal from a short stack before sitting right back down at the table. It was the same journal he had opened earlier that day; and unknowingly, the same exact journal Rayne used on the beast to remove it from Jemma's leg. He sat it in front of himself before its blue trim gleamed off of the firelight.

A deep breath swelled before Rayne shouted, "Wait!" He jumped out of his chair, pointing at the journal. "Wait! Th-that's the journal . . . the one! The one I have been talking about—that has been lost to me for so long! Arnenn, where did you find it?"

Jemma humorously responded by giving her opinion. "He probably just looked right behind that disgusting swash pile of yours!"

"No Jemma, I have looked for that for a very long time and I would've seen it. Arnenn, please tell me!"

"I didn't exactly find it, Uncle . . . it was just on top of the stack right there this morning. I saw something similar to it before, but it didn't have this blue trim around it. It pulled me into it somehow; I think it's what brought me back here. It's also what woke me up this morning and gave me a warning of the thing we killed."

It was a relief to the old man. Throone knew for sure that the time had come and that it was this young Rowe. The Angelic Being who saved his life had said so, and now he saw it for himself. Finally, he had found him after all his long years of waiting and searching. He heard Arnenn speak again.

"Gjone, I didn't tell you, but before I saw the beast in front of me, it was being drawn in this book as if it was a painting. Guys, I'm certain that it was trying to warn me about it!"

"And yet you still didn't see it right in front of you?" spoke Gjone before he laughed in a light manner, not caring to be shocked at the strange thing Arnenn had just said, of course.

Rayne asked jealously, "I have searched endlessly for that journal with those blue edges. Suddenly you find it, and it just draws you an image of this beast? How is that so?"

Throone answered him directly. "It is not for us to know when this or more of these rare creatures of Dark choose to reappear, Rayne. I heavily believe it's been waiting for a particular time to come. And I need to know, where did you get this book in the first place?"

After giving it some thought, Rayne uttered, "—Oh, well, my grandfather bought it for me in some shop back in Vidhera when I was just a kid. It was only a blank journal that looked just like this, except much newer, of course. I used to keep track of the stories he'd tell me as I grew older, but the notes would seem to just disappear after a time. I thought I told you this a long time ago, but maybe I hadn't. Haven't you ever heard me say that in my story?"

Throone took a deep breath. "No, I don't remember you telling me that, not ever . . . nor have I ever been around for your storytelling times, Rayne, which I now highly regret. It would've saved me a lot of pain! But it's no matter. It's coming together now. And I believe what happened is that the blue trim there disappeared as the journal itself began to lose its substance, and also lose the information held inside of it over time. Do you see, Rayne? The information I gave to your grandfather and that he then gave to you was erased! It's just the same as everyone's memory of it long ago! All erased! —At least for the most part. And I don't know why!"

"Wait, did you say that *you* gave to my grandfather?" asked Rayne with a profound look upon his face. The others met him on the very same level of confusion.

Throone sighed. He had never given up so much information and to so many people at one time. "Yes, actually. I have been here longer than you would like to know, young man, but that is not what we're discussing right now." He tried to ignore it. "What I want to discuss, and what I believe, is that that journal of yours is starting to change into—or *back* into something else that may have existed a very long time ago. And yes,

Rayne, I *do* mean the story of which you tell. Are you all getting this? This beast . . . the stories . . . . . this is no joke! At least it's not to me. I have waited far longer to find this book than you, Rayne. Trust me in this."

Rayne had many questions in mind but one stood out more than the others: the same question. "So are you saying that you were the roaming merchant he spoke of so much? Who apparently knew about all of this? How is that even possible? Just how old are you, exactly?"

Throone gave another sigh, knowing he would just have to explain himself.

"I am older than you think or would like to know and I have been a merchant, spear smith, and inventor . . . among many other things—none of which are relevant right now. Look, I more so hold a duty to your family line whether I want it or not. And I used to think your young grandfather was the one who'd be living when Dark returned, for he was a great man. He hoped the same for himself. And for a time I even wondered if it was you, Rayne, since you held so much interest in it all, but I am sorry, it was not the time yet, as unfortunate as it was for the both of us—trust me.

"You see, all along, it was only *me* seeing these things, learning about some of these details myself, coming about random information slowly throughout my long years, most of which I've unfortunately forgotten. But none of that matters anymore. It's all here now and so is this book."

"That explains it! That's why you would come around so much before . . . asking me so many questions and making me more and more interested in this stuff— more than I already was!"

Throone only confirmed with a simple, "Yes."

Jemma grew concerned. "So you're telling us that Arnenn is this, 'one?' What does that even mean?"

"I believe that it means exactly that, Jemma. If all of this is, in fact, happening, those of Dark coming back, then I suppose Arnenn has some type of task to fulfill."

Arnenn felt frozen for a moment as he was hearing it. He needed time to process it all. He almost felt sick to his stomach. He wasn't sure if having some job as such was something he wanted at all, or if it was something he was even close to being ready for.

Jemma breathed quite the deep breath and responded before shifting toward Rayne. "Well, congratulations, Rayne, you've done it, dear! Do you see *now* why I've always been so skeptical about your storytelling and why I had you keep it on the low as of late? I knew something like this would happen one day. . . . You went and filled Arnenn's head and heart with crazy tales and look what it has turned into! I told you about this already. It's why I've always been so nervous when he's around. He's just like you! I was afraid he would turn into the likes of you even more! Nothing against you, Arnenn," she said to him in a lower tone before raising it at Rayne once again. "What are we supposed to explain to his parents now?"

" . . . There's nothing we can explain to them, Jemma, and this is not my doing!" snapped Rayne, outraged at his wife's speculation of it being his fault.

"He's right, Jemma," said Throone. "His stories didn't bring this truth about . . . it was coming either way—and it's probably best that Rayne brought this subject to light because I truly needed all the help I could get to warn you all. Making this family aware of these events coming was to be my doing, and truly, I have done a feeble job of it lately." He rubbed his hands together and continued by saying, "Arnenn, I believe, is the one I've been waiting for—since the book has called out to him, but know this: You are *all* Mourenrowes and I feel that you are *all* chosen just the same in one way or another. You may all have a significant part to play in this and I fear Amruhn's about to change considerably, and many things may not ever be the same. You must accept this."

"What is this family I married into?" remarked Jemma, shaking her head at Rayne.

Gjone spoke up after hearing the conversation going on without him for quite awhile. "Throone, are you saying that this creature I killed is *really* one of the beasts from my dad's stories of the past?" He just wanted to be certain he was hearing it all correctly so that he could allow himself to follow with the same ease as his over-eager father and cousin.

"Must I have to spell it out for you, Gjone? Haven't you been paying any attention? How much have you drunk tonight? Or would you rather believe instead that a creature that has skin like ash and disappears after you kill it is just some undiscovered animal from somewhere on the other side of the Cunnings in Scoth? I hope you all understand this!"

Arnenn only sat, listening to the many discussions and arguments between Throone and his family for some time. He still had a cringe in his stomach. He wondered what this being "the one" is supposed to mean. He thought to himself: *The one to do what? See and hear things I don't mean to or want to? What kind of job is this supposed to be?*

"What else have you seen in that journal?" asked Throone as Arnenn was barely paying attention. He quickly looked up at everyone and then slowly opened the book to the first page, rubbing his fingers across its thick and rough paper.

Nothing showed.

"Well, before it turned a page on me and drew that beast, it started drawing something else here. It began as the outline of some great building, or castle."

"A castle?" asked Throone, a face of interest.

Arnenn continued to run his finger over the page, seeming unaware of everyone around him.

" . . . Arnenn, what on Amruhn are you doing? Snap out of it!" commanded Gjone before laughing to himself.

He peered up, ignoring Gjone's laugh. "I just don't know why it isn't here anymore."

But just as he said it, it started again. The outline of the building came from the left of the page and over to the right, quicker than it had been drawn before. The light of the fire faintly dimmed, causing the room to become darker as a slight wind ran through the room from the open back door, and when the light had finally returned, Arnenn saw the entirety of the building reappeared on the pages in full. Once again, it was magnificent.

"So does this mean we have to keep our doors locked forever now?" asked Jemma. She wasn't paying very much attention to her nephew's gaze into the book as she beamed over to the door and closed it.

Throone was about to answer that it would obviously be a good idea, but Arnenn yelled, "It's back! It's right here on the page again . . . LOOK!" He turned it around and pushed it to the center of the table for everyone to see.

"Very funny," said Gjone, shaking his head. Arnenn didn't know his cousin couldn't see the castle on the page, like himself.

"No, wait, I think I may see something, too," said Throone as he saw the tracings of black ink with white and red fillings slightly coming through within it. He felt a strange need to gasp for breath.

Rayne, who was the most excited of the bunch, looked thoroughly at it, but couldn't see anything. He shouted to it.

"Show me! Reveal your secrets!"

He wanted so badly to see it and for this to be real—to the point of yelling enchantments at it as if a childhood passion was coming back to life within him.

Gjone gave his father a look he had never given him before while feeling to be one of the only sane people left at the table, other than his mother.

Throone looked back at the book after watching Rayne's spectacle. His eyes met the page and saw the picture in full. He was then thrust back in his chair, almost immediately. What felt like a heavy wind from deep within his soul had thrust out of his body like a hurricane. He had to gasp for air as he felt a great weakness come over him. His elbows crashed down against the table and he laid his head in his hands for many moments before someone finally spoke up.

". . . Are you okay, Mr. Throone? Sir?" Rayne's voice sounded.

Throone looked up and glanced around the table after he had partially gained enough strength back to talk. He never answered Rayne. He said only one word after a taking few deep breaths.

"Kulne."

He didn't know how he remembered it, or if he had ever even known it to remember it in the first place. It was the same as how he knew most things he somehow had knowledge about; it was his greatest confusion.

"What is Kulne?" asked Arnenn. He pulled the journal back to himself and closed it.

"That . . . young Mourenrowe, is what's on that page there—" He was breathing heavily. "It is a kingdom of old; a kingdom in the time of your great-grandfathers and grandmothers," said Throone, getting himself back to composure.

It was Rayne's voice that sounded in the silence of the room again, but somewhat to himself this time. "It's true . . . all of it. Everything . . . and this has happened before. It isn't the first time!"

"No, it is not the first time, and yes, it's true," said Throone, breathing more steadily. "And I believe that this journal of yours is exactly what I've been searching for here all along. I'm starting to see and understand something here. I believe that since you once wrote this story in this very journal, it made a connection to the object. It actually may have connected to any journal you could've written these stories within. I never knew this was possible, I just thought it was hidden somewhere as the same exact book it had always been. It's even possible that this book may start to look different than it does now, like it will grow or mold itself into something else entirely. My friends . . . this . . . is the Orrumn."

The other four were lost as he further explained it. "Yes, that's what it's called. The Orrumn. It is what tells about events of the past, and maybe also prophesizes the future pertaining to these types of wars. It is possible that if and when it had existed before, it could have been another journal or book, or who knows. Again, the prophecies attached themselves to this very thing you were given, Rayne."

They all gazed at it as he spoke. It only looked mostly beat up and old and floppy.

"If these creatures are a part of this story from this book and they are going to be attacking everyone, then I'm right in getting the word out there. The people of Harpelle need to be warned!" said Gjone, ignoring the proclamations about the journal.

"Yes, Gjone, the people of all Amruhn *must* be warned . . . but not yet. I don't know exactly how your father tells it, but as I know it, many became unbelievers of these things happening because they had heard of the creatures, but never saw them. We cannot go causing strife amongst our brothers and sisters if we can help it. We have to be careful, and use tact!" He paused in thought. "It makes sense to me now. That creature must have come here to get this journal, not food. It must have been led to the presence of the Orrumn somehow. Just like you Arnenn . . . like you were led to it as well."

"So does this now mean I'm supposed to have some connection with this creature?"

"No, Arnenn!" Throone confirmed in surprise. "I would never say that, but I *do* think this Dark wants it for its own reasons. I believe it would intend to destroy it or use it to some kind of advantage of its own. I don't understand all too much about the Orrumn as of yet, though. Arnenn, what happened on your journey? How exactly did it lead you back here?"

"I, um . . ." He was nervous to say it in front of everyone, but then he thought it couldn't sound *too* crazy with the current conversation happening.

"Well overall, there've been moments of hearing the sounds of someone yelling my name—like they've been trying to get my attention, which is the same thing that happened this morning. It woke me up and pulled me to the book. Anyway, after I left, I heard terrible noises when I came across a bear near a creek, and what I guess is the 'Dark Dust' stuff. It did something awful to me—in my head."

Gjone added in again that he believed it's what made his hands burn on the night of the attack.

"—Exactly," continued Arnenn. "And then I remember having visions or something. One, and the first one, now that I think about it, had a fortress of some sort in the background, similar to the one the journal drew. That happened the night of your party, Uncle, when I fell asleep. Something took me away from the story . . . and you guys wouldn't believe what I saw happen next when looking to the Mountains. . . . Everything changed around me. It was like I was somewhere else entirely." (He didn't feel a need, or want to say anything about the girl he had seen in the same vision.) "It must've made me pass out or something because the next thing I knew, Gjone was waking me up! Then, back to my attempt to go home, I came across some ancient stone statue of a knight on a horse as if it was made brand new again, and then it'd gone back to being old-looking—it was weird. That was the same time I saw the bear.

"The next day, I saw what I believe to have been the exact same one when I almost reached Alderhollow. It roared at me as if I should not be ignoring it anymore. That's when I immediately turned back. Overall, it was just a pulling feeling that there's something here I left behind."

"Exactly," said Throone, shortly.

Jemma wanted to know what he meant by it.

"Exactly what?"

"It's just all too easy to make sense of. It explains it all! I'm not surprised . . . now knowing that it's you, Arnenn," he said as he peered back over to him, looking the Rowe dead in the eyes. "Visions, old things turned to new—the bear that must've been a Light-Beast! The Dark Dust! And to make even more sense out of it, the fact that you saw what you guessed to be the first vision during Rayne's story!

"Listen! It was all a connection waiting to happen. Arnenn, you were close to the book. Rayne, you, a very descendant of Rowe—telling the exact story of all this right in front of Arnenn while the journal itself was in need and trying to reach out, allowing him to see things that it wanted to show him! I also must state that I believe it reached out to Arnenn and not Gjone because he had shown more interest than Gjone. It could've easily even been the other way around as far as I know. The only things I admittedly do not know anything about, are the noises that—"

"Wait!" interrupted Arnenn as he frightened the small gathering. He stood. "Jemma! Do you remember that same night when I was going to go to bed? You saved me from falling on my face when I almost tripped over a book! I remember now. It was this same book! I thought that someone had moved it, but. . . ." Arnenn stalled. "Throone, do you think it's possible it moved itself all on its own . . . and fell off of the stacks somehow? Would you—"

"Perhaps the connection between it and you could've made that possible. That, in fact, is how strong it is. This confirms it for me, if not all of you. . . ." The old man had a wide grin on his face, excited for the young Rowe, and even excited for himself before continuing with a more severe appearance.

"This book needs to be hidden . . . and I feel like it all starts with this castle . . . this 'Kulne.' —I need to investigate it further. But something already tells me I must bring this journal there to keep it out of harm. It's what my heart is telling me. And also, you two young Mourenrowes will be coming right along with."

Arnenn questioned Throone. His mood turned from being excited to concerned. "Hold on a minute. I can't just *not* go home at some point . . . my parents would be even more concerned than they probably already are! And also, why should we go anywhere with you? If I remember correctly, not so long ago you acted like you didn't know any more about this than what Rayne did, and now it's suddenly the opposite? You expect us to just simply trust you?"

"Yes. You *can* trust me, and you will. And I will tell you why. *And,* if you are all wanting to know where I've been, then I will tell you that I saw something which made me believe it all again—truly believe. —Something almost took me in the Palendrian, a creature of Dark even bigger and stranger than your dog, but I survived . . . and was reminded of my task. I was also confirmed in my judgment that it is here now, all about to happen. But more so, it was you, Arnenn, who helped me believe in all of this once more since you said that you were 'seeing' things. . . . Please, you all must understand me. I have lost a lot of hope in this throughout my long years and it was just brought back to life for me. Also, don't you see? This connection means a lot for you all, Gjone, and Rayne, and yes, you too, Jemma! Arnenn, truly, you cannot tell me that after all of this you mean to only go back home to do the same thing you did last year— nothing."

Jemma spoke up after letting the old man get out his explanation, asking, "Even if that's true, then just like that you're going to come here sticking your nose in our business and then take our son and nephew away with you on some journey to some kingdom that probably doesn't even exist? And why can't you do this journey of yours all on your own?"

"Exactly!" agreed Rayne, "As much as I have always wanted to know more about this story myself, I am still a businessman that needs his son around. We will not just so easily give our consent to any such thing!"

Throone answered back with a raise in his voice as he stood slowly from his chair.

"I would guess you think this is something that I *want* for myself, Rayne? To be subject to live on and on, always keeping a watch on your family line? Having to keep my distance well enough to let you live your little lives, but always staying *just* close enough to keep you protected? Is *that* what you suppose I have always wanted for myself? Knowing it's my job to do so? But not exactly knowing why that has to be? You would be wrong!"

The old man had a fire in his brown eyes that none had ever seen before. He almost looked younger than they had ever seen him, even younger than when Rayne would see him during his newer citizenship in Harpelle.

"Trust me. I have had more than my fair amount of times dealing with your thickheaded grandfathers and grandmothers, Rayne Mourenrowe. . . . Why do you think I've become almost obsolete within my task? You think it is easy dealing with your family? Well, let me tell you. It is not! I'm not going by myself simply because Arnenn and Gjone are Mourenrowes and I need their help in this task, and none others' help. I need the both of them. And I've darn well earned my right to it. I will say no more about that."

Rayne was about to speak against it but Throone put his hands down hard on the table and stared at him. "Why do you think your grandfather's life was spared so many times as he traveled the wilds? He wouldn't have all those stories to tell if it wasn't for me. Who do you think pulled you in, Rayne, when you were alone and almost fell off that cliff by the sea as a young boy? And who do you think saved you when you were a child, Gjone, when that wild boar attacked you because you decided to throw rocks at it—which by the way, was just plain stupid! They are coming with me, Mr. and Mrs. Mourenrowe, unless you want to watch everything turn to ruin around you much faster than it already will."

Rayne and his son were speechless from hearing it; it was nothing but the absolute truth.

Jemma was about to respond to his command. But this time, Arnenn interrupted. As frightened as he was, he knew he had to be brave and to accept it all. And he wanted to.

"Sorry, Aunt Jemma, but Throone's right. I don't think I'll be able to go home . . . not after this. This journal's been pulling me into it, and if protecting it from this Dark is what we need to do for some bigger cause or reason . . . then that's what we'll do. Besides, I wasn't too fond of going back home, anyway, even though I do miss my parents."

"I see that you're deciding for me that *I'm* going on this adventure, too?" asked Gjone.

Arnenn shook his head at him, getting ready to talk some sense into his inebriated cousin.

"Gjone, do you not find it interesting that both you and I have always been good fighters? How useless would it be if all that talent and strength you have was never put to good use? Especially at a time like this! And Rayne, I bet you would have jumped at a chance like this in your youth, am I wrong? Would you want to deny that for

Gjone?" asked Arnenn, who had barely ever spoken to his uncle in such a way.

Gjone spoke for himself. "I'm sorry, but when exactly did I say I even *wanted* to go?"

"Do you really *not want* to, Gjone?" asked Arnenn as he raised his eyes at him.

He paused before answering, thinking he had a good point. "I guess I do, actually. I just don't need you deciding it for me."

Arnenn gave a smirk. Gjone answered it back with his laugh (a common way of understanding between the two).

"It is decided then. There is no reason to waste any more time discussing the matter," said Throone with his nose up.

Jemma and Rayne were at a loss for words seeing that the others of the gathering were easily decided on the matter.

Rayne said, "Well if this is how it's gonna be, then you both will be fixing this floor before you go anywhere. And Gjone, you better find and hire someone to cover your shifts while you're gone. And this better not take too long, either, Mr. Throone."

Throone only looked at him to acknowledge it. "I will be going back up to my house for a few days. I need to look into some things about this place in hopes I can find something—and gather some provisions for our trip. It'll give you all enough time to take care of whatever it is you need to. I can assure you that."

"Where's this Kulne place, anyway?" asked Gjone.

Throone answered back, "I don't know just yet, but I will see what I can find out within my own books as I am back at home, like I said. I will also be going to the west side of town to get us some steeds before we leave.

Meet me by the Guard Tower on the very last day of the week in the morning when the sun first rises. We'll head out from there. Whatever any of you do, do not say a single word to anybody about *any* of this. Nobody needs to know yet. And Rayne and Jemma, thank you for your hospitality, and I wish all of you a good night."

They responded partially in question. "You too?"

As Throone was walking to the door and lighting a tiny candle under a stone set within the upper growth of a small and well designed stick, Arnenn yelled after him, saying, "Throone, if there's a black horse named Narmor at the stables, I'll be glad to have him."

Throone nodded back with a smile and a look of approval. Then, his face went back to stern as he said, "Be careful with that journal, Arnenn. And keep it out of Rayne's sight, if you follow."

Arnenn closed the door, but could still hear the old man's whistling before looking at the journal on the table. He felt a bit afraid to look into it and thought it would be best to put it away and only keep it safe until they left for their trip.

He hid it deep within the confines of his travel bag well before he had gone to sleep that night, away from himself, and also, away from Rayne. Just to be safe.

11

AS RAYNE AND JEMMA WALKED THROUGH the main gate of the city near the Guard Tower with their tired son and nephew who had just woke and were carrying all their gear and packed sacks, they saw the old man again. He was standing by three fine-looking steeds that he had picked up on that very same morning. His own horse was gray with many black dots and was carrying one of the largest travel bags on its back that Arnenn had ever seen. Three spears went straight up into the air above its hind legs. It made it look in whole, embarrassingly ridiculous.

"What's with all the spears? He better not expect them to use those," said Jemma to her husband.

Throone overheard her. "It's only just precautionary, my lady, and spears, I find, are excellent for fishing," he said, lying.

Arnenn recognized one of the black horses that stood near Throone. "Narmor, my friend," he said as he walked up and patted the horse's back. He was quite ready for the day of travel with his trusty steed.

~

All the while, Haulfir stood atop the southern balcony of the tall Guard Tower and peered down at Arnenn with great disgust. He wished he could have gone down to tell him what he thinks of him with his fist for easily getting away with his actions at the Nook.

"I take it that's the boy?" asked Haulfir's father, Lenx. "And that that's the old man you spoke of?"

Haulfir slightly shook his head in acknowledgement, angered that his father chose to do nothing at all about the situation.

Lenx Arbowen was known as Captain of the Bear Guard (Captain/Master, whatever you would like to call him—title of "Captain," not equal to any set of order. With the way the government of Harpelle worked under the rule of Vidhera, he governed the entire city in a lot of ways, except for when certain members of the Vidheran government would come down to take a "look" over things). He was a man of justice, and a man that Rayne and many others alike, held at a high regard.

"I'm not sure what reasons you have for your disliking of that young man there, but I would discourage you from making enemies in your position, Haulfir. Also, it would be great folly to have any bad dealings with a man such as Throone. I've known of him for quite a long time and he has lived up in the Mountains for many years now. I know him to have had dealings with many different people in Amruhn, many more than Rayne or I have. I imagine he'd be quite the wrong person to have anything against.

"I urge you, Son, not to take what happened at the tavern personally . . . and don't forget, I got you on the Guard because you said you want to help protect and serve. I did not have you hired so that you can have disunion against the people of this city—whatever you think your reasoning for it is. You may, in fact, be the leader of the Bear Guard one day, but you need to know your place in it *right now*. And *right now*, that is *not* that case," finished Lenx. He was shorter than his son, but more muscular. He grew dark hair—straight and stiff, and never had it curled at its ends as it barely rounded behind his ears. His face, though, was pleasant, as it would rather have taken the form of a smile. Nobody enjoyed seeing a frown upon it . . . it was only the exact opposite.

Haulfir stared down with the same look of disgust on his face. He hadn't cared for what his father said, but knew he was right. It didn't matter though—Arnenn stirred a burning hatred in Haulfir's heart which he just could not ignore. His strife was never against anyone else, not even the old man, but there was just something about Gjone's younger cousin. He couldn't seem to surpass his disliking of him. He had almost a liking to dislike him, and as he stared down, he got to watch him go on some adventure with his good friend and an old man who apparently has something to prove. He didn't like anything about what he was seeing, or what his father thought of it all.

"Guess you're right," responded Haulfir quickly to his father before dashing down the stairs that led to the grounds within the city, deciding it best to be over the matter entirely. He was done thinking of Arnenn or the old man, or any matter between them. He could only hope the best for Gjone.

Lenx raised his hand to Throone as a farewell gesture of safe travels and that they will be welcomed back when they return.

~

"You bring back my two boys very soon . . . and unharmed," said Rayne.

"Unscratched!" followed Jemma with a grave look in her eyes, her hair braided up in a mess.

Throone didn't want to make any promises he couldn't keep. "It shouldn't be long . . . that is if there aren't too many Dark-Beasts attacking us on the road . . . I'm just kidding," he finished with a smile.

Rayne shook his head at the joke and set his hand on Gjone's shoulder.

"Gjone, be safe, especially for your mother's sake. And, if you see anything else unusual out there, tell me all about it when you get back. Same goes for you, Arnenn. I cannot wait to hear about it from you two. Again, be safe, and keep your sights set straight while you're at it."

For what could have been hours and even after mid-day, Throone said almost no words. He led the group south over a small set of hills where a trail used primarily by farmers and single horse ground merchants went on for many miles. The trail rounded hills shaped in sharp and dark-gray rock formations at the peaks, but below, a green grass covered the remainder of them. It was a new sight for Arnenn, but Gjone had been in the high-hill farmland country of Novark with his sword fighting team many times when still in school.

They both assumed Throone knew where they were heading, and wherever this castle was supposed to be.

As Arnenn and Gjone were laughing at ridiculous stories from the previous summer, Throone finally said something. "I know it isn't very cold out yet, but I would suggest you both wear full sleeves and gloves from here on out."

"Why?" asked Gjone. "Oh wait, is it because of those giant mosquitoes out here? I have seen those things before—you wouldn't want anything to do with them suckers . . . trust me."

"Whoa, what?" exclaimed Arnenn, stunned as he remembered how much he absolutely hated insects of any and all kinds, especially if they were larger than normal.

"No. . . ." said Throone, shaking his head. "I wasn't actually joking when I spoke about being attacked on the road by more of those beasts—it's very possible."

Arnenn didn't take it seriously. "Well, I guess I would rather be attacked by another one of those creatures over any mosquitoes. . . ."

Gjone laughed, of course. Throone kept a straight face and said no more about it.

An hour later, they neared a small and abandoned valley of grass with tall trees outlining a small patch of forest to their east. There were three sets of targets and several wooden and hay dummies set throughout the field. Gjone recognized it from his training classes, only, never so dried out and uninviting. He thought it must have been disowned.

"Again, I will bring up what I said about covering yourselves and I'm not joking. As you've learned, Gjone, you don't want them to touch your skin. Now, I found out it doesn't harm the skin of bears or wolves or panthers, or anything with fur . . . nothing but human skin. See, I've been doing some research out of my own books this past week and came across one of extremely rare animals. It's one of the oldest books I have, actually, and in there are recordings of all kinds of strange things from many walks of life. It even talks about beasts from hundreds of years ago, some with a black ash substance, which I say is the Dust. I'm not sure how it wasn't erased or lost, but it means we are definitely in luck!

"It said the only way you can feel it is by immediate contact with your skin. It cannot actually burn you, but you'll feel like it is nonetheless, and the longer you touch it, the worse it feels and longer it lasts afterwards. It's said to be more of a burning annoyance than anything else from what was spoken in the book. Luckily, any material placed over your skin at all should do the job just fine, so keep yourselves covered at all times—as I said," commanded Throone before letting them know something else. "We will be staying here tonight."

"But it's still pretty early . . . we have enough time left in the day to gain a lot more distance," said Arnenn, pulling down his sleeves. He had been enjoying the day's journey while seeing the views of the southern realms of Harpelle and that of Novark. It was a beautiful land, and he would have rather kept on going until at least nightfall; and assumed that the faster they could get done with the trip, the better.

"Actually we are right on time and on track for today," responded Throone as he stepped off of his horse. He grabbed two of the spears strapped to his luggage and tossed them up to a surprised Arnenn and Gjone.

"Now I know you two just love to tell yourselves that you're such great fighters . . . and I applaud you for killing that dog, truly. However, what you two need to know is that the standard slicing and dicing isn't going to cut it anymore, literally. Especially against some of these beasts that are far worse and bigger than the likes of that small dog back at home. Also, if spears are not a current weapon of choice for you now, then that will all change soon. And a spear will become your absolute favorite weapon of all time."

They thought he was joking.

Throone cleared his throat before continuing. "These spears here are unlike any you'd come across in some smith's shop these days . . . these are spears that *I* have made, and that means that they are the *best* spears *ever* made. You'll find," he went on as he nodded and pointed them off of their horses, "they will become more and more valuable to you as time goes on, and you'll see that I'm not going be wrong about that in any way. That is if you two are actually as good as you think you are."

The Mourenrowe cousins were surprised in the old man's confidence in his "special" spears. But he had a right to have it. The spears came to a simple and quick point on both ends instead of just the usual single-headed spear. It made them appear more unique, and especially more dangerous. All three of the spears were colored in a matte black with a very smooth, yet gripped texture.

"Do you not think we can throw a spear and need training?" asked Gjone, studying the one he had been tossed.

Arnenn followed immediately, being a little confused as to exactly what was going on with the whole scenario.

"Is your intention to kill us out here? Why aren't we moving on? You knew these things would be hunting us, and what? Are we just the bait to some kind of scheme of yours?"

Throone shook his head. "Stop it with your ignorance, Arnenn. If you were bait, I wouldn't be training you to protect yourself! And if you don't need my help, Gjone, go ahead and show me what you've got." He pointed at a spot on the ground. "Stand here and aim for the target on the right tree. It's only about sixty-five or seventy feet away . . . so you shouldn't have any problem hitting the center. . . ."

Gjone stepped up to a mark of hard-packed dirt in the grass that was purposely scraped into Amruhn for use of the target. It was one that he had stood behind before.

With the utmost confidence, he gave a couple of aims while moving his arm back and forth. And after slightly stepping back, his body went perfectly in motion with the movement as the spear escaped his hand, sailing toward the target. But however, "toward" wasn't good enough. The spear went far left and missed the outside of the target by a good couple of feet.

With a look of surprise and embarrassment, Gjone said, "I thought these spears were supposed to be 'the best ever made.'" He dumbed downed his voice as he said it.

Throone, standing farther back and off of a straight shot grabbed the third and last spear that was strapped to the pack on his horse and within a second, it was out of his hand and in the air. The spear hit stealthily, going directly into the center of the target and sticking out with its tail end swinging back and forth, taunting the young Rowes.

They were stunned by him once again, but even more so this time. Neither had ever seen anyone throw as fast and as powerfully, and with such a precise aim out of nowhere.

Throone then looked at them and with a serious voice, spoke, "I don't want to hear any more about not being able to trust me . . . okay? And the sooner you two get it through your thick skulls, the sooner we can move on. I am teaching you. Got it?"

The two looked at each other first and then shook their heads up and down at Throone.

"Arnenn, I want to see what you can do as well. Aim for the same target."

After Throone retrieved his spear, Arnenn stepped up to the same mark of dirt, knowing that he would not be able to match the old man's throw. But he always had a better eye for accuracy than his cousin and was feeling proud to show Throone his talent, even though spear throwing never exactly caught much of his attention.

He sent the spear with what felt like an engaging accuracy that would surely hit the target. But somehow, it ended up going left as well, landing next to Gjone's.

Gjone gave a healthy laugh, happy not to be the only one greatly shamed that day.

Arnenn looked back and forth from Throone to Gjone and to the spear that was now hidden somewhere in the woods. He was lost for words; he didn't understand why he had such a terrible throw.

"I would've guessed that spear throwing wasn't either of you two's strength . . . but I had no idea it was going to be *this* bad," said Throone. He began a laugh of his own.

They spent the next three hours learning tactics from the old man. He showed them how to hold the spears correctly, how and when to release when throwing them, and better body positioning. He explained that they could use the rear end of the staff to help steer where it ended up heading. He even showed them some new skills for swinging them at the hay dummies, and blocking.

By the time the sun had little left to do with the day, the abandoned and dried out targets and dummies were practically ruined for good. Both could at least hit the targets on the trees, not having to go on a wild search for missing spears in the shrubs.

Throone also displayed some cooking tactics as the crew made camp and ate a most delicious supper of mighty proportions that night, especially Gjone. And as the fire had died down to one of its last sparks, Arnenn was beaten from all the training, but somehow, the only one still awake. Even though the training was enough to keep his mind busy throughout most the day, he found his thoughts coming across Rayne's found journal: the book he carried that was supposed to be of some great significance, supposedly called "the Orrumn."

He decided that he couldn't be afraid to look into it any longer; and thought that it was about time to do so. A week of patiently waiting was long enough for the young and interested Rowe to keep it packed away in his travel bags. And he knew that a part of him greatly needed to see it.

He thought about the drawings, its pull and the connection he felt; and the noises that led him to it to begin with. He also wondered what they were really doing with this so-called "Orrumn."

He found himself trusting Throone with the matter, but didn't know what was supposed to happen to it. He questioned why it needed to be taken to this Kulne place and just exactly whom it was that Throone planned on giving it to. If he was the finder of the book and it was calling out to him, then why would it need to be taken somewhere else, or to some*one* else?

That and more questions flooded through his mind. He needed to see it again. If it actually is a book of prophecy, then he must see what it wants to show him so that he can know whatever it is he needs to.

He reached over quietly, making sure the other two were sound asleep as he unhitched the buckles on the leather straps of a small bag where the journal lay within his garments.

Putting the journal in his hands, he felt a soothing comfort—such as he was its protector. The blue lines and edgings shone brightly as it again, reflected off of the fire.

Opening the book, he couldn't see much at all. He thought of getting out his stone, but lighting a match to start a fire may have been too loud and he didn't want to wake the others. Besides, his eyes began adjusting quite well to the page all on their own, and this time, the formation of the castle was already there like it had been awaiting him all along with its full colors of red and white. He thought to himself that if the journal is the very thing showing him this place, then *this place* must be where it really wants to go, the same place Throone wants to go. The book did warn him of the beast, after all, and that ended up working out for the better.

Arnenn thought to it: Trust in the Orrumn—trust in whatever it shows.

After studying the castle once more and seeing its great might (a place that looked as if it couldn't have been real), he turned to the page where the creature was drawn. It was now only blank. The beast was gone as if never there. It soothed him. He wanted to see something else, though, see what else can help their journey. Also, Throone never told him that he couldn't look at it, only to be careful with it, so he questioned why he was feeling secretive in the first place.

He gave up trying so hard to keep it on the low and more intently fixed his eyes on the page. Suddenly, a familiar sight started drawing itself. It was the girl again: the same one from the vision he had seen weeks before at Rayne's party. Finally, she came back to him, only in the book, and not some obscure vision. It confirmed the connection Throone spoke about.

He became excited.

Again, she had hair dressed in different colors. Behind her was what had to be the same structure, the same one from the previous vision and the same one on the first page, but much farther away.

Arnenn began to see the page even better than what the light should have allowed. Every color became vivid, each flower, each shade of her long hair, the green grass around the garden she was in, even her eyes. He thought he saw them move, just the same as the vision.

They did, and her head began to lift.

He became confused and even slightly worried, but he didn't want to tear his eyes away from the page. Again, she smiled his way, and at that very moment, something happened. Her smile made him feel a slight jolt and his heart beat faster. He was blushing. He saw her beauty. It was almost as if he could just let himself fall in love with her, but he did not understand how he was seeing her or feeling so much emotion.

He didn't even realize he was no longer looking inside of it, for the Orrumn had cast a vision in front of him as he stared straight ahead: half-living in the journal and half-living in regular Amruhn.

He became nervous and smiled back. It was almost as if she were right in front of him, and in front of the black of the camp behind her instead of the structures in white and red. But she began to fade. He reached out with his hand, trying to grasp at anything he still saw in front of himself, feeling a steady breeze that touched his fingers after dancing smoothly on the grass.

The vision of her was gone again, and there was only the pitch-black between the many trees that Arnenn's eye peered far past.

He realized then that he was looking straight ahead so his eyes traveled back down to the journal. She was there still, but the picture had gone completely still like a regular painting.

Arnenn then flipped to another page, but nothing showed. He decided to go back to the same one, and then the first.

Unsure of what to think and afraid of what to do, he became worried and closed the book; he thought it best to only go to sleep, which worked out well because he became tired as if a drowsiness from the vision had overcome him. It was the same kind of drowsiness felt after the very first time it had happened.

He felt ever more tired, but he still tried to think about whoever the girl in the journal was, and just why it was showing her to him. Bizarre enough, he knew he felt something for her, and that maybe she felt something for him as well, even though there couldn't have been any way she was real.

His eyes closed. He was asleep only a moment later.

Unknowingly, he let the book fall out of his hands and onto the ground.

12

ARNENN HEARD THE DRY LEAVES OF FALL crinkling near his head and awoke to another strange sight: Throone staring down at him while wearing a thin robe-top coat, holding the Orrumn in both hands.

"Did your mother and father forget to teach you to put things away after using them? I won't put up with this type of stupidity, young Mourenrowe. For all we know, these creatures are after this book, and so far as its protector, you've successfully left it sitting out in the open all night to be easily taken. I thought you'd be doing a better job than this. So, tell me, Watchman, do I need to carry the thing for you?" He overwhelmingly stared down and awaited an answer from a confused and embarrassed Arnenn.

"No, no—I just. . . ." started Arnenn with his groggy morning voice.

"No excuses, 'Master of the Orrumn.'"

He tossed the book at Arnenn and walked over to the morning fire. "Here, eat some of this," he said while walking back and handing him a thick piece of bacon. He noticed that Gjone had already woken and was about finished with his own breakfast.

He joined quickly to get his own start for the day since gaining quite the morning appetite. Afterward, they both helped Throone feed Narmor and the other horses some extra fruit.

As they left their camp that settled near the abandoned training field, Throone was much more talkative and chipper than the day before, even after being upset with Arnenn about leaving the Orrumn out in the open all night. He spoke of many things: the different cities he knew about, the true value of currency, how he used to make spears in his early days, and many other things as well. He showed to be getting much more comfortable around the young Mourenrowes, but Arnenn and Gjone were still a bit confused as to what to think of him.

He was always just one of the older folk around town, a drunkard, or a city wanderer from the knowledge of most in Harpelle. But now they learn he was a lot more than that. He was a great traveler that had apparently lived for quite some time—and a skilled fighter of some sort from the likes of what they saw him do with a spear.

"So when you say your 'early days,' how early do you mean? I mean . . . you told us you've lived a long time and knew our great-grandfather. How's that even possible?" Arnenn had to know.

"Long enough ago . . . I can do my best and guess that I'm now to be three hundred and eight, but I could also be wrong about that. It gets hard to keep track after so long. It could be even longer . . . . I know it's hard to believe and sounds crazy, and it's part as to why I've become quite so crazy myself. If I remember correctly and have not become muddled about it, my birth should be sometime within the summer months," said Throone while bunching up his eyebrows. "That's what my foster parents told me anyway."

Arnenn and Gjone peered at each other in disbelief, unsure whether to believe him or not—almost wanting to laugh as Throone continued on about himself.

"Yes, I was an orphan somehow turned foster child and then was eventually adopted by some ol' woman and her strange husband that I've quite forgotten the names of, to be honest. I remember the house we lived in was in some subtle shack—somewhere by a long-gone southern kingdom. I never knew my birth parents, and the world was much different then, too. There were not as many cities or events happening as there are today and Amruhn was, you can say, still regrouping from a time of great strife and loss. I fear it was the war that has to do with what we're dealing with now, but I didn't know much about it then, being a child at the time . . . and neither did anyone else, really.

"Anyway, the 'normal' years of my life went on and I had eventually become a builder of homes, such as my little house in the Mountains. I also became married, which I enjoyed. Such happened here and there in life just like any other, but later in my years my wife had passed away. It saddened me greatly. I loved her deeply. Her name was Porelesce. She died due to her health. I was only sixty-five at the time and didn't know what to do with myself without her, and I hadn't looked my age for quite some time, and soon, everyone I knew was passing away as well. But I just kept living. I felt great. I wasn't getting any older from what I could tell. And people grew curious and began to think me strange . . . and I agreed right along with them.

"I eventually had to move from where I lived before, and then I built my little home in the Cunnings when Harpelle was still in its early days as a city." He gave a quick smile to them. "Ah, now those were the glory days of Harpelle . . . but also, that's when funny things *really* started happening.

"Unwillingly, I came across many findings that gave me information which I didn't care to know at first, but then, became very interested in as time went on. . . ." He roared a great laugh as he said, "It's funny how things you wouldn't have given the slightest care about your whole life start to become of interest when you keep living on and on for so darn long with the need to find new things to entertain yourself.

"I began learning things as if I was being told or taught. And almost mistakenly, I discovered that I had a very strange ability." (They only thought he meant his spear skill.) "I also experienced an encounter once that informed me about the duties I hold to your family line, but we will not be going into any of that right now. From there, I learned bits and pieces of information about the war that'd happened from before I was born — it started mattering to me for some reason.

"About half my life ago while being already an entirely different person than I ever was before, I met a great ancestor of yours. She was fascinating to me and I knew her family line had some great impact in the same war from what I'd learned. But with great folly, I pushed her too far into my belief of it all and sent her almost ruining herself and running away. Learning from that mistake, I kept on living with this entire task to watch over you Mourenrowes while I learn and forget and then again, learn and forget information about the whole thing while trying to decide what I should or shouldn't say — and when or when not to. I have known many of your ancestors, and it has not been an easy task for me at all. And you all look the same as far as I'm concerned. There's really just too much to say about it. And here I am now . . . hello," finished Throone as he jokingly waved his hand as if it was the first time they had ever met. "I am at least happy this part's been figured out . . . finally."

"Whoa," said Arnenn. "You knew a great, great, great . . . I'm guessing to add another great, grandmother of ours? What was she like?"

"Well, she was pretty gre—"

They overheard Gjone in the background interrupting with, "I sure hope you never tried anything with her, because if you did, then . . . not gonna lie, that would be weird . . . and gross."

Throone picked an orange from a tree that he and Arnenn were passing directly underneath and threw it at an unsuspecting Gjone for his unnecessary comment. It hit him straight in the chest. They heard, "Oomph!"

It made Throone chuckle quite wonderfully before he explained, "She was great, like I was going to say . . . a very esteemed young lady. But again, I only scared her away. And to answer the question before either of you two ask, no, I've never tried anything like that and honestly, since my wife, I've been alone ever since and am just fine with it. She was my one and *only* love. I have a task to fulfill and I do not believe it has anything to do with being married again. And *also* before either of you ask, no, I was never able to have any children for some reason, but it is probably for the best. It's bad enough outliving everyone I know, I don't need to outlive my own children along with it."

"But if you were to have children, wouldn't they also inherit 'living forever' just like you?" asked Arnenn.

"Well, I'm not sure about forever . . . I wouldn't say I am to be immortal or anything. . . . I simply just don't have children, and that's that."

They covered a considerable distance that day as they wound through more hills, valleys, and deserted towns. They could also see what looked like the remains of old castles every here and there that sat along the distant mountaintops to their west. It was the farthest south that Arnenn or Gjone had ever been from their homes in all their lives. All they knew of the large lands to the south was that they had either more deserts or swamplands, and many different types of creatures they had never seen, only heard of. But those lands were still much farther down than where they were at the time.

Speaking of the South, Gjone's parents were never able to get enough time away from the shop to have taken their son (or themselves) down the River to the cities of the Lake, or lands any farther since he'd been born. And Arnenn just lived too far away in general; traveling all the way to Harpelle was a great enough accomplishment as it was.

Other than Harpelle, Arnenn took many trips with his family down to areas like the Falls: a vast land falling directly beneath the Kingdom City where the great waterfalls of the west rivers were numerous; and where old cavernous cities once thrived for a rare people long dead.

"What do you really think of this guy?" asked Gjone as Throone led far ahead for a time. "You two seem to be tied together on believing all of this stuff about that book and such—"

"Yeah, well . . . it's not like I meant for all this to happen . . . even though you act like that's the case, and that you just *have* to have a weird attitude about it. Anyway, I'm not sure, but every time I start to disagree about anything he says, he seems to prove us wrong or do something that suggests he's not a liar. What about you?"

Gjone first just stared at Arnenn with lazy eyes for his comment, but let it pass. " . . . Yeah, you're right. Some things don't make sense—like his old age. . . . How are we supposed to actually believe that? It shouldn't even be possible! But then, he kind of just out-of-the-middle-of-nowhere does something impressive that makes you feel the need to believe anything he says."

"Well, we don't really have much reason to not just believe him—and trust him, I guess."

"Yeah, I guess that I guess, too. So also, what's the deal with you and that book?" asked Gjone, quite intrusively.

"Geez, Gjone, I don't know . . . let me try and figure it out!"

Gjone gave an intensely concerned eye toward him. There was a pause. Arnenn then made the mood lighter with laughter, never enjoying nerved conversations with Gjone, or anyone, really.

"Don't act like I know anything more than you at this point. All I know is that I have to try and look into it to see what I can figure out. If I do find something, maybe I'll let you know. But I probably won't . . ."

Gjone smacked Arnenn's shoulder. "Are you even sure you see anything in it at all? I never did. . . . Seriously, are you two just making it up?"

"No, I'm serious! I—saw—a—castle! And also the beast drawn before it attacked us. You didn't see it when you were standing behind me that morning?"

"No, I wasn't paying attention to your dumb book. There was kind of a scary beast in front you. In case you forgot?"

"Oh yeah, that. . . ."

They chuckled together before Arnenn continued with, "Look, I don't know what to think about all of this, just like you. All I can think is that we need to get to this castle and see what happens, whenever that's going to be. And I suppose we'll find out together if it actually exists. That is if you can even see it. . . ."

". . . Alright," said Gjone as he smoothly ended the conversation before they found themselves near a small clearing of the area, away from a set of cliff-bound hills that walled and shaded the trees that grew depressed, desperate for more sunshine. The clearing was a mostly flat land where they passed through riverbeds and dried out washes, and the dirt was very clayish, redder than the usual brown.

The small village they came upon, Throone couldn't even remember the name of, but it was just around the western stretch of the Palendrian Forest's beginning. The old man told them that the Palendrian was the largest mass of tree that existed and that it was also one of the oldest. (Not that all forests aren't old already. . . .) They chose to believe him without question, trusting more of what he would say—much more than before.

He also said that many never ventured far into it because there was just no need to, but also because so many people have gone missing in its vast abyss, that it scared most to go anywhere near it. And those that dared would just end up getting lost and then killed by something unknown. Most all the people of the Lake knew especially well to keep their distance most times— especially since finding out long ago that it was a bad idea to try and take any of its trees.

After more travel and before darkness fell that day, Throone had Arnenn and Gjone take their newfound spears and practice on some trees a little off the beaten path. He suggested once or twice to set the Orrumn out in the middle of nowhere as a trap to see if they could reel in any of the Dark creatures—and have some real practice. They weren't too fond of the idea or feeling daring enough yet, and said they would rather just keep practicing on the trees.

He was merely joking. Throone thought it unlikely for them to come across any because the Light-Beasts of the open lands would probably find them first.

The next day held some of the slowest travel yet and it was all because Throone would come across any reason to pause for a bit, whether it was to give the horses a rest, eat, have them practice more, or tell them all about the area they rambled within at any given time and the hundreds of stories associated with it. They almost began to tune him out half the time. One thing was for sure, though, they were becoming quite used to being away from Harpelle, and with their Keeper.

They ate in a small and almost desolate tavern that night called Wrenck's. Throone said it was the owner's name—a man far-off dead he once knew. He spoke highly of the man before unfolding a map from a pouch and spreading it out on the table in an unorganized fashion, gnawing on a piece of ham and some darker than ordinary bread before pointing at their relation to it.

"Like I said, I've spent many hours in research before we left and found that this 'Kulne' place should be down below in a land of scattered woods near some cliff or wall of rock. As you can see, this map here doesn't go far enough south to show us that area and there really are no maps that do, unfortunately."

Neither thought it sounded very pleasing or promising for their journey to find the place as Throone continued with, "We are still a few good days trip out until we should come across it, in hopes that we do, that is. This city where we are now is called Meens. Soon, we will get to a place that's much livelier than this shabby place, called Strathom, and which I'm sure you may've heard about once or twice in your lives. There, I doubt we'll be allowed to take our young steeds with us any more south, and will have to give them up. I am sorry, but their owner said it's the farthest he'd let them go, and I'm actually surprised he was willing to let them go *this* far in the first place. Like I said, we seem to have some luck on our side!

"We can try and have them held for our return journey but it's not promising. And it's likely they will only get tired of waiting and rent them out to land merchants heading north, instead. It's also unlikely that we'll find anyone who will let us use horses to take anywhere near the lands south of Strathom, at all.

"After that, we will come up to the Pale Mountains. Trust me . . . you'll know them when you see them, and why they are called that. And as you can see, going around will lead us *way* too many miles out either direction to get to our destination. But, I know of a pass between the Mountains! I don't know how often it's used anymore, and doubt it's used at all. Even though it is a pass, it still goes high up and we will get a pretty good view of the land. We may even be able to see what we're looking for; and you can look back and see the whole of the Palendrian!" said Throone, who felt the need to pat both their shoulders and tell them, "It's really quite the sight to see!"

"Back up! What do you mean 'they will get tired of waiting for us?' How long will we be out there?" asked Arnenn, worried and confused.

"There is no telling how long we could be gone, young Mourenrowe. I know no better than you do at this point. We will bring the Orrumn there and then see what happens after that. I am only *hoping* we can leave soon after."

It was the only answer he gave unto it, even after they tried getting more out of him. It led to them spending the rest of the time eating in an awkward silence. And it gave both Arnenn and Gjone a pure fear of what could happen or what was going on.

13

THE NEXT DAY WAS THE SMOOTHEST YET

because a steady road existed all the way from Meens to Strathom. On it, merchants with large wagons pulled by two or more horses would pass by, giving the traveling group of three many different and interesting options for food.

They had this funny-looking delicacy, crispy, yet very flavorful. It was made in different shapes such as pickles or potatoes that were cut into small chunks or slices and then cooked in hot oil by fires that were set safely inside their small carts. The likes of this food was not at all common back in Harpelle where it was served much more "naturally." Throone told them that the cities south and closer to the Lake had much more interesting goods than the lands north, and that it had always been so.

Arnenn and Gjone noticed Throone was excellent at bargaining with the merchants. He got what he wanted and for the exact price he wanted it to be. Sometimes, he would even bargain to pay a higher price than what it was being sold for, which was a very odd thing to the young Rowes. The cousins spoke between themselves and came up with the conclusion that since Throone was at one time a merchant, he understood the business well and had a heart for the poor folk, unlike the people of places such as Harpelle or Vidhera (themselves). And they happened to be exactly on point about their conclusion as well.

They also recognized that any time after he'd buy something, he would say the same phrase, "All good go to Crowlis!" They would say the same thing back, but with even more enthusiasm.

"All good go to Crowlis!!"

With that day's long travel being mostly unexciting, Arnenn's thoughts typically triggered towards the Orrumn and the vision of the girl. He wanted to peer into it and see her again and to meet her somehow, and wondered if she were perhaps real. Arnenn fought the urge to constantly sneak it out of his pack because he knew it would only make the trip harder. He needed to concentrate; keep himself prepared in case of an attack from these so-called Dark-Beasts, if there were more on the loose, that is. And really, use the Orrumn for only that reason, if anything.

He scarily thought about how many of these Dark-Beasts existed and where they were or came from. And, if the Orrumn was, in fact, what the last beast was after, then why haven't they seen any others while being out in the open lands?

He thought of just asking Throone, but there would be even more questions to ask once that question was answered, as there always were. Besides, Arnenn never knew when the guy was going to be in a talkative mood or not. A part of him wished they wouldn't even find the castle and the whole affair would just pass so that he and Gjone could go home. But his other part knew he wanted this adventure and that he couldn't just ignore it, much like he ignored most important matters. Of all, it could be the most important matter of his entire life.

And again, there was the girl. He knew he must figure something out about her. Perhaps there was some sort of connection between her and the castle, and maybe that's where she lived, since the drawing made it seem as such. He wondered if she were there, waiting for him. He needed to know at least *something* else about the book he was carrying, so he decided to speak up and just ask the old man anyway with, "Throone, why do we really have to take the book to this castle?"

"Well, I don't know *every* reason, Arnenn, but I do know it's supposed to be the place it can be kept safe. I believe the Orrumn should be able to lead us to where that is once we're inside the place."

"Okay, so the Orrumn's like a guide, too?"

"I guess so . . . it's supposed to be a book of prophecy, but that's for you to know about and figure out. It has called out to *you* and it's *you's* job. I must be careful looking inside of that book myself. Remember? When you showed me the page with the castle, or fortress . . . or whatever it is last week, I just about felt all my energy forsake me! I don't know what that was all about, so I took it as a sign to leave it to you for now. It's you it called out to in the first place, not me. But I would caution you to still be careful with it. We don't know its power. And speaking of being careful with the Orrumn, don't do a repeat of a couple nights ago leaving it unattended!"

Arnenn immediately regretted asking, for he knew it would lead him to being reprimanded by him in one way or another—the usual case of being subordinate to almost everyone he knew.

They made a stop by another patch of trees for more training as Throone told them what made a great spear.

He explained why using the correct irons, weight, and length anywhere between five to seven feet made a significant difference for each person. He explained that he had experiment with different materials, heats, and shapes until he had perfected the art in its entirety.

Both listened to Throone's instruction and both their aims became more precise; their throws faster, much more powerful. They each found a new liking in using them, just as the old man said would happen. They could be utilized in numerous ways. They could block any blow; and they were even great to be combined with other weapons such as short or long swords, which the Keeper had them doing.

Outside of the newfound spearmen Throone created, camaraderie was built. And it felt great to have it. Even trust wiggled its way into the young Rowes' hearts, knowing that their old traveling companion really cared for their ability to protect themselves.

Most of the time, he would watch them spar while sitting and peeling apples—directing and judging their every move in a stylish fashion, or smoking a long pipe while sharpening his own spear. Throone became proud of them while they in return, were mostly just sore and exhausted, wanting only to relax or to sleep.

Still, the Orrumn was on Arnenn's mind throughout the day and the training only subdued his interest in it by miniature amounts. And even though he had earlier decided to use it for precautionary reasons only, he changed his mind.

After dinner, he had his chance to take a look at it, not interested in the other two falling asleep first. He saw Gjone giving him a strange look as he grabbed it and turned around to face the other direction, but decided not to care about his cousin's opinion of it. Gjone was going to be Gjone, either way, whether Arnenn looked at it or not. And he could tell that Throone was acting like he didn't take any notice.

The night was ominously dark, and this time, he grabbed the small stone from his bag and set it atop a small rock while lighting a small candle for its flame. It gleamed on the book that kept both the castle and the girl. Arnenn stared firmly into the picture, looking directly into her eyes again, waiting for her to look back. He stared deeper and deeper into it, mentally trying to call upon her.

The Orrumn had an entirely different plan in mind.

It went to its third page which was blank at first, but where quickly, three spears were drawn on its rough paper. They were crossed, showing a design in the shape of a star with six sharp prongs protruding from its center, out. One was in the middle, lying horizontally. The other two created an X behind it.

It's not what he was expecting or wanting to see. He only wanted to see the girl. But then he thought it curious that they had three spears with the three of them. And something happened that the book had not yet done. It started to write letters that turned into words, and words that formed an entire sentence. When finished, it read,

> *Three throws of three spears of Rowe are the only way for them to overcome Him.*

The first thing he thought was: *Why would the book say something like this and who is this "Him" it had written of?* He looked back at the camp because he heard rustling noises and saw Throone moving wood around in the fire. Then he thought: *Throone, who is this man for real?*

Could he be leading us into a trap? Or does he intend to take the Orrumn for himself and lock us away in some dungeon in the depths of the castle?

He remembered what happened to the old man when seeing it inside the book. The Orrumn did something to him, almost as if it thought Throone was someone that intended it harm. And now, he was taking it somewhere that no one had ever even heard of; and there was no guarantee he was actually leading them there at all. Especially since he acted secretive about it at times. It was as if he knew more, just the same as he knew more than what he said a month before.

The only thing not adding up within that scenario was that Throone was the third man with the third spear, and really, "Him" could be anybody. Also, who is to say that they are the "Them" it is speaking of? They could very easily have nothing to do with it at all. He thought it might be best not to take any conclusions he could conjure up at that moment too seriously, yet still keep his suspicions about the old man nonetheless.

On its own, the Orrumn flipped to its next page. From the right side, it began drawing a black face with tusks as it continued left, creating the rest of a tank-like body. It was just like before. His ears were full of yells and in waves they came as he heard his name called the clearest he'd heard it yet. And there was a whole new beast on the page in the form of a terrifying boar wrapped in black. Its coat was the same as the wolf of Dark they had killed.

Arnenn realized he needed to tear his eyes away from the page and look up because it was most likely right in front of him, just like before. And when finally doing so, he found that he was correct. The creature from within the book was staring directly at him, standing no more than twenty yards away in the midst of the dusk that was fading second by second.

"Guys!" he yelled, looking back and pointing ahead of himself. He saw a ready Throone throw a spear to Gjone and command, "Arnenn, put your book away!"

Gjone walked ahead as Arnenn jumped back to where his bag was set. He quickly hid the book inside one of its pouches, proceeding in covering it with as many other items as he possibly could. He then grabbed his spear before walking out to where the now-known-to-be Dark-Beast was awaiting a fight, and where also, two more of its kind had just come out of the trees to its sides.

He became nervous, worrying if his skill was up to par enough for the encounter. And for some reason, he felt a need to impress the old man.

"One for each of us!" shouted and laughed Gjone who had decided to be shy of any nerves, like usual.

Throone threw his spear the same exact way he had before. It went through the head and all the way to its back, sticking within: creating a clean hole and instantly killing the beast. As he ran up to it, it turned to ash in the dark before him. He took hold his spear so quickly that it was in his hand before it could fully fall to the ground. He then headed the opposite direction of the beasts—to the left. The pair of cousins could no longer see him as he struck his spear deep into the loam at his feet.

It had gone pitch black away from the fire, but Gjone was still ready to take his throw.

A flame sparked in the same area that Throone had gone. And they saw what looked like two bright lights appear. One by another, they made Throone's hands look like two great lamps. They rose up and created light that beamed out to where the other two beasts were standing.

Gjone, shocked at what he was seeing, still took his aim—right away. The spear flew out of his strong right and caught the creature to its left, making only a slice across its side. Gjone gave a shout of anger, once again failing to kill one of the forsaken Dark-Beasts on the first try.

The third beast (the one Arnenn guessed that he was responsible for) started making its way directly for him. He, also, did not understand what he was seeing to his left, but knew he had to focus. He wasn't going to try the same tactic as Gjone, though. He ran up to the beast with spear in hand instead. When nearing it, he jumped high into the air and came down with his spear pointing directly down at the beast's body before it even had the chance to jump at him. The spear went right through it: clear to its underbelly, and so hard that it stuck into the ground beneath it.

After the creature disintegrated into nothing but the Dust, Arnenn withdrew his spear from the ground, tossing it over to Gjone, and looked over at Throone, shocked.

Gjone's beast now stared at all three of them but was significantly angered with him. It took charge and jumped, but Gjone blocked the beast and tossed it aside with Arnenn's spear. It charged back. And this time, he knocked it on the head with the middle of the staff and angered the thing even more.

Arnenn knew what he was doing. Gjone always liked to anger his opponents. He would play with their calm, get them to have only rage and no tactic, and then make his move.

"Don't toy with it, Gjone!" yelled the Keeper, who still held up his hands of fire above serious eyes.

Gjone took little notice of Throone's comment and this time even kicked the beast in the face. It gave a dreadful snarl—such as they had never heard an animal or beast of any kind make. But with it being only three feet away from him, he drove the end of the spear through its mouth before it squirmed relentlessly, not yet turning to ash.

Throone quickly ran up and kneeled to the beast. And with his bare hands of fire, he touched it. Its whole body turned yellow and then red before igniting into flame and eventually disappearing. He did it with a sense of care for the creature.

The fire in his hands went out before he stood and all had gone back to pitch black again. He spoke up with intensity in his voice. "First, Gjone, do not play around with these creatures. They will get much bigger and much worse! Second, the body, Gjone, the body! Not the mouth, you big fool! Third, you savage, show a little decency, will ya?"

Gjone was only in shock by what he'd just seen and gave almost no thought to his actions.

"Fourth, we need to leave, now. It's obviously not safe out here. We need to get our horses and ourselves to safety. Basically, we must get to Strathom as soon as we can!"

"Wait!" exclaimed both Arnenn and Gjone. "How did you do that?"

"We have no time for questions, let's leave!" He ran to the camp, and the two young Rowes could only follow in true disbelief—lost in wonder. Even Gjone.

They snuck through the night on the smooth roads and trails that wound through mounded hills with holes as the old man held a lit purt stone to guide the way (even though it was apparently not entirely needed).

The two didn't know what to think about what they saw him do and wanted to know much more about the guy, more than ever, because he just used what must've been magic—real magic, and right before their eyes.

It was in the dead middle of the night when the roads and hills became steeper, but Narmor and the others were eager to handle it well. And whenever they passed a traveler of any type, Throone warned them to be alert for unexpected animals in the area without giving any further detail.

Coming to the peak of a particular hill seen from far away in the dark with a glow that'd showered its form, they finally gazed upon their destination. Many lights were located at the very center and bottom of a valley. They had never seen so much of it in one small area as when they peered into the festive city called Strathom. And where it was cradled happened to be so cold from its winds that tunneled around inside, Arnenn could almost feel his bones crinkle beneath his skin.

Reaching the stables, which were luckily right next to a seeming to be popular and warmer-looking inn, they patted their friends a good night and rushed into it. Inside the building, they found warmth, and much of it. For if the fires that lined all the walls of the Strathom Inn weren't keeping the place cozy enough, then the number of bodies huddled together inside definitely were.

Arnenn and Gjone were surprised at how much was going on inside the little city. Food settled all about and ales were flowing everywhere. Many different types of folk were playing many different types of games. Shouts surrounded the entire bar in the inn and the place had an unexplainable joy mixed within its presence—along with the air-meandering smell of hot-spiced pumpkin drinks and pies. And it felt like they were back at the Ivory Nook, but that it had grown almost five times in size.

The group was then led to a table in the far back by a young woman whose only job was to take people to their assigned tables of the restaurant, which is another thing (other than Throone's hands of fire) that neither the of young Rowes had ever witnessed.

The walls were lined with heavy browns covered by shelves that held up the seasonal pumpkins. They had many different shapes carved into them—mostly suns or stars—but some created a swirling projection that could create you a daze if stared at too long. And within each one, a candle and purt stone rested safely inside. The carvings gave off all kinds of different purple-tinted projections that went in all directions, giving more light unto the room than what was needed.

"Quite the place, isn't it?" asked Throone as the two still made expressions as blank as bricks at him.

Gjone started right in. "So you're a wizard! That explains why you're so old!"

Throone closed his eyes. His hand rested on his forehead. "I'm not a wizard! And try keeping your voice down," he said, angrily shaking his head. "I shouldn't have even done that for this very reason . . . stupid comments as such. . . ."

"But your hands were full of light . . . and fire! You must be a wizard! Or some type of druid or something. That's not a normal thing, you know?" stated Arnenn in a slight whisper as he tightly clasped the end of the table.

An older lady with tall and curly hair came by at that time to ask what they would like to eat. They paused as Throone ordered some ales and warm chicken soups with crackers for all. When she had walked away, he answered back. "You think I've lived as long as I have and not realized that? I know what happened. I don't need your help telling me what I just did. I also realize it's not normality. And can you two grow up and stop acting like this? You better not go telling anybody, and I mean it. Only a small handful of people know about it and it's going to stay that way."

He took a deep breath and slowed himself down. "I don't know why or how I have the ability. Never have. And, that's *all* I can do—I cannot do anything else. I don't have a wand or a special staff, and I don't do spells. I also don't mix potions and I cannot control lightning or water . . . and I don't want any stupid questions about it. I can handle fire and heat in a variety of ways and that is all. I think it's probably best for you two to know from here on out for certain reasons to come, but *only* you two, got it?"

They assured him the secret was sealed.

"On the more important subject, I'm unsure of how many of those Dark-Beasts are out there. I know there are to be wolves up in this area that should be able to ward them off, but I guess there may not be as many as up north. It's at least safe to say that we're being followed for the Orrumn."

"What about the people in this city, or any other cities or towns? Shouldn't they be warned?"

"I don't believe they'd be attacking any big cities—at least not yet. . . . Understand, Arnenn . . . Gjone . . . at one point that may be possible, and we will need to figure out what to do to stop that from happening, yes.

But right now, these beasts are being drawn to the book so until the book is safe, we'll just have to fight them off. I believe what's best to figure out after this particular journey is where they're coming from. That will at least help us know what cities would be in need of extra security."

As Gjone kept trying to reason the whole wizard thing with Throone, annoying him greatly, Arnenn's thoughts drifted back to the Orrumn. He remembered the spears drawn before the attack and how it made him question the old man. He couldn't decide if his ability meant something good or bad, but he still felt Throone could be trusted overall. He also felt it would be a good idea to not anger him in any way since he was even more dangerous than with having only his amazing spear skills alone.

After eating and feeling like they were *somewhat* on the same page with things, they walked around the other interesting parts of the small and cold city and discussed more matters of their travel for the day ahead, such as the provisions they would need.

As Throone walked around with his arms tightly molded to his body, he told them it would be their greatest benefit to buy as much food and water as possible. It was because they still needed to cross the Pale Mountains and there were to be no other towns or villages at all before they reached the castle they were in search for, wherever it may be. He also said they should get enough to last them for quite some time after they arrived as well, just in case they happened to be there for a while. They stalked up on many pounds of dried meats from the small food stands.

The cousins didn't mind; they didn't spend any of their own money. It was one of the agreements Throone made with Rayne and Jemma. He didn't seem to mind either and apparently had more than plenty of money to spare. Again, he would say the same phrase as he purchased the items. "All good go to Crowlis!"

It was obvious that Gjone enjoyed Strathom much more than Arnenn, and Throone noticed it easily as he watched him walk around and gaze at the many sights and intricate characteristics of the city.

The young man was found enamored by the new and old houses with many caged purt stones on strings that swung across to each and every one of them, along with the small fountains of unique designs with water given from a small creek that drifted down and east through the city. In the middle of the walkways, people were playing games that looked like loads of fun; and many pretty girls roamed about around his and Arnenn's age, which Gjone would smile at, and they, right back to the tall man of Harpelle.

Arnenn also thought there to be many interesting little nuggets about the place, such as the trees that bent over all the buildings and the many lights; and the lifting lives of those in ragged, yet put-together clothing. But that which was in the Orrumn clouded his vision of it all, and really, he just wanted to know what else could be found within it, what other knowledge or secrets it held for him, and the interesting girl: who she was, and again, if she were real.

He wasn't able to do any of it that night due to being tired from their gathering of goods for the days ahead. Also that night, they shared a room where none slept very well due to the loud noises of the exciting city outside their room's walls.

14

STRATHOM'S LOOK IN THE MORNING WAS

almost even more surprising. The only dry-seeming valley at night ended up being one of the most pleasant surroundings they had seen on their journey as of yet. And on top of the still green grass and outer fields were flowers of the brightest autumn colors.

"I'll just stay here—you two can go on without me," joked Gjone as they walked to the stables carrying their overloaded quantities of luggage and food.

Throone thought of everything he could to reason with the stableman about getting some horses to take south, but the owner was persistent in saying no.

"There's no good reason to have any of my steeds going into those lands. There's nothing for it or for you to venture into those old and desolate places. You'll get yourselves and my steeds lost or killed! I will not be having it!" argued the stableman, justly.

As Throone eagerly kept reasoning with the man, explaining how careful they would be, the young Rowes found themselves walking into a small clothing shop for what seemed to be the average merchant, farmer, or villager. There, Gjone bought a ridiculous blue hat that had a long and round brim, and a top that went to a pointy end, high into the air. It seriously must have been about two feet tall when fully pulled.

"I'm not sure if this is the best look for either of you," said a young girl of blonde hair at the counter, flirting.

"What do you mean? I think it would look great on my cousin, here."

Arnenn gave him a slight push in his embarrassment. "It fits your massive head much better than mine. . . ."

Gjone gave her an extra smile as they walked away— Arnenn had already invested too much interest in another girl to have any left for others.

As they walked out the shop's door, they noticed that Throone was able to get an almost-broken pull cart with two wheels that would carry their goods, and without a horse to pull it. It truly didn't help them look forward to the remainder of their journey to the wherever-it-could-be castle.

Before they could ask, and right when Throone wasn't looking when confirming, "Yes, this is the best I could do," Gjone set the hat he had just purchased inside the Keeper's luggage.

Traveling away from Strathom, they had to take turns pulling the cart on a road that had not been used for many long years; and they could see that it traveled into a range of mountains that almost looked to be glowing in a radiant white. Arnenn knew them to be the Pale Mountains that Throone had mentioned days earlier. As it was his turn, and after pulling the cart for only half of an hour, he grew tiresome of all its weight and realized he'd never asked a question that had an excellent point to it.

"Why do we really need all this food? Won't there be food where we're going?"

"I wouldn't bet anything on it. I don't think there'll be any people there so food will be very scarce unless you want to find and pick fruit from trees all day long," said Throone. He wasn't even sure if trees bore fruit in the Southlands.

"Wait! What? So it's an abandoned castle? You never told us that . . . how is this book going to be kept safe if there's not even anyone there to watch over the thing?" asked Arnenn, stunned at what he was hearing and that he was now just hearing it.

"I don't know. We will all just have to figure it out together," Throone responded, very calmly, keeping the Mountains inside his tunneled vision.

"So that's your great wizard plan?" asked Gjone. "Just go all the way to this far-off and abandoned castle and stick the book under a pile of rocks?"

"Pretty much," Throone said easily, not caring to have any better answer for the two. "And I'm just going to pretend I didn't hear that comment about being a wizard and stop answering you two's stupid questions. I'm serious, no more wizard talk from here on out unless you would like to be lit on fire!" He rolled his eyes and let their question and his main answer be as it was and nothing else. He muttered something to himself that they both heard: "Darned Mourenrowes. . . ."

The day went on and the road became harder to conquer and the many rocks made pulling the cart a real pain. Its chopped up wheels of wood bounced and kicked around and would even skid and skip amongst the rocks that stuck underneath them from time to time, which was an extreme annoyance. They went through gullies with brush hanging down from the trees that were more than willing to scrape at their arms and faces. Gjone and Throone walked ahead with some short blades to cut off limbs hanging down into the gullies from the abrasive plant life up above, clearing a path for Arnenn who gained a new nickname: Captain of the Cart (that is until he couldn't carry it any longer).

Eventually, Throone took over Arnenn's job as he explained that the road they trod would start becoming even tougher than it already was before they were up and over the beginning slopes of the Pale Mountains.

As they crept closer to the smaller hills that bore around the mass of rock, the road changed to whitish dirt and they were led through a canyon. They came upon a hole in the mountainside but could tell it wasn't a cave because they could see light coming through, far away from its other end. It was a tunnel that ran up into the slope of the Mountain's beginning.

After practically crawling through the stuffy and dusty hole, and pushing the cart together through its darkest parts, the trail inclined through an area that was last walked upon over fifty years before for mining and hauling over cut trees from the southern slope to cities north such as Strathom—or even over to the Lake's many different towns.

But nobody used them anymore because the large, angry, and scary animals of the land would continue to run them off. It happened continuously for years and years until everyone eventually got the point and gave up their steady efforts.

Not talking for quite a long while, only helping push the cart up the steep trail, Throone said (he figured they would eventually be asking him more questions), "There's been word that all kinds of large mammals protected something in the area. Nobody knew what it was they were protecting, but they drove many of the people that settled and built there for a short time, away. Even here in these lonely mountains they tried to mine for things such as Medolathe (what they use to create purt stones) but they never found much in these hills, so the consensus was to move north and to put these lands to rest until further notice of attempting it came again. There's a slight possibility we may have a run-in with some of the mammals, but I also have a way with them so we should be okay. I'd assume some of them would be Light-Beasts."

The Pale Mountains became rockier as evening was abroad, until it was almost bereft of dirt and only stone showed through its thin crust, reflecting the coming moonlight. Rain came in hard from the west as the trail became more and more narrow. The water made it slippery and harder to pull or even push the cart, even with all members working tirelessly together.

Gjone and Arnenn kept thinking it was a mistake going with Throone's advice to go over the Mountain, and that it may have been a better idea to pick going all the way around, instead. They figured that it would have at least been an ordinary flat walk that way.

A nice break came when Throone said they were about to reach the peak of the pass. They waiting out the light drizzle and snacked on dried fruit and edible berries found on some of the nearby bushes, and were at least happy to start heading down the other side of the Mountain—down, and thankfully, no longer up.

Half an hour after breaking, they had come upon the top of the pass. It allowed them to see the distant south under the falling light, which set west behind many dark clouds. It was dense in green and what looked to be an almost swampy land from what they could tell, and as expected. Past that, they couldn't see very much at all . . . especially any castle. Arnenn had even stepped atop a massive rock formation he'd seen from a distance while they all trailed about the area to find their own better view, but he still couldn't see any castle while the now lighter rainfall still muddled what his eyes could see.

That's when Throone said to them both, "My friends . . . take a look behind you."

Arnenn turned and saw the expansive lands of the North, along with the great size of the Palendrian Forest. Its sheer mass was breathtaking. Even Gjone widened his eyes at it while his hand beamed atop his eyes to cover them from the rain, but Arnenn could see something that the others could not from his higher standpoint.

"Throone, what's that blackened area supposed to be?" he asked as he pointed ahead.

"Blackened area?"

"Yes! It's far out in the center. Come up here and look!"

Throone and Gjone stepped up and saw that Arnenn wasn't joking. In the very center of the vast forest, many miles out, there was a spot of black where they believed the trees were under a sickness of some sort.

"Is that part of the Forest dying?"

"That forest is ancient . . . so for all I know, it could be!" replied Throone. "But we must continue on. We should still be able to get through half the Mountain down and find a good place to camp before nightfall."

Though not saying much about it, Throone thought relentlessly to himself of what could be going on in the Palendrian. It was, in fact, the same forest he'd been led into a few weeks prior where he was attacked by a some strange creature of Dark, although he never ventured far enough into it to know any more about it. He definitely never remembered seeing this discoloring when he had stood upon one of the Pale's eastern ridges some years earlier.

It began making some sense to him, though. If he never knew for sure what was in there, then how would he say it doesn't have something to do with Dark? They could have even been there all along. But he couldn't just turn around now; he knew that the Orrumn would need to be protected first.

He had to take one more glance north, wondering if he should be concerned for those of Strathom.

It was almost two whole days full of pulling the cart strenuously through the mud while in the wet and almost humid areas south of the Pales. Sleeping in its settings wasn't easy, either. Many bugs flew at their faces which woke them up over and over again, especially Arnenn, who was more than distraughtly disgusted by them the entire time.

They felt they had to have passed the ending of Throone's map already and should surely be at the place, but it was still nowhere in sight.

The cousins were also afraid that some of the larger predators such as crocodiles would come and sweep them away in the middle of the night, but luckily, it never happened. Throone laughed and said it was a very unlikely hypothesis. They also hadn't seen any large animals—definitely not any Light-Beasts. And so far, it hinted that they might have removed themselves from the area long ago. It may as well have been the case. Arnenn couldn't really imagine what they could've wanted with such a place by the looks of it.

Throughout their time in the lands, Arnenn started taking full advantage of studying the Orrumn. The same pages of the castle, the girl, and the spears still appeared as if they were always there, but no visions or anything else ever happened.

Over and over again on the page with the girl, he tried, but still, nothing. He was at a loss and thought he had reached the surface with it. He couldn't show the old man because he was too afraid of what it might do to him. And then Gjone was just Gjone, and didn't care—besides the fact that he saw nothing in it back at the house, or bothered to retry.

Arnenn eventually decided it was no use and gave up as the task of traveling went ever on, being hard enough as it already was.

Even as the sun shone bright after the clouds had finally drifted away, the trees around the swamplands still made for a dark road. The area was scary more than anything else and Arnenn understood why people had given up existing in these lands long ago, other than the animals that would run them off. He could sense an almost age old remnant of magic or spirits that lurked around the area in a strange way; and wondered if there were some who lived in the swampy woods from an ancient time. There must have been, because condensed were decayed and abandoned homes that were mostly hidden inside the decomposing trees around them. And the odd noises of the many unknown creatures didn't help, either.

For a while, they had to lightly tiptoe across thin paths running between moldy-looking ponds surrounded by tall grasses. Every here and there they would get their boots soaked on accident or almost fall into one of them. Their feet squished into watered socks as they kept their eyes peeled for any type of predator willing to take advantage of their clumsiness.

"It should be around here somewhere," said the old man, gruffly, long after they were shy of any path or trail, but still walking through the bare swamplands—searching endlessly for any signs of a structure. The ground had at least dried up a lot more than it had the previous day, since the rain took heed elsewhere.

"Should we just keep walking until we run head-into something?" asked Gjone with a touch of humor.

"I'm not sure we really have any other choice," replied Throone, seriously.

Arnenn withdrew the Orrumn from his pouch again and opened it to the first page to look at the drawing of the castle. This time, something was finally different. Its small flags of red were swaying back and forth, holding on to dear life as the wind attempted to take them for its own. He then looked up at Throone and Gjone with excitement as he pointed to the page. That's when Gjone saw an image through the trees in the far distance, which he had not noticed a second before when looking ahead in the very same direction. "Wait, I think I see something—"

They began following.

Arnenn thought his cousin might have only been fooling with them since it was very likely, but he was wrong because he saw a wall of white through the thick trees all on his own. He also noticed that the wall went high, and that there were shades of both white *and* red.

They became excited. If it wasn't for the fact that the three had found what they had been searching for after the entire week's travel, then they were at least happy to be *somewhere* other than nowhere.

The cousins and the Keeper sped up, darting from tree to tree while crossing each other's winding and abrupt paths; they gained ground until being closer and closer to the large wall, running right into it—such as Throone had suspected.

There was no clearing, no open glade, no field before the castle. Only trees ran right up against its walls, and some looked as if they had been ripped out of the ground all along its distance with piles of extra brush left all over the place. As the three gazed up, they could see even more ripped trees that settled along the many ledges. It looked as if the building had uprooted itself entirely out of the ground, or was unchallenged by a great natural disaster.

But even with the brush and trees along and on the top of it, the members of the small company could see its beauty and magnificence as the structure stared back at them.

It was *so* large: HUGE. They didn't understand why they couldn't see it from far away in the distance. It was more like a newly built palace than any old and broken castle; and within the many tiers it had were bridges and staircases going in all directions, connecting them sturdily where bronze and silver statues of enormous animals set along all sides of the many stairs. It was perhaps the largest structure they had ever seen: twice, or even three times the size of those in Vidhera. And behind it was a high wall of rock like a cliff almost as tall as the castle's highest tower that bore thinner and thinner as it went higher into the heavens.

They looked to their right and saw a set of dark colored doors that stood above an almost unending flight of stairs.

"Guess you were right, old wizard," said Gjone while staring up at its tallest tower. His head had to set almost completely behind his shoulders to see it.

Throone gave no response to Gjone. He had only a look of great awe upon his face—again, as if he had remembrance of the place. His jaw dropped open.

"I know this place somehow. Or it is perhaps some memory of mine. I cannot make sense of it."

Arnenn looked back and forth between the building and its painting inside the Orrumn: double checking. From what he could tell, everything was in order. It looked to be the very same castle drawn and in all the same colors. He looked around him, seeing if there was anyone else. There was absolutely no one. But he did see that they had officially arrived at their destination. His and Gjone's trust in the Keeper had grown exponentially in that moment.

"Are you sure no one lives here? . . . It looks like it was newly built—just painted yesterday . . . other than all these trees lying around everywhere. . . ." said Arnenn. He put the book away and began running his hand across its clean outer wall.

"Oddly, I'm pretty sure of it," answered the Keeper, pointing to his right. "We need to go over there . . . where the stair to that entrance is so we can find out more."

They left the cart with all their food and luggage up against the face of the wall and climbed over the fallen trees and brush that lined the fortress, and for a good amount of time.

At an exciting pace, they came at last to its very steps where the fortress was engulfing their vision in every proportion. The mighty presence of it loomed over them as nothing had ever done before. As beautiful as it was, it was also frightening, almost ominous in its own way. It had such wonder and might added to it that it was plainly humbling for the small group of three to look upon its greatness.

They came to a short but wide bridge before the stair. It ran over a creek. And it looked like there may have been a stealthy flowing river that ran underneath it at one time.

A large tree settled all the way across the bridge as if it had fallen from space, and as they walked up to it, Throone decided he wanted it moved. All three helped each other push it to one side and together, rolled it over the short wall that outlined the bridge. Down into the creek, the tree went. And it pleased them all to do so, for it wasn't necessary that a place of such great magnitude should have such shrubbery subduing its presence.

Throone wasted no more time after that. He became too excited to wait any longer. Almost with the same enthusiasm and energy of a child, he dashed up the stairs and reached the doors before both Arnenn and Gjone, who fell ever behind while trying their best to keep up.

They were a dark copper and black metal that quite impressively had the imprints of hundreds of hands molded into them. They were all different sizes, too. There were large handprints about twelve to fifteen feet high, which were much bigger than the ones below, almost the hands of some great giants of old. Also, the doors were surely locked, because even after both young Rowes gave a great push and pull, the doors didn't give a single bit.

Still heavily breathing from trying to keep up with the old man on the stairs, Arnenn held the Orrumn in his hands. He looked down. It turned to a fresh page once again where an image in black ink began to appear. He became startled as if it was about to draw a beast of Dark again, perhaps one that could have busted right out of the castle. Instead, though, the same large doors with the hand imprints were now being painted before his eyes. He gave a great breath of relief.

Gjone stood next to Arnenn and stared into the book, but still saw only a blank page and then shook his head.

Arnenn didn't care, though—the castle was enough to reason with any of Gjone's doubts of the images in the book.

Throughout all of the imprints, one in the center of the right door began glowing a familiar blue, but only inside of the Orrumn. Arnenn looked up and matched the handprint on the door to the imprint glowing in the book. He then crept quickly forward and reached for it. It touched. And surprisingly, every tiny protrusion of the imprint fit exactly into each of the creases on his palm and fingers.

He looked up at the door, expecting something to happen, but nothing did. Gjone pushed and pulled the door again, and still, they didn't budge. Arnenn looked down at the Orrumn to make sure he touched the correct one. He was sure he had.

He didn't understand. The Orrumn called out to him; it showed him this castle; it brought them this far; it revealed an image of this handprint on this very door. And then nothing? He only glanced at the other two who were just as confused.

But it didn't last long.

Suddenly in his right peripheral, Throone's hand found its way to another imprint that was next to Arnenn's, almost as if he knew exactly how it worked. When the old man touched it, a rough sound began. The doors were slightly shaking and about to explode or crack, but still, they did not open.

They became frightened, but Throone yelled, "Arnenn . . . the Orrumn! What do you see?"

He looked back down while the book was still open in the crease of his left elbow. The imprint Throone was touching was flaring up like fire in the Orrumn as his own stayed blue.

And then another imprint on the page began to glow in white where Arnenn looked back at Gjone who had a concerning look on his face about the shaking doors, almost about to run back down the stairs for his safety.

"Gjone! Put your hand on the door, right there!" said Arnenn, aggressively.

Gjone looked at them, and then the door. He was utterly confused. The imprint on the door itself also started to glow white, which even *more* so made Gjone confused as to what to think.

But after his moments of hesitation while looking back and forth between Arnenn and Throone who were yelling and pointing, Gjone's hand found its way and perfectly molded to the glowing imprint.

Light glared around all the creases surrounding the doors. They shook even harder. The three could feel its rumble beneath their feet as if the stone was about to crack and go crashing down.

But the doors stopped shaking; all went silent and still.

What sounded like the regular unlocking of a door by the use of key, was a click. The doors then beamed open abruptly; they had to leave their hand imprints and run at full speed backward toward the stairs, dodging the two doors' massive swings outward. They creaked relentlessly until they couldn't swing open any farther, slamming against the wall as they stopped.

The three could see nothing but darkness inside.

Arnenn closed the Orrumn and looked down at it where it now had an even brighter blue lining around all its edges. He asked, "Throone, how did you know to place your hand there?"

The old man only responded with a questioning stare on his face. "I just felt it was the right thing to do."

15

"BEFORE WE ATTEMPT TO GO IN THERE,
you two should go back and get the gear. I'll keep a
watch up here to make sure nothing weird attempts to
creep in . . . or out," said Throone; he didn't want to end
up lost inside the castle without the food and supplies. It
meant that Gjone and Arnenn had to go back—far out
and around into the forested sections where no fallen
trees were lying about to get the cart and bring it to the
stair's beginning. From there, they left it on the bridge
and journeyed back up while carrying the food and
luggage for three, hoping they weren't found to be
locked outside. Throone had done no such thing, but
they still gave him quite the dirty look for making them
do all the work while he just stood there, peering into
the place. But, their feelings weren't his greatest concern.

As Gjone passed Throone his bags and spear, the old
man pulled out his stone and set it atop his stick. "We
don't know what could be in here so we need to stay
close and look for a place where we can safely put our
things. Keep your spears and blades with you at all
times until we get a better sense of this place." He said it
like he was trying his best to contain his excitement.

Throone walked in first, holding the light, which
glared its bright purple against a wall of half pillars
holding large candles studded out on fixtures. They
weren't lit, just as they wouldn't have expected them to
be. But when shutting the doors, the light reflecting off

the stone almost filled a vast expanse that showed a lengthy, dark tunnel.

It was brickwork at its absolute best: Stone tablets were arranged to depict people, animals, or even symbols that even Throone had never seen or knew the meaning of— and large creatures of the underwater realms, or perhaps above the waters. They paced ever slowly as the hallway looked to go ever on, running only into emptiness. And through emptiness they walked for many a minute, swelled inside the dark and cavernous path, perceiving themselves to be only insignificant.

This time going down a flight of stairs, they saw a possible entrance to a larger room farther beyond and could hear the sound of pouring water. There were no hints of the castle being in any worse condition than it was outside, nor were there any bad or uncommon smells filtering through the chilled air. If anything, more of a sweet fragrance existed, like a garden were planted somewhere inside.

The hallway's exit at the bottom of the stair was near, and from what they could tell, an enormous room was before them. But Throone's lit stone couldn't cast light far enough to know just how big it could be, or exactly what the room's purpose was.

As they landed on the last step, the Keeper noticed a lamp on the wall, not so far away to his right. His arm reached with great length with help from the short stick that held fire, and it shined on the lamp. It was bereft of any candle. But when Throone held the fire's flame underneath to get a better look, a particle of the fire was stolen from the stone and the lamp's glass quickly flamed and filled itself with yellow.

Then about fifteen feet down the wall, a different lamp stole the same particle of the flame from the original one.

It somehow danced its way slowly over as if traveling on an invisible thread. It kept happening and continued to the next lamp, and then over to the next. It moved faster and faster each time, like the old fortress was waking up.

The flame also went to lamps above as it continued its many movements across, sustaining the large chamber in firelight. Farther and farther and up the wall it went to wrap around the room's entirety.

Above its visitors, the lamps had ignited themselves all the way up to a towering ceiling before the light began in jumping movements to the top of five grandiose chandeliers. The streams of light had flickered down and around until eventually, all the rings of candles held a steady fire.

Every lamp was ignited, but the room still existed in a modest dark. And it suggested that they were looking at a night sky surrounded entirely by the most radiant stars ever seen. They began shining stealthier with every passing second before the company saw that the room had set in thorough illumination. All they could do at first was stare. Speechless.

There were openings to many small corridors on the long walls to both their left and their right, and directly underneath each chandelier that hung mightily low, were stone fountains set in a polished and light-blue tint. They had intense moving water within and amazingly, they didn't flow from a stream or river coming from elsewhere, but all on their own. And they existed with the clearest water ever seen. It made little sense, but Arnenn was filled with delight and wonder as his soul became lost within their free-flowing waters. He also saw that clear on the other side of the large hall, was an almost colossal throne veiled in white, which he guessed must've been meant for a king at one point in time, or maybe even still. Taking up more of its epic space were long tables scattered along the walls and in its corners.

The nearest fountain carved an image of a great moose lying with two of its young on a mound of grass that surrounded a rock with water fiercely streaming out of the middle: erupting like a volcano. The size of the moose alone was fantastically larger than any moose they had ever seen in real life.

They continued walking into the hall where they also passed a fountain of a great bear with a live fish in its mouth. The way the eyes on the bear looked at Arnenn gave him a great fright, along with a familiar feeling. The fountain's flow came out from underneath and over a thinly-layered rock; its current drifted so harshly that if one of the members were to have plodded into it, then they would surely be swept away and spun helplessly around and around until the very end of their days.

The central fountain was the largest—tallest, and most prominent of all, definitely the main focus. It was of a man that bore long hair and a short beard. He was shy of any tunic except for the bands that wore across his chest and back, and the mold showed his muscles vividly. He was looking straight ahead with his arms down to his side. In his right hand, he held a wildly designed lance of some sort in which the head of it pointed down at the ground, and then into the water below. In more stone, children and baby animals surrounded the large man in great joy. It portrayed all of them to be splashing up its water that bounced and shot about in every angle and direction.

Throone looked up with great fear and reverence to the great man in the fountain, pondering who he could have been. But he also felt a comfort being inside the great fortress. He stood in awe of its miraculous details that he longingly gazed at. It didn't even make sense how any of it was there at all, but for once, he felt he wasn't the only magical force existing on Amruhn and that the castle had some large part to do with it. More so, he felt oddly at home.

The last two fountains were not as miraculous as the one in the middle, but they were interesting in their own way. One was of men and women with the tail of what looked like a fish (they had never heard of such things we call mermaids) and they were holding hands in a circle halfway out of the water. The other was a great leopard atop some compromised branch of a tree that was hovering above the group, and both had their own unique waterworks as well.

After passing the fountains without extra stops, the group came to the white chair seen from the other side of the hall. Arnenn and the others thought it slightly amusing, for it was much too large for any regular sized man to ever fill it correctly.

"There must've been a great king that lived and ruled here," said Throone before also saying, ". . . a king of great size, too . . . if I may summon up the words. . . ."

"Are you sure there's no one here?" asked Gjone. "This place is very lively. What if it's a trap?"

Arnenn looked at Throone in a worried way over Gjone's question.

"I don't believe, young Mourenrowe, that *that* would be the case. What I *do* believe is that this fortress just now appeared and that it hasn't existed for any time before we began our way here. I just know it. It seems like it uprooted itself—if you couldn't tell from outside. But whatever spirit lived within this place from before has continued as if no one had ever left. That's the feeling I had about this place when I saw the picture of it in the Orrumn. I could feel the presence of this great fortress as if it'd come out of me like a ferocious wind and stole all of my energy away. But now, I feel as if it wants to give it back to me. I don't see how this could be a trap in any way. Quite the opposite, if anything. . . ."

Gjone glanced at Throone for the crazy answer he had given, but was still in quite the shock from what just happened back at the entrance. He had never seen any sort of magic before this journey began, if it was magic at all. But if so, it could be the very same magic his father spoke of, which he always thought was only absolutely ludicrous.

His notion about joining in on this trip was only to help his cousin and his father's old friend deal with some prospect of his family line, which he himself held absolutely no importance. But for once, he had to greatly rationalize against all that and reason directly against himself. He found that the doors weren't going to open unless *he also* touched them; and his hand fit perfectly within the imprint that gleamed in white, calling out to him; he felt its power. It's as if it made complete use of his presence in the company and that it critically needed him there.

He thought to himself what it could all mean and it made him want to start paying more attention to the whole scenario and everything happening. But he still knew to keep his wits about him; he wasn't about to let the possible magic fill his head with anything that it shouldn't. He thought to himself: *Arnenn's already doing a wonderful enough job of that all on his own!*

"Where's this book supposed to go? You said this is the place it can be kept safe. Is there some certain area I should be going?" Arnenn was more than ready to start venturing around the mysterious place—wanted to look for someone.

"That, you will need to ask the Orrumn! I have already told you that it's *your* job, not mine!" said Throone as he continued to walk along the walls while studying the designs and colors on the hall's surfaces, also slightly ignoring him about it otherwise.

Arnenn realized he'd asked the same question before so he said nothing else, not wanting to anger the man with fiery capabilities. But he didn't know what to do or where to go so he quickly opened the Orrumn. Turning around, he no longer faced the chair, but the hallway they'd taken leave of minutes ago.

Just like before, a new drawing started on a new page. It began to paint the very image of the hall they were in, just as he had hoped. It drew the fountains, and also the many corridor openings that led to the castle's many unknown destinations that Throone kept peering into.

Then unexpectedly, he saw people—many different people walking around, dancing, and speaking to one another inside of the Orrumn. They appeared and then disappeared in no set time or order. Some were much bigger than others, and some were much smaller; some were closer to his height from what he could tell, but even a few of the children that came in and out of the page were taller than he.

Arnenn tore his eyes away from the page and looked around the room, but there was nothing but stillness along with his companions staring eccentrically at him. He then peered back down to the movement in the book and could not figure out if they were memories of what had happened there at one time before, or things that would someday be. By the looks of objects such as their clothing, he thought it had to be of the past, and quite possibly a very long and forgotten past. But maybe even some kind of unforeseen future.

Their movement continued as Arnenn then noticed something familiar, something he was surprised he had not noticed right away: All had long hair that held different shades of color, exactly like the hair of the girl seen in the book, the one he wants to find. But he thought to himself that if it were showing him things of the past, then she must have existed there at a time long before his own.

It absolutely crushed his soul. He thought right away that she was someone who no longer lived; he had no luck of ever meeting or knowing her.

His knees were weak and he felt as if his usual hopeful spirit had completely left his body, gone forever. He wanted only to drop the Orrumn and walk away from it all.

But, he also couldn't be too certain about anything just yet. It was all only speculation. He kept his attention to what he was seeing inside the Orrumn. The taller people looked much different than those who were shorter. They had a brighter or darker colored skin and wore clothing in tight rob-like fashions. And they reminded him of the ancient paintings he had seen as a child in school, that he and his fellow classmates were told to be only made up for "art." Naturally, it was everyone's belief.

He watched as objects would appear mid-air.

He saw a woman that must have been eight feet tall, moving dust particles on the floor with just the wave of her hand, controlling the wind above and around them, sending the dust up into air pockets of heat and then combusting it all into nothing. And there was a man even taller than she that wore a black robe shining mightily over his already dark skin. Arnenn watched him walk gracefully; he was holding a small gem that contained what must have been energy inside.

He was wholly confused as to how they were doing these miraculous things. He thought these people might even have something to do with the likes of which Throone came to exist.

Then, something else caught his attention. It was a young boy of seemingly average height. He wore an older-style green tunic with dark-leather leggings. He appeared quite abruptly, waving at him. But then, he disappeared. Arnenn looked up again to make sure the visions weren't coming to life about him like they had before. They still were not.

A part of him wanted to tell the others what he was seeing, but as Throone said, it was only *his* job to figure it out. Also, he knew how Gjone would react.

But Gjone said something anyway as he had noticed Arnenn staring very intently into the book. "Arnenn, seriously . . . what's going on?"

He ignored his cousin while continuing to study the drawings. The boy reappeared and waved to him again, but this time by one of the corridors on Arnenn's right. The youngster ran eagerly into its lightless entrance.

"I think we're supposed to head into that corridor, right there," He eventually pointed to the second one on his right that headed east. The other two didn't question and followed easily into its emptiness.

Arnenn asked Throone for his stone, its fire still stealthily lit. But as he neared, they saw that the stone's light was not going to be much help. The same thing happened with the lamps again; flares of fire came from the main hall and then danced themselves over to the ones in the small corridor.

They left their luggage on a table near the entrance, except for any smaller weapons; for they figured they wouldn't need any spears—being that the place for the most part gave off a comforting vibe. And as the three moved at a slow pace, the lamps lit up only one at a time while waiting on them. They could sense that the castle was welcoming them, helping the boy lead them to their destination of the Orrumn's resting place.

The walls of the corridor had the same designs seen in the entranceway that were set in brickwork. And while studying them closer, they began feeling like they were heading down again.

At first, they terrified Arnenn.

Stone figures that looked to be some supposed "indoor" gargoyles were set on the walls at opposite sides of the corridor. There were new ones about every fifty feet and all were very different and scary-looking. They gave the members a new hunch of wonder. But they couldn't decide on what type of sensation they were adding to the place or what they meant. Or, if they were perhaps creatures made up, or possibly real.

Eventually, the corridor made its way to a descending staircase that spiraled. Arnenn looked down, again, and saw that the Orrumn began drawing exactly where they were as the boy waved them farther ahead. Arnenn gave in and told them what he was seeing. Both gave him a look of suspicion, questioning if they should trust in the book and whoever this boy inside it happened to be. They agreed to it, though, mostly because they didn't know what else to do.

The stair became darker as its dim lamps didn't give much light. And Throone's stone came into good use once again. Anything said echoed to the point of almost nerve-racking fright as they must have gone deep into an underground abyss where many passageways trailed off to the right into barracks or maybe even dungeons. And anytime they came upon a new opening, he had to double check and make sure that straight ahead and down the winding stair was still the correct way to go.

The boy would run ahead until out of sight, but would then reappear and wave, and continue the same process as if wanting them to follow even faster. But they were already going as quick as they could within the dim lighting of Throone's stone that encircled them in a purple glimmer.

Continuing, the echo of their conversation died away and another sound was heard. It was water again. But this time, it was much louder and stronger sounding: rushing—almost thunderously. The place had become vibrant with a natural light and the stair had eventually stopped its steady winding. And ahead, they could see the sun's beam shine in from small openings in a rocked ceiling above, creating many more beams to all of the vegetation below. Descending farther down on the stair that now had no walls to its sides, they came into an open cave of Amruhn's best soil. It was most marvelous.

As the falling from what had to have been a large body of water that went far below to maybe thousands of feet into the world's center, large and vibrant trees and plants and grass grew abundantly in every corner of the self-gardened cave. All three felt a wave of cool and clean air as a spring of energy spun around the place and inside their bodies. It filled their lungs with a power that ignited their souls and fulfilled their hearts as they breathed it in entirely.

Throone had a smile on his face as they paused to see what was around them. He felt like a child again, yet also, some great man of power at the same time.

The boy on the page stood still for a moment before he continued running, or jumping from step to step as they took the stair's sharp right. But Arnenn's attention was leaving anything the youngster was doing as he pushed through a series of overgrown plant life to see an open glade with tall grass that ran out to white sands, which then sunk into a clear blue and open sea.

"I'm not looking forward to our trip back to the top," said Gjone. Arnenn slightly chuckled, but the old man wasn't paying attention to a single word he said. The Keeper had learned to tune out most of what the older cousin would say days before, and he wasn't interested in being distracted from his moment of existing in pure astonishment.

There was a single stone platform in the middle of the glade and Arnenn thought to himself: *Is that where I'm supposed to put it? Out here in the open? This is where it can be kept safe? Where anyone can come from this sea and snatch it right up?*

It made less sense than ever before.

He looked again at the page to see if it could explain any more, or see if he was perhaps wrong about his whole conclusion with the platform. This time, the boy was nowhere to be found as the wind flipped the pages both forward and backward. It then settled on the one of the girl. And Arnenn somehow knew that the Orrumn was entirely responsible for it happening, more than just the wind.

Arnenn was dumbfounded as to why it would be going back to this particular page. He had just worked himself through dealing with the fact that he had no hope of ever seeing her. And he was growing angry at how the Orrumn was toying with his emotions. He felt the same frustration as when he tried leaving Harpelle—

when he couldn't pull a single word from his uncle, and how he was completely lost as to what to think, annoyed and done with it all.

But just like before, during the first night of camping near the woods, she gazed up at him with a smile. He felt his heart sink into his stomach while drifting into the painting again—a daze as the picture became a vision. He almost forgot where he was when Throone placed a hand on his shoulder, causing him to jolt out of it.

Arnenn studied him in question, distressed. "WHY DID YOU DO THAT?" he yelled at the powerful man— somewhat accidentally, yet also on purpose.

"Collect your wits, Arnenn! There's something in here!"

The next moment, he saw what they did: some object move from behind a large plant that had practically grown itself into a tree.

"Should we investigate it?" asked Arnenn, thinking there was little chance he'd leave the Orrumn on the platform with whatever was helping itself around in the area.

Out of the corner of his eye, something peaked from behind the plant, almost wanting to reveal itself, but unsure if doing so was the best idea. It surely wasn't any creature of Dark or any species of animal that he could tell. Arnenn thought, *Maybe it was the boy in the book who had led them there. And maybe he needed rescuing.* But next, he saw a long strand of hair hanging down from behind, just like the hair of the girl, or the others he had just seen inside the Orrumn, definitely not the boy who only had short hair of blonde.

Getting over any fear left of whom or what it may be, he paced forward excitedly. The others stayed contently where they were.

"You can come out. None of us are going to hurt you. Are you here alone? Or are you with others?"

There were no answers to Arnenn's questions. Instead, she only walked out from behind the plantation.

Arnenn felt his heart stop.

She was real. There. Right in front of him. He could tell it was her; he knew it for sure; his interest and almost obsession with her caught up to him immediately.

He couldn't think of a single thing to say. He couldn't believe it. How could this be real? He only stared, impolitely. He tried to say something, but she spoke instead.

"Do not I know you?"

Her voice was soft and smooth, pleasant.

"Yes—well—no. . . ." stuttered Arnenn, overtaken by her. She was even more beautiful than what the picture had led him to believe. He felt like he needed to hold himself back from embracing her in his arms. He hadn't felt so childish about a girl since he was twelve when surprising Pearlin with a kiss, where she had only responded by slapping him. He thought about how foolish he would look if anything similar were to happen.

"I saw you in the book."

"What do you mean?" she asked. Her face gave just as much question as the question itself.

Throone and Gjone stood back while listening to the conversation, both confused by what was happening or who she was, but funnily enough, could tell that she and Arnenn were drawn to each other.

Arnenn walked to the platform in the middle of the area, closer to where she still stood and where the grass was lying softly underneath his boots and her thin leather bracings that wrapped around her feet and between her toes. She slightly stepped back from Arnenn as he only set the book down on the stone, saying, "This."

The very moment it touched the platform; it changed even more. It began to mold into something different. The dirty-brown shades of the Orrumn began to appear red while its blue edges grew thicker and shined with little help from anything around it.

"The Orrumn!" she exclaimed in suspense as she walked closer to Arnenn and studied his face.

Next, the young woman asked a question, wasting no more time.

"Are you Arnenn?"

16

WORD WAS FLOODING HARPELLE ABOUT
the event of Gjone's killing and how he ran off with the
crazy old man that lived up in the Mountains. It actually
became the principal talk of the town in the last couple
of weeks. And due to it, some Harpellians had gone on
searches for similar creatures around the east end of the
city to see if they could find anything, and just for the
fun and interest of it.

Parents became concerned for their children's safety
and travelers would hear of the story and bring word
along to other cities as they gossiped and laughed about
it. In fact, there was one shop on the east end of town
which had a horribly-made stuffed animal of a black dog
as a joke for the all the kids, and they were flying off the
shelves. (This was most likely due to the words at work
from people like Cezz, with many contributors such as
Simeon.)

People would ask Rayne and Jemma questions about
the subject and as much as they wanted to speak up and
tell them all about it, they kept their word to the old man
that had taken their son and nephew away. It wasn't the
easiest to handle, especially since it had now been weeks
since their venturing away.

Haulfir assumed his usual position in the Ivory Nook
with his boots atop the table after his guard tasks were
finished for the day. "I know *exactly* why Rayne and
Jemma are being so quiet about it all, Cezz. They're

embarrassed about the whole thing! They've never been this shy about any subject the entire time I've known them . . . it isn't natural."

"I just think Rayne's stories have finally caught up to him, but I don't necessarily disbelieve them one bit!" said Cezz, as Rimland sat shaking his head in agreement after taking a big gulp of ale just set down before him.

"It isn't whether I disbelieve them or not, it is just that I feel sorry for Gjone . . . having to go on that stupid adventure. And the fact that they have been gone for weeks now is more than irregular."

"I don't think it's up for us to decide whether it's irregular or not! It's not us that have anything to do with any of it. And I'm pretty sure Gjone can handle himself and his own situations in life without any of our help." Cezz's blonde haired arms were crossed as he leaned back in his chair and continued. "The only concern we need to have is if the story about this beast is true. I believe it is . . . because Gjone's not a liar. It means that we need to keep watch for now on. Especially you, Haulfir. You're the one on the Bear Guard, now . . . after all."

"I know what my job is, you dimwit!" scolded Haulfir toward Cezz, whom he knew to be much smarter than himself. "I'm not worried about Gjone or anything, but I do kind of hope Arnenn doesn't end up making it back. Maybe he'll get lost in the woods somewhere . . . I can only hope. The same for that awful old man, too!"

Cezz and Rimland rolled their eyes.

"What is it with you having it out for Gjone's cousin?" asked Rimland. He finally stopped sipping on his wooden mug for one second. Rimland was almost as large as Gjone, but in a not-as-healthy-looking way. And the best way to explain his voice is that he always had too much air stuck in the back of his throat, disabling him to get out a full projection.

"He isn't a bad guy at all . . . and none of us have ever had a problem with—"

"I just don't like him, okay? I never have!" answered Haulfir, gruffly. "You two idiots should have already figured that one out by now!"

"Are you still on about being sent over the table by him? You need to get over that, Haulfir. No one here even remembers that anymore."

"Apparently *you* do, Cezz. And yes, I am, actually . . . it's bad enough that little rich kid has to come down here every single summer to do basically nothin'. And he only helps out Rayne and Jemma on the docks when they make him, if you two don't remember." (They all used to help Gjone a couple of years back in their teens as a first job.) "What's more annoying is that he thinks he has more fighting skill than anyone here—which makes no sense at all. No other in any place on Amruhn has more knowledge of fighting than the people of this city in my opinion . . . no one from Vidhera could ever even come close—no matter what they think! I would love to have an actual one on one with him some time, and I'll show you who will win. And let me tell you . . . it'll be *me*."

Cezz started to speak up—but Haulfir felt he had more to add to the matter.

"Also, I'm a guard, and he should have respected me! The people of this city need to know they have my protection, so when they see me being pushed over the table by some little no-one brat, I could lose their confidence, and I'm not fine with that—"

"Haulfir," interjected Cezz, who shook his head with rolling eyes. "I don't think you know what you are talking about. . . . You're confused! If you want to be treated with the respect because you're a 'guard' . . . then you may want to address others with respect even *more* so. Like it or not, Rayne and Jemma are happy to have him here every summer as if he's one of their own. And now with you being on the Guard, you are to be his protector while he's here. For now, you should be more concerned about losing the *respect* of the people of this town rather than their confidence, and you definitely aren't starting in a great direction so far. . . ."

Haulfir gave him his signature scowl, but knew Cezz had a point as he remarked sarcastically, "Gee, Cezz, who made you the wise one?" (Cezz was popular. He was also the smartest; he received the best grades in school for all inactive subjects. He was very levelheaded and the most reasonable out of the small group of friends that grew up together on the east end. They all assumed he'd end up being a doctor, or something like it.)

Haulfir knew that neither Cezz nor Rimland, nor anyone else would understand him or agree with his feelings about Arnenn, and he also knew nobody cared to, either—there was simply no need for them to since they all liked him just fine as he was. It's just that *he* never liked Arnenn. And for some reason during the past summer, the young man from the Kingdom City had been on his nerves more than ever before. Haulfir wouldn't tell anyone, but he sometimes thought Arnenn might decide to settle in Harpelle and do something like join the Bear Guard—completely rule over his territory. (There was never any claim to this from Arnenn or anyone else. And really, it was the last thing Arnenn would've ever cared to do.)

Also, he wasn't actually too sure or confident that he really *could* conquer Gjone's younger cousin in a fight. Arnenn did always surprise everyone when they would gather to spar around the Bear Guard's training fields— although, Haulfir would still love to try nonetheless.

At times, he questioned what it really was that fired him up about Arnenn. All he knew was that his annoyance with him had become something similar to hatred. He couldn't stop it from happening—nor did he care to try. He would do anything to get him back for embarrassing and disrespecting him in front of his friends and all the others in the Nook. And beyond that, he was upset that his father wasn't even on his side about such subjects more than half the time.

Lenx Arbowen was a good leader—almost *too* good in his son's opinion, or at least too kind. Haulfir knew all about how people would get away with things in the city that they just absolutely shouldn't.

The disrespecting boat merchants and common thieves would steal food and supplies from the shops and then never seem to get caught. Then, they would sell the stolen items in that crappy Crennan town or the junky areas of the Lake. It was a well-known issue. No secret at all. Plainly, there just weren't enough guards around to catch them all. And the punishment was never severe enough; a week of jail inside the Guard Tower wasn't much a change in the life of the usual thieving merchant.

He and the others of the Bear Guard were told by his father and the many elders that Harpelle was made through the strength and greatness of its people long before their own time, but Haulfir felt the city no longer lived up to its name of what it used to be. Not even close. (Sadly, he was all too correct about this.)

In fact, if he were given the opportunity, he would track down any and all that stole from Harpelle and rightly cut off their hands for their punishment. It was the little things like excessive burglary that bothered him the most about his father's guarding tactics, but one day it would be different; one day, he would be Captain of the Bear Guard, and Harpelle will be even greater than what it once was at a time long before.

He left Cezz and Rimland at the Nook earlier than his usual that night because his father had him and some of the other guards going out into the provinces between Harpelle and Alderhollow. They were to question word received about the sightings of strange creatures. Haulfir thought it was only due to the hype going on and that probably nothing at all had been seen—people were becoming afraid of any creature that moved at all, and probably their own shadows as well.

Even so, he was glad his father was at least doing *something* about it as he continued walking home in the black of the night.

The Bear of Dark gazed from a small set of hills that overlooked Harpelle, settling just to its east before the River. He had sent a strong servant under his order to find the Orrumn and retrieve it. But his servant had greatly failed him, and now, the Orrumn was no longer sensed to be within the city.

What he did sense within it was the Rowe that resided there. He would need to find and rid the city of the descendant. But he would have to use care. It was one thing he had not been seen yet by the great Light-Beasts that guarded the cities of the putrid realm, and he needed to keep it that way: keep his creeping secret through the dark of the nights and staying hidden during the day.

He remembered and hated the treaty made between men and the pathetic animals that allied themselves with them. He forgot it long ago. He had a greater purpose now; he served the Dark Angelic.

There would be no failure for him. He was going to gather himself an army to rid the land of its Light-Beasts if that's what it took. And he would continue to let the city fall to disunion, to be broken and lose its strength even more than it had already done so on its own. He could feel it beginning already. His master's words were becoming truth. He saw it for himself. The seed of hatred was growing.

He watched a courageous young guard with red hair and in a black uniform, walk alone that very night—he would need him. He watched him from behind the thick oaks covered by the black of the evening that hid the oaks well enough themselves.

The Dark Bear finished up with the helpless deer he'd caught and destroyed and turned south, knowing he would be back soon enough.

17

LOOKING INTO THE ORRUMN AS IT DREW

the picture of a young man with all black hair was the last thing Essria remembered. It would show him again and again as she'd stare into it, looking for a sign to save the Kingdom and its people. But the more time she would spend within it, the more attached she would become, until infatuated with the picture of the young man. She would watch profoundly as the Orrumn would show him placing a hand on the great doors of Kulne. It would also give his name anytime it showed the image, as if it was important she knew it. And it would read his name in full: Arnenn Mourenrowe.

It made little sense how she was able to see into the Orrumn while others could not. None, other than King Madelmar, or the one who discovered the Orrumn could see inside it. But those two chose not to do so anymore. Why it was, she couldn't be too certain.

She spent many long days down in the Garden Cave. Sometimes, she was sent there to see the Orrumn by request of the King or his advisors, while other times, she would sneak down to it and search out her own questions, questions such as whom the one named Arnenn was. She didn't understand how his hair was all black, but his last name was that of another she knew: Mouren Rowe. It meant that Arnenn could have been directly related to him—the one that knew the King better than any other, the same who'd originally found the Orrumn.

She heard about the great strength of Rowe, such as everyone had heard about within the great Kingdom of Kulne: a kingdom that tirelessly rebuilt itself throughout the last half-century. The King himself knew the family well and had shared with them in life. Sometimes away with them in far-off lands, just as he was doing at the time she remembered: fighting a great war against an even greater evil right before making its way to the Kingdom's very doorstep.

But before that, and to things which were otherwise her interests, Essria loved learning of Kulne's history; and she'd often read any book she could in regards to anything about it since it was where she had decided (after proposed by the King's officials) to attend school.

She had an interest in studying the magics of old—along with any magics still left within the world, and in great depth; and she knew of them better than most did (even as a child), to the point where her many mentors believed her interest and wonder, along with her natural knowledge, is what allowed her to see what the Orrumn kept inside. She saw the same types of images Arnenn would; she saw people much larger, radiantly beautiful, wearing the ancient garments of a world long gone—and magic used in ways that would both amaze, yet also frighten her.

Essria wasn't raised where Kulne resided but on the island of Ionsdi, which was only thirty miles of sea from the northern lands of Amruhn. Her people's numbers were decreasing fast with their attempts to fight off the great serpents that inhabited their island and destroyed their ships. It is what first sparked her interest in the Kingdom to begin with, save for that of magic.

She wanted to escape and live in a place of freedom and strength, far away from the scattered people of the island that had grown weaker throughout the years. She hoped that one day she would get the help her people needed and prayed it would be found in the magics. Being so, her parents agreed to let her go, wishing they would one day see their deeply-loved daughter again.

But even less peace than what remained on Ionsdi was found at Kulne after only a year of her studies. A power and substance called the Dark Dust had come where shortly after, Amruhn, too, became a divided place.

Certain magics of the elements that were unknown or uncommon grew, and not all of which were good.

It was at this time she would study the Orrumn in great depth and detail, doing almost nothing else but trying to understand its prophecies and helping the King in any way she could—becoming one of the his greatest young pupils.

Months had passed and almost an entire year of the war had set into time until she heard they had victory. But something happened then that she had never experienced when getting lost in the visions of the Orrumn: She felt as if she'd transported from one world to another—taken back in time, maybe, to a place she had never been, but that had somehow always existed. It was as if she fell into a long sleep.

In it, she had consciousness, but not entirely, and could tell that she was not alone—yet was apart from any others that were with her—like she was never supposed to be there at all, and stuck. And, whom they were, she did not know. She was only able to summon up enough thought and memory to cling to the one thing she missed the most from her last thoughts: the vision of the one named Arnenn.

At first, neither were sure of what to say to each other. Arnenn didn't want to come across too strong or lead on that he was entirely interested in her from just the picture in the Orrumn, and Essria felt the same toward him, but she, too, didn't know what to think. She wondered how he was suddenly there in front of her—then, and exactly when "then" was. She believed she had been somewhere else for what could've been many days. With so much running through her head, and after just waking up, Essria was afraid.

Even though, she stepped in quickly at Arnenn and wrapped her arms around him. With no hesitation from the other, he did the same. It was like they had both been waiting centuries for the moment it would finally happen.

Throone and Gjone did not understand what they were seeing between Arnenn and this girl they had found. But they, also, found her and her hair fascinating; along with the different clothes she wore.

"Was it you? Did you save us, Arnenn?" she asked. She was ready for him to say yes. It was the only answer she thought could be true.

"Save us? . . . I don't understand. We just got here."

"But . . . I heard we defeated them—and I saw you in the Orrumn."

"I'm sorry . . . defeated who? What do you mean you saw me? . . . I saw you."

He couldn't imagine whatever it was she meant—or how she knew him—or how he saved her, or whomever "us" was.

"That couldn't be. I've been here with the Orrumn, watching you . . . I have been waiting for you to finally come."

The others were just as confused as Arnenn.

"Wait, exactly how long have you been waiting for me?" he asked her.

"I—I'm not sure . . . what am I misunderstanding? What's going on? You are Arnenn . . . are you not?" she asked, becoming concerned. She thought she must have been tricked. Perhaps one of her friends or some of the other students were up to something.

"Yes, I'm Arnenn, but I'm . . . confused as to—"

Throone and Gjone had heard enough. They walked together through the brush, both tired of trying to figure out the situation by the two's confusing conversation that was quickly going nowhere.

"—What he means to say . . ." said Throone as Essria's attention turned, "is that we would like to know who you are, and for you to know us as well." They crept nearer to Arnenn. "I'm Throone, and this here is Gjone Mourenrowe, Arnenn here's cousin." Gjone nodded his head to her as Throone continued. "I see you've met our youngest member here, Arnenn. What's your name, might I ask?"

She was skeptical to answer at first, but then thought there couldn't have been much harm to do so. One of them was he that she felt deeply for. And the others wouldn't even be there at all if it wasn't for Kulne's very consent of it.

" . . . I am Essria." She paused. "But my friends—my friends call me Ess."

"It's nice to meet you, Essria—or Ess, if I may. Please come! It is a bit windy and becoming slightly cold down here. We should all go upstairs to the main hall." He stepped aside and held out his arm for her to pass.

Stalling, she looked at the two strangely. The one named Gjone had hair even longer than Arnenn's, yet still all just one color—all brown. But he looked similar to someone she had seen before. And when she first saw Throone with his whitish hair, she thought it normal for an older man, but there was also something familiar and peculiar about him as well. Maybe it was his eyes . . . or the way he spoke. She couldn't decipher what it was as she stood, unmoving.

"Come. Let us all get some warmth and something to eat," Throone stated again before Arnenn grabbed the Orrumn from the platform. She watched him reach for it as if it were his own.

"Arnenn, what are you doing?"

He was puzzled by her question. ". . . I'm grabbing the book . . . the Orrumn. Why?"

"You need to leave it there . . . the platform is the safest place for it! That's where it belongs," she replied slowly and meaningfully.

"She's right, Arnenn. That's why we're here . . . to keep it safe," said Throone, looking back with an agreeing face.

Arnenn paused and stared at the Orrumn as if it was trying to take hold of him as well. He felt he'd be lost without its presence. That they all would. He thought again about the situation, how the book is what brought them this deep into the fortress in the first place.

He let the questions bounce around inside his head. *Would we not need it to find our way back? How would we know to protect ourselves with all these beasts out in the wild? How would this cave of all areas be a safe place for it?*

As they waited for him to set it back down on the platform, he thought he should just trust them. Throone was right after all; it was exactly what they were there to do, as hard as it would be to let it go. And there was the girl, the very one in the Orrumn. She was there with him—she was practically the main reason he kept looking into the book in the first place.

He set it down slowly, and with only little assurance for its safety.

~

They discussed matters no further that day, as strange as it was. Essria only went up to one of the common rooms in a tall tower where she stayed after many awkward moments of walking the stairs and showing them where they could find small chambers in which to sleep—before they gave her some food for the night in exchange. She afterward sat in thought and wondered where everyone else had gone and why the castle was so quiet, and wherever the King could be. She needed some time to herself to figure things out on her own. This Arnenn she had seen in the Orrumn was there and she was excited, but also quite anxious and nervous about it. It was all very off to her. Everything felt unexplainably different. And she also felt it best to be careful with what she said or did during the days to come since everyone else she knew was nowhere to be found.

~

Those days did pass—maybe even weeks. It was hard to tell because they'd easily lose track of time inside the massive fortress.

It was mostly unintentional; it was just too hard to want to leave.

There was so much to learn about it, so many things to do, so many rooms to find and get lost within, and so many areas to share in wonder and to wander about.

Even Gjone found the castle to be of great interest. There were courtyards covered in fast-growing grass on the rooftops—full of training equipment: shortswords, broadswords, and longswords; axes, knives, bows, more spears, you name it. There, he and Arnenn would continue improving their throwing (when not on duty for tree debris removal). And their skill using Throone's spears had become quite impressive to the old man who had made it a point to continue with their lessons (at least more towards the early part of their stay, until Essria had become more comfortable being around the three).

She had begun showing them all around the mighty fortress—all the way from the lowest depths of random small caves and abandoned studies with strange names to the highest towers of concerning heights, which took numerous days to fulfill. Still, they had only seen the half of it. And watching the magical activities such as the lighting throughout castle's depths was amazing. They never grew tired or bored of it.

To Throone, it was intoxicating in the best possible way. Here and there were the most random tiny doors that led them through cramped and tunneled caverns and passageways before coming to underground rooms even bigger than that of the main hall. Numerous libraries, courts, studies, and stuffy labs filled with maps upon walls put all the visitors in complete amazement over Amruhn's geographical fashions of old, though hard to read. There were also ancient scrolls rolled up in what were practically fossilized parchments. They were sitting about in the fortress's tens of deep and darkened chambers where the need of purt stone was in no way "optional."

Getting Throone to move on from *any* of the rooms was a task all in itself, mostly because there were strange-looking devices used for such things that the old man couldn't possibly imagine the purpose for, but would still try to figure out anyway. They were either lying on the ground or suspended from the tall ceilings in its basements that were more like tombs for antiques and rare artifacts; and enough passages were going here and there to even more oddities of old to fulfill the Keeper's interest for any amount of his long years left to live. Also, more waterworks of the castle were ever flowing whether inside, outside in fountains, or in human-made streams where it left and must have worked its magic elsewhere.

The fortress was so epically massive; each member of the company could have had an entire average sized palace all to themselves. The place just conveyed itself entirely endless. Arnenn thought that if he had ever lived there at a time before, he would never have needed to depart anywhere else throughout the rest of life.

Essria explained to them what the designs made out of brickwork throughout all of the halls, alleyways, and corridors were all about and how the magics of the elements were celebrated in a very high regard. She said the students of the school would be selected to perform their arts within the particular season they were born (at least most times) and that their magic worked best within. They would practice all other seasons of the year to display their performances in respects to their forms of magic.

"The King says it was one of the old traditions. He did his best to bring it back but it had unfortunately never lasted long due to the war that came," she said as her hair of color swayed from side to side while leading them through the lit ways of the fortress. Going on, she explained, "There are four different symbols made of the brickwork and they are scattered throughout the many different quarters and sectors the castle. They represent the seasons and their certain magics of the elements. They weren't here before us, but many things were. The designs were made by some of the other students to keep remembrance of the traditions of old." She gave them the names of the different forms, but they sounded unusual, and none of them believed that they would've remembered them without taking precise note.

As time continued, she became even more comfortable with the new members since they were all she had to talk to in the endless place, which still confused her greatly. They did their best to give her the time alone she needed but were growing ever impatient to find out more about her and how or why she was there.

One morning, Throone raced himself into the main hall to meet the younger three for some breakfast. (It had become a tradition within their time at the place.)

Coming right at them, he held a strange blue object which he waved about in his hand.

"What is this? And how did it end up in my luggage?" He pulled it entirely apart; it was the broad-brimmed and pointed hat Gjone had snuck into his bags when back in Strathom.

"It's your wizard hat!" said Gjone as he and Arnenn tried to hold back their laughter before almost bursting out of themselves.

Throone had a questioning and sour look on his face. "What did I tell you about the wizard talk?" he asked, grimly.

"Look . . . Throone, the sooner you accept it, the sooner we can all move on with it. It's better not to live in denial of what you are."

Throone raised his brows at the comment. "Well, the sooner you two stop it with this joke of yours that is just

SO hilarious, the later I will throw you in the fountain with the bear and watch you spin endlessly around!" He laughed right back at them before walking away as if his pathetic response was somehow better.

Arnenn explained the joke to Essria later that day when walking the many tiers of the castle, enjoying a day of such wonderful weather. He and Gjone had already told her about his hands of fire, even though Throone had never given them any permission to do so. And he wasn't happy about it at all. They also told her about his long age—supposedly being over three hundred years old. When they told her these things, she was stunned to hear he had magic such as that, and partially didn't believe it. She had heard of that sort of magic before, but it was extremely rare. There was much to know about the magics of the elements from previous ages and she'd read about many of them while spending most her time studying in the Kingdom's many libraries.

She explained to them both that he was possibly a descendant of someone great and powerful, if what they said was true. But Gjone told her the man had never even known his parents, so there was no way for him to know if that was even a possibility.

She became interested in the old man and his power and wanted to know more about the fire, for it was a mighty sign of magic. It was said that only high kings and people of old that ruled and fought the great wars against ancient beings existing no more were the only ones able to sustain those types of powers through the elements—able to wield the elements, rather than only will.

There was much talk that King Madelmar was able to do such things but it was only of speculation to most; he never showed any to Essria until the war and he vaguely practiced it in front of the students or any others just the same. She wanted to understand it just as much as the old man himself did, and just as much as she questioned the current situation in which she found herself.

It all came to her mind for the hundredth time. Where had everyone gone? Where was the King, the teachers, the villagers and the citizens? All of the staff, the other students, and her friends—her best friend, Loramae— surely she wouldn't have just left her there.

The one thing that her mind kept going back to was the remembered feeling of being asleep for a long time. It was as if she were given some sort of rare herb and drugged. Who would have done something like that to her? Was it perhaps long enough that they had all moved on and left her there to be alone? Had it been months? And why would they leave after winning the war? And this old man Throone she meets has some high form of magic. She wondered if he had come from the past. But that made no sense. The other two that showed up were unlike any she had ever seen, heard, or read about before. And other than Gjone, neither was very tall.

Since meeting down in the Garden Cave, there was no shortage of being drawn to each other. Essria wanted to understand much more about him, and he wanted to know more about her and why she was there all alone, just as she wanted the same answer for herself.

They were almost inseparable from the early hours of the morning until the moment at night when departing for sleep. And over the days, she would show Arnenn the many other secret places of the fortress without Throone or Gjone; and they would talk late into the evenings while staring out at the moon and stars.

The two spent a lot of their time together outside, endlessly walking the many stairs and bridges of the castle or having picnics on the courtyards where they would talk for hours upon end.

"So explain to me, Arnenn, how is it that you two's hair is all one color? It's confused me long enough now . . . and I really must know!" she said, excitedly. She had to understand it.

"I can ask the same for you, Ess. How's your hair in different shades of color and not like everyone else's?"

"What do you mean 'like everyone else's?'"

Arnenn didn't wait to answer. "You're the only person I've ever seen with different colored hair . . . in real life, anyway, I mean . . . I saw some people inside the Orrumn with the same when we arrived here. Don't get me wrong . . . I think it is spectacular and brilliant! But how does it grow like that?"

"Wait, Arnenn. I'm the only other person you've seen with different colored hair? How can that even be? Are you not from here?"

"Well, no actually . . . like I told you, we came here from Harpelle in the North. It's a major city. Haven't you ever heard of it?"

"No . . . I've never heard of that place at all. Not in any of the books of Amruhn have I ever read about a 'Harpelle,' and there are no major cities in the North anymore . . . as far as I knew. Is it mostly winter there year-round? Or is it just frigid all of the time?"

"No. . . . It isn't winter all year-round at all." He wondered why she would ask such a question before he continued in more questioning of his own.

"Really, Ess? The city in the realms of the Light-Beasts?" He was confused as to how she had never heard of it. He thought to himself of how she was found in this close-to-nowhere castle, all alone; there has to be many things she doesn't know, no matter how many books about Amruhn she's read.

"I know of the Light-Beasts, Arnenn, yes! Everybody does! But never this place you're from. . . . Anyway, it's just the same as our eyes. Every season they turn a new color. Yours do as well, do they not? I mean . . . yours are brown just like mine, right now."

"Well, yeah," he agreed, "—but not hair. . . ." He almost laughed.

She answered him back seriously. "Yes, Arnenn—hair too! At least everyone I know does. . . ."

"Well, unfortunately, I don't know *anyone* that you know, and you're the only one I've ever seen like this— except for like I said, the ones in the book—the Orrumn, I mean."

She basically ignored his explanation. "It's like the poem; the children's lullaby." She began.

> *"Summer comes and yellow sums as the animals eat their food.*
> *In fall the leaves drown, deep down to the ground, where Amruhn dies to brown."*

"Yes I do know it, Ess," he said before finishing for her.

> *"When winter is due, we all sink blue, and gather close for warmth.*
> *Then spring flowers, green showers, and the waters of Amruhn cleanse anew.*

. . . What about it?"

221

"If you know it so well," she said, "recite the one about our hair," she quickly commanded right after.

He only sat there—as silent and still as the castle itself. She quickly began again as a smile lifted her cheeks.

> *"The fire of the sun shines bright in summers might, reminding us of our own Light.*
>
> *Then fall comes around and the birds fly abound, where all the leaves of Amruhn once again, die to brown.*
>
> *When winter is back, the wind and the snow make our roots grow black.*
>
> *And as spring blooms in series of reds, the water and flowers begin to wed."*

" . . . . . Um, I've never heard of that one, Ess, no."

"Together, they explain the seasons and the magics they bring. Like I said before: It's Peldia in summer, Negnya in the fall, Holgorenth in the winter, and Setsia in the spring. We're Negnya right now—brown hair and brown eyes. That's why I asked if it's cold in Harpelle year-round, your hair is all black. It's confusing to me. It's like you haven't changed out of Holgorenth for almost a year or maybe even longer. And Gjone . . . it's like he's been suspended in the magic of Negnya for a *very* long time!"

"So according to you—and if I have this right, my hair should be brown right now instead of black? And then turn black in the winter when my eyes turn back to blue?"

"Exactly! Holgorenth," she said, nodding her head. "And then red hair and green eyes in the spring when all is renewed—Setsia. And then blonde hair and yellow eyes in the summer when the sun shines its heaviest light: Peldia."

Arnenn was still; he was studying what he was told, trying his best to remember the combinations correctly, yet still perplexed by it. He stared at her hair again and noticed that almost every four to five inches exactly, it had changed. And her long hair must have been five to six years in the growing without being cut. It all lined up with what she said; it went in the series of colors she explained: red, blonde, brown, and then black; and then all over again.

After gazing for many seconds straight, he heard, "You said that you saw these and other things in the Orrumn. That's another thing that makes no sense. When and how did you have it? The last I know, I had it, which is where I saw the image of you, and everyone I know was still here."

Trying to figure out an answer to a whole new subject after the one he was still trying hard to understand, he said, "Well, I can assure you that you didn't, actually. I found it back in Harpelle weeks ago. The three of us journeyed all this way with it just to put it here. Ess, no one has even heard or known of this place. And as far as we knew, it didn't even exist until the book had shown it to us. Throone said this is where it is to be kept safe. I saw visions of people with your hair color in it, yes, but that was after I saw you! It also warned me about these beasts that are of this Dark . . . that tried to attack us and take it."

"The Dark-Beasts?" she asked. "Wait, so the war is still going on?"

"Ess, there've been no wars going on for many years now—many decades, actually. But Throone has talked about one coming, and that's why we're here . . . from what I know at least. . . ."

Essria paused and looked over the outskirts of the castle where open fields and beautiful glades once existed and where now, only foliage and tree dross replaced all in sight.

"I have been trying to make sense of this, but I haven't been able to. There were wide-open fields here, Arnenn. But now there are only trees where there weren't any for at least a mile out. I don't get it. My schoolmates and I— many would garden out there. There were crops we would gather and bring to the kitchen as an activity to help out the staff. And some of us students practiced magic out there, also. But now it's all gone and you say that I'm the only one who has hair like mine and that no one even knows of this place. What am I missing?" she asked. "We seem to be from different worlds, or more like different times. And I really hope there isn't a war coming . . . the one I knew of was the most terrible, Arnenn, more than you'd imagine!"

Arnenn let it all sink in, remembering his thoughts and questions before ever meeting her. "It sounds crazy, Ess, but you may be right about that."

She looked at him with a questioning face, thinking she couldn't have been correct in her wild guessing.

"When I saw the others in the book, I believe it showed me things from the past that were memories. We may be wrong, and I'm sure there must be a better explanation to all of this, but I think we need to talk to Throone to get to the bottom of it. He may be able to help make sense of it all. This was all his idea anyway. . . . Also, I— too, hope no war is coming. I've never lived during any of those times and always hoped I would never have to. But, just that alone explains many interesting things about this confusing situation. You've lived in a time of a war, Ess. I haven't. That doesn't exactly make much sense."

"Yes, you may be right, somehow—and I would love to get to the bottom of all this. I'm ready to know." She smiled his way gently, but with much worry. He could see it behind her long lashes as he also felt it within himself.

There were so many things to figure out about each other and the situation of the Kingdom, the missing people, and the Orrumn. But they still lived in what was almost a world of their own.

Arnenn explained how he was only visiting Gjone in Harpelle from a city called Vidhera, which was the capital of all Northern Amruhn. Essria had never heard of Vidhera, either, and she explained to him that she'd come from an island south of the shores of Amruhn, which Arnenn had heard of but was always told that nobody existed on. The confusion of the lost worlds almost bound them together in a passionate curiosity for one another—one that neither had ever shared with any other.

Although Essria didn't seem to know too much about Arnenn's world, she did know of many things. She would continue telling him what certain flowers, plant life, or rare animals that scurried around the area of the castle were called; and she even told him about magics she had seen or read about. She would tell him facts, such as people that were ten feet tall or more who could move water or fire with a wave of their hand, breathe underwater, bend metals with their mind, or even pull lightning from the sky—harness it, or use it to perform terrible acts, and a great many other things.

Arnenn didn't know whether to believe most of it or not but loved how excited she became when talking of these things; and every time, she would laugh a little and finish it with a smile as she glared at him. He found himself to be more awestruck by her each and every day he saw her.

Essria had found in Arnenn a rare handsomeness. He looked different than anyone she'd ever known before. His all jet-black hair made him look sturdy and his seasonal brown eyes showed dark against his already dark hair. She found herself interested to know what he would look like in the other seasons, as well. He was also her very same height, which she found comforting because most of the boys she knew towered completely over her, for she had never been very tall—even when compared to most the girls she knew.

She also loved how Arnenn would be so interested in all that she had to say, and he seemed to have an adventurous and somewhat non-worrisome spirit about him. She felt that they could run off together and leave all matters of the world and of magic behind and be perfectly content.

18

THROONE SPENT MOST OF HIS TIME DOING
the very same thing Essria did with her own at Kulne.
He poured over the history books both day and night,
taking in as much information as possible (if he wasn't
on mad searches around the castle all on his own). It was
nothing but complete excitement for the Keeper. He had
spent hundreds of years looking for further information
and could never seem to come across enough to satisfy
his thirst for knowledge. But now, he was like a child
that had gone into his favorite store and was told he
could have whatever he wanted and as much as he
wanted.

The two young Rowes noticed a difference in him. The
sometimes gruff man would turn chipper again, and
when they'd gather, he would tell them about the many
different things of a past Amruhn he had never known,
along with cities and kingdoms he never knew existed.
Most of it had little if anything at all to do with magic,
but he didn't mind; he just loved the history that had
been hidden from him for so long. When it did happen
to be about magic or anything similar, he would say,
"You think *I'm* a wizard? Think again!"

He and Essria connected well on the subject and would
talk back and forth as Arnenn and Gjone would sit quiet,
just listening and learning all kinds of new things about
the past.

Essria would ask Throone about his ability, but he only
continued with the fact that he didn't know and never

had. He told her that he hoped to find out something, and soon if at all possible. It was surprising he hadn't already—he just about destroyed all the libraries.

What were once the most majestic rooms with tall stacks of books in proper fashion on elegantly designed shelves and in alphabetical order, were then disheveled and in a state of chaos and disrepair. Books were resting open, one on top of another—in corners, on chairs and tables, and even sometimes in the corridors outside the rooms.

"I have been waiting for this very day, when you two wanderers would finally come around to discuss this whole confusing matter in more detail," said Throone as Arnenn and Essria surprised him inside of the main library one mid-day; his eyes glued to a book practically no farther than three inches away from his nose. "What would you like to know?" he asked, making it seem as if he could answer any question ever asked.

"Throone . . . sir, I would like to know where everyone has gone, and what it all means."

"Ah, now *that* is a good question. And just Throone will be fine, Essria," he stated. "Now, what it all means, we can only speculate. But, I understand you'd like to know what happened to all your friends and family— and I will definitely be giving you my best answer to that, so please . . . take a seat!"

He paused, setting his right leg over his left in the chair he had been using before taking a sip from his hand-heated cup of tea, such the same as the average day in his little shack of a home on the mountain would be spent. He offered some up to the others as well but they politely declined and sat on a close-by bench that was built right out of the wall in an unusual fashion. The room was much darker than it should have been for reading, lit by only a few candles along the magical lamps in the far back of the room when he finally said it.

"They are gone."

"Well, I know they're gone . . . that they're not here, but *where* are they?" Essria pried deeper.

Throone took a deep breath and looked down at his lap before his eyes made way to her again. "My poor girl, I'm afraid you don't understand. They are gone and they won't be coming back, ever. —It's not that they wouldn't if they could, for I believe they would love to! But they just simply cannot. You see, Essria . . . they are all gone because they are, in fact," he looked at the both of them and finished with, "dead."

A tear came from Essria's eye almost immediately. She wondered how he could say such a thing to her and be so inconsiderate.

"You're lying . . . you couldn't mean that! It's not possible!"

Arnenn gave Throone the most disapproving glare and comforted Essria as best he could, though somehow believing it was probably the very truth. At just that moment, though, Gjone found himself in the corridor outside when he heard the sound of Essria crying. He gave a sigh to it, but thought he should make sure she was okay. He ended up finding more than only her in a place he would rather have nothing at all to do with: the library.

"Gjone! Glad you are here . . . come and take a seat! There's something you all need to know," said Throone as Gjone reluctantly sat himself near the other two.

He continued by saying, "Now, I'm sorry, Essria. You may find me completely insensitive. I don't mean to be, but we've been here for far too long without discussing matters of any actual importance as you two lovebirds have been adventuring off around this castle non-stop! Don't think Gjone and I haven't noticed. . . . But we have not yet chosen to talk about all of this. Now, I admit that I'm partial to blame for it, but we must waste no more time!"

He repositioned himself again. "First, Essria, I'm going to tell you another thing you will find hard to believe. You, much like everyone else you once knew, are also not supposed to be here, or be alive at all. But you are. That raises some questions. And I must ask. What year was it when you studied here?"

Being so shocked by what she was hearing, she didn't answer for a few good moments. When ready, she told them, "It was the 2,743'rd year of the recorded."

Gjone and Arnenn looked at each other—in just as much shock as when seeing their first Dark-Beast turned to Dust.

"Ess, right now it's the 3051'st year of the recorded," spoke Arnenn with deep concern.

"There's no way that could be right!" she screamed softly with watery eyes.

Throone answered her by shaking his head up and down slowly, keeping steady eyes fixed on her.

"There *is* a way that is right, actually, and I didn't believe it at first, either." He peered back between Arnenn and Gjone, getting their agreement of what he was about to say. "We had no idea you were going to be here, Essria, but since we found you it has had me thinking, and the only answer I can come up with is that you . . . well, you existed inside, and came *out* of the Orrumn."

It must have been ten seconds that lingered slowly by before she responded and tried to correct him in his misjudgment. "No, I did not come out of the Orrumn . . . I was only reading it for the King's sake."

Throone took a deep breath. "This is going to be tough to explain, but I will try my best; and I will need you to hear me out without question." His eyes held even more intent. "The Orrumn, from what I know, is a book that is connected to future prophecies, and even past events. But also, it's somehow able to preserve that which it holds—information, also objects, and as we see now, even human life! I feel it, too—through my skin. I'm able to absorb some of the things it does, or feel what comes out of it—just like this very fortress itself! And I cannot put words to it."

He turned his head and looked at Arnenn. His eyes were the widest the young Mourenrowe had ever seen. "Arnenn, when you showed me the drawing of this place in the book, I felt it come out of me! I now know that's *exactly* what happened! In a way, it came through or out of me as if it were a spirit!" He held his hand out in pause. "This again, I don't know how is possible . . . but Essria, I also didn't know that you came through it . . . just as much as every other detail inside of it! Don't you see? Somehow your life, Essria, was preserved within the Orrumn and you came out of it with this place! It has some type of strong magic that contained you and it's simply amazing that you are here! You have, in fact, been stuck in the Orrumn just about as long as I've been alive . . . which means that the great battle against that of Dark was in fact the war that'd happened when you were here. I have always speculated that the ending of it was when I was born . . . born right after that exact event!"

Essria's face suggested that it made sense to her. She remembered feeling as if she was attached to something or somewhere different for quite a while, but for how long, she couldn't tell. She told them about the strange experience of being "inside the Orrumn," —if it was actually the case.

"I remember feeling lost for a great while, asleep but not asleep, and in a place filled with a soft light; and alone, but not alone. —But I'm not just going to believe what you are saying. And if I and this castle were somehow 'preserved' in time, then why wasn't everyone else here?"

Throone attempted to answer her question with a question of his own. "Well, what's the last thing you remember before it all happened?"

"I snuck down here right after hearing we had victory. I wanted to know where someone was . . ." She was worried to say what was next and met the eyes of all three at least twice before speaking again. Arnenn's, she met three times. "The King would have me go down to the platform inside the Garden Cave and see what the Orrumn would give about ways to defeat Dark before the victory. But I thought that after it ended, he wouldn't need my help anymore. It made me anxious because I had already become attached to the Orrumn and I somewhat forgot about my original purpose of why I was here, which was to save my people that remained on Ionsdi. Then," she steadied herself, "I took it upon myself to go down and see it—see the picture of Arnenn at least once more—see if there was a way to find him— to be with him." She gave Arnenn a nervous glance. "That's the last I can remember."

"Well that explains quite a lot," said Gjone, peering impolitely at Arnenn and Essria. Arnenn blushed inside and out, beyond thrilled to hear it. He wanted to say something back to confirm he had the same feeling towards her, but he only stared with a smile.

Throone replied hastily. "The war against Dark you speak of . . . Essria, it's because of that war that the Orrumn existed and even exists again! Arnenn, Gjone, it's the same war within the story Rayne tells, and that I've been here talking and living on about all along! There is a great connection between all of these events both then and now which wasn't in between. Listen carefully to this!"

He made a slight squint with his eyes before speaking again.

"When that war was won and the threat of Dark was gone—at least for the time, the need for this entire kingdom and many other things to exist was done, and the Orrumn took it all, along with you, Essria. And from what you just said, it seems you had a deeper connection with it than anyone else did . . . or tie to something in our time, you must have . . . thus being Arnenn here, or maybe other things as well. That could be why it took you and nobody else. It's very intriguing to say the least. As far as your people are concerned, they were probably driven out of this place . . . or maybe some were killed in battle before you found your way down there. This is beginning to come together now."

Throone stood and then slowly paced, entirely thrilled to understand.

"I believe that when this kingdom was gone, they became scattered and were only known as non-dwellers. I remember that's what they were called—if they are the people I'm thinking of. They were strange to all others in the regions, both north and south. They were wanderers. They roamed Amruhn homeless, leaderless, and also kingless. They must have never remembered where they came from. It makes sense that most had forgotten all about their home, being this place, along with the events of the war. It's as if the Orrumn, or perhaps something else, had taken their memories of it all.

"There were many off happenings and events with those people as well because most others had shunned them out until they were all gone, thinking them to be freaks of some sort. I remember hearing about some of those people during my youth, a people of rare abilities they were as well . . . more than most people that still studied magic . . . though I never knew any myself or gave them much thought at the time, I must admit. I now even wonder if I am a descendant of any of them and that maybe they had lost me. Anyway, I'm sorry you have to hear this, Essria. I do greatly apologize . . . I would have never before guessed that's who they were, or that this is where they came from."

Essria took some time to herself to mull it all over as Throone said another thing. "It is in fact, happening all over again, three hundred years into your future and three hundred from my beginning. That same threat is coming. I am sorry, Essria."

There was a concerning look in Essria's eyes. "But were they not already defeated?" she asked. "I can remember hearing that those who were supposed to kill the Dark Presence succeeded . . . and I heard that right after it'd happened.

"Perhaps some aspect of it *was*, but ridding Dark . . . all of evil for good . . . I don't know if that's possible."

"What of King Madelmar? Surely he wouldn't have been some wanderer . . . he was too great! You couldn't imagine! And some of the people I knew of, some of them were strong and were powerful within their forms of magic. Even some of the students!"

"We don't know what happened to the king of yours, however great he was. I have never heard of him specifically by name in all my time. But it seems that once all that happened, a large part of the magics were lost to all people in Amruhn. If I'm not mistaking it, it explains why your hair is made of different colors and ours is not. It is a side effect—a side effect of magic that no longer exists in Amruhn or in the world at all today. It hasn't existed since your time here long ago, Essria. We now only exist within the very last remaining remnants of that magic."

He said that and looked at Arnenn and Gjone. "You two, there have been many different speculations and misconceptions of why our eyes change for the seasons and I have believed a great amount of reasons as to why it is, and by many different experts of recent sciences. But the *real* truth is that it's one of the only remaining magics left in the world at all. All others have been erased! Except that of my own, of course. . . .

"But what I've noticed in some of these books I have come across here is that they suggest these kinds of wars have happened more than once. Yes, even before your war, Essria; and each and every single time they happen, another remnant of magic is stolen—taken from our world and lost completely! There also seems to be much confusion in the history books about Amruhn when these events would happen. Years or chunks of time would be lost. Some of the recorded years may not even be correct! It's as if the world had periods of complete confusion and had to 'renew' itself. Only remembering normal things not of magic.

"They would speak of a battle and Dark things that came out of the depths. But the details are hard to find and I believe it's because after the Orrumn takes what it does, the many details are forgotten—as unfortunate as it may be. It is possible that even the magic in this very castle itself may be lost, or frighteningly worse, changed! Though I sure hope that's not the case."

"So do these lost magics still exist inside the Orrumn?" asked Arnenn, entirely enthusiastic to know more.

"That may be so," Throone answered. "From what we've seen it do so far, I wouldn't doubt it."

Essria thought of what it actually meant if everything she'd just heard was true. Her parents, her friends, the King, and all the others she had ever known were gone, forever. She couldn't understand how to get through it, forever miss them while being forced to exist in a world she knew nothing about—and right after having learned that she is to live through another war.

She wanted to cry. She wanted to run and hide, but knew she couldn't.

Sitting in the library, the only people she knew now were Arnenn, his cousin, and the old man of magic. She thought of his supposed ability and how he knew so much, proclaiming her life here forth for her. She did not believe he was being honest and wanted to get to the bottom of the matter, demanding answers of him.

"What of you? You seem to know so much . . . and you have a magic of your own, very rare magic, too . . . from what they have told me. Who exactly are you? I want the truth!"

"The truth?"

Throone laughed as if she were entirely ridiculous. He leaned forward, still standing. "I was hoping you could provide *me* with some truth yourself, young lady. You can question and interrogate me all you want and I will give you the same dang answer I gave these two here that were never even supposed to say a single word about it in the first place. —I don't know how I have the ability, just like I said a minute ago. But what I *do* know, is that it's my job to watch over the line of these two kids here . . . the line of Rowe. They are important to me. I have been around for far too long watching over their family simply because there's a magic in me that says I must. Arnenn came across the Orrumn and I helped him bring it here where it belongs, and as far as I know, my job's done! Speaking of their family line, you can go ahead and tell us what you know—since you knew of a particular Rowe before your war ended." He crossed his arms and tilted his head back after taking seat again.

She took her time to begin speaking as they made her uncomfortable with their constant staring. Figuring that she wasn't going to get any answers herself, she went on.

". . . I knew of only one, the one named Mouren. He came here from time to time. Somehow, he was a great friend to Madelmar, the King. I saw him only once, though. He was a bit taller than you are, Gjone, actually looked somewhat similar—now that I think of it," she said to him. "But older, and with a beard of color—like many other grown men had."

Gjone became more interested. "Yeah . . . it must be the one my father has always spoken of," he added while straightening his back, seeing more and more truth to his dad's wild stories.

Essria continued. "I was told that the King had him bring the Orrumn here in the first place, long before my or anyone else's time here. He would seek it out in the Garden Cave for a while, but after some time, he had stopped, refusing to look at it anymore. I don't know why or what happened. I just know that he was of some great importance to the King. All of us were to revere and respect him. He was said to be powerful. It was actually him and some of his followers that stopped the Dark Presence, or at least, I thought so. . . . ."

"Who were his 'followers?'" asked the Keeper.

"None of us knew for sure, but they were unlike any we had ever known before. We never saw them until the war had come and even then, they were very obscure, secretive . . . different. And we never found out exactly where they came from."

Arnenn justified it quickly and excitedly. "So it's right then? I mean . . . Throone, you said this has happened before—I believe it! Mouren brought the book here, read it, and then fought against Dark. Is this exactly what I'm supposed to do as well, or both Gjone and I together? Are we supposed to gather others like us?"

"Why must you insist on continuing to ask me questions which you know I don't have the answers to, Arnenn? If I knew, I would have told you already! But, I would say you'd have a part to play whether it's that or something else, as I may myself. And Essria, for whatever reason the book took you and brought you back, you may also have a part to play. I suspect you have no choice either way. . . . If a war is coming, then all on Amruhn are going to have a role in at least one way or another."

Throone took another deep breath before speaking again; he was ready for the long conversation to come to an end.

"One thing I'm completely positive about is that we cannot stay here any longer and that includes you, too, Essria. We are running out of food and have been gone for what could've been many weeks altogether now. On top of all that, both your parents, Gjone and Arnenn, are likely worried sick about you and at that, very upset with me! It wasn't my intent to be gone this long. Now, it's either all or none of our faults and I'm sure we can all agree to it, but we must start preparing to head back to Strathom to get some steeds and some more supplies. And I may be departing on my way back, too. There's something I must see to in the Palendrian. I have to find out what's going on and what is hiding in that rare abyss. I hope you two Mourenrowes have continued practicing as I've advised you to, you may surely need it for safety on your way home when I leave you.

"Pack your things tonight. We must leave first thing tomorrow morning."

Throone then stood up again, stretched, looked around and sighed, took a large sip of his tea, and finished the conversation with, "It will be hard for me to do it, but I will be removing myself from my research. Good day to you all!"

19

RAIN AND WIND HIT HARD ON THE LAST
night of their stay. Loud thunder and lightning clashed
as if it were a battle, making sleep for all four quite the
strain. Each member slept in his or her individual room
such as he or she had done since the very first night.
Arnenn's room was near a large window that was being
heavily hit by the hail and wind. Within the moment, he
wouldn't be surprised if the castle were infested with
ghosts or vampires with how dark and spooky it had
become. Within all reality, he knew that the rain's heavy
downfall would only make for a harder journey out and
that getting some sound sleep would be most beneficial.

But it didn't matter what he knew would come; he
couldn't seem to stop his mind from racing about things
that were.

He thought about the entirety of time since his summer
stay in Harpelle where he first heard a part of his uncle's
story, but was interrupted by a vision of Essria. He tried
to go back home, but that didn't work because he saw
more unusual things and even heard screams that led
him to this book called the Orrumn that has a power and
a magic beyond his own comprehension. Then, it turned
out that a man he heard to be hundreds of years old, led
him to a massive fortress that came from nowhere in a
place farther from home he had ever been.

He also finds himself falling in love with a girl who is
supposedly from the past and who was kept inside the
book he found; and he is also supposed to be some

chosen member of his family line to defeat some demon or something of a great terror called Dark, from what he had gathered.

He thought about what was to come and was only frightened. He didn't know how he was going to handle the situation he found himself in and he couldn't just ignore it like he did most things back at home. He also didn't know if he was going to be able to defeat any God-awful demons or whatever else may be entailed if a war would come. Sure, he was aware that he could fight since he'd grown up training—simply as only a hobby— or something to do—but at what cost? And just how good did he need to become? Why wasn't some warrior chosen for such a task? And could he even slightly compare himself to this "Mouren" that Essria said was of great strength and power, someone who was bigger than even Gjone, and that apparently had still not defeated those of the Dark entirely?

He thought of the Orrumn and what it showed him: Kulne, Essria, and how they have been brought back to life. Then there were the beasts that the book had shown him, or more so *warned* him about.

He asked himself how he'd be able to see anything else if he didn't have the great book in his possession. How would they be warned? And again, how would the Cave in the depths of the fortress even slightly be a safe place for it? He didn't want to accept it. He simply could not.

He then thought of the other page it had shown him. The three spears. The prophecy. It was the one thing he had yet to understand. He forgot exactly how it went but remembered that three spears of Rowe are supposed to defeat someone. He thought it must be someone of the Dark he had heard about through Essria.

He put aside any previous thought of it being Throone. The old man was becoming more and more trustworthy throughout the whole thing.

He wanted to know more about the prophecy and was not going to be able to rid himself of his wonder for it. He began to feel its pulling again, even though it had been weeks since the last time. He needed to look once more before he would leave it there, leave it for what could be forever.

He knew he'd be able to make his way down unheard with help from the storm's rambunctious noises. But he thought against it for a moment. Maybe he should let it go and trust the word of Throone and Essria to leave it there and let the book be. But he knew it would greatly bother him to not at least have a peek and to see what else it may want to show him.

It was decided.

Grabbing his stone after getting up and putting on some extra garments to cover from the fierce cold of the Garden Cave, he slowly opened his door to peek out into the corridor. It was empty as he had hoped and suspected it to be. He saw the lamps on the walls that awaited his presence and knew they would magically flicker on as he made his way down. He strode a quick pace as the passage led him to one of the corridors coming from the main hall, the one that would lead him down to it.

As expected, the lanterns sparked on right away, feeling his presence as they stole strands of light from each other. Arnenn became quite used to the castle's antics throughout his weeks there and knew it was going to be different being back somewhere where the lights didn't automatically turn themselves on and off.

The lighting came to its end in the corridor where it again led him to the gargoyles before the spiraling stair. He lit a candle placed within his small stone, ready to start his venture down into the far depths of the castle's dungeons and into the Garden Cave.

Walking alone inside the huge place was much more frightening than when being with any of the others. The gargoyles stared as if warning him to stop in his path and to turn back. But Arnenn had already convinced himself that there was more the Orrumn had to show him—and he still felt its pull. He also felt a rush of cold wrapping around him. It made the corridor feel much larger and more hollowed than it actually was. And it reminded him that he was only one small man.

He began his winding down the stair while feeling pressure to turn around. Every step held a guilty feeling, but the tension was strong and the book was evidently calling out to him. Arnenn thought of where the guilt was coming from. Neither Throone nor Essria, or even Gjone had ever said he couldn't look into it throughout any of their time there, but he still felt that it was wrong somehow, and that they would not want him to do so.

He tried to reason why the castle was a safe place for the Orrumn if it wasn't supposed to be used. Then, he began to feel the resentment. It snuck in and sunk deep down as he went over and over it in his head.

Why was it up to them what he did with the book? It didn't call out to them, only him. They are not the ones who found it. Who were they to tell him what he could or couldn't do with it?

Long minutes passed and the guilt slid farther and farther away from his consciousness. He held his head up as he entered down the straight stair that began into the Cave. He could feel its piercing cold under each of his coverings. It didn't sway or slow him.

This was his right. His task. No one else's.

Entering, he looked down and out and saw the book from far away, given a faint light by the moon's shining through the holed ceiling of rock. He thought even more about the whole situation. Perhaps Throone and Essria were up to something. Perhaps they were waiting for it to be taken by someone else. Maybe it was all a hoax, a set-up; they had schemed him and planned it all out to fool him into handing it over. Many different and outlandish possibilities skimmed his mind of what else could be happening.

Winds swept through from the high tide on the shore outside as they only tunneled around inside, blowing around the many large plants. His pace became faster and his determination to open the book became fiercer. Finally, he stepped close to the platform where he held up his stone to the Orrumn that sturdily held its place, unscathed by the Cave's strong breeze. It was even more magnificent of a sight than when he had last laid it there. It had somehow grown; its blue edges glowed radiantly and its rough and frayed corners were now perfectly repaired as if brand new. It had completely changed from when he'd first found it at his uncles—not showing even a single trace of resemblance.

He wasn't going to wait any longer. It was time to do what he went down there for.

He opened it and skipped past the page of the castle to the page of Essria. He saw her again as he held the pages down with a hand on each side, the wind wildly trying to flip them over, back and forth.

For the briefest moment, it caught him off guard and surprised him. He remembered his feelings for her; and he felt he was betraying her in this very moment. It was the last thing he would have ever wanted to do. The guilt came flooding back in. He thought he should close the book, turn around, and pretend he never went down to it at all; forget about his assumption of her or Throone doing something bad to it.

But he had come this far already, and wanted to know what else it could tell him before they would leave it there for good.

There couldn't be any real harm in that.

He skipped past the page of her—as hard as it was to do—and felt the guilt through each second as the page slowly turned. He then saw the very page of the star formation showing the three spears, the one he wanted to see again. The letters were written on the page as if speaking directly to him.

Three throws of three spears of Rowe are the only way for them to overcome Him.

He read it aloud, again and again, as if reading it more would give him the answer to whoever this *Him* could be, or whoever *They* are, or that maybe it was a riddle of sorts that he needed to work out. It didn't seem to help, though. He turned past the page, over to the one of the doors of Kulne, and even past that to a blank page to see if there was anything else it could tell him. There was nothing.

He found it interesting that the pictures which helped lead him to the Cave no longer existed, and neither did any of the beasts it had drawn to warn him from before. It made him think that he was perhaps wrong all along and that there was nothing else important to see within it. The task that the Orrumn had required of him was finished. All he could do was leave it there and go home. Perhaps this was his one and only task.

He found that he was fine with it. An enormous amount of relief came, and it surprised him. He smiled. There was nothing else for him to know or that he could be told. He knew the prophecy and would find out what it meant if needed to. He didn't need the book anymore; Throone and Essria were right. It needed to stay where it was on the platform in the Garden Cave.

The young Rowe started to close the book, but the empty page began to show color seeping through. He stopped his hand and opened the Orrumn again. His heart began racing. He wasn't sure if he wanted to see what it had to show him, or not.

A figure of a man appeared on the left page—again with the same hair as Essria, but braided in the back; and his tied beard had grown in different colors. But even with, he was fervent and rugged-looking, more than most he'd ever seen. He held a spear horizontally in his right as he showed to be walking through an empty field of tall and dead grass with many trees and mountains outlining the far distance. He wore warrior-like robes dense in dark greens drowning in gold and black cottons that buttoned firmly to his posture against the wind that tangled his hair. The look of the man reminded him of Gjone, yet older. Even more bruiting. He remembered what Essria said about the descendant of Rowe she had known about—the same one Throone had talked about long before. Mouren. It must have been him.

The drawing went to the right page where it began creating something new. This new figure was prominent beyond belief. It was an older man with long and white hair that grew underneath a bronze-colored crown upon his head while an also white-braided beard reached almost down to his stomach. His garments were of blood reds and sheer blacks that flowed smoothly behind and around him in many series. There was something about the man; Arnenn couldn't match his mind correctly to whatever it was. He was brilliant, yet scary-looking. He felt he was looking at the wisest man he had ever seen and possibly, who had ever existed in all of time.

In the background and again on the left page, it started to draw two other tall people in darker clothing. A man and a woman. They held spears as well, but were too far away and behind for Arnenn to make out any of their detail.

The drawing began to move as if watching life in real time as the two men in front were walking both toward and beside him. They stared directly at Arnenn like they were angry, or just very direct and serious. Then, the shouting noise started inside his head like before—but almost protruding from inside the picture itself.

He could see the first man drawn shouting his name while waving his spear in the air, desperately calling out.

It all became a vision set before his eyes.

The wise-looking man in red stared without saying a word while walking fast, more than running. The others kept shouting Arnenn's name and he heard them say something he did not expect. The same man that looked like a prospect of Gjone yelled the words,

"Bring us out!"

The vision stopped and he came back to his reality. *Bring us out.* He said it to himself and knew he must do so. It was important. He felt it and was right about the book; he must take the Orrumn with him. How else would he bring them out? And also, he needed Throone to do it; somehow, he was going to have to convince him of it.

The book slammed shut. Arnenn grasped it and up the stairs he raced for many long minutes before silently making his way back to his room and sneaking through the door as if he had never left.

He had the Orrumn back in his possession and he was going to have to figure out how to deal with his decision to take it.

He couldn't help but feel he was betraying them somehow. They came all this way to do one single task, but now it was all for nothing. But he was not ready to let go of it. Arnenn knew he had to bring them out. He saw the importance of it in their eyes as they told him how serious it was. Above all, he felt he needed them. He needed them to help him defeat the evil that was coming.

He slid the now larger and much heavier Orrumn into the same pouch it was held within before and though still raining, the storm had died down. Only a light drizzle was hitting against the window, making it a bit more comforting. Even so, he sat awake through most of the night thinking about what he had done and what it now meant for him. But also what it meant for Gjone, for Throone, and especially, what it meant for Essria.

20

OTHER THAN THE USUAL WORK ON THE
docks, Rayne and Jemma stayed in most of the time,
even though it was unlike their usual selves. Their
neighbors thought it strange to see them only leave for
work, go straight into their house at the end of the day,
and not come out until work came again on the next. It
was for a good reason, though; the story was out and in
full speed ahead. It was even being posted on small
papers all around the city.

> *Gjone the Throne-Thrower (otherwise known as
> Gjone, the son of Rayne and Jemma Mourenrowe,
> who own Remma's) has defeated a mythical beast
> before taking off on a mad adventure to kill all evil
> and magical beasts that exist!*

They were mostly ads to reel in customers for all
various types of sales, and it was working.

Gjone had become quite the celebrity around town and
was more known in Harpelle than ever before, though
he had no idea it was the case and obviously wasn't
around to enjoy any bit of it, which he really would have
loved.

It was all the well different for his parents. At first they
thought it a simple task to hold back on promoting the
fact that their son was nowhere around, or just telling
others he was off visiting family elsewhere, but people
had caught on too quickly and the talk of the beast

started too big of a roar around town—to the point where they didn't want to say a single thing about it at all. The Mourenrowes became at the same time the most interesting and applauding family, yet biggest laughing stock of Harpelle. The whole city had to be in on it, too. If one person weren't trying to pull information out of them about the occurrence, then another would be making fun of the story or enjoying themselves while telling their very own version of it.

"He finally gets what he's been sowing all along!" people would say as they passed by their shop that had sadly become slower than normal. Everyone was usually a big fan of Rayne and his stories, but since a similar story was possibly true, it backfired on him in the way he would never have imagined. He only shyly thought that he'd ever be ridiculed about such things since he was always shown respect leading up to that time. Of course, there were some who still respected him and left them alone, such as those that worked for him or did any sort of regularly needed business at Remma's.

All they wanted was their son back at that point, but were also afraid of how others may ridicule him. (Not that Gjone would even put up with it . . . I'd like to see what would happen if they tried any such thing.)

They were becoming ever too concerned and thought they would've been back already, but had not received any word in their regards—not even a single letter from one of the southern realms. They knew Gjone was strong, though, and the same with their nephew, but they would not ease up on their emotions until both returned in one piece, and alive.

Rayne had even considered heading south himself to search them out, but he didn't know exactly where they had gone which meant he didn't know what to be looking for in the extensive lands of Amruhn. And Jemma didn't want to be stuck with running the shop all on her own. They would just keep confiding in each other that everything was okay and that their son and nephew would be back soon enough.

Jemma felt the need to send a letter of her own to Arnenn's parents, explaining that in their deepest regrets, the two boys had gone off on a journey of their own matters. But she didn't go into any detail or add any mention of the old man they had left with. After dropping off the letter and before heading to the shop for opening, both Rayne and Jemma stumbled into Haulfir, who had just returned from his trip to the outer provinces.

After a warm greeting, Rayne spoke first. "I heard you and your father went out to some neighboring towns to investigate sightings. Tell us, Haulfir, did you find anything interesting out there?"

"Interesting you can say—just a bunch of nut-jobs if you ask me. . . . If anything, the whole story has reached too far out. People are saying that they've seen these creatures, but there's no proof or evidence of it at all. I think they're just scared or bored for the most part and want to have some kind of involvement if they can."

Rayne laughed. ". . . I can see how that would be the truth. . . ."

Haulfir had more to say about it, though. He felt for them and their situation.

"By the way, I'm sorry about the whole affair, really. I know it's been tough for you guys with Gjone being away and everyone giving you a hard time about it and all. And I miss him being around—too. Hope he's okay. And just so you guys know, I don't believe any of it, myself."

Rayne and Jemma halted for a moment. "I will thank you for the apology, Haulfir. But there's no use not believing it," spoke Rayne, gently.

Haulfir was amazed that they would be latching on to the story while being as quiet as they've been. He thought that giving his opinion was the best approach, but then remembered that he was still talking to the same exact Rayne of old he'd always known.

"Well, what do you mean? You think it true? You think there actually *are* strange beasts out in the wild?"

"Young man," said Rayne, standing in a more upright position, "that's why we've been so quiet lately! We're more than happy to share it with *you* because we know we have your word on the matter; you are, of course, one of Gjone's best friends—and a member of the Bear Guard . . . and the son of whom we fully trust. . . . Thing is, though, if it was just a joke, then we'd love to play along! But we know what we saw that night when Jemma was attacked by something that was entirely unexplainable. And Gjone has no reason to lie about killing the beast, either. We didn't raise him to do something as such. And I believe something different *is* happening and it's not just because of the stories I tell or even because I believe them to be true! Though I would beg of you to keep it quiet, still. A running joke is all good fun right now, but if people believed it any more true than they do already, they'd be knocking down our door or going out to look for more beasts—only getting themselves hurt, or worse, killed!"

Haulfir was a bit shunned for words at Rayne's absurd response but tried to be the politest he could, still. "Oh, I see. Well . . . I hope Gjone comes back soon. Sure is different here without him. Anyway . . . let me know if anyone continues bothering you or anything. I can handle them for you." He didn't know what else to say.

They both looked back at him as Jemma said, "Okay. . . . Yeah," while tilting her head to the side.

They quickly departed afterward.

Haulfir thought his meeting with the Mourenrowes could have been a little less serious, or at least less awkward. He had felt sorry for them about the situation leading up to that very moment, but wasn't sure if he was going to keep feeling the same way anymore. He sure didn't want to after the way their conversation had gone.

He continued across the bridge before feeling an odd presence. It caused him to look up at one of the smaller hills outside the city's walls. Turning his head right, he saw a smoke-like substance come up from its backside, and then onto the top. It was as if a bear had grown into something almost as tall as the trees that surrounded it, and in pure black, its skin was unsettling. It was moving around like ash in the wind, yet it was swimming in fire and dirt and water.

The great beast looked directly down at Haulfir and stared into his eyes. But it was not the kind of stare that instilled fear. He felt more soothed than frightened. Strangely, it felt that the monster of a bear was confiding in him somehow before slowly turning around and taking leave to the backside of the small hill.

He looked around to check if he was the only one who had seen the beast; he noticed to be alone in it.

As he turned his head back, he saw smaller creatures with similar black and ashy fur that looked like large dogs or wolves following what he guessed to be their master.

Haulfir suddenly knew for himself that his friend's story was, in fact, true. He didn't know what to do, though. Should he warn everyone of what he had seen? Was he ready for the whole town to be in shock? Should he keep quiet such as Rayne had told him to? The beast didn't seem to bring or mean any harm. There was something about it. Haulfir wasn't scared a single bit—even if he should have been.

He thought of going back to Rayne and Jemma as he could see them at their shop in the distance. He could at least tell them about what he'd seen and that he believed them, for they would surely believe him—at least Rayne, if not Jemma, but stopped just as he began running.

The way that the conversation had gone with them questioning his judgment after only trying to apologize, and how the strange encounter with the large bear went, made him think it best to say nothing at all and just let the matter be. Also, he didn't want any publicity—bringing himself, his father, or the Bear Guard any embarrassment. He decided to make his way back to the Tower as if seeing nothing at all.

The Dark Bear had a specific plan for the young man of red hair and knew he was somehow connected to the Rowes, but that there was also a seed of hatred growing inside his mind toward them. He could sense it—almost smell it. He could use him; he could use the seed to tweak and adjust his heart for his master's purposes.

He gathered his minions, the many animals consumed by the Dust both long ago and even just recently. They had overturned some of the Light-Beasts that watched over the realms of Harpelle. The others, those not of the Lights, they turned easily, or simply only killed them to let them rot and decay.

But the Beasts of Light became aware of their presence, and many of the Dark they had already torn into oblivion. Some left their secret structures within the Sculths and gathered to increase their watch around the towns and cities. People would notice more and more wild animals than the usual, and closer to the city than ever before. Some were worried, but some thought very little of what it could mean.

The Light-Beasts knew what it meant, though. They knew it meant Harpelle was in grave danger.

21

THEY WERE A BIT BUMMED TO LEAVE THE castle; having the entire fortressed mansion all to them was going to be hard to give up, but they knew they couldn't stay forever.

It became much colder toward the end of their stay as the winter months drifted closer. So with little hope, they searched the castle for any extra clothing before leaving. But it was unfortunately stripped bare, which meant that any of Essria's (or anyone else's of old) belongings no longer existed. It wasn't a surprise. It was as such since they had first arrived. It was found that anything like clothing, blankets, food, or really, any softer materials that were not a part of the castle's original structure and its rare items, no longer existed within. The fortress had been stripped bare by everyone or simply just disappeared and never returned: Essria was forced to wear and wash the same clothes she appeared in since the day she came out of the Orrumn, the same clothes Arnenn first saw in the picture, the only clothes he had ever seen her wear.

Arnenn let her use his warmest coat as she responded with, "Thank you," with a smile. Sure, he was doing something nice, but his actions from the night before made him feel guilt such as he had never felt. It was almost pointless.

He thought about it all again. He was nervous. Why did he feel the need to have to look, and especially, take it? He wanted to forget and pretend it never happened and that he didn't have the Orrumn, but it was not the truth. And he had no time left to sneak it back. He thought about speaking up right away, telling them right then what he intends to do with it. But he could only sense that it would frustrate them all and that Throone would only have it put back.

He thought there would be a better time to bring it up, perhaps a time when they were in true need of it. But for now, the Orrumn was with him, the only one that needed to know of its whereabouts. And it was staying that way, leaving Kulne that very day.

After they closed the doors that sealed up with the structure's unknown source of magic, they made it to the bottom of the staircase outside where the misplaced trees still lined the castle's tossed-up soil (along with the new batch of trees they were able to clean off of the great fortress).

They again saw the shabby cart left on the bridge. It had been rained on and weathered over many days and nights. Arnenn, Throone, and Gjone, just stood, staring at it for quite awhile, each with gears turning about whether they needed it, or not. They had far less weight than on the trip in, and while looking ahead at the muddy and murky lands about to be trekked, they gave each other quick acknowledgements without need of word, going right past the shabby cart with their packs on their backs and starting ahead on their journey home.

The lands were exactly as they expected: muddy and filled with puddles with flying critters everywhere that spun around in a dense air that held a touch of cold murkiness. Their arms moved just about as much as their legs from swiping them away, just like their time within the area weeks before. At least this time, they didn't have the cart to slow them down or to help them fall into the waters while trying to balance it atop paths that didn't exist.

It was a blistering sight for Essria who ever only saw the outside lands of the Kingdom to be lush and well maintained with lovely homes that scattered amongst the many gardens. Being down in the raw and thick of the undergrowth of trees dressed in algae or maybe mold, confirmed to her that time had truly done its work. She now certainly knew to have set foot into an entirely different age of Amruhn.

Again, every here and there, Arnenn and Gjone would see unfamiliar animals or rare birds souring around that they hadn't seen before, and even the common toad or frog; or little webbed-foot critters that Throone knew not what to call. They looked as if they were interested in the group—or someone, or something in it.

At one point, Essria laughed with delight as a strange water-living squirrel-type creature had come up to her and excitedly ran around her feet in circles. After about five minutes of that, it finally left. Essria found it cute. The others only found the thing to be weird and very annoying.

They didn't speak much except for when needed and they ate barely any food just in case they were to be held up somewhere and needed it for any type of emergency. And other than the heavy walking through the mud, the first few days and nights passed pretty simply; and on the morning of the third day, they had made it to the Pale Mountains. It glared down at the group again with its whitish stone.

As they headed up to its peak, the swampy forest was left behind and their boots trod upon dry ground once again. They scaled up the barely existing serpentine trail that ran over jagged rocks that slipped beneath them. And when they had made it to the pass's peak, a now familiar sight for the three, they looked out and over the lands of the North and the entirety of the Palendrian again. This time, none had to step up any higher rock formations to see the black spot cradled in its midst.

It had grown larger.

"It's safe to say that forest is dying. . . ." said Gjone.

"Either that, or it means something even worse. It wouldn't just now start dying after so long, and even so, it wouldn't turn black like that. Neither I nor anyone I have ever known has gone into the very depths of that forest, but I would consider there's something growing in there. And I undoubtedly believe it to be our enemy, the Dust," said Throone.

"So that's where it's coming from?" Arnenn tried to confirm.

Essria answered without giving the Keeper the option to be the only one that knew anything.

"I don't remember if that's where it came from before, but it can choose anywhere to grow and harvest itself. It may have been here before, yes."

"Harvest itself?"

Essria answered again. "Yes, in a way. The creatures of the Dust are not just ravenous beasts from nowhere. It is more of a lingering substance that grows on them. It can convert regular animals into savage beasts and then turn them as if they are demons of some sort. Whether they actually become or *are* demons because of it, I'm not certain. But they are harvesting the elements of Amruhn to grow in number and strength. The Dark Dust is a part of the elements—at least those elements which it steals."

"That's where I'll be going after we get to that small town we were in with the stuffy tavern called Wrenck's.

You three will head back to Harpelle, and you two cousins will keep Essria safe, you hear?" commanded Throone.

"I can defend myself just fine, actually," said Essria, confirming her ability to help herself just fine on her own with no "man's" help.

Throone glanced at her. "Good! Then it's the less I need to be concerned about!"

The next evening when dusk was on the horizon, they came nearer to Strathom.

"You are in for a real treat, Essria!" confirmed Gjone. "I don't know what types of things existed in your day, but what you are about to witness here should be pretty different!"

"I think they'd be more interested in your hair, to be honest," Arnenn said to her.

It only made her nervous, not excited. She thought about what to expect from the new Amruhn she was now a part of and what everyone would think of her. If this city were different than anything else she had known of before, then it even deeper confirms that it's true—all of it—that she is three hundred years into the future. The aspect of it still frightened her greatly and she wondered how much could have changed since her time, but she had never been to any of the northern lands over the Pales, anyway, even in her own era, so she realized it would end up being a surprise whether it was three hundred years later, or not.

Throone thought he'd give some guidance to the young ones of the group. "Whatever you all do, be sure to say nothing of Kulne," he said; "no one should know that place exists—at least not yet. We don't want people learning about it and trying to house themselves there or fighting over it. And if anyone asks who we are, tell him or her we are only travelers from the Lake on our way to visit our family in the North for the Changing of the Season. And Essria, if anyone asks about your hair, just say that you had it died at the Lake at some strange booth or something like that. I don't feel it's necessary to have to hide it in some obnoxious hat."

Throone was beginning to not care much for the idea of concealing everything *too* carefully. He had done so his whole life for the most part, and since many things were now coming about, which apparently had so much to do with his existence, he was ready to let it be, let the people see strange things, because they will only get even stranger.

It was dark again as they showed up to Strathom from the opposite direction. Throone gave a great sigh of relief, happy to see the place was in no danger of Dark forces from the Palendrian.

Gjone excitedly led the group to the Strathom Inn after they rummaged through the crowded streets full of merchants, tented shops, and always-open food stands.

There were many large stones inside of glass jars and other such objects where Essria saw people doing things she had never seen people do before—both inside and outside buildings that were designed in the oddest of architectures. From the very corners of the buildings, thin sheets of wood were protruding over everything else around, holding all sorts of oddly shaped purt stones that were glowing many different colors, not just the usual purple.

A woman she passed by was drawing the face of a child that sat opposite of her. It reminded her of the types of drawings she would see in the Orrumn. The skill of the artist was impressive. There were also large crowds of obnoxious people playing simple games, like throwing tiny bags into little holes and yelling with utter excitement anytime one had made it in. It was in no way magical, but was the most vivid life she had ever seen outside of the magics. It didn't seem to need magic; it was fine on its own. And its spirited aesthetic lifted her soul—even as she received strange glares from people every here and there.

There seemed to be a celebration or special event happening, almost a circus of sorts. But it was really just the everyday character of the place. The hair of everyone around was the same, all one color, but of different colors. They had all red hair, or all blonde, and others' all black or brown like those Essria already knew; or all gray or white which was at least familiar to her. She was just as impressed by their hair as they were with hers.

Upbeat music with the likes of which she had never heard played loudly in the far distance of the street as four small girls came up to her, wanting to play with and braid her hair. She sat down and let them as she gazed in pure amazement at the little town of complete strangers.

For a moment, it made her forget about her troubled past, the war, and everyone she missed considerably. It was a comforting change to be around so many others instead of all alone, or only with the three she knew.

Those very three saw a large crowd forming around her to watch the little girls braid the most unusual, yet most beautiful hair they had ever seen. The people of Strathom would talk amongst themselves and ask how she did it, or where she could have bought such odd-looking clothes.

She would look at Arnenn and laugh and smile as her hair was given a whole new style.

When the group finally sat down to eat, Essria tried various foods that were new to her. These so-called "fried foods" were nothing but a mouthwatering delight to the younger ones of the group. They ate fried zucchini and squash, pickles, and even chicken served with buttery potatoes. The server told them it was a favorite around Strathom and it quickly became theirs as well, especially since they had eaten nothing but the same dried foods for weeks, practically starving. But they had put down enough that very night to set them as being comfortably prepared for the next couple days ahead.

Throone didn't hold much fancy to that type of food, though, at least not anymore. He told them he'd eaten too much of it when living around the Lake and at one point in time found himself larger than his usual. It led him to thinking it best to stop and to stick with the standard foods he was used to.

Strathom was a pleasant stay for the small fellowship that had been alone in the castle for many days and nights. Arnenn and Gjone were happier to at least be a bit closer to home and with other people to talk to about things going on around Amruhn—other than their own journey.

Gjone kept a good look out for more girls to talk to, which worked quite well, like always. And Arnenn was just happy to know that the girl he had found himself interested in, which funnily enough, he knew only from within a book during his last time there, was now there with him in real life. It was still hard to believe it true. He had to pinch himself at times.

Though he felt his spirit rise a bit after the journey to the exciting city, he still felt the guilt. He thought he should just say something and come clean about having the book, but he was afraid Throone would have them journey all the way back to the castle. He didn't want to deal with the humiliation that would bring upon him so he just kept the book hidden deep within his luggage, as deep down as he put the guilt and shame he carried along with it. Still, he felt a right to have it, nonetheless, and there was a task that needed done. He knew he couldn't hide it for much longer and neither did he really want to. But it would still have to wait.

Gathering provisions that next morning, they heard it again.

"All good go to Crowlis!"

Narmor and the other horses were unfortunately gone, taken by a fleet of merchants needing a pull for their carts to the surrounding cities, just as Throone said would happen. But there were others still—they were going to have to make some new friends. It saddened Arnenn, though; there was something about that horse he liked.

"Who is this 'Crowlis' you speak of?" Gjone finally asked as they just started riding north out of the flashy city where he would have rather stayed and taken up permanent refuge.

"Crowlis? Oh, he's an old friend of mine . . . and a friend to many others as well. Crowlis Jepp is his full name. Let me explain; it's more of just a saying that directs appreciation to the people around the Lake more than anything. See, the towns that encompass the Lake— and also places such as Strathom, are governed a bit differently than places like Harpelle or Alderhollow.

Crowlis isn't any type of king . . . or ruler . . . or anything, really, he's more of a well-known and wealthy inn-owner, or inn'keeper' you can say," answered the old man.

"So does the saying mean that all the money of the Lake goes to him?" asked Gjone, even though knowing it couldn't have actually been the case.

Throone laughed. "No, not quite. You can say that a lot of money goes to him because he *is* rich beyond all desire—since the inn he runs brings in a lot of business for him, but you'd never think it if you met him. Mr. Jepp spends most of his time working as a bartender because he's friendly and very, very talkative. I have known Crowlis since he was all of you three's age and he is one besides you all that knows about me and my, uh . . . 'rare capability.'

"Again, he's no king since, technically, the Lake is still run under the rule of Vidhera, but he's something similar. He takes care of and serves the people around it rather than the other way around, which by the way, is a lot of people. And he even has others that are not of the Lake on his side—both north and south. He is a slave to no one and no one is a slave unto him. He only makes sure everything runs nice and smoothly around its crazy towns because from time to time, people can get a little out of hand and you can say he has a way of uh, 'taking care of it.' It's a good idea for most to treat him and his followers with the utmost respect if they value their lives at all. I'm sure you understand what I am getting at. . . .

"Anyway, it's quite easy to show him respect. He's a very excited and happy fellow who would do just about anything for you. The meaning behind all good going to him is just another way to remind those of the Lake he has their backs. It's not a scare tactic if I made it sound that way, but a saying that the people want to succeed throughout their many business endeavors and other such things—whether good or not so good—since it's the largest trade source of all Amruhn, as you should already know.

"Many merchants know it well and they mean it when they say it. They're truly grateful for him and what he's done. He and his men ran those who were causing nothing but bad business and trouble out long ago and the people of the Lake have thrived ever since! In fact, I may have been more than some help in certain ways to those events a great while back, but I still say it to show my respects for him and the many people, you see."

To put it simply, Gjone liked what he heard.

Essria shared a horse with Arnenn as the group moved faster than when heading south a few weeks ago. The only difference was that it had become much, much colder.

Arnenn continued doing a fantastic job of concealing the book during the travel, not constantly going through his stuff or changing clothes as much as the others. But it became increasingly difficult as he and Essria would get even colder and absolutely needed more covers to put on.

The plan was to stop somewhere close to the western edge of the Palendrian where Throone would give his horse over to Essria and walk the rest of the way to its entrance, and early the next day if possible.

That exact thing happened as they eventually came upon, slept in, and left the little town called Meens one morning into a slow ride.

Throone stepped off his horse and gathered his single bag and spear right before saying to the group of young travelers, "I want you all to get back to Harpelle as soon as you can, so ride fast. And when you stop for a night, one of you should keep watch. You don't have the Orrumn in your possession anymore so those beasts shouldn't sense it at all."

Arnenn felt his stomach sink.

"Nonetheless, I want you two to be careful and to keep your spears near you at all times, and Essria, that short blade I gave you will be useful enough for anything you should come by between here and Harpelle if you don't run into any Dark-Beasts. I'll be seeing you all there soon enough, but only after I investigate whatever is happening to this mass forest and see what Dark we are dealing with, if that is, in fact, what's in there. I'll let you all know about my findings when I see you next, and again, keep your mouths closed about Kulne and the Orrumn. I know I can trust you to keep your word this time. Am I correct in knowing that?"

They assured him he was, a second time.

"What of Essria?" asked Arnenn, "How're we going to explain her to everyone?"

"I am leaving that up to you three to be as creative as possible between one another. Also, I'm leaving you all quite a bit of food so you should be set to go for your travels without me." He walked even closer to the three. "Arnenn, Gjone, thank you for your assistance on this trip. It was highly needed in more ways to me than you could know; and Essria, it's been more than a pleasure to meet you—more than you'd believe, and I think you'll like Harpelle. Anyhow, the book's now safe and secure, and we'll figure out what's best to do from here on out. Everything seems to be a bit back to normal, which is great! I wish you all farewell!" ended Throone before he started walking east with the Palendrian in sight.

"One more thing, Throone!" shouted Gjone, throwing him the hat he had bought for him weeks before. The Keeper caught it as his hand flared into a fire that turned it to nothing but ashes.

The traveling joke was over with.

Essria was stunned—glad to have finally seen his magic for herself and to know all the talk was true. It was impressive; and for some odd reason, it was the first time she had fully trusted in him. She found herself caring strongly for the old man of magic and wanted him to stay. She hoped he would be alright all alone. He was beginning to become somewhat of a second father to her.

Throone then smiled, turned around, and walked again toward the Forest's wall, whistling a tune that all three have heard him whistle before.

They watched him fade away into the green mass. Neither Arnenn nor Gjone expected to feel the way they did about him leaving, for the Keeper had set their quest in motion with his leadership and guidance and knowledge. They didn't realize it, but they depended on him greatly for many things, and the farther he walked away, the more they understood what they no longer had. They both would have rather gone into the Forest with the old man if he had given them any chance to, but they also knew they must be getting home—the amount of concern their parents could be experiencing was weighing heavily on their consciences.

Adding to Arnenn's, was again, the Orrumn hidden in the deep parts of his pack, along with the fact that the very man he needed to see into it was now leaving his presence for an unknown amount of time. He had no idea when he would see him next. It could be weeks, even months. But he was nowhere close to persuading him to do anything of the sort, or even telling the other two. It would be hard enough to explain why he even had it at all. He looked at Gjone and Essria as they started north and thought of what they would say if he told them he had it, and also, about the picture he'd seen inside of it the night before taking leave of the castle.

Would they understand? Could he get them to agree with him that they needed it? His mind raced again as his soul lowered into the depths of the affair. He decided that if he were to be wrong in having the Orrumn, then he should know the exactly why it was.

He asked right away.

"Ess, why did we have to leave the Orrumn there? I mean . . . we came on this long journey just to set it on some platform in a cave and then only leave again. What do you know about it? You and Throone seem to know something we don't."

" . . . But you're the only one who really cares," supplied Gjone. Essria slightly laughed and then looked at the boy of dark hair she had affection for.

"Well, I definitely know it can be dangerous, Arnenn. At one point, I began going down to it whenever I got a chance—like it was growing some obsession in me. That's what the King said would happen, and it seems he was right. I always wanted to know more. There were even things it showed me I can't remember. I would try to get answers out of it, which is what he wanted me to do, but he still warned me about going any further. I had betrayed his trust in the matter, and look what has happened: I find out that I came three hundred years into the future and everyone I know is said to be gone—forever."

She looked down and then closed her eyes in sadness, partially pausing in disbelief before opening them to speak again. "One thing about the Cave itself . . . is that it's said to be the farthest, yet closest point of the world."

Arnenn and Gjone were truly confused by what her statement was supposed to mean. Gjone explained that it made absolutely no sense at all and that she should consider revising it.

She explained it in more detail to the two unbelievers. "From what I know, and stay with me on this . . . the sea you are looking at from within the Garden Cave doesn't exactly exist on Amruhn's geography. If you look at an original map of Kulne, there's no ocean for miles and miles south. Even stranger, if one were to sail from the shores of the Garden Cave, they wouldn't come across any of the islands that exist below Amruhn or anywhere else around it. And when sailing near the edges, they would only see more and more cliffs that go miles up into the sky and on. Most who've tried to find anything only just continued sailing out to nothing at all and turned back. More that tried had either died or perhaps found something no one else had. It was never known for sure, but the King confided in us that there was no reason or need to have any dealings with the matter and that if we cared for our lives, we wouldn't dare such type of travel. Although, he wouldn't stop anyone who truly wanted to try and would tell them that they'd have to build a ship all on their own to do it. It was a part of his rare sense of humor, you see." She giggled to it.

"I don't get where it all goes, but no one of this world can steal the Orrumn from those shores because they can't get to the Cave. That explains why it's the farthest end of our world and the closest to another. That's what the King had always said."

Gjone asked, "Why don't they just climb the cliff to see what's up there?"

"I knew you'd ask, Gjone. The wall goes too far up and is made only of stone so any who've tried only stumbled and fell to their death. It is truly the most terrible thing to think about!"

Arnenn followed with, "That's interesting, but I don't know if I'm ready to believe that, even after everything we've seen already. . . . But even in the Cave, how's the book any safer if it's in an unguarded castle?"

"You're wrong right there! There's no single better-guarded place than Kulne—whether in the Cave or right behind the front doors! Its magic allows only those that it accepts to enter. No one else!" said Essria, looking directly at the two.

"But what if the magic's worn off, just like Throone suggested?" asked Arnenn.

"How did you get through the doors?" she asked back quickly, expecting the question.

"Well, the three of us touched our hands to some of the imprints on them that lit up with color."

"—Exactly!" she exclaimed, happily. "Throone is wrong about that. Those imprints were made exactly for you! It is a powerful magic; and a prophecy that only the King understood. But the fact that you were allowed in without anyone else's permission means something great! It has always been that way! It means you were *all* supposed to be there—both of you—and Throone as well. You see, Kulne's magic is just as intact as ever due to that reason alone! Anyway, if the book is safe, then so are we. And if a war *does* end up coming and there's any need for the Orrumn again, then we all know exactly where it is."

None of it made him feel any better—mostly worse if anything—upon being even more confused about it all. He had possibly caused the group great harm by having it and he could only hope they would not be attacked on the road again. Not so much because he was frightened by the beasts, entirely, but because he would have to explain himself. He still felt like he wasn't ready for that, even though *now* would by no doubt be a great time to do it.

Camp that night was near the northwestern edge of the Palendrian where they ignited a large fire to get through the almost-freezing cold. Settings of snow rested about in spotted sections around them as they talked and planned to get an early start the next day; and agreed that with a fast pace they could make it home before sunrise the next morning. They also came up with a plan to conceal Essria. They would take her all the way around the eastern wall of Harpelle and sneak her through the fields and the farms—through the River (somehow—maybe swim across?) to Gjone's house. From there, they would only introduce her to Jemma and Rayne and not delay to tell them the truth about her and everything else, and then find her some regular clothes to wear and something to hide her hair.

With no hesitance, Arnenn offered himself up to keep watch for the first part of the night as Gjone would then follow until morning.

He peered over to Essria after she had drifted into the night's slumber under a young fern. As bad as he felt about having and concealing the Orrumn, he still gazed at her in pure amazement. She was so beautiful and had the most freeing spirit about her. It was almost as if she were meant for him, even though they shouldn't have existed within the same century.

He reflected upon the many moments they had shared during their days at the castle while discussing their childhood, their traditions, and the many other aspects to know about each another. They had grown close. But the strength of their bond was now only in question.

He asked himself why he had to create such a mess with it. It was confusing. Essria had been brought back from the very book he was now concealing. None of it should be a secret at all; it was all on him, but surely, they would understand soon enough. He sure hoped, at least.

He watched the sway of leaves and branches of the trees that set widely apart from one another for quite some time while the others shuffled around in their blankets, finding warmth. Now that they were both asleep, he could once again look into it.

He grabbed his stone to see within the night shadows and slowly retreated a few yards from the fire with his pack in hand, still hiding the Orrumn inside before withdrawing it. His eyes felt soothed once more as he glared into its playful colors on the thick parchment. The same picture he'd previously seen was still showing as a painting on both pages. He awaited it to move again, but the page had only turned itself, where a picture was drawn of the Forest from the very same perspective of when he last looked into its scattered oaks and spruces. In the very middle of the page, a hole began developing, making a section in between two trees. He guessed it to be a path the Orrumn wanted him to follow. Arnenn hadn't felt a need to question what the Orrumn would tell him to do any time before, so no trace in his mind gave warning otherwise.

Again, he looked back at the camp where both Gjone and Essria were sound asleep. His job was to keep watch and he meant to do just that, but he needed to follow the path first, at least just a little to find out what the book wanted to lead him to. He felt he didn't need his spear. The shortsword he carried would be good enough, for he didn't think he'd be gone very long. Plus, he didn't want to wake either of the two at the camp by trying to grab for it.

Carrying his lit stone while walking the path that the Orrumn had set before him, he looked up and down from it and to the trees ahead. He passed into the Forest, farther away from the camp as he heard the fall leaves crackling underneath his boots with each step.

A very cold draft began as soon as he reached it while each breath created a cloud of steam from his mouth. Arnenn gave thought to turning around, but they would soon be leaving the Palendrian for good. He must do this now.

He wondered what could happen to Essria by him not keeping watch. *What if any of those Dark-Beasts were to draw near to the camp?* But he knew his cousin would be able to handle anything that came their way, even half asleep.

The path looked welcoming and he wondered what possible things it could be leading him to. Perhaps there was some other remnant of magic he needed to discover, some new relic, or maybe it was trying to lead him to Throone so that he could release the men in the book.

He considered the possibility that he didn't need the old man to do it at all. Maybe he could draw them out all on his own. As far as Arnenn's thoughts went, if he was appointed by the Orrumn, then *he* should be able to carry out any task it had—not needing Throone or anyone else's help at all. He could at least try.

Oaks of great size became thicker and closer together as he went farther in and as the minutes flew by. The Forest was shrouded with shrubs and overgrown trees and small ferns with berry bushes all around. The wind grabbed at their fallen leaves and permeated their scents that gave off an aroma that kept Arnenn interested in whatever he could find within, for he was sure that something awaited him.

Taken out of his enjoyable daze, he heard what sounded like the snapping of a branch about fifteen feet to his right, and stopped in his path while turning his head, raising his light and peering into the darkness to see what moved. He saw nothing. Peering down at the Orrumn, the page had turned on him once again. The path was gone.

All that went through Arnenn's mind at that moment was *Oh-no*. He knew what it meant, and he was startled. This beast was similar to the one back in Harpelle. The yelling began again, they were calling his name. At that point, he recognized they were the very same yells he had heard through the book just a few days prior by the men on the page. They were the very ones calling out to him all along: always trying to protect him.

Almost bare of light with just the small purt stone in his left while under his arm was a closed Orrumn, he thought it best not to wait and to outrun the beast, wherever it could have been.

He ran fast in the direction he came; his lungs flared up from the cold of the night. He saw the campfire in the distance but he only slowed while thinking he must try another tactic because he was leading the beast straight to his camp where his companions would see him with the Orrumn. At a standstill, he removed his shortsword from its sheath, which he held steadily in his right, still knowing he may not be able to kill the beast in whole with it.

Arnenn was unsure of what his next move was going to be. He could either hide or he could find the beast and lead it away from the camp, try to lose it. Or, he could continue to the camp anyway—get his spear and wake the others, just as if he were doing what he was supposed to in the first place.

He felt so foolish. He couldn't believe he had found himself tied up in an all-new mess with the Orrumn on top of the other mess he'd already created.

In Arnenn's stall, the beast appeared, coming out of a set of trees between him and the camp in the distance—the plan to go back became much more difficult. He could try to get around it, but even if he had, the beast would follow him straight into it. He was over trying to figure it all out and began to shout for Gjone, unsure if his cousin could hear him or not. And he could barely see the beast as it stood within the black of the Forest.

Due to his movements, the light behind his stone had expired—only a thin reflection of the moon gave a dim light to the area to watch the beast leaping at him.

Arnenn ducked underneath its jump at the very last second where an opportunity to make a run for the camp came about. He hesitated not a single moment to do so. But with the Orrumn still held under his arm and the blade in his hand—his stone lost to the ground, another beast jumped out of the trees before him.

He was bound to them.

He had to do something.

He continued yelling for Gjone, but he could not hesitate any longer. Not knowing what to do and unable to go forward or backward, he ran left into the many trees. He even started shouting Essria's nickname while sprinting as fast he could through the brush in every direction while twigs and branches scraped at his arms and face; the sharp prongs of the bushes below cut easily through his leggings.

Again, the many oaks became denser and he found himself running through messy streams and gullies that weaved in and out through trees whose roots grew far into the path, causing him to stumble, going chest first into a single wide-bodied growth of the Forest, losing both Orrumn and shortsword to the ground.

Hurriedly, he picked up the book as it gleamed bright blue off of the moon, but his blade he could not find. He could hear the beasts not far behind while also seeing a large root from underneath a tree leading to another gully filled with brush. Not having enough time to find and gain back his blade, he jumped into the gully, ducking low where he heard the snarls from the Dark creatures now walking a slow pace—knowing he was near, sensing the Orrumn was close.

Arnenn sat as quiet and still as possible, which was difficult due to his lungs that only wanted him to gasp heavily for breath. And his scraped hands bled and trembled while holding the Orrumn against his chest, concealing its blue glows.

Minutes passed, and luckily the beasts had not yet found him. He could hear them growl lowly like the old and rusted gears heard from the first one when back in Harpelle. He wasn't sure what they were even waiting for, but he was glad they had not attempted anything just yet, for he wouldn't have had any way to protect himself. There had to be something he could do, though. He was getting ready to run into the brush within the oaks behind before hearing something else, something familiar.

It was the sound of a spear weaving its way through the thick, cold air. And it suggested it had hit something dead-on before a sizzling noise overtook Arnenn's ears. He heard the same set of noises once more, and knew the beasts to be dead.

He peeked out and over the brush and saw Gjone looking straight his way in deep question, his arms up and open wide as if he were some great hawk of a man in the dense shadows about to swoop in on its prey. Two spears lay on the ground to Arnenn's left as Essria also paced in his direction, carrying both a shortsword and a lit purt stone.

Arnenn stood up entirely so that they could see him, but kept the book low beneath his waist, still concealed by the brush that grew upward.

"I thought you were supposed to be the one watching out for us!" spoke Gjone, heated in the moment. "What's going on? And why are you out here? You weren't supposed to leave the camp. We had to find you due to your screaming—and I had to use *my* spear to kill *your* beast!"

Arnenn didn't say a word. He only put his head down and thought to himself that he had to let them in on his secret. He had no other choice. He couldn't conceal it forever by standing behind the brush and he was tired of it being a secret anyway. He lifted his head and spoke. "Ess, Gjone, there's something you two need to know . . . there's something I have done."

Gjone and Essria peered over at each other with a quick look of concern and then right back to Arnenn whose hands came up from beneath his waist. The others saw the outline of a large book wrapped in blue glows of moonlight.

Both knew exactly what it was.

22

MORE, RATHER THAN FEWER WORDS WERE

said that evening. They were beyond disappointed to put it mildly, if not feeling entirely betrayed. They went back to stay until morning, moving their things many yards away from the trees of the Forest. And it didn't take long for Gjone to show his frustration, grieving, "So I guess this is all just your own secret mission you're on here then? All this way, Arnenn, all that we have done, for nothing!"

Arnenn didn't exactly fight him back. He kept his head low, understanding of the punishing words directed at him. He looked over at Essria. She wasn't even willing to look his way. He could only imagine what she was thinking. Perhaps it was: *This boy I had known of for so long and thought was honorable has shown to be anything but through his actions of taking and concealing the Orrumn, something he and I share in common.*

He tried talking to her instead of answering to Gjone's shouting. "Ess, you said that even you at one time found it hard to put the Orrumn—"

"First, it's only *Essria* to you . . . and second, it was *because* of you, Arnenn. I thought you were someone who'd be better than this. . . . I told you myself that the book needed to stay there."

"Seriously, Arnenn," interjected Gjone as he paced back and forth while the firelight bounced off his short-bearded face and long hair. "What are we supposed to do now? Go all the way back so that you can properly leave it there? Do you need us to watch you and to make sure it happens? I don't even want to know what Throone would think of this. What's our plan now, chosen one? Where's your obsession with this book going to lead us next?"

"Look, guys, I'm sorry that I took it and concealed it from you. I just have my own reasons for why I think it's important for us to have," he replied in the nicest manner he could, still partially staring at his feet.

It made Gjone even more upset. "Really, Arnenn? That book could've gotten us killed tonight and it was *me* that had to save you by the way. . . . I would rather throw it into these woods and let this Dark have it—and let them do whatever they wish with it!"

Arnenn was about to speak up about what he'd seen in the Orrumn before Essria shouted, "—You two need to stop! We need sleep so we can leave in the morning. I say we do exactly what Throone told us to do which is go back to your city, where I will decide what to do with myself. And Arnenn, you can do the same for you and your Orrumn since you just *had* to take it!" She sat down right after to settle into sleep.

Arnenn felt the pressure of her anger all upon him. The worst he thought could happen came true.

Gjone gave a fierce look and took seat on the ground himself; also deciding the discussion was over. "You can continue to keep watch . . . and this time it would be smart for you to *actually* stay here." He settled into his covers and simply closed his eyes.

Arnenn was defeated. He wished now, more than ever before that he had never taken the Orrumn, hadn't done something that he only *thought* was a good idea, not even consulting the others—knowing not for sure. Essria and Gjone were beyond upset with him and he felt every ounce of their anger. He thought all night of how he could have stopped himself from the dishonorable act, but he also couldn't help but think of the one thing that remained to be the greatest trouble of all: the Orrumn itself.

It showed him a way into the Forest as he placed all of his trust within it. He didn't know where it was leading him to begin with, but it had also led directly to the beasts that found him. Could the Orrumn have been playing him all along? Or, was it really trying to lead him somewhere he needed to go and the beasts were just bad luck? The book still warned him of them after all, and it had never led him astray any time before. He still wanted to trust in the book, and he believed he had figured out what it wanted him to do.

As terrible as he felt towards Gjone—especially Essria (who seemed to have lost all interest in him), he still needed to reason with them and somehow turn the whole situation around. He was tired of being yelled at, scrutinized, and apologizing for his action. He'd had enough. Doing his best to keep himself awake, stuck in drowsiness, he decided it would be his turn to speak when the two awoke the next morning.

He would convince them of his plan, as difficult as it would be.

When the sun had finally decided to give its presence, along with its very first glows on East Amruhn, they ate a small bite of food without paying much attention to Arnenn who had had no sleep and was far beyond the bounds of tired and cold, but who was also determined to go through with his plan. He wasted zero seconds as he could tell they were trying their very best to pretend he didn't exist.

"We have to find Throone."

They both looked up at him in confusion. Gjone almost laughed.

But Arnenn had repeated it. "We must find Throone. We must find him and bring him the Orrumn. There are things that he needs to see . . . things he needs to bring out of it." It was most straight-forward.

Gjone spoke first. "Wait, Throone's the one who had us take that thing there in the first place. And now you want to bring it to him after all this time? The only thing he's going to do now is just kill you himse—"

"—Stop it, Gjone! It's MY turn to talk and both of you need to stay quiet and hear me out!" he said as the other two scrunched their necks back in disbelief. Arnenn was done giving laughter to serious moods around his older cousin like he'd always done. "I'm going to say sorry only *one* more time and that's it—because I have done enough apologizing and keeping quiet up until now. I. Am. Sorry." He paused and started walking about as he went on with his argument.

"I didn't take it just because I wanted to be a jerk or something. This thing called out to me from the very beginning, warning us, bringing matters about, and things back to life that haven't existed for many years— you being one of them, Ess, and from what Throone says, a great war is to come. You say that I'm supposed to just leave it there because *there* it can be kept safe? No! I need this. We *ALL* need this to help us. And we can't hide it away near some other place or 'other world' that it has nothin' to do with. It's not another world this concerns as far as I can guess. . . . It's our world . . . it's in Amruhn where this Dark is, along with . . . who knows what else."

"Yeah? Well—" tried Gjone.

"—You guys need to know what I saw and the reason why it's with me in the first place. Ess, the man you explained that is of Gjone and I's line was in the book. I saw him! He called out to me to bring them out! How was I supposed to just leave the Orrumn and ignore it all?"

"Whose 'them?'" asked Gjone, crossing his arms.

Arnenn answered hastily. "I couldn't see them all. But like Ess said, there was one man that looked very much like you, Gjone, but with colored hair like hers! . . . The other was older . . . white hair . . . he was dressed in dark reds and black. He also bore a strange crown of—"

"Madelmar!" screamed Essria, leaping up steadily. "You saw the King?"

"Maybe. . . ." he said as he grabbed the Orrumn and showed her the page. The picture was still there again, unmoving, but just as colorful and alive as before.

"Yes, that's him!" she frighteningly confirmed.

"Let me see this," said Gjone, walking over and then peering impolitely into the Orrumn. It was just as he assumed. There was only another blank page to his eyes. He shook his head in disbelief. "I don't know what this book's problem is with me and why it won't let me see anything. For all I know, you're all making it up and have been all along!"

"I don't understand why you can't see it, Gjone, but he's not making it up!" said Essria, explaining it to him excitedly. "I can see it myself, and that is them! Trust me. I would know Madelmar more than anyone!"

"Exactly! Don't you guys see? I couldn't just leave it there. They need to be brought out! I just know they do! I heard them shouting it to me! There must be a reason they need to come out and be here, just like you are here, Ess. Don't you guys get it? We have to find Throone so that he can release them—just like he did Kulne. He's the only one that can do this as far as I know, unless I'm able to . . . which I don't believe is the case. . . ."

Gjone answered it justly. "So you think we're going to just find him somewhere in this mass of a forest where this Dark is growing? Any time we've been in a close proximity of the place, we've been attacked . . . just like last night. Also, if you haven't noticed, it's always while you have that book. And what do you suppose we do? Ask these creatures if they've seen some weird old man wandering their forest and friendly have them lead us to him? Oh, yes, that will be easy enough. Why don't we just do that? And what if you're wrong, Arnenn? What if we bring them out and they're not who you believe they are? No. We will not be going in there even if you're right about your book. Besides, you could've just asked him to do it before he was gone! Throone told us we need to get home and even said he'd be seeing us there. So all we need to do . . . is stick to the plan and not do anything else unexpected, or stupid."

"He's right, Arnenn," spoke Essria. "There's no need for us to go in there."

Arnenn knew they had a point, for it was a much safer plan. But really, nothing was "safe" anymore. And there was something else he had to say.

"You must know what else I saw last night." He said it simply while looking both directly in the eyes. "The book was trying to lead me into the Forest. It created a path for me to follow. That's why I left the camp and why I was in there! I was only going to see if I can figure it out. And I believe it wants us to go to Throone! I just know it's what's right! I mean, what if he's in trouble?"

"It's probably a trap!" said Gjone, walking back to his side of the morning campfire. "We don't know if we can even trust this book! And I don't care how much the two of you think that thing's useful . . . it led you in there to get eaten up by those beasts, Arnenn. It obviously has control over your mind. You didn't even bring a useful weapon with you! Also, Essria trusted the book about you—and look how that went for her."

He scowled at Gjone.

"What, Arnenn? It's true! Your stupid book won't even let me see anything in it, so how can I trust it at all? How can I trust any of this? I want to go home. And right now."

Arnenn was dumbfounded for words, and also felt like punching Gjone. There had never been so much tension between them other than fighting like brothers as small children. Arnenn wanted nothing more than to make things right with him, but had to stand in what he truly thought needed to be done.

"I get you're frustrated with me and that you don't trust in the Orrumn, Gjone, but I'm going in there whether you two are coming, or not. And I am only doing it because I know it's what's best for all of us. There's nothing for us in Harpelle right now. I will be finding Throone, and I'm not waiting any longer to do so."

Arnenn placed the book back into his pouch before hearing something which he entirely did not expect, something said after the deepest sigh of question and emotion he'd ever heard.

"I am most confused about this—frustrated with you, Arnenn. I don't know what to think about you . . . and all of this to be honest; and I don't know when or *if* I will forgive you." She walked closer to him, saying, "I also do not know if this is the correct thing to even do—and it honestly sounds like a complete nightmare! But I am going with you. And I will be whatever help I can to save Throone."

She looked at Gjone. "I'm sorry, Gjone, but I have my own history with the Orrumn. And to be honest, if it's showing something, it must be important! It has never led astray!"

It didn't prompt Gjone to think any differently. "Well, perhaps it explains why you two are meant for each other! Go in there if you must! Follow into the book's trap! I'll happily be waiting in comfort at home." He paused for a moment, and began walking away, but turned around again. "Come to think of it, I don't fully understand why I needed to come on this trip in the first place. Farewell!" he shouted as they watched him walk off with his horse and belongings.

Arnenn felt deeply troubled about his cousin, but knew Gjone wanted to leave and that he was going to do nothing else but let him, even though he hated to see him go the way he was after the entire journey they experienced together. It was a saddening moment as he watched him walk down the trail leading home. He stared with crossed arms until he could no longer see him through the trees.

They spent the last few minutes putting out the remains of the morning fire and strapping their luggage to their horses. Arnenn still received a bit of a cold shoulder from Essria, but was beyond happy she had decided to stay with him.

"Don't think it changes anything between us." You're just lucky I have nothing better to do."

He said nothing back. He only smiled to himself as they prepared to leave.

As they walked beside their horses and southeast into the Forest's western wall, he took the Orrumn from its pouch (happy it was no longer a secret to do so) to see if the path still remained inside. The book was, indeed, showing it running right between the same trees while capturing the daylight as well, making it much more pleasant and much less frightening to follow. This time he kept his spear at his side, ready for any kind of beast that could come about.

But just as quickly, they heard the fast thudding of hooves coming from behind. It startled them to where both shortsword and spear were ready in their hands.

And as Gjone stepped off of his horse, he said, "Ugh, dang it, Cousin . . . you'd better be right about this . . . or you'll have something much worse than these forsaken Dark-Beasts to deal with . . . .

Me."

23

THE KEEPER RAN AN IGNITED FINGERTIP

over the bark, marking his way, just the same as when first coming upon the trees of the Cunnings near Harpelle, long ago.

His feet moved the fallen leaves as they roughly graced their settling. His spear held tight in his left while its head hewn deep into the loam. With every step, he whistled a tune he had learned in his youth that was made more of his own with each year of his long life, almost a theme that he had unintentionally created for himself. There was nothing quiet about his movement and he intended it that way, for if there was something of Dark watching, he would want it to come out and face him right away. He'd kill it, and follow its tracks. The way was bereft of any so far. Still, he led himself farther in and continued his tune, keeping his eyes of season peeled for any sign of them.

Throone remembered well his previous venture into the Palendrian, the transformation of newness he had seen in the Forest after finding the Dark insect that almost took his life and the Angelic Being who saved him from it. But it had not changed the whole of the Forest—not that he could tell.

The Keeper kept wide eyes as he felt the rough texture of each old oak he passed. A part of its bark was cleaned away where the body underneath stained easily to a black marking. There was a renewed confidence about him. He now had the comfort and protection she had somehow given him. And there were no intentions of getting caught in a similar trap, even when being so close to the very same danger.

He thought about everything he had seen as of late, the many appearances or *re*appearances brought into the world, remnants of a past Amruhn come back to life: the Orrumn, Essria, and all else there was to know of Kulne that he hadn't even scraped the surface of. The Keeper also wondered how old the Palendrian actually was and why he never wandered very deep into it in all his long years, and if the threat of Dark had been growing there all along, ever since he was a baby.

It became denser and greener until instead of stepping on fallen leaves, he was gracefully walking on a soft grass. It was more pleasant than on the outskirts, which was the opposite of what he expected to find in this particular set of woods. Deeper he went as each step felt as if he was traveling into an older realm or world, and there were more birds than he had ever seen before, and of many colors. They flew from tree to tree while the wind above blew their canopies back and forth. The sound it created gave a ringing in the Keeper's ears as the birds would land on branches and tilt their heads to watch him pass as if never seeing a human.

He went on for what was almost two whole days— mostly because of the slow pace that he carried and the naps taken every so often, hidden away somewhere in the underbrush or behind some great oak and its leaves. Or, because there was just so much ground to cover whether it was going uphill, downhill, or even along the many winding areas where paths had never existed.

He kept his whistle as the birds began to sing along, learning the tune as he kept at it. The ground started pointing down and the oaks grew taller, making up the difference in elevation between crust and treetop. And with every yard he crept into its center, the more roots appeared along its floor. It forced the Keeper to be mathematical with his steps to keep from tripping. Shallow streams ran in the same direction the Keeper was heading, but to where exactly, or where they came *from*, he was not sure.

The Keeper was enjoying his stay inside the large mass so far. It became more shaded as the trees almost knit together; their brush and vegetation mingled with others in greens and dark purples and their roots strangely weaved over to one another.

He knew that daytime was leaving him and soon all would be darkened where he would have to be more cautious again. He steadied his pace to find out what he could before light would ultimately fail the day.

He knew he was getting close to something but was also growing impatient as the winds picked up and created more unnerving noises. But then even the song on his lips died as he noticed the eerie silence that had fallen over the Forest only a moment later. There were just as many birds as before, but they had no song in them, and their color was faded. He could sense that this part of the land had life and cheer at one time, but was long forgotten. For these trees, unlike the others he had recently passed, grew weary and depressed, and so did any life evolving around them.

It implied to the Keeper that they meant each other harm, for the roots of one tree would be seen strangling another. They would scurry and crisscross their way everywhere along the dirt and then wrap up and around the body of its brother or sister as if they meant to suck out each other's souls. Some roots would come from far away to grab hold another, and it continued from tree to tree and on into the distance. Throone took a swig of water and started to put it away, but then decided to pour a bit on the ground, instead. He briefly watched as it sunk into the dirt.

As expected, the roots began to move as if they were snakes, fighting for the water, creaking when moving. He also watched as one tree's grasp on another would tighten. He stepped ahead and said aloud, "I'm sure glad it-aint raining right now. . . ."

He understood what was happening. The trees were dying and fighting for any water they could get. Any around them would somehow be stolen by something else, just as the rivers and creeks were losing their steady stream. It made sense to the Keeper that the Dark would use the water for its own purposes, since it was part of what it was.

There was nothing but complete silence now without Throone's song and the birds that sung along with him. Farther in, birds still existed, but in a whole different way. They were up high into the trees that grew tall and bent where just a thin blanket of them existed within.

He happened to come across one that had died for some unknown reason. It was entirely blue and had a beak of bright yellow. Throone couldn't help but feel sorry for it and thought it might have flown into this sector of the Forest unintentionally, and was then caught by something else. He looked around as he continued walking and noticed that more and more birds and of many different colors rested lifeless on the ground. The ones that still flew about in the trees were only black as if crows had found their way into the deep of the land, but Throone knew they were no crows.

The deeper he dealt, the worse it became. The black birds carried in their talons the much smaller and colorful birds. They would toss them aside as the others of their kind would alight and begin to feast on them. It was a horrible thing to watch.

He began smelling a gassy substance, which he knew, meant he was surely getting close to something of Dark—and close to the black spot seen atop the Pales' pass. And he also began noticing what he knew to be Dark birds trying to ascend down on him, but he set them ablaze as they even neared him and into Dust they would quickly turn, affirming his guessing.

The Keeper weaved himself in and out of the tall and strangled mass of oaks before seeing a sight that he had never thought to be possible. It was like the trees were floating. Of course, they were not; the ground beneath them had been dug out and deep down below a pit set before him. The trees held on for dear life to one another by their strangling roots, yet still tried to kill their brothers and sisters while at it. It turned them into the oddest of shapes imaginable and it looked to go on and on, possibly for a mile out, or possibly even more.

Throone turned his attention into the forbidding pit. He couldn't see very much due to the darkness that had overtaken the day, but the smell of gas grew strong within it. His choices were to try and journey down into the pit or balance on the roots above going from tree to tree. He decided the latter option to see if he could get a better view of what he was dealing with inside. It was the very reason he was there at all.

After minutes of balancing along the tangled roots that hovered above the pit, he saw walls: stone walls that could have lined the whole of it, which almost came up to some of the tangled roots of the trees in the distance. He could also see cylinder-shaped towers that beamed toward the sky about every hundred or so feet, and the walls of the structure had surrounded another opening within.

Still floating along the thick roots that held the trees high, he fiercely struck one with a sharp end of his spear. It stuck sturdily. He then attained his purt stone and held it wholly within his palm before his hand enflamed into a bright fire. It allowed him to see far down into depths of the pit below where an open courtyard was spread wide, scattered with his stone's purple luminescence. It was held within the remains of some ancient structure that must have wrought away thousands of years ago and was then somehow buried underneath the crust of the Palendrian.

It was a breeding ground—a most horrific sight to see. It festered abundantly; it was like looking into a locust's nest. It bred Dark creatures of all shapes and sizes, lying asleep. Likely waiting for something to wake them. It was a collection of the many beasts subdued by Dark, who were to be forever prisoners to its will. Some were creatures captured by it long ago that had grown larger and stronger throughout time.

The Dark's abundant existence was now only an axiom to the Keeper.

The Dust had crawled its way up to the roots where Throone was standing before making its way over the tops of the trees, festering and stealing the elements all about. He did his best to avoid touching or stepping on any of it, unsure of its capabilities.

He breathed in his environment, and alas, took his opportunity.

He placed the stone into his pack and withdrew his spear from the floating tree. With his left, he grabbed the same tree and set it to fire. It convulsed into it, turning orange before its canopy was wrapped in unyielding flame. The Keeper made his way back to solid ground and watched the seeping fire spread from oak to oak. He saw them awakened by the fire and the branches that fell and crashed far down. It did not yet burn the beasts, but made them angry and concerned enough to run amongst each other in discontent.

Throone slammed his boot on the nearest root to shake the trees, helping them fall into the pit and freeing them from their strangled existence. It took longer than intended. So long, in fact, that some of the Dark-Beasts had already made their way out of their nesting. He could see them running up a flight of stairs that circled a wide pillar of the hidden castle before meeting level ground on the far end of the pit.

A large, black bird that had noticed the old man from earlier swung down on him as hundreds of its kind followed in its path. They tried to pick at his head, arms, and shoulders. His hands kept ablaze as he grasped his spear tightly in his hands, igniting it in whole. It became so hot that it flared a bright orange as he swung it around himself, scorching every bird that came into its proximity, its constant circular movement unending.

More trees began their fall and some of the beasts had went up in flame with Throone's powerful fire as the courtyard started filling itself with Dust. He saw even more that had made their way out, and knew he should retreat from the gaping hole.

The fire dancing on the roots began spreading closer to the edge where Throone killed any remaining Dark birds that had come close. Its flame was giving way in all directions among the trees and their limbs, though it still burned brightly within the overgrown mass as it continued to drop in on the evil below.

Most all of the suspended trees had fallen by then, and only the smaller ones near the pit's edge still remained by the time the fire had created a cleared mass that had filled the midst of the Forest.

The Dark-Beasts that stirred within the pit were twisting about in torment, being scorched. They clawed and scratched at each other, trying to free themselves from its burn that was consuming them more and more each second. Those that it had already touched had little luck of surviving the extreme wrath that was spreading throughout their bodies, for Throone's fire burned with the utmost force and power.

He had finished his work of finding the Dark's resting place and killing off many of them. He turned around to leave while his hands were still ignited, and he waited no longer for the beasts running his way to catch up and find him. Making his way out, his fire sustained sturdily off of his spear that had also shined against each tree he had made his mark upon when on his way in.

But he heard a voice from yards behind. It screeched in a profound and low-toned voice when it spoke. And it quickly caught the Keeper's attention.

You came to burn me. But you have already succeeded in that, old friend

Throone stopped in his path and walked slowly back to the pit's edge, though knowing it best to only be running away. The voice made him want to cringe in terror, yet it still happened to draw him in.

Parts of the trees that had disembarked from their limbs were on fire within the courtyard and among the moving Dust below, allowing the Keeper to see clearly within without his stone. He could not see whom or whatever said the words, but then heard it speak again. This time, it said his name.

You came to burn me. But you have already succeeded in that, Throone . . . .

It continued in names he'd never heard.

. . . Symuth . . . Vorrunth . . . Belud

Throone noticed that mostly all the beasts had made their way out, except for those already burned up by the fire, and that existed no more. He knew he must flee. But again, there was something about the voice behind its roughness and terror that grabbed at him. He had to know what it was.

The Dust that now rested on the very bottom of the courtyard began collecting in a wind with a circular rotation. It concentrated and spread its way up, creating a head followed by shoulders, and finally, a body that must have been more than fifty feet tall when it had stopped. The being peered up at Throone while its Dust flickered with a flame darker and smokier than that of any beast he had so far seen. It sparked at its ends, suggesting that the Keeper's fire wouldn't do a single bit of harm.

Throone became frightened.

The Dust on the head of the Dark Being began spreading from the middle as if a face hidden inside was determined to escape. He could see parts of a face, a nose and an eye. Its skin underneath shone bright like crystal as it spoke again.

The Orrumn is on its way to me. I can sense it. Again, you thought you could trust them. But the one named Arnenn comes with it in hand. I will destroy it and all of the Pull within. Then I will come for you.

You came to burn me, old friend, but you have already succeeded in that . . . .

It paused before speaking something that ignited the Keeper's soul into a raging fire.

. . . old one of Madelmar.

Throone's entire body flamed up such as he had never experienced, and on parts of his body that had never been ignited, even his arms and legs. It started burning through his clothes. He couldn't move. It was a feeling of a memory. And he could almost tie himself to this Madelmar he'd learned of. He thought about what it was he had to do with the king from her time, but he couldn't conjure a connection. He also thought about what it said of the Orrumn. It wasn't true. It couldn't have been. It was left at Kulne. It was safe from this Dark, and from this terrible foe he was staring down at.

He cried out.

"NO!"

The Dark Being collapsed to the floor, turning again into the Dust on the courtyard where the fire of Throone had gone out entirely. But the flame on his body still burned about, giving light unto him and himself away to the beasts on chase. He could only kneel on the ground, cooling his temperature before doing anything else.

He noticed just a moment later that tens of Dark-Beasts had found him, and had begun surrounding him. He searched about, seeing if there were openings to escape. There were none. He only stood in sheer terror for his life, all over again.

He grabbed his fallen spear and slowly took his stand, ready to take on any that stepped even an inch closer.

It is exactly what they started doing.

His face filled with rage, but with determination. He would not be able to wield fire any longer. He was too weak and had been drained of his magic. But even in his weakness, his spear struck directly through each beast, going all the way through them with a fierce stealth and accuracy. It was the Skill of Throone.

One after another, he fought them off. It came to many long and enduring minutes. His spear became hard to hold while sweat beamed profusely from his palms. And he knew that at any moment he could entirely fail and collapse.

They backed him up to the edge of the pit that dropped down eagerly like a cliff, and the only choice he had was to jump past them and make a run for it; but he did not know how far he would get or where he would end up going, instead.

Confusion and weariness had completely set in as he was fighting for his life with only little luck of survival. She, the Angelic Being, would not be able to come to his rescue again, not like last time, as that is what she said. He knew now that he would only be able to fight his way out, taking one Dark-Beast at a time before they would consume him.

He questioned why he had to make his way back into this dreadful forest again. He should have known better and used better wisdom. He was stuck, bound to the chasm of the Palendrian by his significant loss of energy, surrounded by Dark about to take him. He felt a wave of nausea and dropped to his knees. There was little hope left for him; little hope for those that he had counseled and found himself caring deeply for; little hope for Arnenn, Gjone, and Essria.

A spear with an almost white glow came whistling through the air from his right, going swiftly by his head and through three Dark-Beasts that were about to steal his life, creatures which he couldn't even make out the type of before becoming Dark. And then another spear came from his right, its blueish tint stuck into a beast that looked like another giant insect. It was pinned to a tree before turning to Dust.

He notched his head straight, and saw her.

She stood in front of him after stepping atop a great rock that was lying in his way, cradled within the thick roots of the trees about it. The girl looked Throone directly into his eyes before slashing through a Dark-Beast that had noticed her from below, proving to him her skill with a blade. The beast did not die, but went tumbling down the rocks toward the old man. He finished it off in confusion, yet with hope.

The Keeper saw that she held in her left, a book of great size. It was beaming a sheer light off of a close moon. "The Orrumn!" yelled Throone aloud, wholly confused: scared. "Get it out of here!"

Ignoring his request, she opened it up and placed her hand on a page. Throone felt his drained energy being used once more, and again, not by his choice. He watched as a page from inside the book shined a bright red—the likes of fire. She was somehow using his magic from within him, and through the Orrumn.

Every part of her face had shown bright and before he could tell what was happening, any beast that was still surrounding him caught flame and then turned to Dust.

24

HE WAS ALMOST TOO WEAK TO STAND.
Arnenn and Gjone helped him up and then took him in
a different direction than that of which he'd come. He
raised no question of it; he was more startled about
seeing them and wondering why he was looking at the
Orrumn.

More beasts from farther away gave chase as they
crawled through the maze of trees and crossed roots in
the dark. Essria took over helping Throone walk as the
other two ran behind to fend off any beasts that had
come too close. Throone gained back enough composure
to hold his own as he ran beside Essria. They headed
north where they returned to the horses, and where
there was a deep pond in the way and the mass of thick
trees came to a short end.

One had caught hold of Gjone's leg. It looked to be in
the shape of a heavyset leopard with teeth larger than
normal. It reeled Gjone back as he slid along the ground
in the opposite direction of the horses. The group could
hear him shouting (somehow still with a shred of
humor), "What the heck's with these things and people's
ankles?"

They yelled for Gjone as Throone could barely function
enough to know what was happening.

Arnenn had only a small chance of luck saving his
cousin. His aim had to be straight on, and it needed to be
quick. Waiting too long, or making any mistake, could
mean Gjone's ending.

He steadied his eyes and breathing. His arm swung back lengthily, keeping his sights on the Dark cat that was about to pull Gjone back through the dense brush.

Essria watched as the spear flew gently yet quickly out of Arnenn's hand: sailing directly above Gjone's head; missing him by only inches before going straight into the cat's belly. It ended the beast. Gjone's shocked and scared face looked back and forth at Arnenn and the spear now lying on the ground right next to him. He picked himself and Arnenn's spear up before reaching to grab his own, thus limping and running with both as best he could, then lifting his wounded leg over his horse—in pain, with a great grunt and yell.

They waited no longer to escape. There were still more approaching when they rode atop their friends and into a pond that went far wide to its ends, both right and left, but short to the other side where the dry ground lay. Throone was surprised to see that any bodies of water even existed in the Forest anymore, and it was deep enough to reach up to the steeds' bellies.

There was great luck. The Dark-Beasts behind stopped, not attempting to cross it. Some decided to run along it on both sides to find a way around its far ends, but most only decided to yelp and screech in many strange sounds at their guests' departure. Only one Dark-Beast dared to jump it, but its failed attempt led its feline figure into the water's deepest part. They never saw it come back out as they barely peered back, hurrying on. The beast was to stay forever submerged, taken by the water that entirely consumed it.

Essria led the group after making their way through the small body of water—just as speedily as when the three had come to Throone's rescue.

<

Following the path that the Orrumn had revealed, they traveled a fast and steady pace through the Palendrian to find him: They wanted to reach him before he had gone deeper into the Forest and harder to find. They had not run into any beasts the entire day, which was great luck for them, but it also made them concerned for their old friend. And they worried what it could mean for him.

At one point, during mid-day, they came across the tops of what must have been old bridges of great stonework, ravaged by the Palendrian's overgrowth. Vines hid most of what existed of everything else and many broken statues lay about in disorder, wrapped in thorny twigs, yet yellow flowers grew around them; and most were showing to be partially buried underneath the grainy soil. There were more heads of stone lying about than there were bodies and most bore royal crowns that had only worn away or chipped off.

The travel became slower, and here and there, Essria would catch sight of abandoned buildings in rare fashions, which had just about sunk into the ground. They were odd to the Mourenrowes, but a bit more familiar to her compared to anything she had seen since being awoken into her new days on Amruhn so far. However, they were in no way accessible to the group to see what kind of gems hid inside; neither did they have time to do anything of the sort. Arnenn asked her if she knew anything about the place from her past, but all she did was shake her head in a way that said no.

The sun shined far to the west and its light gleamed upon the stony substances within the forested coverings of stark colorings. It's where they were forced to walk slowly beside their four-legged friends and also where they had to cross over sections of narrowed or almost broken pathways. Some were made of wood and rope that bridged over gullies or even cliffed walls that dropped scarily down. They crossed over them just fine; though some looked as if they had turned into a substance that a single fly of just the right size, could easily break.

At times, they questioned what they were trailing on, for instead of bridges or pathways, they showed to be the rooftops of many old homes that had been deeply buried beneath the crust. Carefully, they went on until the area was just about flat ground again.

They gained back their pace and stormed into even busier parts of the Palendrian where it still kept happening. They had to consistently stop and start up all over again due to walking across more sketchy things. But the day still kept drawing by in impatience, along with their own that settled in with their cold and fatigued bodies. And when almost losing any hope left as the night began closing in, they witnessed a fire, far away in the direction of which the Orrumn was leading them.

As Arnenn looked into it, he saw a different, yet still strange sight: Throone standing along fire-burning trees and roots that were somehow suspended high into the sky above a sheer darkness below. It startled him. He thought the old man must have been in danger, just like he was afraid of. They pushed forward as he explained to Gjone and Essria what he was seeing, shouting and pointing. "Throone is in there!"

As they came closer and made their way through the pond and then beyond into terrifyingly whimsical trees that looked hollow, with roots weaving in all directions that grabbed at each other and blocked their paths, they saw Throone surrounded by a large gathering of Dark-Beasts. They were about to take him.

Arnenn placed the book into his shouldered pouch and ran forward while both he and Gjone threw their spears into the mass of Dark near the Keeper (doing their best not to hit him). Then, quicker than he could see Essria in the act, she opened the pouch that hung from Arnenn's back and grabbed the Orrumn as if she were a thief of great skill.

"Ess! What are you doing?" shouted Arnenn.

She easily ignored him while speeding through a set of trees. He was unsure of whether to chase after her or go into the area of Dark-Beasts to help the old man. He wondered why she would try stealing the Orrumn, and questioned who else she may just be. He ceased to move a muscle while in consideration of what to do.

A bright red light suddenly flashed. And then, all the beasts went up in flame and disappeared.

>

Their quick speed continued out of the middle parts of the cold and spooky Palendrian as there was now a whole new set of questions about Essria, Throone, and to Throone himself, how the Orrumn was in their possession. They were not being chased anymore, but still knew that the farther they went, the safer they would likely be.

Gjone eventually had to cry out, "We need to stop!" where he came to a halt. The others followed his halting before turning around with weary looks. Gjone got off on his good leg and sat on a large rock of stone. "I have to do something with my leg! It hurts and has been bleeding ever since!"

"Yes, you do! And we need to give these steeds a rest, too," said Throone.

The fellowship tended to Gjone's leg with water, an ointment Arnenn had in his pack ever since leaving Harpelle (the same kind Stalk had put on Jemma's leg), and a thin, white tunic they had to rip into strands and tightly wrap around it.

Gjone let Throone know he could use the big coat he had lying in his pack to keep warm.

While unhitching Gjone's bag and shaking due to the cold wind from riding at high speeds with no more than rags for clothes, he wasted no time to raise the question.

"Any care to explain why we have the Orrumn?"

Gjone and Essria only looked at Arnenn, waiting for him to answer.

"You think you may want to be a bit more grateful? We just saved your life with it!"

Arnenn felt he had grown quite comfortable around Throone, enough to speak in any tone he felt necessary, changed from his usual attitude of being too respectful.

"I *am* grateful, Arnenn . . . very much so!" he said, seriously. "But I'm also highly confused as to why you have it with you when we just left it where it belongs days ago. It's supposed to be there! Not here where it can be taken by these creatures and destroyed! How do you have it?"

After a pause, he said, "I simply took it with me. And as much as I would love to, I'm not getting into another argument of why I did. I have already done that. I will just say that I'm supposed to have it. And you . . . you need to bring something *out* of it."

"You expect me to do *what* exactly? This is dangerous stuff, Arnenn! I am not bringing *anything* else out of that book!" replied Throone while raising his brows even more than they already were.

"Wait! I need to show you something!" He glared over to Essria excitedly and asked, "Ess, what did you do with the Orrumn? Can you get it for me?"

"It's Essria!" she corrected, squinting her eyes at him and retrieving the book from her pack.

"I cannot just look into it! I don't have enough strength for that! I've been drained of it entirely!" cried Throone, looking away as Arnenn began peeling it open.

He then stopped and let it close. "Well, I suppose you don't have to right now . . . but eventually, you will. Throone, we can't just hide the book at Kulne and run away from it. I saw an ancestor of Gjone and I's. The one Ess—I mean, Essria spoke of! He's been calling out to me through it—from the beginning! And I saw and heard him say to bring them out before we left! I swear on this. And I don't believe for a single second the book is supposed to stay at that place forever. We need it to help us—to protect us!"

"You want me pull *people* out of it? Like I did her?" He pointed her way. "Arnenn, you don't even know for sure who these people could be!"

"I tried telling him that myself. . . ." added Gjone.

"No, I don't know them . . . but Ess does. She knows *exactly* who they are," he hastily responded. "Throone, it's the one you told me about before . . . the one named Mouren! It *has* to be! And the King too!"

Throone made a questionable face. It was loads to believe. He continued his original argument. "Look, I am not running from anything. But that book needs to be kept safe in the place where it belongs! . . . That's what I know to be sure of. There are all these creatures and . . ." he paused, "other things in here that can sense the Orrumn. And sense that you have it, Arnenn." He continued slowly. "They know who you are—and who *I* am."

"What do you mean they know who I am?" he asked, bewildered. "And what do you mean by 'other things?'"

Throone looked at the three like he was about to say something they themselves wouldn't believe, as if it was hardly worth mentioning. "It's hard to explain . . . but I saw something in there—something tremendous, almost human form. It spoke to me. It knew my name! And yours! It told me you had the Orrumn and that you are bringing it to him, and he was going to destroy it . . . and then come for me. But it also said something about your king, Essria—your 'Madelmar.' I couldn't make any connection with it all though. I don't know what he has to do with it. There were other names he said as well, as if they were names I was supposed to know, but I did not."

Arnenn was stunned by the consideration of him doing anything bad to the book. "I'm not bringing it anywhere—or to anyone . . . especially not this *thing* you speak of. . . ."

"I know, Arnenn. I know you're not trying to destroy it, but this is why it's dangerous to have it with us. This is why it needs to be kept safe! Many Dark things and magics are going on in this place, many things we don't yet know," confirmed Throone.

" . . . Speaking of things we don't know. . . ." said Gjone, looking at Essria. They stared at her, wondering how she used the Orrumn to kill all of Throone's beasts.

Arnenn set the book back into his pouch, away from Essria as she spoke.

"Well, I suppose I need to say something. And I'm sorry if it seems like I've concealed this from you all, but I just now remembered I have the ability."

They peered at each other as she sat down on a fallen tree with her arms straightened to her side, tilting her hands and shoulders back and looking up at all three.

"I remembered that sometimes the King would send me down to the Garden Cave, and it wasn't always just to find information. The Orrumn was able to show me creatures of Dark at times, many of them, and I was able to kill them simply by touching them through the Orrumn. It wasn't a magic I always had; the King gave me the ability to do it if I'm not mistaken. But it didn't work on all of the Dark, only some. I promise that I didn't remember until right before it happened, and I'm not sure why it just now came back to me."

"Just when I thought I wasn't the only normal one. . . ." Gjone commented again.

"You pulled my magic right out of me—bending it to your own will!" said Throone as he walked forward with a good set of clothing on to put over the burnt up rags still worn underneath.

"I'm sorry, I didn't know that was going to happen," she said, and wondered if it may have worked the same before, that she was perhaps taking energy from another. But she could only speculate. The King never discussed the specifics of the magic with her, only entrusted her to use it carefully at her own will.

"Well it is all the same frightening! And there seems to be a lot more about you than just your hair color, Essria. Are you sure there's nothing else you'd like to share about yourself with me . . . or any of us?" Throone had his hands on his sides and his elbows pointing out while pacing.

"No, at least not that I remember. . . ." she said truthfully.

All three looked at each other in amazement as Arnenn said, "Well I'm impressed . . . and intrigued in the least," still trying his best to ease onto her good side.

"Is what Arnenn says true, Essria?" Is it Mouren . . . and this Madelmar you've seen in this book?" the Keeper asked.

"Yes. I have seen them with my own eyes. It's surely them." Her voice was practically monotone, layered in truth.

Throone muddled over it as he walked a bit into the distance and then paced back. He felt he would have to do what Arnenn needed of him at some point, but did not understand why these people would need to be brought out of the Orrumn, or even more crazy, brought *back* to life at all. He had his suspicions about what it all could've been connected to—something the Angelic Being had said to him, as well as the Dark Being he just saw as well: something about "the Pull." And then there was Essria and her most questionable power. But he had other questions of concern on his mind for his young friends.

"So how are you all in this forest? Didn't I tell you to get back to Harpelle? Have you three done *anything* I've asked at all?"

"We came to find you!" spoke Essria. "It was all Arnenn's idea, really. And he was right in thinking it. There's a need to have the Orrumn with us whether it's for one reason or another. Arnenn seems to be convinced and I'm starting to agree with him on the matter." She thought it best to be the one to speak up so that Arnenn didn't have to be alone in his response, especially since she was one of the very people who'd told him to leave the Orrumn where it was in the first place.

Arnenn was surprised she had spoken up for him and hoped it meant that things were becoming a bit back to how they used to be. But his mind went right back to having to question the old man.

"What were *you* doing in here, by the way? Why was there a great fire set to the trees? Weren't you only in here to investigate and then leave?"

"Well . . . yes, investigate their nest . . . and kill as many as I could, of course," he responded, scratching at his beard and looking out into the distance.

"You didn't think it a bit dangerous to try all on your own?"

Throone came right back into himself, straightly saying, "Of course I did! But I also knew that I could at least trust myself to do it! And I was right to because apparently, I can't trust *you* to not have the Orrumn in your possession at all times, Arnenn."

"If it wasn't for us, old wizard, you wouldn't have even made it out!" screamed Arnenn while pointing back to the fire. "So I don't know how much you actually *can* trust yourself, at all! —Also, you should be happy I have it with me at all times . . . it saved your life today!"

Gjone watched his cousin in his over-confidence, knowing it wouldn't end up anywhere well for him.

Throone came close to Arnenn's face and said, "Don't be so quick to show me disrespect, young Mourenrowe. I *am*, in fact, thankful you all were here to help me, but if you had even the slightest idea of how many times I have saved the lives of your temperamental bloodline, you'd be bowing on your knees in thankfulness right now instead of talking down me like I'm some lowly servant of yours in all of this. The point is, none of you should've come; and you should all be back with Rayne and Jemma who are probably worried sick about you at my expense!"

Arnenn was about to respond until Gjone thundered, "In that case, let's be going! My leg is doing fine and I'm over hearing you all argue!" It was truly terrifying, even to the Keeper.

Gjone had Arnenn help him up before slightly limping over to his horse as he said to him in a quiet whisper, "Thanks for saving me back there, Cousin. That was a close one. . . ."

Arnenn shrugged it off like it was nothing, of course — being a boy — and not wanting it to be too big a deal when Gjone would once again have to save his life in return, most likely. And with that, his mind was still racing and fired-up about his argument with the Keeper.

"Sounds good to me!" said the old man, quickly. "I want out of this forsaken forest as soon as possible myself. And we won't be stopping again until we have reached treeless ground where we can give our friends here a *real* break and ourselves . . . some real sleep." Throone patted the brown haired horse he had been returned to. "Let's try to go a little easier on them for now on so we can return them in one piece."

"We'll have no choice. There are parts here where we'll need to be walking delicately, which we came upon earlier, some abandoned city of stone within overgrown trees," said Essria. She took notice of how Throone always gave a great deal of concern for their horses. She enjoyed his caring nature for them.

Throone relit his stone after making his way atop his steed. "There's more to know about this place than I ever thought possible, but it's no matter now. We have no time for sightseeing. The only thing we'll be seeing is the glow of our stones. So light them up! We move now into Darker times."

Arnenn wasn't very satisfied with the conversation and still felt heated over it all, but held himself back from opening his mouth about anything else, which he knew was smart.

Things had changed, and overall, were coming back together for him. Yes, Throone was angry—Essria was still upset. But he was found right in his idea to follow the Orrumn's instruction. They had succeeded in the search for the old man and saved his life. Gjone wasn't even mad anymore, and Essria was at least beginning to warm up to him again as well—at least it seemed to be the case—he wasn't sure if it was for the better of him or just the situation where having the Orrumn was proving beneficial. Either way, there was much going on inside his head. And he was determined to make things right. The Orrumn, the Kingdom, learning about magics he had never thought existed. It was all new to him, just as much as most things in his world were new to Essria.

They finally made their way out of the Palendrian's western wall around noon the next day and found that the farther north they headed, the colder it became. They started to wear more clothes than the usual, stopping to pull items out of their bags one by one to keep warm and sharing whatever they had, mostly for Throone and Essria.

It was long since any of them had any decent sleep (especially Arnenn, who hadn't slept for two entire nights) and the piercing cold wasn't making it any easier. They stayed as close they could to the fire Throone had made while Gjone kept a watch out and continued to rub the ointment on his leg. They made camp inside a large ditch for warmth holding brittle dirt within. Arnenn whispered over to Essria, itching to know how she felt. "Ess, can I speak to you alone?"

She felt a bit awkward, but agreed to it.

"Yeah, I suppose so. . . ."

They walked a bit into the distance, somewhat outside the ditch with their blankets protecting them from the chilled breezes blowing above as Arnenn asked her a question in the worst possible way.

"So are we even now?" He didn't intend for it to come across so uncaring, and he realized how awful it sounded after saying it.

She paused. "What do you mean 'are we even?' Even about what?" Her face stern.

"Our secrets . . . me with taking the Orrumn, and you with your powers . . . or are you still upset with me?"

His explaining made it no better for him. She couldn't believe that this would be how he would ultimately try to mend things with her. She contemplated that perhaps men of the future had no idea how to treat a lady.

"No Arnenn, not exactly. . . ." She took a deep breath and looked about before continuing. "You intentionally withheld the fact about you taking the Orrumn when you weren't supposed to, and put us all in danger by doing it. For me, I only just remembered I have that ability with the book. That is in *no* way close to even. And yes, I'm still upset with you—you purposely lied to me!" She said it as if she had been holding it in, wanting to get it out. She needed him to remember it.

"Ess, is there any way we can move on from this? Like I said, I didn't mean to hurt you, or anybody. I was just doing what I felt I was supposed to, and I'm sorry I

didn't say anything earlier, I should've just been honest .
. . I—"

She kept her comments short-said. "I get it, Arnenn . . .
you felt it was right. Okay. I get it. We ALL get it now.
But you could've just said something. You didn't have to
conceal it. All you had to say was that you disagreed
about it being kept there, nothing else. We would've
understood, maybe even agreed!"

She stopped and only shook her head, looking away
with her arms crossed underneath her blanket of thick
wool. "I can't help but just feel so distraught about it. I
really like you, Arnenn, but it just makes me wonder if I
can even trust you at all! And I need something to trust.
I need to trust in you! I'm new to everything here, in
case you forgot. And I'm scared. Everyone else I know is
gone and I need something to hold on to in this world. It
would be nice if I knew I could hold on to you, but now
I'm just scared. Scared *and* confused. And stop calling
me Ess!"

Arnenn's voice softened as he closed his eyes and
spoke slowly. "I am sorry, Essria. I really am. I really
have no good excuse for it. I became selfish; I didn't
understand why I couldn't take it with me, and I just
assumed you and Throone were right about it and that I
would've been wrong somehow. But then I questioned
it, and in my questioning, I made a quick decision. The
Orrumn tends to have an effect on me and it's hard to
resist it. I'm sure you have felt the same way before,
from what you were saying."

Essria also softened her voice. "Yes, I have, but it was
because I wanted to see *you*."

"I wanted to see you, too! Just like I said before!"
Arnenn began again. "You don't even want to know
how many times I searched out the picture of you on our

way to the castle. It's almost embarrassing! You are—" he paused, thinking if he should say it or not. But with jumping nerves, he told her, "You are the most wonderful girl I have ever known, met, or seen . . . and I find you entirely fascinating and beautiful and I feel a connection to you like you wouldn't imagine—like I never have with anyone else! —It hurts me to hurt you like this. I didn't mean to do it with such malice, even though it's what happened. —Ess, I thought you and Throone wouldn't want me to see it for some reason, and I became upset and thought wrong of you and took it all upon myself. I see now that it would've been best to just say something in the first place. It was just so stupid of me.

Ess, I lo—"

"—That was a terrible thing for you to think of me. You should know right now that I am better than that and that you can come to me with anything—ever. Anyway, do you think I don't feel the same way about you? That's why it hurt me so much! I saw something special about you in the book and our entire time together at Kulne. You showing up at the castle was a dream come true to me! I do feel the same way, Arnenn, but I'm not apologizing for just remembering the magic I have. Besides, it saved Throone and maybe all of us as well. Understand. This is all extremely confusing to me right now. It's still hard to believe. Just imagine if you were in my place! I barely remember half of what I used to know!"

"You don't need to apologize at all . . . it's *me* that needs to." He asked it right away. "Will you forgive me, Ess?"

She said nothing for a moment, only thinking. The forming of Arnenn's question didn't help—it irritated her that on top of everything already going on, he would keep calling her "Ess," even after she would tell him not to. She gave into it, though, ready to accept. She secretly really wanted nothing else but to.

"Yes. I do. —But this doesn't mean I'm not still upset with you . . . so don't start acting like all is perfectly fine," she needed to add.

Arnenn wanted things to be just like before but knew he had screwed that up and needed to be patient. "I understand, Ess . . . and I agree."

He gave her a light hug again before hearing them.

In waves, they came like before. Loud, and clearly yelling his name. He looked at Essria with wide and confused eyes, startling her greatly.

Gjone stood up with his leg still in pain as three cats of Dust (like the one that'd previously taken hold of him) had found them. He was ready with spear in hand and shouted out to the others. Arnenn and Essria were at his side with spear and shortsword as Throone tried to wake from the slumber he had just fallen into. Tired, freezing cold and irritated he bounced up quickly, rubbing his eyes in confusion.

The beasts were ready to make their attack and so were the four members of the small fellowship. But it would equal to being unneeded.

Quickly from their left, a large wolf in white fur jumped at the cat farthest from them, sinking its teeth into its neck. The beast disappeared into the Dust immediately, such as it'd never existed. More wolves of the pack came from other directions and killed the other two with less ease.

The white wolf walked slowly up to the group and lowered its head, almost bowing to all of the members, yet frightening them greatly. From behind, smaller and younger wolves went right up to Gjone in excitement, then going to Arnenn and then Essria as they pet them questioningly, confused as to what was happening while laughing.

Suddenly, a great bear taller than Gjone walked up from behind the wolves and out of the night's darkness. All laughter stopped. Arnenn noticed its eyes to be familiar, similar to the one seen many weeks ago, or even similar to the bear sculpted in the fountain back at the Kingdom. He kept walking toward them and even surpassed the white wolf.

They nervously watched Throone stepping forward, almost trying to stop him before he and the bear were only five frightening feet apart and staring directly into each other's eyes that had just turned the sheer blue of winter.

Then, the old man nodded his head before speaking to his group. Turning back to them, he fretted, "We must get back to Harpelle . . . and as quick as we possibly can!"

25

MORE SIGHTINGS OF ANIMALS ENGULFED

Harpelle and its provinces. However, they were that of which no one would have ever wanted to see. Wolves, moose, and deer; smaller animals such as squirrels, foxes, rabbits, and mongoose, lay dead. It was a horrific sight. Some knew there to be terrors of some sort on the loose whether it were the strange creatures heard about around town, or not.

The bite marks were absolutely horrifying. Any that would find one of these poor animals in the realms would bury them out of respect and honor—or at least reasonable dignity and decency, while those who believed the age-old treaty between man and beast would be more than happy to do so.

Word about the killings reached only a select few in Harpelle as it became lost talk in the busy city (even with the popularity of the Mourenrowes' story going around about practically the exact same thing: failing to make the connection). There were also humans every here and there that had gone missing, but unfortunately, they never lived to tell the tale of why and no one had yet found them. If so, the folk of the realms around Harpelle may have taken the sightings a bit more seriously, rather than only something to laugh about in the taverns or markets.

The eyes of all in Amruhn turned blue as the cold hit Harpelle early in the year. Its people awoke to the color white surrounding their city, giving a surprise and delight to some while those who dreaded the snow looked outside their icy windows in despair. But it wasn't the only different sighting that day. The other was one that none in the city had ever before seen, but maybe only heard old tales about from people such as their great-grandfathers, or Rayne himself.

Wolves, bears, mountain lions: any large beast who could wield a deadly bite lined the walls near the Guard Tower, looking south as if protecting the city from something even more terrifying than them. They were the Light-Beasts, and bigger were they than most the animals seen around Harpelle. They stood among one another as a force never imagined, and frightening were they as they trailed and circled about with their eyes just as cold blue as the people they were protecting.

The citizens spoke amongst each other about what they were seeing, and even visitors and merchants were surprised about the appearance along with them. Trade had halted due to the beasts' interference (except for the River merchants since it wasn't stalling them at all—yet) and they made quite a fuss about it. They ended up just turning around and heading their way back along the River or to the lands west. Everybody worried about what it meant, and those that had any sense at all knew it meant something else was out in the wilds, something of great harm to them.

Some began displaying for Rayne and Jemma an entirely different attitude that morning about the story of Gjone and the beast; and those who thought it to be only a joke took it somewhat seriously for the first time in their lives. Others would ask if more were there to make an attack on the city, or if the very beasts outside the walls were there to do that exact same thing.

"Have you seen the beasts hanging around outside the Guard Tower today, Rayne and Jemma?" They heard it all morning long. One after another, people wanted to have a regular conversation with them instead of just shouting random absurdities their way. But it also made their part of the docks busier than they had been for weeks.

Rayne was concerned about his son, but not so much worried. He knew Gjone and Arnenn were no weak ducks, never have been. But wondered if they had run across any other Dark-Beasts and what it could mean if they had. He also knew there better be a good explanation for their prolonged absence.

Whenever he'd find a moment alone in the back of their warehouse, he would again ponder his son's killing, the strange sightings in the provinces that some still claimed to be true, and the supposed Light-Beasts surrounding Harpelle that very day. It made him excited to say the least, because all he had ever wanted was to prove the truth of his grandfather's story: of his previous kin rising up against a great evil. And it was beginning to happen all over again, just like the stories he had told so many times before. But he also knew it came with aspects of bad: many deaths, the separation of people from their lands, the Dark creatures of terrible measures, and again, what it meant for his son and nephew—and everyone.

He questioned why he let them leave so easily and why he didn't have a stronger opinion against their journey to begin with. To him, he was entirely at fault, and knew why it was. Jemma was (partially) right. His longing spirit for wild stories made him excited for his son to leave on his own adventure, perhaps too excited. Rayne always wanted more for Gjone (regarding such things) than he was given the opportunity, so he didn't try too hard to stop him at the time. He deeply regretted it, though, and felt he must do something to change it. Only, he didn't understand what that should be.

Jemma was finally smiling due to the heavy traffic of business, but it was the first time she had smiled in a while. The thought of where her son and nephew were and whatever could have happened to them killed her inside. Her worry had come to the point of aggravation and she swore that if she ever saw that old man Throone again, she would put him in his grave, or at least something close to it. Still, it was nice for her and Rayne to have something else to keep their minds occupied. Especially since first thing that morning, Jemma received a letter from Arnenn's mother. It went as such:

> Dear Jemma and Rayne,
>
> It is with deep regret I have to inform you that we are a little more than entirely confused as to the reasoning of all this. It has now been almost five months since I have seen my son who has gone off on some other journey that you did not give any detail about. I don't know what to think about all of this.
>
> Alandis is upset as well. Arnenn was supposed to be back at work by now, and my poor husband has had to fill his spot with one of the neighbor kids who might I say, "lacks the least bit of skills necessary for the job." I am in deep hopes and concern that our Arnenn will be returning to us soon and in one piece. If not, Alandis and I will have to go over there, or on a mad search for them on our own.

Know we are not upset with you two. We understand that Arnenn and Gjone are both adults and can decide what to do on their own, but as you know, it is hard as parents not to worry. Even our cat Jenkas seems to be concerned.

We send you our love and hopes that they return soon, for all our sakes.

Sincerely,
Kershpa and Alandis

The letter made Jemma feel guiltier than ever, but she had no time to write anything in return with how busy the shop had become. Also, she wasn't sure what to say back. There was no use in any letter of apology or explanation. The best and *only* thing that could happen was simply one thing: for Gjone and Arnenn to return. There was nothing she, Rayne, or anyone else could do. They would unfortunately just have to wait even longer.

In the meantime, they had work to get to; and Harpelle had its own news going on with the Light-Beasts at their doorstep. The talk of the wild animals near the Guard Tower had people stocking up on things like loaves of bread, vegetables, and longer lasting foods such as dried poultry or pork. Also, ales.

A fear surrounded the city, but a feeling of new and exciting life was also in the air, for only through old tales has such a sight been seen.

Many came together in the cold and fires were set all around the city for people to huddle up next to for warmth and community. Some places had even decided to close down for the day because there was just too much excitement going on about the so-called Light-Beasts outside to make focusing on routine tasks such as day jobs, easy to do. Even the schools were letting children stay at home with their parents. Most were hosted up on Mom and Dad's shoulders to see the zoo that'd come to visit. It was an entirely different way to enjoy a Changing of the Seasons celebration.

Day and night had passed and the animals still lingered, huddled together in the cold with the same determined look in their blue eyes—suggesting something was to come over the hills in the distance at any moment.

People had different feelings about their presence as the days went by. Some would mock the beats, shouting at them to leave and go back to their homes or to wherever in the wilds they had come from. (These were mostly drunkards who would stay too late at the bars around the southern end of town.)

Others that actually had any small amount of respect would throw food over the wall to help feed the beasts. Even the Bear Guard got in on this by striking up a deal with most of the taverns and restaurants around town to gather all unsold foods and scrapped-up leftovers. The Captain had his men all over town, collecting and carrying the food in the city's many signature wooden bins.

Lenx Arbowen and some of the Bear Guard's bravest decided to make a point to the public while going out to feed the giant beasts on the snowy grounds where they stayed, being joined with them as one, nervous beyond all belief. Many watched as they weren't harmed in any way while walking through crowds of massive bears, cats, and wolves. It was no easy task to be done, but the Captain needed the citizens to know that the beasts were on their side and that the treaty made long ago was as real as ever before. (Even with their own doubts, they bravely did this.)

Still, some people thought it didn't mean a single thing and that the Captain of the Bear Guard was only out of his mind—if he even had one left. They would whisper to each other that the only reason he and his men were not attacked was due only to feeding them and that otherwise, *they* would have been their food that day.

The largest of crowds gathered near the Guard Tower later that same day because the Bear Guard had been receiving questions from everyone, everywhere.

"Why are these animals surrounding our doors?"

"What's going on out there?"

"Are you sure these are the Light-Beasts?"

"Are we safe or are we going to die?"

"Why aren't you doing anything else about this?"

They just kept coming.

Some folk expected the Guard to know more than anyone else did, which of course, they did not, and Lenx even had some of his men scour the lands once again to see if there was anything to be found. But they again saw nothing and decided to stop the search entirely to focus on the bigger matter at hand, the Light-Beasts.

Lenx made his appearance around mid-afternoon to answer as many questions as he could. Haulfir stood by his father's side, along with three other trusted men of the Bear Guard atop the Tower's highest ledge where two large carved bear heads beamed out and over a small circle of dead grass and snow. The Captain had to shout as best he could for all to hear him clearly.

"Folks. . . . Friends, please calm down! Please! We have been just as concerned as you all! First and foremost, know that none of these animals are here to harm us in any way! As you should all know, there was a treaty made long ago between man and beast! They are our protectors while we keep their lands free! And that is how it's always been! These here are Light-Beasts!"

An elderly man in the crowd interrupted him, yelling, "That's all fairy-tale! —Nobody believes that anymore! They're here to take over our city! You watch!"

Shouts of agreement came from half the people in the crowd as Lenx shouted back, "I can assure you all they are not here to harm us or take over the city! If that were the case, then they would have done so already, and as you saw, they did not harm us when we went out to them! They are looking out at something in the distance! That's what we need to discuss—I believe it's for the best you all stay near to your homes and wait it out! If there is something out there that would mean us any harm, the animals will take care of it, and the Guard will step in if need be. But you should all begin by keeping yourselves safe in your homes!"

"The stories are true! Rayne Mourenrowe's son killed a strange beast, and now there are going to be more here to get back at us, and kill us all!" shouted someone else in the crowd that Lenx couldn't see. The other half of the crowd shouted in agreement.

"WE KNOW NONE OF THAT FOR SURE!" continued the Captain—louder than before. All went silent. Lenx didn't have to shout as forcefully anymore.

"Stories and strange sightings are one thing, but none of us have seen these creatures yet. Not the creature the young man killed, or anything else. Now, that's not to say something doesn't exist out there, I believe there definitely *could* be something, but we need to keep our focus and wits about us. And we need to play it right by first keeping ourselves safe!"

They kept at it by either agreeing or disagreeing, and arguing amongst each other. Haulfir looked at his father, agreeing with him in his attitude about it, though he himself knew the strange beasts to surely exist. As he watched the expression on people faces from what his father was saying, he thought about the sighting of the giant bear he had seen atop the hill, the one he had yet to say a single word to anyone about.

He went back and forth about whether he should say something or not as he stood upon the ledge. Most of him still thought nothing of it, but the other part of him had a concern about what could happen to the people if the beast he'd seen had found its way into the city. He knew it was his direct duty to do something. But again, the great beast had looked at him to keep it quiet, and he gave word to it that he would. They had some kind of understanding between one another. It was a crazy thing to think—he questioned if it was just all in his head.

In his thought, he looked behind him, out at the animals from atop the ledge that he, his father, and the other guards stood. That's when he saw him again, along with his followers, the many smaller beasts beside him. Only now, there were much more that came over the tops of many sets of hills, far into the distance to the south where a bluff steeply ran its way up to them. They covered almost the entire width of it with their ashy blackness. And he also noticed each and every animal surrounding the Guard Tower quickly take their stand, for they saw the Dark-Beasts at the very same moment as he.

This time, he didn't have much of a choice of whether to speak up or not. He smoothly glided over to his father who was still reasoning with the citizens—he nudged him on the shoulder.

"What, Son? Now's not the best time," said Lenx.

"Father . . . you may want to look behind you."

Lenx hesitated, but when finally turning his head, he saw the hilltops far away to be lined in black. A faint smoke rose above. The Captain squinted right before holding a special made purt stone up to his right eye that allowed him to see far into the distance where the black was made up of the figures of many large and distraught animals. They looked to be the same types from Rayne's stories, and Rayne's son's attack that all have been in excitement about during the days leading up to the Light-Beasts' appearance. So immediately, he informed the guards standing around, who also peered out in shock, seeing that something they did not expect to happen, had, in fact, happened.

"Hey! What is going on? What are you looking at?" shouted half the crowd as another half ran to both their left and right to have a look through the slight openings in the main gate. They all saw it right ahead of them where in a matter of seconds, anyone still concerned about the animals on watch quickly lost that concern and redirected it.

"Haulfir, the alarm . . . now!" shouted Captain Lenx to his son.

Haulfir then ordered the three guards to his right to the Horns of Harpelle as he ran up the stairs to ring the alarming bell.

"Inform the others!" shouted Lenx. Just as he was trying to avoid, the people became frantic and started pushing and shoving in all directions. It's the reason he wanted everyone to go back to their homes; he thought they were only going to get in the way of the Guard and cause something worse to happen. "Everyone, get back to your homes! Go back! But stay calm! Remain calm!

Grab your children and go safely back! Do not push each other!" he continued while waving his hands wildly above his head. Some listened and began walking a quick pace back to their homes while most still pushed and shoved anyway. Others stayed by the fences peering out at what was soon to be a battlefield.

More guards came out from within the Tower dressed in their black uniforms with the bear head insignia shining brightly upon their chests. They ordered the people by the fence to get back, explaining that it was not a safe place for them to be. Most pretended not to hear.

Haulfir reached for the rope. It was quite the stretch, but as he took hold of it, the bell struck loudly in his ears and anyone who wasn't part of the commotion going on in the south end of the city was then alarmed and knew something must have happened regarding the Light-Beasts outside. Some walked ponderously out of their homes and into the streets, seeing others run quickly and worriedly into their own.

One after another, the sounds engulfed Harpelle. The horns of the city blew mightily into the cold wind with a majestic ringing; the dust collected over the years left their tubes at once. They sat high in their towers of steel and stone, causing the sound to reverberate off of the metals and shake into the depths of the ground beneath and around them. Some heard thumps as many of the Bear Guard ran about in order.

Lenx ordered his guards to take their places on the platform atop the city's thick, wooden walls. They situated and became ready to fire their arrows on his call as the Captain rounded up other guards with swords in case the beasts of Dark were to make their way through. He was even considering taking them with him outside the walls to fight alongside the Light-Beasts that had come to protect—feeling an unexplainable need to do so—to fight beside them, but only if it was what had to be done.

Nerves were heavy. The Bear Guard knew the treaty called for them to be strong and honorable, and to bind together and to never back down from a fight. They knew this well because they were reminded of it many times, more times than they ever needed to be reminded. It made them no less worried, though; the Dark in the distance was a threat beyond any other they had ever known or thought could exist. They had no idea what they actually were other than some looking even bigger than the Light-Beasts, and cloaked in a savage and ashy blackness surrounded by a cloud of smoke. The Guard had absolutely no experience fighting a force against any that weren't human—because they never thought they would need it—especially against a force of something much scarier than anything they had ever known to exist.

Having no time to plan or create an objective didn't help much, either. The beasts came from nowhere and with little warning other than what was thought to be make-believe tales, but now the people and the Bear Guard alike, saw it. And all the while, it was entirely hard to believe any of it was actually happening, no longer a joke.

No longer was it only a tale told by strange men of old. They saw now that it was all very real. And on that day, they were to experience something more than that of which most the storytellers themselves ever had, and it could very well mean it to be their last day, if not including everyone else they knew as well.

They were brave, though, and as frightening of a battle they knew it would become, they found great purpose. They could tell a connection existed between them and the Lights. It fired and toiled within their hearts and souls. It ignited an energy within them. They knew they were meant to fight alongside each other and also, that they were a part of some greater epic, greater than any other which wonder could provide.

Fighting with all their will and might and honor was exactly what they were going to do. Even those of the Guard who had never actually believed in the Light-beasts and thought it was all foolishness, were suddenly, completely changed to it.

"Son!" yelled Lenx as he ran to Haulfir, "I want you to stay within these walls and help lead this part of the Guard. Keep these people within their homes! And if any of those things get into our city's walls, do not hesitate for a second to eliminate them with all you have! And keep yourself alive! I may have to go out there and meet them head-on."

All he could say was, "Yes, Father!"

One thing he knew and liked about his father aside from his usual tactics of running the Guard, is that when desperate measures were at an extreme imminence, there was no one better to depend on, no one braver.

He had forgotten all about making a decision to tell the others since it was already made for him and he cared no more for the giant beast of a bear he'd seen before, or whatever connection he felt there. He left it all behind him; he was going to do whatever was right. He knew his duty on the Bear Guard and was going to protect the people of his city: kill as many of these terrors he could manage, ready to fight and have honor of his own; and ready to take the very beats that could've taken his good friend Gjone.

Rayne and Jemma heard the horns. It was the first time they had ever heard them, for they were never needed in the days of trade in Harpelle. They saw the guards ordering people into their homes and wondered what could possibly be going on. With the sight of most being frantic, Rayne saw their weakness and felt nothing but shame. The strength of its inhabitants had for the most part, left. It made him angry, guilty to be any part of it, but also saddened for them.

Harpelle. It was always known to be the great city of strength. But he saw it happen over the years. The city came to the mercy of money and commerce with the many merchants that came from all lands throughout Amruhn, and he indeed knew he played a significant part.

He and Jemma were already making their way south through the packed alleyways full of people and stacked whiskey barrels as a well-known guard by the name of Herring came running up, heavily breathing under his short, dark, and curly hair. He commanded, "Rayne, Jemma . . . you need to go back and close the shop . . . and stay inside of it."

Jemma asked with the utmost excitement, "I don't understand . . . what do you mean, Herring? Tell us. What's going on out there?"

Herring and the other guards were given an order from Lenx not to inform everybody about the beasts on the hills if they could help it, but he knew Rayne and Jemma well enough to tell them calmly.

"Black creatures . . . like the one your son had killed. More are here . . . and I mean *a lot* more. They are on the top of the hills that head into Novark as if they are going to attack. You need to stay inside and keep safe in case they get in somehow and—"

Shaking his head with his eyes closed in confusion and disagreement, Rayne interjected. "I'm sorry, Herring, but I will not be cowering from these things. I won't. Not like everyone else here. Look around you. All these people, so afraid—no strength or courage. I cannot let it be so for myself."

"I thought that's what you might say, Rayne," said Herring before Jemma partially laughed at his response. "Rayne, you couldn't be serious . . . I know you're strong, dear, but you need to stay with me. Let's do as he says and close up, or at least go back home."

"She's right," agreed Herring. "We have got it under control. It is best for you to keep your shop safe and closed up, for now at least . . . if anything, help some of these merchants make their way out of here and down the River before you lock up. You know just as well as I that the last thing we need is any of them hurt on our grounds, ending up with nasty Lake dwellers knocking on our doors. . . . having to deal with them. . . ."

Herring didn't wait for any other response and ran off with a commanding shout. "Keep yourselves locked in!"

Rayne wasn't ready to let it be. Nor was he planning on locking himself inside his shop or anywhere else for that matter. But Herring was correct about the merchants. "Come, Jemma, let's get them out of here."

The very same moment they made it back and walked through the open door, Rayne clearly and loudly stated, "Everyone, get yourselves somewhere safe! You can stay in here if need be, but we are locking up. Any of you that have come on boats, I suggest you get back to them and take your leave to Crennan . . . and as soon as you can!"

They hastily helped any and all of the many customers carry their gear or purchases out to their boats or on their way somewhere else. "Sail quickly!" spoke Jemma as the crowds around the shop ran here and there.

"What's happening? What's the big rush here?" the boat merchants would ask while setting their gear inside their boats or loitering within the shop. Rayne easily and eagerly gave the truth.

"We are under attack."

It was enough said. No one questioned anything more about it, even though none could even imagine why they would be under an attack, or by whom. Many of the merchants hurried into their boats at once to quickly take their leave down the Cunning. And when the last of them had finally drifted out and everyone's movements were a little less chaotic around the shop, Jemma yelled after her husband. "Rayne, come on! Get in here! We need to lock the door!"

From the docks, Rayne ran straight to her as she held it open. But he stopped right before her and did not make his way inside.

"What are you waiting for? Get in here already!" she said, rolling her eyes.

He only stood still before her. "Jemma, I'm sorry, but I won't be staying in here with you. You just keep yourself safe."

She reluctantly paused. "No—no, Rayne, get in here. Don't do something brave, or stupid!"

"I love you, Jemma. But I will not. Take care of these people. Understand, I must go and be what help I can out there." He felt sour that he'd said nothing to Lenx about the Dark-Beasts, the warning he could have given instead of trying to keep his word to the old man Throone, word that only brought further harm to the people of Harpelle.

He began to walk the other direction, but Jemma ran after and grabbed him by the shoulder, stopping him in his path and abruptly turning him around. Her blue eyes looked deep into his for a few moments before igniting her lungs to say, "Please don't tell me this is what all your stories lead to, Rayne. I know you have a heart for these things. I get it. And I know you want to be part of this more than anything. But . . . if something happened to you . . . I just couldn't bear it. Please, come back and stay in here with me!"

All he did was kiss her before setting a hand upon her face; a face he'd love staring into more than anything else. He then held her hands in his and said, "Jemma . . . what if those beasts out there took our son?" He asked again in a different way. "My love . . . what if our Gjone is dead because of these things?" He only paused and awaited her answer.

Jemma's eyes darted back and forth with thought at first, but closed swiftly after. Then, with a deep breath, they opened.

"Then that's that, I guess." She looked back. "Telt! Sarra! Keep it locked! And keep it safe!" She then turned back to Rayne and told him, "If I can't stop you from going, then in return, you won't be stopping me, either."

He smiled and agreed, and quickly they closed the door while everyone inside rustled about to get set into their places. Telt locked it from the inside as the owners of Remma's Produce set off toward home to grab a set of weapons that they had buried away somewhere in their room, many years before.

They were weapons even Gjone didn't know about. One of them, a sword Rayne had secretly inherited from his Grandfather.

26

THE DARK BEAR GAZED DOWN FROM ATOP

the bluff of the hills that lined the northern edge of Novark, the start into the realm of Harpelle. He watched the Light-Beasts surrounding it come slowly forth, waiting to collide with his Dark army. It reminded him of his own time as a Light-Beast, fighting against the exact thing he now was. But those days were long gone. He knew he had grown ever stronger. And he had no fear of them anymore.

Far away, he snarled at them behind his glowing black wrought in a clouded mess of the elements, elements mixed with something far more terrible.

He gathered more Dark who had snuck their way through the scattered trees, all the way from the central parts of the Palendrian to the lands farther north during the nights of cold until existing in the boundaries of Harpelle. They crept in and made quick work of the protectors in the provinces. Hunting in packs, they would find a lone Light-Beast and turn them over to Dark, or kill them. And in the Lights' very own lands they did this. And there in the city, they would do the same: move into it and kill all and destroy, or convert any they could, beast, and even man if it was possible. They were to weaken the people and their sturdy structures standing in any remembrance of the Light.

He remembered the old strength of Harpelle that existed hundreds of years before when first built, but now, he saw it only confused with trade and worldly pleasantries. It would be an easy city to destroy, but he was more concerned with one of his other tasks: killing the descendant of Rowe, the one he sensed weeks before.

He knew there were others, too, more than the one he already knew about. There was a son, or perhaps even two sons. And he'd heard the story about the killing directly from the many serpents and small insects of Dark that would crawl beneath the grimy holes and crevices to listen in on the conversations spoken loudly about. And he learned they also existed in Vidhera, but knew that that city was far too great in size to attack just yet.

He waited for the correct time: when the city was cold and its people were their weakest. Harpelle would be overrun, where after, he would move on to find the others. But there was one more task to be done before he would leave for good.

There was the young man with red hair, the one he sensed a seed of hatred growing within; and the one he decided to use to lead his master's armies of men. He had stared into his eyes and let him know it was his task, even though the young man couldn't fully comprehend it.

He roared into the fields like thunder. It stifled any down in the valley both before and even far into the city. At that, the beasts of Dark walked slowly north, jumping their way down the cliffed hills. And even more kept creeping their way up and over from the hills' backsides where those of Harpelle could see its army growing in hundreds, second by second.

The many citizens that refused to stay inside their homes and had found the strength to fight alongside the Guard watched the Dark coming down the bluffs. And those who knew Rayne's stories knew also that the terrors he spoke of were real. These were the beasts of Dark. And they saw the sheer size of what must have been their leader slowly making his way down one of the hills. It's where a deep fear had finally struck their hearts. A terror they never knew existed was now on their very doorstep.

At once, all understood the importance of the treaty and the truth about the Light-Beasts surrounding the Guard Tower. They watched them creep southward to the oncoming evil while the Bear Guard handed out old swords and knives and spears to those willing. They saw some who quickly denied their courage, running back to their homes after being handed a weapon, realizing that they had very little chance of survival against such an overwhelming threat of evil.

Many other leaders of the Guard took brave citizens to the thick walls and rare openings surrounding the city from its very east to its west, just in case any Dark lingered closer north, nearer to the River, hiding within the trees, attempting to make secret attacks on the city.

But it wasn't only the Dark who brought a tense ferocity to the fight. The Light-Beasts showed their teeth in warning to their enemy, and even some of the Guard saw it. It was a monster that none would have ever wanted to be up against. In their great size, they seemed to have magic of their own; and in great strength and power, it had shown through them.

"If you intend to stay, then you intend to fight!" shouted Lenx to the citizens after he and his guards took up their shields that shined in bright silver with the Harpelle Wolf Head imprinted on them. The shouting of the Bear Guard roared thick in the ears of everyone around who quickly followed.

He decided to go through with his plan and gathered those to go outside the city walls. He couldn't keep himself locked inside the city (just the same as how Rayne couldn't stay locked inside his shop). But before he could get very far, he ended up seeing the Mourenrowes running up to him. Each had a flashing bright sword kept in excellent condition. It barely surprised the Captain.

"Where can you use us?" asked Rayne.

Lenx had never seen them so determined in his life. "Rayne, my old friend . . . Jemma," he said, tilting his head toward her. "We can definitely use your help. Stay inside these walls with Haulfir. Keep the people safe in case anything gets in." He ended it, running off to the Tower, ready to lead his men and women past the gate and into the clearing when he heard, "Wait! There's something more you must know about these beasts!"

Rayne caught him again, heavily breathing. "The only way to kill them is to pierce them all the way through. There is no other way!" He gave Lenx a blank stare of seriousness right after.

Lenx stalled for a moment before laughing, "Ha, Rayne . . . I don't know how you'd know that, but of course, only *you* would know it."

He did not disbelieve or question it one bit. At this point, anything Rayne said was nothing but solid truth.

The Captain ran off again, telling as many he could as Rayne and Jemma did the same. Person to person they told, and them to others: spreading the word.

This time, a bear of Light gave a great roar. It ignited the souls of all the wild Light-Beasts, as they, too, howled and roared along with him. The citizens looked out at the two mass armies with dread, yet giving a great shouting together as well in support for the protectors before the gap minimized quickly between the beasts of Light and Dark. Then it happened.

They collided.

Teeth dug deep into each other. The Light-Beasts turned some of the Dark into ash with just a single bite while the Dark-Beasts' claws and teeth like knives ripped and tore at their enemies of Light whose blood splashed clean on the snow-laid ground.

Everywhere, beasts fought sporadically, going to and fro to make new attacks. It was difficult for the people to tell which side was overcoming the other, for it was more a skirmishing of carnage leading to bloodshed and Dust. And there was equality in number of deaths.

Some of the wolves of Dark had made their way past the first onslaught and raced toward the city, but the stealthy arrows of the Bear Guard from atop the Tower took them down—that is if a Light-beast hadn't already succeeded in doing so. Some disappeared into ash right before the guards' eyes, and some made their way back up onto their paws as if nothing had happened, or weren't hurt in any way as arrows protruded from their bodies.

The people shared confused looks as to what they were seeing. If it wasn't bad enough that the creatures didn't make any sense by looks alone, then seeing them disappear into a black ash made them feel like nothing they had ever known was real. But at the same time, it was encouraging to figure out how to kill them, and noticing that they had a chance to rid themselves of the terrible foes, they grew ever eager to take them out as their arrows soared.

The Light-Beasts were holding quite well, but there were more and more members of the Dust that would make their way down the bluff of the hills, which meant the army of Light could only hold their blocking of the city for so long. In seeing it, Lenx knew what he had to do.

Shortly after, a couple hundred guards and brave citizens followed him single-file through a small door set underneath a battlement of the Tower to help out their Light-Beast allies on the fields beyond the city. On the shallow snow, they walked with fear that couldn't be ignored, fear that wisely shouldn't be.

"Remember, all the way through!" said Captain Lenx Arbowen as they grouped together in their stride. The army of the Lights began to dwindle beyond, and more Dark would get through their protective shield every here and there. They saw people outside the city gate, and savagely darted for them, going in for the kill.

Again, they didn't get far due to being hit by another stealthy arrow, or given a straight sword that went all the way through them. But the people found out quickly that it was a difficult task. Sometimes, it would take many tries to burry them through the thick of the beasts as they bit and clawed ferociously back, ripping at them and charring their skin with their bodies of Dust. It terrified all, both brave citizen and Bear Guard alike. Those on the fields held their ground firmly, though, and began learning new tactics and techniques from each other. They found it worked best to run their blades down into the creatures from above, or from underneath the chest and up. But really, cutting off their heads was what worked best.

But it wasn't so easy to kill any Dark that were much larger than wolves or cats, however, because any bears whether large or small that'd come their way would quickly demolish any men around them. Swords and arrows, or even spears were of little or no use. Some citizens even ran back to the city, scared and confused beyond all their being, for they did not understand what they were up against.

The Dark Bear took his stride after waiting for some of the Lights to die off. His creep turned into a run and he barreled through and over everything in his path— either Light or Dark, and almost without notice. It didn't take him long to find his way to the people of Harpelle, swiping some to their deaths.

Arrows flew from far away as he neared the Guard Tower, but they only either partially stuck within him or bounced right off his fur of thick flame as he made his way up to two large, yet smaller-than-he bears that were ready to bring him down.

Both jumped at the larger one coming their way, but the Dark Bear made quick work of them. He snapped the neck of the one to his left by catching it within his great jaw. The other clawed at its side and tried to get a good bite on his leg until a pack of Dark cats came and dragged the Light-Beast to the ground, ending its life in agonizing pain by thoroughly being bitten.

The people watched in sadness, grieving for the poor beasts, but in despair at the one of Dark who had easily carried on toward them.

The brave people upon the field kept at it, ridding more creatures of Dark than they first thought possible. But still, Lenx saw those he cared for dying all around him while the great beast of a bear was inching ever closer to his right flank. He saw an opportunity for space and began shouting to all.

"Pull back! All of you . . . make back into the city!"

Those that heard followed his request without hesitating, running full speed away from the battle and the terrors trailing behind. But most who did not hear, did not last much longer. They had gone too far out into the field and were overtaken by the Dark.

One who had barely survived was one of Lenx's lead guards, a man taller and even more bruiting than Gjone by the name of Kedd. He was almost taken by a Dark wolf that had already began its leap toward him, but was quickly saved by a feline who turned the wolf into ash with a simple bite in mid-air. The great cat paused and stared at Kedd, warning him to continue back to the gate; looking at him—suggesting they should have never left the inside of the city.

He ran swiftly, planting his feet deep into the snow and wet dirt with all his might, and was the very last to make it back to the walls before Lenx closed the small door of the Tower behind him.

He was almost too late. A pack of Dark wolves had scratched against the door right after making his way through it. It greatly frightened those within the walls that had yet to have any part to play in the battle, and the pounding and scratching became heavier against the sturdy main gate.

The Lights had dwindled, and the Darks now gathered entirely upon the tall city gate and walls around the Guard Tower.

The four had at last made their way to the top of the ridge on the southeast line of Harpelle after the long day and night it took to rush their way through the hilly farmlands of Novark. They tried to make as much ground as possible by leaving the road and going through fields with small riverbeds and patched forests, but they felt it made little difference in the end, even after finding Essria a horse of her own to help with speed.

It was a suspected surprise but a saddening sight. It grieved them. What was once an open glade of grass and wildflowers where they last saw many ground merchants traveling in and out of the city with cheer was now filled with Light-Beasts, men of the Bear Guard, and regular citizens of Harpelle, lying dead. It was also covered in Dust and blood that set atop a thin blanket of snow.

Essria stared at the strong city in which the men of her group had traveled. It was beautiful. She saw its heavy wood and stone. She'd never seen a city so sturdy-looking, even when compared to Kulne. But the death she saw around it was dreadful and stole most of its beauty. It broke her heart. And it reminded her of similar things she had witnessed before, such as the hundreds of Dark-Beasts that'd made their way up against the city gates, fighting the few Light-Beasts still remaining. A familiar view.

Arnenn grabbed the Orrumn and peered inside to see if there was an answer to any of it—anything that could help; anything at all. He thought it could reflect the scene in front of them where Essria would kill all the Dark-Beasts at once with just a touch of her hand, just like she had in the Palendrian when saving the Keeper.

Nothing came about. He turned it to a new page and then another, trying more blank pages and hoping one would reveal something. But as the many sets of seconds passed by, it gave him nothing. The most he was given was the wind that blew around the pages, annoying an already impatient Arnenn, who yelled, "COME ON!"

All it needed to do was show the battle on the grounds, then they could easily be killed—all of them.

That simple. Each and every Dark-Beast would cease to exist and everyone would be saved. Rayne, Jemma, all would stay alive for sure.

He thought then that he had it all wrong. Why did he believe it would show up for him if it were not his magic? It made him feel even worse and slightly embarrassed in front of her. She only stared at him, confused.

"What?" she asked.

He didn't respond; he only attempted to hand it over to his left where she began holding out her hands, understanding what he'd been trying to do. But his carelessness and anger caused him to fumble the Orrumn in between their steeds.

It only fell to the ground on its spine, spread open.

"You're wasting time, Arnenn! We need to get down there!" said Gjone. He was about to give the order to ride ahead. However, at that very moment, the Keeper who sat behind the others upon his own steed had accidentally caught sight of something inside the Orrumn as it settled upon the pebbly surface of the ground, and on a very particular page: one he had recently heard about. And somehow, the wind's drift did not seem to exist below where the Orrumn laid itself on Amruhn's crust.

He saw for himself the ancestor of Rowe and the older man in a scarlet red: the one Essria had spoken of. And just like the moment when feeling Kulne peel out of his soul, the same thing happened. But with even greater power behind it now.

More energy drained from his body. He saw visions of the man with a beard of color in different settings and images that had flashed back to Kulne again, like old memories, not of his own. Something burst out of him like fire and just like the Orrumn, he fell to the ground.

The others saw Throone in his agony, realizing he had seen the picture.

Arnenn was unsure of what to do. His own face went blank and white as he felt the raw bite of his foolishness.

The Keeper's breath moved the dirt and snow as his face rubbed the pebbles beneath his cheek. He could only shyly hold himself by his elbows, trying to get a knee up. "You two, get out of here. NOW!" he yelled in what was almost a whisper as he pointing ahead, and in pain, added, "Go to the city . . . and get your book out of my sight!" and where he then lay, only coughing.

Essria had already stepped down from her own horse and made her way to him. She had to help him; had to take care of him. And she could see the loss of energy throughout his face. But even while feeling the shame, Arnenn wasn't convinced that her not at least trying was a good idea. He had to speak up.

"But what if we—" tried Arnenn, but Throone grunted, "Arnenn, you cannot wield the Orrumn to your desire! Leave now! Please! Get out of here!"

Essria said the same. "Please go, Arnenn. It won't work . . . I just know it. I can't explain!"

He kept giving her a blank stare in question, but then turned to Gjone who was growing ever impatient, about to leave on his own.

"They will be fine," he said to Arnenn. "We have to get down there!"

Arnenn stared back to her one last time, and she to him. It was strange to realize that it would be their first departure since meeting. And there was no guarantee they would be seeing each other again. A heavy mixture of feelings boiled in their hearts for each other, existing in an old and rare magic that words could only flirt with—almost a bond of others from a world long gone. But there were no words to confirm their love, only a stare of understanding. It was going to have to do.

* * *

The young Rowes began racing towards the terrors when they noticed them forming a tide up against the gate, creating a ladder of themselves for their leader to crawl to its tall top. It's when they quickly realized that no plan and only brave determination would only sum to great folly.

Arnenn slowed before coming to a complete stop again. Gjone had to follow. "Maybe we should go around—back to where the house is and go in from there. I don't know what use we'd be up against all of them. We'd only get lost within that army, and ourselves, killed."

"I think you're right, Cousin," replied Gjone, smiling before going through with his plan. But that plan didn't last long after hearing the great roar of a bear on the hills to their west. Atop the bluff where those of Dark previously awaited the battle to start, a whole new legion of Light had come and cleared away any still lingering.

The Dark-Beasts heard it and some turned around, but most just kept piling themselves at the gate, making it look as if they were a swarm of insects. They were clawing, pulling, and even biting each other to create a better hold. Many yelps of pain came from the mass of Dark. It was a mess of heat and smoke and ash that rose ever up, creating clouds above. The people on the other side could feel the heat through the thick wood of the gate, protruding sweat from their foreheads and melting the snow beneath their feet.

Sadly, the arrows of the Guard were barely making a difference anymore when the Dark Bear began his incline on the backs of his many minions. They screeched and screamed even more as his claws dug deep into their backs, pulling farther up until almost on top of them, ready to go over the gate.

The people could see his large head peeking over. It instilled a great fear for all those standing with weapons and shields, but no skill handy to use them correctly.

His weight was much too great for them, however; he began to slide: falling into the mud made from the melted snow in a failed attempt. He responded by swiping at the many others as they flew up against the wall for their punishment of failing him. Some, he'd even knocked unconscious.

The Rowes watched it unfold and saw the sheer size of the Dark Bear in the distance almost make his way into the city. It gave them great concern, but they also found hope as they watched any remaining Light-Beasts on the field retreating south to their new host.

"Well, we can stick with your plan . . . or, we can ride with them," said Gjone, nodding past.

Arnenn raised his brows. "Oh . . . and what of that large bear-looking Dark-Beast? That thing's massive, Gjone, I—"

"Arnenn, if Throone's taught us anything through this entire debacle, it's how to use a spear." Gjone set his left upon his cousin's shoulder while holding his spear in his right. "All our life, our training . . . we can take him. Arnenn, we can save our city."

Our city, thought Arnenn. For once it wasn't just the summer home of his cousin, but it was his own to save as well. He was ready to fight for it.

~

Three, four, five times the Dark Bear rushed at the gate and collided with it: weakening it, each crash better than the one before until a large arrow of steel flung from the battlement caught him right behind the shoulder. He gave a great screech before falling to the ground.

~

The new legion was ready to begin their pace northward to the city when they saw two of Rowe-kind heading their way. Just then, a great bear had walked up from behind many different animals in front, and Arnenn and Gjone noticed it was the same one they had seen the night before; the one that somehow let Throone know that Dark was to attack their city. Its serious blue eyes behind its sheer brown fur gave them a stare. It then turned its head to the many Dark upon the gate of Harpelle. Its intensity shoveled itself into the Rowes' hearts. It looked once more at Gjone, and then, took off.

They began their pace at full speed ahead, waiting no longer for the Dark to make their way inside. The others followed, as did both Arnenn and Gjone who had been accepted into their fierce army.

The Dark-Beasts were unaware of their coming for the most part. Only a few noticed. But the mass of Light-Beasts heading their way was even greater in number compared to the Lights who had previously protected Harpelle, for they had been gathered throughout many different areas of the realms.

New creatures were running within the army from big to small. There were fantastically large moose with great antlers to small foxes, which were unknown by the

Rowes to be Light-Beasts, or not, but showed confidence within their stride.

None of the Dark yet dared to run up against them, and backed closer to the city's wall where the Dark Bear had returned to his massive paws, paying no attention to the oncoming attack from the south, for he felt assured they would be handled. Besides, he had a job of his own to do, one of greater importance. But the others of Dark had no choice but to meet them head on. And they began turning around in concern at the very same time their master had finally made a significant crack in the gate. Once it happened, they ignored the Lights and raced to the gate, pushing.

It finally crashed into the city.

27

THE DARK-BEASTS FUMBLED OVER ONE

another to make their way in. It was the worst thing Harpelle had ever witnessed—a force that told them they were over for good. The terrible beasts had entirely rummaged their way into the city as the Lights ran ever faster to catch up.

The people watched as many variations of Light and Dark came thundering through the broken gate, biting and clawing at one another. The sounds alone were enough to cause those inside the buildings to faint while outside, citizens and guards alike fought and scurried around their screeching.

Light-Beast killed Dark-Beast and the other way around. Teeth dug deep into raw elements of Dark until gums became condensed in Dust. Humans swung their swords and axes, slashing and deepening their blades into the flesh of beasts whose souls burned heartily inside. People's skin was seared from contact with them, blamelessly ignorant to have covered themselves, feeling the excruciating pain of the claws and teeth that had sunk deep into their limbs and mid-bodies, sharing in the pain with the beasts of the Light.

Alone and almost unnoticed, the Dark Bear kept his eyes peeled for the descendant of Rowe to come before him as he made his way slowly down the street with tens of arrows protruding from his body, along with the large steel arrow caught behind his shoulder, causing him to limp.

Jemma made sure that any and all others and their children were clear of the streets and locked within the schoolhouses, shops, and taverns. Dark-Beasts who had not already found and killed those willing to fight were quickly trying to break through the doors or windows, but they would likely not succeed, for she would use her sword to stab straight through the neck of any creature coming into her proximity. Rayne and Haulfir were with her, making sure the same thing happened, all watching over each other, for the Bear Guard had been broken up around the city after the Dark had made their way in.

Haulfir could see the same great bear from before who walked slowly, disappearing into an alley as if looking for something specific, uncaring about anything else around. It was even larger than what he remembered—almost half as tall as the many stacked houses he limped by.

The feelings rushed back to him; the confusion started. He wondered again why he felt a connection with the beast. He should only want to kill it—nothing else, but it wasn't the case. He felt the thing wanted him to fall into some kind of mental trap, one that welcomed him—one he felt could be accepted, though it couldn't have been possible.

Either way, he wouldn't let it happen.

Haulfir snapped quickly out of it and hid from its sight. He couldn't fight him alone; he had to first do something about the many other Dark-Beasts trying to find their way into the buildings.

All three stabbed deeply through them, or cut off their heads and legs which did the job quite well. But none were unscathed by the treacherous demons whose skin rubbed and flamed at their own.

Cuts and scrapes set deep as they peered down at their wounded arms and bleeding hands that tightly held on to their swords. And there wouldn't be enough of Stalk's healing gel to help anyone from the burns and bites of the Dark-Beasts and their Dust.

He then thought of Gjone, where he might be, and what could've happened to explain why he wasn't there. He thought of the story that'd been told around town, the joke it was, and how he cared little for it; and how suddenly these creatures were full blown on their very doorstep with barely any time to prepare, or better yet, what to prepare *for*. He also thought of the many stories Rayne had told over time. Ones he'd never liked: all the talk such as demons and great serpents. And especially, the one from the summer night when Gjone's cousin had fallen asleep, and how they were probably all true.

A part of him felt silly for not believing Rayne, but the other part was still angry about it all. His stories led on to this somehow — as if the very belief itself had woken these creatures, and it resulted in them coming — as absurd as it sounded.

And then there was Arnenn who came to his mind, once again. He had no intention of feeling bad about hating he who came from his smug capital, led Gjone on to these stories, and then took off with him, maybe ending his life. He hoped that he were killed, too, if Gjone being dead had to be the case.

"I'm moving ahead to take care of what I can by the Tower, you two stay back and protect these people," said Haulfir as he dashed away.

Rayne didn't appreciate the command a single bit but kept his mouth closed and helped his wife fend off the beasts. He was quite surprised how well they were doing against the creatures, especially the bigger ones.

He began to know his strength, finding more confidence in the depth of his wild and outlandish heart when slicing through them and seeing them turn to Dust.

Throone gained back most of his composure, but was tired of constantly being drained of his energy, over and over. They were all the most terrible losses of strength to have ever overcome him. And this time, it was even worse than when he had come upon the Dark Being in the Palendrian. Every time, he felt almost years of youth leave his life that he had recently gained back, lost; amnesia set it, but then new memories were given.

He wondered what it all meant: Arnenn's talk of letting out his ancestor of old, and if it had actually happened. He also thought about the older man he saw: Kulne's king, Essria's king—Madelmar. And maybe he, as well, had come out of the Orrumn and was then hidden in some far corner of Amruhn, or Kulne itself. He somewhat felt he was. But there was no way for him to know for sure or what plans they had there. He could only carry on and meet the beasts in battle and save his fellow people of Harpelle. Especially the line of Rowe, for it was the only thing he'd always felt he must do.

He questioned why he sent them off to battle so quickly and so easily, but trusted that Arnenn and Gjone had the skills and knowledge necessary to stay alive. He hoped he had trained them well. At least he prayed it was so. As all he now felt was guilt. As he left the city without giving any warning about the Dark. As the many people of Harpelle could be dead because of him.

"Essria, I intend to go into the city. I do not ask you to go with."

"And I do not ask your permission," she said back.

The Lights and the men of Harpelle had lost many, but the Dark's numbers had dwindled considerably as well. It was mostly due to the new company of deadly Light-Beasts, but also because of Arnenn and Gjone who put their spears to great use.

Now returned, they were showing the crowds their newfound skill of fighting. And the people shouted cheerfully. It made some finally find their courage from deep within. They came out of their hiding places, ready to fight—together upon the many Dark-Beasts behind the Guard Tower.

"Gjone, Thrown-Thrower! Gjone, Thrown-Thrower!"

Gjone and Arnenn were fighting in full with the Skill of Throone. And it gave most in that part of the city a new hope as they watched their spear work.

They were killing Dark-Beasts left and right. They would throw their spears with a steady accuracy and a blazing speed while hastily chasing after them. Then, they would watch their spears run clean through the beasts that quickly turned to Dust, and into the wooden walls beyond they stuck sturdily. The Rowes would grab them back, block if they had to, stab another all the way through, and continue it all over again.

Impressed, more people came around corners, out behind barrels, jumping from the rooftops while shouting, "Gjone, Thrown-Thrower, the man that kills beasts is back!" They would try their own hand in going up against the Dark. Some succeeded. But most had unfortunately failed in their spirited attempts.

Even Cezz and Rimland (who were never fighters) made their way out of the Ivory Nook with many others, running out with objects such as chairs and small table stands, anything that could be used as a weapon—even though they would be of little use against the Dark. Still, more numbers meant more numbers and a better chance at ridding the city of its enemy.

At the same time, the people became completely comfortable with the presence of the Light-Beasts while running by them with complete trust, because anything that wasn't a black-wrought creature, was well known to be no opponent. But they had to use care. Just one unsteady move in the wrong direction would only mean destruction for a small human around any great beast, whether Dark or Light, who deathly thrashed at one another.

They had fought and killed most in the area when Rayne and Jemma heard the shouts of their son's now well-known nickname. Their faces ignited in hope and they immediately left the schoolhouse they were guarding without question, running farther up the street where more Dark still lingered, but were dying off quickly.

"He's back! They're back!" shouted Rayne to his wife and she in return as they kept their eyes of season peeled for their son and nephew.

Gjone heard the many shouts of his name and noticed how people he'd never known before, somehow now knew him. Arnenn watched as it fueled him on. (Gjone never shied away from being a showoff.) It was quite the impressive sight, though, and he had well earned it. Gjone killed many of the Dark—one after another. Each one that tried to attack him went up in Dust with the quick piercing of Throone's well-made spear. There were no more failed throws from Gjone anymore. The spear would go all the way through their very centers as he moved with an ultimate strength and speed and intensity.

The young woman and the old man had made their way into the city and fought alongside the Light-Beasts and the people of Harpelle, not yet finding the sons of Rowe. Throone saw the city in almost ruin about him and it broke a part of his soul. But it also fueled his fiery anger. Many of its citizens were killed along with the many creatures of the Light. The only things that had sufficed the best were most of its thick buildings. Only here and there were some waylaid, and barely at that, and even one had caught fire due to reasons unknown.

Having to ignore it for the moment, he made his own quick work of the Dark with his spear, and those who saw the Keeper were even more surprised by his expertise of fighting than they were Gjone's, who himself, had moved away from the area.

Essria was given a strange stare from anybody not currently occupied with a Dark-Beast, or by those who peered out through the Nook's windows. And to her, they were just as strange, and just the same as Arnenn or Gjone or of the hundreds in Strathom and in between. Though she took small interest in any of that, for the amount of death around her broke her heart of magic, the same as it did Throone's.

She had a skill of her own, knew how to use a sword. She had found one stray, and with it, was able to kill the Dark-Beasts by running it through them—even though a few times, there were close calls. Their Dust would rub against her, almost burn through her thick clothes; and she could almost feel their inner-torment within the burning sensations on her arms.

She had never been in a battle such as this since most of her time during the war at Kulne was stayed inside the castle. Also, she didn't have the Orrumn to help kill the many Dark creatures, feeling like it would be useful to her again. She could sense it now, unlike before. It made no sense. But it didn't matter. It was with Arnenn now, the Orrumn's new master.

She thought of him and could only hope him still alive and that she'd be seeing him again. She didn't like how they had departed, and felt she was ready to forgive him for taking the Orrumn, ready to say how she truly felt.

Throone called her to follow farther in to find the others. She quickly hurried after him through the sturdy city, seeing its many impressive buildings and designs of carved wolf and bear heads everywhere she turned her own, along with the real wolves and bears whose heads were just as large and frightening—especially the ones engulfed in the Dust.

28

HE MADE HIS WAY THROUGH THE CITY: limping down alleyways, knocking over the crates and barrels along the walls to sniff out the descendant of Rowe. The citizens remaining inside the shops and houses looked out their windows as they watched the terror creep slowly by, peering in at the many inside before moving on as if uninterested in the cowards.

They could hear his noises. They were like the scraping of metal blades as he breathed his fog onto the windows. And they could feel his heat on the other side of the wall. They hid under tables and kept as quiet as possible unless there was desperate need to whisper. Children would irrationally let out words and their parents would have to cover their mouths, nervously saying, "Shhh, just keep quiet and still."

From building to building he went, looking around. The alleys he walked were shaded and dark, and he could smell that he was getting closer to where the Rowe had spent much of his time. He inched closer to the rear of the city until making it to the River where the streets had become desolate of any soul.

He came up to what was believed to be the spot and sniffed at the building.

The merchants and employees inside knew less of anything that had happened as they pretended no one existed inside. What they did know, however, was that a massive terror was trying to look through the windows. And they would have guessed that everyone else in the city had already been killed by it—only they were left: the terror would finish them off and be done with Harpelle.

He knew the Rowe was either inside or somewhere near, for he was.

Rayne held his grandfather's sword tight in his hand when the Dark Bear turned his tumultuous face and saw him as he screamed,

"GET OUT OF MY CITY, DEMON!"

He felt brave and strong and confident, ready to be a warrior like his ancestors—knowing now that the stories were always true, and that he would be just as strong against the terrors of the Dark.

<

They had been searching for their son and nephew before catching sight of Haulfir again. The young man of the Bear Guard directed them to stay away from the fight around the Guard Tower.

"Gjone has it covered up there, and there's a massive beast running around inside the city. We must find it . . . and kill it!"

"We haven't seen our son in weeks . . . get out of our way, Haulfir!" screamed Jemma as Rayne finished her statement with, "And stop telling us what to do, boy!"

"Listen to me, please!" shouted Haulfir, most seriously. "It was seen heading towards your shop! It's going to tear it to shreds along with anyone in there! It's looking for something . . . we must take care of it! Gjone will survive and you will see him again. I promise you! He's alive—and doing well enough on his own. Trust me. I saw him!"

"This will be the last time you will try to persuade us, Haulfir!" she exclaimed, again.

"Wait, Jemma . . . he's right," said Rayne.

She was more confused than ever this time.

"Gjone has made it this far. We can trust he'll be safe. We must help save those we can! I saw the thing, too. It's horrifying . . . we have to do something!"

"Rayne, you cannot be serious this time. You cannot do this all alone!" she cried out.

"—You're right . . . I have Haulfir to help me."

"Please don't do this. You're not a warrior, Rayne, please!"

"Jemma! The beasts are almost all gone! Go to Gjone and Arnenn and lead them back here! And get as many guards as you can! Go now—hurry!"

She stood, almost paralyzed.

"Please, my love, GO!"

At that, she left without question, running as fast she could to embrace her son.

>

Arnenn and Gjone had finished almost any Dark left within the area. Some even started running out of the city and back to the hills, but most were struck by fast-flying arrows that went cleanly through them—if not already caught in the teeth of a fierce Light-Beast.

There was a mixture of cheer and sadness as Gjone killed the last one in the area with a powerful throw of his spear. When it died, there were none left. There were only those of the Light, which were scarce.

People swarmed about and surrounded Gjone and Arnenn, and some started shouting Gjone's title. Even some who saw the skills of Arnenn asked his name as they would awkwardly repeat it with, "And Arnenn, too!" for they watched him fight just as well, even while something seemingly bulky inside of a bag had consistently bounced around on his back the entire time.

Others were too sad and bewildered by the battle. Cries of dread came from many around that'd lost loved ones and friends. They could barely handle it—and neither could Arnenn. He watched as some folks ran to find any injured and then looked back to the celebration of Gjone, who had taken heed to those shouting his name, holding his spear in the air and shaking it endlessly while shouting in victory.

Rimland came up to his good friend. "All hail the killer of all beasts . . . the great, Gjone, Thrown-Thrower!"

Arnenn was confused. He wanted to join in to help those around him and didn't feel celebrating was appropriate. He also wanted to know where Essria was, and even Throone, and if they were still out in the hills—or if they had ever joined in the battle.

He wanted to search her out, find her, and take her in his arms. He had to know she was safe, along with Rayne and Jemma. There was no guarantee at all that they were even alive.

He also thought of the Orrumn and if he needed to be using it somehow—seeing something inside of it. Perhaps it could show him if they were okay. But none of those thoughts lasted much longer as he saw his aunt running up the street.

She continued in full speed at Gjone who was caught unaware by her hug. When he saw it was his mother, he embraced her back, shouting, "Mom!"

She held him for many long seconds, thrilled to have him back and knowing he was safe.

"You're finally home, my son!" she said as she hugged him once more, right before seeing and heading over to

Arnenn as well, telling him right away about the many concerns they had for him, along with his parents' concern—as if it were to have mattered at the moment.

She then turned her head and saw Gjone again, his leg wrapped in a dirty-white cloth patched in dried blood over his trousers. The old man had not brought them back unscratched (just as he never exactly promised he would). Then, she and everyone else saw a set of figures running up from behind a corner of broken food crates. One, the old man who had taken the two away. The other, a girl with long hair of many colors, spectacularly beautiful.

Arnenn held a smile and a sigh of relief as Jemma's expression quickly changed to being furious. "Who do you think you are, old fool?" she asked loudly, creating a scene.

The crowd's noise died down before becoming almost completely silent. Everybody looked at the old man they had seen from time to time in one area or another who traveled his way around town for many years. They noticed he looked a bit different, though. His beard was unkempt and longer, and he showed to be even stronger and keener than ever before. It was easier for those to notice who hadn't seen him for the last few weeks of his pardon.

He was unsure of how to respond to her obscene question, at least right away, so Jemma spoke again, instead. "You had us worried half to death! How could you take them away from us for so long?"

Throone was about to answer, but Essria stepped ahead of him. She felt the need to speak for the Keeper, and interjected. "I am sorry. They found me, and their journey became longer than intended."

"Oh, so *you're* who's to blame for this? Who exactly are you anyway, strange girl?"

Throone ignored the question and stepped back in front of Essria.

"Jemma, please . . . none of this is I, her, or anyone else's fault. You saw what came about this city today . . . and that is the very reason why we are now just getting back!" He was getting ready to raise his voice as he stepped atop a small crate to look deeper into the large crowd that gathered around Gjone. "You ALL will know soon enough what has happened! But right now," he pointing to the north end of the city, "there's a giant beast still remaining in here, if any of you have been paying attention!"

Jemma suddenly realized she had forgotten all about the monster due to being so lost within her son's return, as both Arnenn and Gjone had forgotten as well. They darted intense eyes at each other before running as fast they could with spears ready in hand.

He shouted loud the words again. "Get out of this city . . . . . . NOW!"

The Dark Bear looked eagerly into Rayne's eyes. There he was, the descendant of Rowe he had sensed all along.

"GET AWAY FROM MY SHOP!" he yelled again, holding tight his grandfather's sword with nothing but confidence.

Haulfir stood beside him, staying quiet—not knowing how to kill a beast of such size, impressed by Rayne's unwavering courage.

The Bear clawed at the shop in anger, leaving deep marks on its wall before shoving himself against it, creating a slight crack. If it was made of anything less

364

than the sturdy wood of Harpelle, it would have easily caved.

It gave a great roar that echoed through the alleyways nearby. Almost the entire city heard it while those inside the shop couldn't help but scream. It made Rayne even angrier, fusing his temper. He waited no longer to run at the beast and to set the blade of his sword into its heart.

But Rayne was no match for the Dark Bear's speed, strength, and knowledge of fighting. The Bear quickly stepped aside and swiped its great paw, throwing Rayne against the wall of his own shop. The Rowe bounced off of it before landing close to the entrance of a bridge that crossed the Cunning. His chest was clawed in a deep and bloodied mess: scared forever, and the wind had been entirely taken from his lungs. He had to wait through the many excruciating seconds until he could breathe again.

He had also lost control of his grandfather's sword, remembering the sound it made as it chimed against the stone tiles into the distance.

Those inside the shop were terrified. They heard his yell and were far concerned for him, yet also far too afraid to go outside for fear of being killed by the great terror.

The Dark Bear paid little attention to the younger one who stood behind. His only concern in the moment was killing this descendant of Rowe. But he had to redirect it. Without pause, the young guard stepped right into his direct path to Rayne: courageous, yet, deathly afraid.

Rayne saw Haulfir's back above him and grew worried. With little breath, he struggled to say, "Haulfir . . . brave young man . . . don't do this . . . leave me be!"

Haulfir ignored his friend's father. He only held up his sword in both hands with a focused face toward the

Dark Bear, and lifted them slowly above his head in position, ready to strike at any moment, awaiting the perfect opportunity to take the beast down.

He was more skilled than Rayne, and knew it. He could kill this beast if he played it right.

"Haulfir, NO!" screeched Rayne, but Haulfir was almost ready.

Something else was happening, though. It was the very same, very confusing feeling. It came upon him: the connection he'd experienced with the Bear, just like before. Haulfir lowered his sword as if he were willed to do so. He also felt an ultimate surge within his body and mind. It was a feeling of fierce power and worthiness. An importance. And it was mixed with the deepest emotion in which one that was only human could ever experience.

He couldn't help what was happening, but he also didn't fight it. He didn't want to fight it. He only turned toward Rayne — slowly.

He heard him say, "Haulfir . . . what are you doing? Get out of here!" His voice and breathing trembled excessively.

". . . Save yourself!"

Haulfir looked at him with a stark white face and only said,

"I am."

The young guard's arms lifted high again with the hilt of his sword nestled in his palms. The blade pointed down at Rayne.

And then, Haulfir felt himself pulling, and next, watched his sword dive past the clawed mess, right into Rayne's heart.

The Rowe's eyes flashed open — his body jolted and jerked. He stared at Haulfir in deep thought, confused.

But his concern did not last before it went only to his wife and son.

His eyes flickered, and then they closed.

He was woven into the blue light—a color and an image of memory seen only in rare dreams throughout his life before being high above the grounds of Amruhn. But it was more. It was time. It was presence. It was beauty. And it was real.

Forests came and went, growing and dispersing before being wiped away into deserts, then green again. Rivers came and went, turning into canyons before filling into flat land. He saw kingdoms and cities, structures—lost. He saw their existence in a matter of seconds before a new one took its place, and then another, gone.

Every form of weather existed as one. And he could feel the power, the magic in the elements within the heavy clouds pulling strength from the ground far down below.

He heard the shouts of men and woman, and then he saw them. They were beyond him in every way, and all different. Yet he felt their love. They tried to grab at him, take him, and bring him in: exist with them forever.

But he couldn't stay. He was not the same. He was not given a chance to kill the Dark Presence such as they. He was not one the Orrumn would prophesy. He was not like Arnenn. And he was not like Gjone.

Haulfir came back to himself and noticed what he had done. His face was as stone and his heart was flooded with horror. He pulled free his sword from Rayne's body, falling over him and losing it to the Cunning—throwing it in disbelief of what he had done.

He was on his back and looking once again at the Dark Bear, seeing himself lying right next to Rayne's body. Horrified, he said under his breath, "What have I done?"

The Bear crept closer, drilling into Haulfir's soul with steady eyes. He could tell the beast wanted to answer. And that, it did.

A voice spoke clearly inside the young guard's head.

You became great

Gjone's spear ran entirely through the Dark Bear's gut from afar. But it did not yet kill him. It looked over while screeching and saw two more descendants of Rowe heading his way—he knew his life as over, but he welcomed it. He had fulfilled his purpose and done his master's will.

Arnenn threw his. It went directly through its neck. It fell, but the burning only slightly began weaving throughout its coat that had wrought thick throughout many ages of collecting Dust. He was not yet dying. He only struggled—kicking his legs around.

The upcoming crowd of guards and citizens saw the beast as they also saw the body of Rayne in lifeless form, and Haulfir, they saw lying on his side, almost knocked out.

Throone ran up to the Dark Bear quickly, laying hands on its side as they glared orange with bright fire in the winter cold. The beast turned red before finally disappearing into a clouded mass of Dark Dust: dead Dust—only ash.

All stared in amazement at what they had seen the old town dweller do.

"NO!" came their cries.

Jemma wrapped Rayne in her arms, as did Gjone. And Arnenn bowed his head and closed his eyes in disbelief as tears dripped from them.

Essria held Arnenn's hand and comforted him. He held hers quickly back before embracing her in his arms. But it was not the way he wanted it to happen.

Gjone couldn't handle it. He looked at Arnenn and Throone with watered and determined eyes and spoke between his tightened teeth. "I will kill each and every last one of these beasts . . . NO MATTER WHAT IT TAKES!"

The disgust on his face was such as Arnenn had never seen. It was an entirely new side of Gjone: a well-deserved hatred, a revenge that would steal his heart.

Haulfir stood up around the carnage. The only thing he could do was walk away from Rayne's dead body and grieving family. He was unable to handle being any part of it.

He couldn't speak, or look at Gjone, or anyone else.

He walked through the large crowd of his fellow guards and citizens. They patted him on the shoulder with care as he saw his father limping up far behind, being walked by two other men of the Bear Guard.

When he came close enough to Haulfir, the Captain cried out, "Son! Thank goodness you are okay!"

29

JUST LIKE THE DAY HE SAW IT DISAPPEAR,
when they were right about what they said; when the
ancient kingdom was there and then no more as he took
his leave from Amruhn long ago, Mouren awoke inside
the Garden Cave.

It took him a few moments to remember the area and
to again feel what it was like to have a physical body. He
ran his hands over the large leaves and his toes melted
into the grass as a smile of remembrance appeared upon
his face. Even the wisps of extreme cold were inviting as
he looked around with his eyes of Holgorenth that hid
behind his great beard portraying the seasons.

He saw the stone platform where the Orrumn once lay;
and where he would look into it, losing countless hours
in its presence before deciding he could do it no more.

He had breath again, no longer bound to the void of
blue light, trapped as he could only watch what was
happening around him—as if he were a ghost and dead
of life—able to do nothing but shout. No longer was he
bound to the Pull.

He walked the stairs and paths he'd trekked many
times before, delighted to see the brick art of the
students and the age-old architecture of the libraries that
somehow, were in a complete mess.

The lamps lit up in the darkness, lighting his way;
welcoming him and remembering his presence.

He entered for the first time in hundreds of years, the Hall of Nevruine which celebrated the elements like nowhere he had ever known.

He saw the statue of a young Madelmar. He gazed at it, remembering the old king's brilliance, his mysterious ways, his strengths and weaknesses, and how he missed him so.

He pushed open the Kingdom's doors that were built of magic thousands of years before. He looked over the expanse of trees where once beautiful fields of color had settled; and where he thought he had defeated the Dark Presence, but where he was wrong like all the others of Rowe before him.

He knew what he must do: find his kin—find the one of his line that he could see from inside of the Pull itself.

Find Arnenn.

Acknowledgements

Nox + Quills Creative (Cover art and Map)
NoxandQuillsCreative.com

Shealin Ashley Photography (Bio photo)
ShealinAshley.com

Characters

Alandis: (Uh-lan-dis)

Arbowen: (Ar-bow-en)

Arnenn: (Ar-nen)

Cezz: (Sezz)

Crowlis: (Krow-lis)

Essria: (Es-ree-uh)

Gjone: (Jown—sounds like the name: Joan)

Haulfir: (Hall-fur)

Herring: (Hair-ing)

Jemma: (Jem-uh)

Kedd: (Ked)

Kershpa: (Kersh-puh)

Lenx: (Lenks)

Loramae: Lor-uh-may

Mourenrowe: (Mor-en-rowe)

Narmor: (Nar-mer)

Porelesce: (Por-el-ess)

Rayne: (Rane)—(sounds like "rain")

Rimland: (Rim-lind)

<u>Places</u>

Alderhollow: (All-der-hall-oh)

Amruhn: (Am-rewn)

Crennan: (Kren-en)

Disdon Sea: (Diz-Dun)

Filman: (Fill-min)

Gathralim' Waters: (Gath-ral-eem)

Harpelle: (Har-pell)

Ionsdi: (E-owns-dee)

Kingdom of Kulne: (cooln)

Meens: (Meens)

Hall of Nevruine: (Nev-rew-ine)

Novark: (No-vark)

The Palendrian Forest: (Pal-end-ree-ann)

Strathom: (Strath-um)

The Sculths: (Skool-ths)

Vidhera: (Vid-air-uh)

Wrenck's: (Renks)

Other

Setsia: (Set-see-uh)

Peldia: (Pel-Gee-uh)

Negnya: (Nen-yuh)

Holgorenth: (Hol-ger-enth)

Thank you for reading Book One of
The Prophecies of Rowe: **Reappearance**

Be sure to keep your eyes of season peeled for
more to come

ThePropheciesofRowe.com

.com/ThePropheciesofRowe

@ThePropheciesofRowe

@DennisCooleyPOR

Dennis J. Cooley

"What's that?" is what I would've answered with if you told me about anything written by J.R.R Tolkien or Terry Brooks before I was 18 years old. I was far too busy riding my bicycle or playing drums and I wasn't interested in reading in any way. That is until I was suggested to read "The Hobbit." I said I "guess" I would. But that's when it all changed and I couldn't seem to get enough of the story and the many unexplainable feelings that came along with it.

14 years later and still never getting enough, a friend suggested I write a story that could be used to make a film. The very next day, I began, just to see what would happen. But in the midst of it all, I became more carried away with the actual story and just had to keep writing it. It all leads to here: The Prophecies of Rowe.

I live in Arizona (US) with my wife Danielle and our hedgehog. And I'd always rather be outdoors than indoors.

Made in the USA
Lexington, KY
30 September 2017